WHATEVER IT TAKES

By Adele Parks

Playing Away
Game Over
Larger Than Life
The Other Woman's Shoes
Still Thinking Of You
Husbands
Young Wives' Tales
Happy Families (Quick Read)
Tell Me Something
Love Lies
Men I've Loved Before
About Last Night
Whatever It Takes

Adele
PARKS

WHATEVER
IT TAKES

headline
review

First published in Great Britain in 2012
by HEADLINE REVIEW
An imprint of HEADLINE PUBLISHING GROUP

1

Cataloguing in Publication Data is available from the British Library

ISBN 978 0 7553 7133 4 (Hardback)
ISBN 978 0 7553 7134 1 (Trade paperback)

Typeset in Monotype Dante by Palimpsest Book Production Limited,
Falkirk, Stirlingshire

Printed and bound in Great Britain by Clays Ltd, St Ives plc

Headline's policy is to use papers that are natural, renewable
and recyclable products and made from wood grown in responsible forests.
The logging and manufacturing processes are expected to conform to
the environmental regulations of the country of origin.

HEADLINE PUBLISHING GROUP
An Hachette UK Company
338 Euston Road
London NW1 3BH

www.headline.co.uk
www.hachette.co.uk

For Alex King and Will Moore.

JULY

1

Sun-faded, handmade bunting fluttered in the breeze. The floral triangles artfully framed the patio door that led out to the small but stylish deck, the prequel to a minute patch of grass that only Londoners (and *very* ambitious estate agents) would dare describe as a garden. There was a slim border around the edge of the garden that in February boasted delicate snowdrops and in March hosted stout daffodils and tulips; sadly the roses never took. There was only one tree, a birch tree, and on close inspection it became apparent that even it didn't belong to the Hamilton family but was, in fact, rooted in their neighbours' garden. It was not pruned and, like an errant and curious cat, it had jumped the fence and adopted them. The overhang effectively took up a third of their space but the Hamilton girls were all too happy to nurture and call it their own. Nurturing, in this instance, took the form of adorning it with vast amounts of white fairy lights that caused the burdened branches to bow and scrape.

There were several pretty pastel-coloured lanterns lined along the garden walls. Like the fairy lights, the lanterns would come into their own after dark, they'd glow beautifully later that evening; everyone was expecting it to be a long party.

Their last party.

Eloise glanced at the barbecue that was beginning to sizzle tantalisingly. She reassured herself that the table was stacked with cheerfully coloured plastic plates, beer and wine glasses and that there was a huge tub of ice tucked neatly underneath. People did not eat from sagging paper plates at Eloise's events, she always hired in. She tutted as she noticed a small and incongruous assortment of discarded toys scattered about, including a slightly deflated football, a cracked plastic bucket (with turrets) and a doll that had clearly had the dubious 'benefit' of being victim to one of her daughters' make-over sessions – she was bald and wore glitter eye shadow on her protruding plastic belly. These toys had obviously fallen beneath the children's notice and had not made it into the packing boxes. It had been a ruthless cut. Other than the abused toys the effect was perfect. Just what Eloise had hoped for. The bunting, fairy lights and lanterns said whimsical, yet fun and inviting. She always worked hard at recreating the sort of tableaux that might be seen in glossy magazines.

The Hamiltons threw a lot of parties. They always had. They were party people through to their souls. The house-warming party – way back when – had been legendary. They'd bought food from the Bluebird food emporium and only served champagne (which set a precedent for all their subsequent dos). The Bluebird didn't have a food emporium now; it had been replaced by a frighteningly exclusive designer shop that sold expensive clothes and, somewhat disconcertingly, chandeliers. Eloise frankly preferred it if a shop did one thing or another and she was always baffled when they didn't abide by this rule. Of course, John Lewis sold both clothes *and* chandeliers but only very ordinary versions of both, which upset her less. Over the years, Mark and Eloise had thrown lavish Christmas, birthday, Easter and summer holiday parties here in Muswell Hill. The accent on the impressive catering had been modified on occasion. For a while, when the girls were tiny, the sushi was swapped for mushy but they'd continued to serve champagne and El always took care to do something notable; a bubble machine, colour themes, a magic show, a bouncy castle (squeezed into the postage stamp-sized garden). She once hired a lady who gave manicures and another who gave massages for one of her birthday parties, and they'd had pole-dancing lessons in the sitting room for their tenth wedding anniversary (Eloise still harboured vague feelings of disquiet about that one; she *thought* the guests loved it and she *hoped* they knew she was being ironic). Yes, the Hamiltons' parties were something of an event among their many friends. Eloise was known for her attention to detail and generous hosting. She wouldn't want to disappoint. Especially not today. First impressions, last impressions. It's what it was all about.

Of course, this wasn't going to be their last party *ever*, at least, God, she hoped not. But it was their last *here* in their Muswell Hill home. The home Mark and Eloise had bought when they married. The home that they'd scampered back to following the hospital births of their three babies. Eloise could barely recall the tiny, precious, overwhelming bundles when she looked at the faces of the confident girls, now aged eleven, nine and seven. This was the home that, in a constant attempt to be ahead of the curve and impressive, they'd initially decorated with oxblood red and royal blue, then with impractical ghostly white hues and finally muted taupe and complementing mauves. Would the next owners redecorate? The thought caused Eloise to gasp. Probably, she admitted to herself. Face facts.

Eloise didn't hold the fanciful notion that a house was one of the family; not exactly. But she did think of it as the backdrop for the family, the safety net. It was the measure of their aspirations (their debt), their triumphs (their disasters). It had acquired a personality of sorts and, certainly, a pulse.

And Eloise had loved it here. Loved *being* here. Being in the true 'to be or not to be' sense; the sense of existing, living. Here. They were moving out. Not just out of the street or even out of Muswell Hill but out *out*. Out of London. Out of the M25 concrete girdle and, frankly, she was terrified. Yes, of course she knew there were other places to live in the world. She was aware that there were almost seven billion people on the planet and the last census showed that only approximately seven million of them lived in London, but the problem was . . . the truth was . . . she wasn't sure there were other places for *her* to live in the world.

By contrast, Eloise's husband Mark had wanted to move out of London practically since the day he'd moved in. His heart was in

Dartmouth where he'd grown up; bobbing on boats, clambering over hills and paddling in the sea. Yes, Eloise realised that, put like that, a Dartmouth life did seem idyllic – probably *was* idyllic and exactly where their family ought to be – but she'd grown up in the urban jungle and she maintained it had never done her any harm. Mark always raised an eyebrow when she said as much but resisted mentioning the fact that, following a spate of violent break-ins in their road, she slept with her handbag and the fact that she couldn't swim – water terrified her (unless it was the sort she was sluiced with at a state-of-the-art spa). He didn't need to say these things; they were a deeply intimate couple who knew one another inside out and as such they understood the value of not pointing out one another's frailties on too regular a basis.

Eloise was a *Londoner*, born and bred, and that was fundamental and formative. If she was to be cut wide open, the traditional system of nerves and arteries wouldn't be revealed, rather it was more likely that the Tube map would be found. She knew the roads, the parks, the shops, and the signature of the individual zones that made up the whole. She could describe in detail the fastest way from any London destination to any other. It was her party piece. If someone were to say, 'Tate Britain to Camden Market', she'd say, 'Exit Tate Britain, six-minute walk to Pimlico Tube station (nine-minute if you were an out-of-towner), take the Victoria line – five stops – change at Warren Street, a further two stops on the Northern line, get off at Camden Town station and the market is just a few minutes' walk along the high street.' And that was not even a route she'd deigned to follow for over a decade (she was rather more Islington High Street than Camden Market now). London was what Eloise knew. What she was.

Mark had long since argued that Londoners were some of the most closed-minded people on the planet because they didn't want to travel the world. Eloise always counter-argued that was because London was *the* destination, it *was* the world.

'Where else can you find streets with dozens of different cuisines, numerous places of worship for various denominations, couture as diverse as the sari, the mini, and the burka and yet still expect a decent cup of Earl Grey?' she'd demand.

Mark also often commented in passing that it would be nice not to have to park his car approximately two miles away from his home because of the overly enthusiastic yellow-line daubing that the local council seemed to indulge in. He'd frequently mentioned that it might be grand to have a garden where the trees were actually rooted.

'But there are beautiful parks in London,' argued Eloise.

'Yes, but trying to secure a space in one of them, any time from April to late August, requires SAS tactics and foreign office diplomacy skills.'

It was true that sometimes when they were picnicking on Hampstead Heath, they'd had to sit so close to other families that it looked as though the two families were dating or even mating. 'Space is at such a premium in London,' Mark had stated, with increasing regularity, over the past year or so.

'Proving I'm on to something with my theory that everyone wants to live here,' Eloise would counter swiftly.

'But the problem isn't just in the parks, streets, Tube, bars, shops and schools, we've run out of room in our house too.'

Eloise couldn't deny this. When they'd moved in they'd had so much space, entire spare rooms, but they'd since stuffed those rooms with babies and, well, plastic things. Mark was a solicitor and as such he often needed a space to work from when he was at home so they'd had to turn the box room into an office. There was room for his desk, books and files although when El took him a cup of coffee she did find it a bit claustrophobic, especially if the cats followed her. It was such a small room that some might call it a large cupboard – indeed, before all the breeding, they'd used it as a cupboard.

The girls had two bedrooms between the three of them. Officially, Poppy and Erin, the younger two, shared one and Emily, the eldest, shared the other with the toys (and spare jackets, boxes of old CDs, books, photo albums and the camping equipment). Over the past year Emily, in particular, had become increasingly resentful of how everyone's possessions seemed to smudge and bleed into someone else's personal space, and her resentment had often taken the form of her flinging her family's things out of her bedroom window. El had been particularly embarrassed when the elderly gentleman who lived next door returned a bundle of her greying knickers; they'd been in a laundry pile that had found itself on the wrong end of one of Emily's tantrums.

'We need more space,' was the sentence Mark uttered most frequently (that or maybe 'Have you seen my iPad?'). Eloise finally stopped arguing with him and simply sighed.

'I know, you're right. You almost always are, which, frankly, can be as annoying as it is useful. I don't think any of us could bear to live through Emily's teenage angst years without at least two more rooms to which we might be able to run for cover.'

'Fact is, we simply can't afford two more rooms in London. Last time I checked we didn't have a spare several hundred thousand pounds in loose change hiding down the back of the sofa,' stated Mark. 'And then there's the school problem.'

'Well, yes,' Eloise had admitted.

'I just think that kids should go to schools that don't require either a criminal record or a trust fund as an entrance prerequisite,' Mark had mumbled.

Emily was due to start secondary school next academic year. The local primary school was fantastic, full of focused, ambitious, worthy, funny, education-is-important types, but sadly Emily didn't get into the secondary school the Hamiltons had been hoping for. Disappointingly, she'd been allocated her sixth choice; an alternative that required a bulletproof vest as part of the uniform. Eloise had been secretly and unrealistically hoping that the girls might be privately educated once they reached secondary school. This plan depended on a lottery win; Eloise didn't even do the lottery. Mark's salary as a solicitor was decent but could never cover school fees; sometimes El had difficulty making it stretch to cover babysitters – London was so expensive.

Then the phone call came. Mark's father, Ray, was also a solicitor, the managing partner of a small practice in Dartmouth. He was long past the age of retirement but took pride in the fact that his name hung above the door and he employed two other solicitors. Ray had always harboured the dream that his son would one day take over the little practice and make it a family business; maybe one of the girls would follow on in time. So last spring, the same day as Eloise had received the letter to say that Emily would need to be fitted for a bulletproof vest as well as netball shoes, Ray had rung to make Mark an offer. Ray wanted his son to carry on the family business. He was willing to sell it at a steal.

'I had no idea you were ready to retire, Dad.'

'Well, I am. I need to spend more time with your mother.'

'Very romantic.'

'Something like that. Will you consider it?'

'Of course.'

'You'd be doing me a favour, son.'

Mark doubted this. From his viewpoint all he could see was the life raft his father was flinging at him. He could do the same work in Dartmouth that he was doing in London but it would be *his* practice. *His* profit attached to *his* reputation. He relished the challenge.

Mark quickly worked out that if they sold up their three-nearly-four-bedroom terraced house with storage problems, a temperamental boiler and signs of damp on one of the connecting walls, they could buy a fine example of a mid eighteenth-century Grade II Listed house in Dartmouth. To be precise (and Mark always was), they could buy a house with all the original features (flagstone floors, moulded plaster cornicing and window shutters), enough bedrooms (one with an *en suite*), a reception room, a dining room, a kitchen/breakfast room, a family bathroom and a cloakroom. Their new home would have river views from most south-facing windows and from the sizeable rear garden. The estate agent didn't mention the free babysitting that they'd benefit from but Mark knew that would be thrown in.

Eloise had made token verbal objections but she'd bowed to the inevitability of the economic sense.

'I'll miss my gym.'

'You can get fit walking along the beach. You won't need a gym.'

'What about the girls' tennis classes, fine art classes, pony club?'

'El, you don't need a class to enjoy those things. We need to simplify our lives. It will be good for us. All the Sunday supplements agree,' he'd added with a beam. He knew Eloise was a devotee of Sunday supplement magazines.

So, Eloise finally agreed to sell up; it seemed a no-brainer after roughly fifteen years of Mark campaigning, two bottles of wine and a particularly surprising but satisfying orgasm.

She worried whether that made her sound weak.

Or shallow.

Or both.

Or, perhaps, simply married. Eloise wondered whether it was just her or did other women agree to things that they didn't really want to do just because they didn't want to look like spoilsports in the face of their husbands' overwhelming enthusiasm? In the past she'd found herself agreeing to a snowboarding holiday when she'd known before they'd arrived in the French Alps that it was just an expensive way to get bruises and mind-numbingly cold. She'd even once agreed to a sponsored bungee jump but that was a long, long time ago.

Despite her passion for London Eloise had to admit to a tiny bubble of excitement gurgling somewhere deep inside her. She reasoned that since she had agreed to move, the only sensible way forward was to throw herself entirely into her new life which, after all, shouldn't be too difficult because she liked Dartmouth very, very much. The Hamiltons usually visited five or six times a year. Eloise loved to stand on the embankment (a safe distance from the edge) and watch the endless streams of fishing and pleasure boats teem in and out of the harbour. She couldn't fail to appreciate the rolling hills, the vivid, rugged shorelines, the town's quaint cobbled streets. She had no problem at all with moving closer to her in-laws, whom she loved very much.

Her father-in-law, Ray, was an old-school gentleman who kept his own counsel and was never anything other than impeccably polite and hospitable. He'd worked faithfully and discreetly to service the legal needs of most of Dartmouth's inhabitants for years and was well respected in the community. The couple lived modestly but then, rather splendidly, spent most of their cash on flamboyant holidays. They liked to go on world cruises. Eloise thought this was particularly brilliant as not only did such hols prove that her in-laws had wide interests but also the cruises provided an endless source of easy conversation. If chatter ever faltered all El had to say was, 'I can't imagine waking up to the sun glinting off Sydney Opera House', and Ray would pick up the mantle.

'Fine sight, and I was actually breathless when I caught my first glimpse of Hong Kong Harbour. Breathless. And as for taking my first steps on the Great Wall of China . . . tremendous. Tremendous.'

Eloise earned extra brownie points whenever she asked to see Ray's photo albums. He handled the leather books, with acid-free tissue paper, like newborns. She'd make the appropriate 'oh's and 'ah's and he considered her to be the perfect daughter-in-law. Which, on the whole, she was.

Mark's mother, Margaret, also adored Eloise although it had taken longer to win Margaret round as she'd carefully weighed up whether Eloise was good enough for her only child. Eloise had been patient, she understood that mindset. Now Prince William was married, Eloise couldn't see anyone ever being good enough for any of her girls and even if Wills had proposed to one of them she'd have worried about the potential problems that may have resulted because of the big age gap. Margaret had been a sterling granny from the moment Eloise had seen the little blue line on the pee stick. Eloise's own mother already had three grandchildren by the time Emily had been born, so while she'd clearly been pleased and proud, she'd been immune to the charms of a baby blowing bubbles with its own spit and she'd refused to declare Emily a genius for rolling over at just four months; instead she'd smiled approvingly and said her development was normal. Normal! Eloise had barely been able to speak to her mother for several weeks after such careless cruelty. Anyway, her mum's involvement with the girls was limited as, just after Poppy was born, Eloise's parents emigrated to Portugal, to enjoy a sunny retirement. Margaret readily stepped into the role of surrogate mum and supreme granny. She had genuinely viewed every gasp and gurgle that fell from the rosebud lips of her three granddaughters as significant historical moments; most of which she'd recorded in her diary and on camera. Margaret was kind, patient, generous and good with the washing machine. She was a lovely lady to be around.

Besides, Eloise (a die-hard shopaholic) had to admit she was excited because if she was going to be living in the country she was entitled to drive a 4 x 4. They were going to buy a BMW X5 and she was ecstatic. Eloise dreamt about new car smell. A new house meant new furniture, new crockery, new bedding, and new tea-lights. Yay, lots of shopping! Although her best friend, Sara, had somewhat tactlessly pointed out that opportunities to spend, spend, spend would be limited. Unless you were looking for fishing hooks or pastel-coloured prints of boats, then Dartmouth wasn't necessarily the place to flex plastic. Mark maintained this was a good thing. He'd repeatedly pointed out that their mortgage would stay almost the same. 'Same' in this case was still a stretch, so Eloise wasn't to get 'carried away'. Eloise was currently assessing exactly what was the definition of 'carried away'. For example, would it be classed as carried away if she repainted every wall and bought a few new scatter cushions? Probably not (as long as no one ever found out that the paint was Farrow and Ball and the scatter cushions were White Company). Would it be classed as carried away if she threw out every stick of furniture they possessed and dashed to Heal's for replacements?

Possibly.

Eloise glanced around the garden and took a deep breath. It was not the money or the upheaval or even the sentimental attachment to their house that was stabbing her in the gut and causing a scratching feeling in her throat, meaning there was a definite threat of tears tonight. The most difficult part of leaving London was that she was moving away from all her friends; her giddy and amazing friends. Sara, her old colleagues, her school-gate mum friends, the friends she'd made at her book club, upholstery class and the gym and her brother Ed and sister-in-law Fran all lived in London. To be accurate, these people all lived within three Tube stops of Eloise. She had a village here, a community here. She was finding it hard to accept that she'd agreed to leave it all behind.

'I know what you are thinking.' Mark's voice interrupted her thoughts.

'I was just wondering whether I need to bring out more chairs. The stripped deckchairs will look brilliant but they take up so much room,' Eloise bluffed.

Their home was sold. Their new house was bought. There were one hundred and forty-four boxes of packed belongings languishing upstairs waiting for the removal men to arrive on Monday; there was nothing more to be said on the matter.

'Yeah, chairs, that's what I thought you were thinking about,' said Mark. Eloise didn't believe him, he didn't believe her, but this gracious pretence was love. Mark stood behind his wife and wrapped his arms around her, she leaned her head back against his chest. He was six foot one and she was only five four so he could cradle her comfortably. He put his lips close to her right ear and his warm breath made her shudder. After so many years this, Eloise's friends assured her, was miraculous. He whispered, 'You're doing the right thing, El. Thank you.'

She didn't know what it was exactly, maybe it was something about the husky, sincere tone of his voice, or maybe the way the sunlight caught on the hairs of his tanned forearms, but she knew that he was correct again. She was doing the right thing.

2

'Are you ready?' Charlie popped his head around the bedroom door. He flashed Sara a broad smile but since he and Sara had been together for seven years she knew that the smile was strained and his patience was stretched. He'd already asked this question three times in the last hour and a quarter. They'd been fashionably late when he'd first asked, now they were just plain rude. 'Eloise is on the phone. She wants to know if we're going to be much longer.' Charlie ignored Sara's frantic hand gestures that clearly indicated she couldn't face talking to Eloise at that moment and he passed the phone to his wife.

'Hi. You're late,' stated Eloise flatly.

'I don't want to come,' Sara replied with equal frankness, the sort reserved for closest friends.

'Sara!'

'I'll miss you. If I come I admit defeat. It's over, that's it, you're off.' Sara wondered whether Eloise could hear the tears in her voice.

'I can't have a party without you. If I don't have a party, I can't leave,' said Eloise gently.

'My point, exactly.' Sara wished she didn't sound like a rejected child, friendless in the playground, but she felt like one.

'But I've got to leave,' Eloise murmured; she was using the same tone she'd used when she'd broken the news to Emily and Erin that there was no Father Christmas.

'I know.'

14

'Please, Sara. I need you here.'

Neither woman spoke for a few seconds while Sara dug into her reserves of determination.

'OK.' Sara hung up and handed the phone back to Charlie.

'So we're going?' he asked hopefully. He'd thought Eloise might be able to motivate Sara even though he'd failed to do so.

'Suppose, but I don't know what to wear,' Sara groaned as she flopped back on to the king-size bed, lying with her arms and legs spread wide on the eggshell-blue three-hundred-thread sheets that had cost a fortune and (happily) felt as though they did. She was only wearing her underwear. Sara didn't suffer from stretch marks or post-pregnancy flab as many other women did, nor did she have a Caesarean scar and she did enough aerobics and yoga to defy time and gravity. Sara was aware that she had the body of someone about a decade younger than she actually was; people were forever commenting that she looked terrific for her age. Her height helped. She was five foot eight and she'd never been afraid of it. She didn't understand why some tall girls slouched. She walked with a ramrod straight back. She knew the compliment that she looked good for her age was genuine (whether it was given generously or grudgingly) but, either way, it was a compliment that she struggled to accept as gracefully as she should. The truth was, Sara would have willingly worn a bit of fat if it was the sort of fat that came about because of mindlessly eating up the leftovers off the kids' plates or if it was the sort of fat that simply wouldn't shift after the birth (no matter how much breastfeeding had occurred).

There were no kids' plates in their house and Sara had never felt what it was like to have a tiny baby's mouth clasp on to her nipple; she'd never had the opportunity to nurture in that intimate and raw way. That was why, despite the fact that she was nearly naked and spread-eagled, Charlie knew she wasn't being provocative. It was not the right time of the treatment cycle to have sex and they only *ever* had sex when a doctor said they could. Anyway, whilst she was definitely in *a* mood, she wasn't in *the* mood. Quite the opposite.

'What do you wear for your best friend's leaving party? A shroud? Certainly black,' Sara commented sulkily.

Charlie's eyes swept round the room and he clocked the piles of discarded clothes that his wife had tried on and cast off; they were liberally scattered across the usually pristine and minimalist bedroom. The beautiful and expensive garments had a strangely spiteful and angry air about them, they were a bit like chickenpox on a child's soft skin – glaring, obvious, unwanted.

He didn't ask what was really wrong although it was clearly unreasonable for a grown woman to be sulking because she was having a clothes crisis. He knew what was wrong.

Eloise's leaving party was insult to injury. Both Charlie and Sara had been to enough of Eloise's parties to know what to expect. This party, like all her other parties, would no doubt be stylish and memorable and impressively OTT. There'd be obscene amounts of delicious food and decent drink, a swathe of beautiful, individual decorations and an outright glut of interesting, impressive friends.

All of whom would have a Walton-size family.

The place would be heaving with screaming babies, sticky toddlers, precocious kids and sulky teens and none of them would be Charlie and Sara's. That's what was really wrong. That was always wrong. Sometimes, when Sara was feeling blue she tried to pretend it was because of something more mundane; she might say she'd had a tough day in the office, or she'd lost her Oyster card, or (like today) she couldn't find the right thing to wear for an important event but, in fact, it was never any of those things that caused her bad moods. They were doing their fourth round of IVF and the pressure was insane.

Charlie carefully sat down on the edge of the bed. Nowadays, he often circled Sara as though she was a wild and unpredictable animal; it wasn't a sex game – it was fear. 'What about this?' he asked tentatively, as he bent and scooped up a scarlet strappy dress which was usually considered to be one of Sara's favourites.

'Hate it,' she muttered. It was not Sara who replied, actually, it was the human menopausal gonadotropin; this was the drug that a few weeks ago she'd injected into her body every day, for a week. The hormones in HMG stimulated the ovaries to produce and mature eggs for successful ovulation. Too much information? Sara shared that much and more with old ladies at the cheese counter in the supermarket. She found it difficult to talk about anything else nowadays. She wanted a baby. What else was there for her to say?

Sara believed that the hormones meant that nice Dr Jekyll became a snarling Ms Hyde almost the instant the cold steel needle punctured her skin. Charlie didn't accept that his wife's often hideously unreasonable behaviour was all due to the drugs she was ingesting. He thought that the *instant* transformation proved that Sara's reaction was psychological. She was blind with anger, frustration and desperation and therefore she was irrational. Sara feared he might be right. All she knew for certain was that she was often a tearful, stressy, bitter woman who made Snow White's stepmother look calm and sorted; whether this was because of drugs packed with hormones or because she was so livid at her insanely disappointing body, the result was the same.

She was hell to live with.

They both missed the old Sara.

Sara glanced at Charlie and caught him in a rare unguarded moment. Normally he froze his face into an expression which was supposed to look buoyantly optimistic and eternally unconcerned; in this instant she saw him as he really was – weary and worn. Fragile.

Pity and affection flooded through her body and Sara tried to rally. They'd learnt to do this for one another; it was a delicate balancing act. It was like being on either end of a see-saw – if one sank, the weight and strength of the other kicked in and pushed the despairing partner back up. Sara hated to think what would happen if either one got sick of this exhausting balancing act, and stood up and walked right away. She remembered the throbbing pain through her coccyx when she was a kid, when the see-saw crashed to the ground if the other kid stopped playing. She couldn't begin to imagine the pain if Charlie walked away.

Sara took a deep breath in and then breathed out, slowly. She visualised expelling the negative thought as Dr Alison Glover said she must. Sara thought Dr Glover was the best doctor she'd seen so far and there were many to pick from. Dr Glover exuded calm and patience. Her huge brown eyes were at once reassuringly intelligent and yet eternally sympathetic. She was one of the most earnest and respected professionals in her field but she had a holistic approach to the process that sometimes bordered on the hippy. Dr Glover had said Sara must start thinking more positively because if she were to become pregnant she wouldn't want the baby bathing in negative thoughts, would she? The image was a seductive one. So, even though Sara's legs felt as though they were encased in cement boots, she stood up and forced one foot in front of another. Left right, left right. As she pulled on the scarlet dress she tried to offer up a reasonable explanation for her wallowing. Sara hadn't the energy to consider whether it was truly pathetic that the kindest thing she managed to do for her husband nowadays was lie.

'I'm going to miss Eloise so much, that's why I've been so funny about going to this party. How can she do this to me?' She forced some humour into her voice and then added, 'Will you zip me up?'

'You mustn't take Eloise's decision to move to Dartmouth so person-ally,' said Charlie, tactfully choosing to accept that it might be her friend's move that was leaving Sara so low. 'You must see that she's not abandoning or rejecting you.'

'I know. Obviously, on a rational level, I'm aware that she's not rejecting me, that we are both grown-ups and we have to make inde-pendent decisions.' Sara grabbed a chunky necklace and popped it round her neck, added several heavy bracelets and slipped her feet into her shoes. She ran her hand through her bobbed, chestnut-brown hair and then undertook her final but signature act of preening; she applied a slash of scarlet lipstick. Sara was never seen without it. She had chubby cheeks, despite being generally slim, and the startling red colour punctuated her face and, she believed, stopped her looking like a hamster. Sara took a cursory glance at her reflection. She looked fine. Charlie beamed, thrilled that she was finally ready and that there was a chance that they might get to the party and actually have a good time. Good times were no longer guaranteed and therefore all the more precious.

'She has her family to think of. Imagine it. A childhood in Dartmouth. The girls are so lucky.'

He hadn't meant to but Charlie had just punched his wife in the gut and the pain pin-balled around her head and heart. She would miss Eloise, she wasn't lying about that, but she'd miss Emily, Erin and Poppy even more. Sara adored the girls. She never arrived at their house without bringing little gifts of sugary sweets, glittery pencils or stickers and she'd happily take them to the park or play games with them, even after Eloise's deep reserves of energy and patience had been used up. The girls accepted her treats and time willingly enough, but they had doting parents and were used to being the centre of everyone's attention. Eloise was the most grateful for Sara's affection and the extra pair of hands she provided. Sara would occasionally be called upon to make tea for two of the girls, while Eloise took the third to the doctor's or an optician's appointment. Sara and Charlie occasionally babysat so that Eloise and Mark could have a night out. Few of Eloise's other friends were ever available to do this sort of favour, as they all had children of their own to manage.

'It's really, really kind of you,' Eloise had always gushed on these occasions.

'No problem at all,' Sara had reassured her. 'Think of me as an auntie. I know it's sometimes difficult to get sitters and with your parents living abroad and Mark's parents living in Dartmouth you don't have much help. You go out and enjoy yourselves.' Secretly, there was nothing Sara liked more than to be curled up in Eloise's couch with Charlie and the girls. She considered it practice for when she'd have her own family.

If.

As Charlie and Sara walked towards Eloise's house it became clear that the party was well and truly underway. The upstairs windows were wide open and jazzy lounge music drifted down the street; bursts of adult laughter and childish screeches of delight (or feigned fear) erupted spasmodically. They had to slam the enormous silver knocker against the glossy black door three times before anyone was aware of their arrival. Eventually, Mark flung open the door and launched a broad, relieved smile their way. As he kissed Sara and gave Charlie a manly but warm back slap, he gushed, 'Thank God it's you two. If it had been the Robinsons with their four little buggers I think I might have run away.' He pointed his thumb behind him and rolled his eyes with good humour. 'There are more kids in there than adults and, to be honest, it is manic bordering on dangerous.'

Sara had to remind herself that Mark wasn't being insensitive. In his boyish way, he was trying to make her feel particularly welcome.

Still, she wanted to claw his eyes out.

He opened the door wide so that Charlie and Sara could shuffle past him into the long thin hall and as they did so he dashed out on to the street, muttering something about nipping to the corner shop to get some Tabasco sauce for the Bloody Marys.

Charlie and Sara loitered in the hallway for a moment. Neither of them was particularly confident in social situations such as this. Charlie didn't enjoy meeting large groups of Londoners who, within moments of shaking hands, invariably demanded to know what he did for a living. He was a plumber. A good one. Reliable and honest enough. But that didn't seem to cut it with the people he met at this sort of party. Mark and Eloise were the type of couple who had exciting friends. They knew countless stirring writers, influential politicians, important journos, rich bankers and interesting TV producers, many of whom had been invited to the party. Charlie and Sara were pretty sure Mark and Eloise only knew one plumber.

Eloise used to work in advertising but had given it up when she had Emily. In theory Sara supported a woman's choice to work in or out of the home after childbirth but in reality she was surprised to find that she was a bit irritated by the fact that Eloise didn't have to work. Sara had given quite a lot of thought to how much Mark must earn to support them all, and of course his parents had deep pockets; the latest offer to hand over the solicitor's practice for not much more than pocket money proved as much. Eloise occasionally said she missed the buzz of the trendy Soho office but Sara noted that she obviously didn't miss it enough to actually go back to grafting. Eloise kept up with her old colleagues by having lunch in expensive, widely reviewed restaurants so Sara fully expected the party to be stuffed full of pushy brand managers and earnest market researchers. The people who worked in advertising were easy to spot as they were the ones speaking a foreign language. A language scattered with phrases such as 'early adopters', 'brand integrity' and 'statement platforms'. The women in advertising drank beer and swore like sailors, the men wore purple knitwear and if they talked to Charlie at all it was to ask him to come and look at their leaky tap.

Sara tried to comfort herself with the thought that Charlie numbered amongst the sexiest men at this party. He had the most stunning green eyes that were flecked with gold and sparkled when he laughed; he worked out and so had resisted the cliché of becoming a tubby plumber, too hefty to get into most London *en suites*. He had dark curly hair and from the moment Sara had seen it, all she'd wanted to do was run her fingers through the said curls. Sara tried to catch Charlie's eye; she wanted to receive and bestow a look of mutual support. He avoided her glance. He preferred to pretend that there was nothing that could faze them in Eloise's sitting room.

Eloise suddenly appeared in the hallway; she flung her arms around Sara and yelled, 'At last! Here you are! Now the party can really begin.'

Eloise was surrounded by little girls with bunches and small boys with bruises, who were mobbing her. All of them were demanding something or other – ice-cream bowls, the TV remote or the loo. Erin and Poppy were among the rabble but they paused in their stream of demands to plonk gratefully received kisses on Sara and Charlie. As always Sara gasped at their beauty and felt a tug of love and longing in her chest as she hugged them to her. Eloise dealt with all the kids' requests and the baying crowd eventually melted away as she led Charlie and Sara through the sitting room towards the garden.

As expected, the house was full of bright and bubbly people quaffing champagne and nibbling the delicious canapés that were being passed around by Emily and her friends; tempting scallops wrapped in Parma ham, halloumi with chilli and mini goat's cheese tarts were proffered and accepted. Instantly, Sara knew that Eloise had employed caterers because, despite having many talents, she was a self-professed disaster in the kitchen. Sara had sometimes found herself wondering whether Eloise made such a big deal about just how terrible a chef she was because she relished rejecting an element of the stay-at-home-mum stereotype. Sara was not a good cook either but she rarely drew attention to the fact. She believed there were enough people in the world who were keen to point out others' faults; why help them along?

Eloise slipped through the guests, asking everyone whether they had enough to eat or whether they needed their glass refilled. She introduced Sara and Charlie to a number of people and, with helpful tact, reminded both parties if they'd met before.

'You remember Sara and Charlie Woddell, don't you, Josh? You last met at Mark's birthday party.' Eloise bestowed a smile on everyone, like a film star walking the red carpet; she didn't appear to be in the least bit concerned about leaving London. Sara thought El was probably counting off the moments until she had a place for her solid oak, wall-mounted wellington rack. The women had hunted high and low for a rack that had enough spikes to accommodate five sets of boots.

As Sara had expected (and dreaded), there were children everywhere. Some were sprawled in front of the TV, others were huddled around a Wii or iPod, there were a few eavesdroppers dotted between adults, keen to glean something useful from an inappropriate conversation and those with a sweet tooth were hovering near the enormous five-tier cake stand that was crammed with brightly decorated cupcakes. Sara was not so desperate for a child that she was incapable of distinguishing between good kids and the ones that would end up resting at Her Majesty's pleasure. She noticed the kids who were sulking, sniping and nipping, but it didn't diminish her appreciation of the ones with the cute smiles and adorable chubby legs, which of course was the type she was planning on producing if the IVF worked this time. When Sara saw a dimpled knee it took all her self-control not to swoop down and kiss it. She realised that kissing the legs of strangers' kids would be deemed as inappropriate so, on the whole, she played safe and kept her distance.

Sadly, most people interpreted Sara's self-restraint as a sure sign that she was not very maternal and generally quite standoffish. She knew lots of people thought she and Charlie didn't have kids because she had prioritised her career above and beyond raising a family. Eloise had never assumed as much and had always been sympathetic to Sara's situation. It was one of the reasons Sara had become so close to El. Sara didn't have any other friends who were quite so sympathetic and supportive.

Charlie noticed his wife's gaze lingering on a cheeky-looking red-haired boy and he quickly suggested he'd go and find some alcohol. Eloise had struck up a conversation with some guy who could do with a shave, although Sara instantly forgave him his slovenly appearance when she clocked the plump baby he was bouncing on his knee. A lump of longing, as indigestible as coal, sat in her throat. Worried she might not be able to control her ever-threatening tears, Sara turned away and headed out into the garden on her own.

Sara soon found herself jammed between two practically indistinguishable women, wearing Boden, blond bobs and benign smiles. One introduced herself as mumble mumble, Lucy's mummy, and the other woman said she was called something ending in the letter 'a' and was the mum of Dana and Harry. Sara quickly gathered that Lucy and Harry were in Poppy's school class. Eloise had been a school rep for Poppy's class for the last two years and, according to the blonde ladies, she'd been a marvel.

'We're going to miss her so much, aren't we?' said Lucy's mother, sadly shaking her head with regret.

'Absolutely, I was hoping she'd stand as Secretary next year, or even Chair,' added Harry's mum.

'Oh yes, she would have made a marvellous Chair.'

Sara didn't tell them of the times Eloise had occasionally commented that her role as class rep was a thankless, endless task. Sara wondered whether El considered leaving the role behind as one of the advantages of leaving London; maybe even a deciding factor. She didn't have a chance to say as much because suddenly the conversation moved on and, before she knew it, Sara was fielding the inevitable question of how she'd met Eloise and Mark.

'Through my husband's work,' she said vaguely.

'Is your husband a solicitor too?' asked Harry's mum. Sara could see how this conclusion had been drawn. She considered whether she should explain that Mark and Charlie met when the Hamilton boiler blew up. Like most Londoners the Hamiltons had endured mice, spasmodic patches of damp and, for a brief period, living next to noisy, argumentative neighbours. They had not been too worried about any of that but Mark and Eloise did see hot water as an essential. In desperation Mark had turned to the *Yellow Pages* and Charlie had responded swiftly to the call-out. Mark had been so grateful for Charlie's efficiency that he'd suggested, while the central heating was beefing back up to full capacity, that he should take Charlie for a thank-you drink. Sara had since learnt that Mark and Eloise often invited people for drinks or to dinner or out for a coffee. They were both confident that their invites would always be accepted and they always were.

Mark and Charlie got on like a house on fire (which in boy terms meant they supported the same football team and both enjoyed a curry). On hearing Charlie was new to the area Mark had insisted that Charlie call his wife to ask her to join them in the pub. After they'd had a couple of pints Mark suggested they all go back to theirs so that Sara could meet Eloise and their girls.

'You'll love her. Everyone does,' he'd said with a confident beam. Then, almost as an afterthought, he'd added, 'And she'll love you. She loves everyone.'

Sara hadn't expected to love Eloise. On the short walk from the pub to the Hamilton home she'd imagined that Mark's wife would be one of those over-confident, overwhelming types because her husband's introduction was nauseating. However, Sara found that after just fifteen minutes in Eloise's company she was indeed intoxicated.

Eloise, a warm, generous and spontaneous hostess, didn't resent her husband getting tipsy with the plumber and his wife while she made tea for three young girls. She'd called Charlie her knight in shining armour, she'd insisted on giving him a sizable cash tip, and then she'd practically demanded that they stay for supper. Eloise filled the kitchen with compliments and (despite her claims that she was an appalling cook) she produced big batches of pasta and an irresistibly wholesome and simple tomato sauce. They'd quickly drunk a bottle of Merlot and then Mark had nipped to the local off-licence to get a second bottle. The evening had passed in a haze of excited chatter and loud laughter. When finally they'd left, Sara had a list of useful contacts that Eloise insisted would be invaluable (including the number for the most wonderful chap who framed pictures at very reasonable costs and the best fishmonger for miles). They had also received an invite to return on Sunday for lunch. Eloise had said she'd invite a bunch of neighbours, a spontaneous welcome party for Charlie and Sara.

Sara had thought Eloise was too good to be true. Her perfect figure, manners and family must be faulty on some level, she reasoned. How was it possible that Eloise had managed to reach her mid-thirties and yet be so full of excitement, optimism and bonhomie? But as one invite led to the next and then to the next, as the weeks rolled into months and then, finally, years, Sara had found nothing in Eloise's character or actions to suggest that the petite, blonde, friendly woman was less than perfect. Eloise was generous, patient, pretty and bright. She darted around like a small fairy sprinkling magic dust on everyone she met. Sara noticed that people clustered around Eloise as though she carried an invisible, enchanted umbrella that might protect them from the big bad world. Sara had huddled under that charmed brolly for four wonderful years and she didn't know how she'd cope without it.

Sara didn't rush to clear up the blonde ladies' assumption that Charlie was a solicitor. As it happened, Lucy's mother lost interest in the conversation before Sara had to explicitly state that Charlie was a plumber. Sara had noticed that people did that a lot nowadays; questions were asked without an answer being genuinely demanded or expected and, even if one was delivered, it was rarely listened to.

Lucy's mother started to talk about a nasty rash on Lucy's front bottom. Sara was aware that it was not this woman's fault that, after approximately 130,000 years of the existence of *Homo sapiens*, humankind had failed to come up with a dignified name for female genitalia, but she really couldn't help but roll her eyes when Blondie repeatedly uttered the words 'front bottom'.

Harry's mother clocked Sara's expression and chuckled unconvincingly. 'Are you one of those mums who find the slightly twee nomenclature tedious? Do you call your little girl's parts her vagina?' she asked without any sign of irony, embarrassment or hesitation.

'I don't have a little girl,' Sara replied.

'Penis, then?'

'I don't have a penis.'

The blonde women giggled; they carried on laughing a little longer than necessary and they tried to catch one another's eye without meeting Sara's. No doubt they had her down as a 'character'. People expected to meet 'characters' at Eloise and Mark's parties; characters of varying degrees of amusement and acceptability. Sara wondered whether the blondes had categorised her as mad or eccentric; she knew it all depended on how wealthy they'd decided she was. Lucy's mum had checked out Sara's Chloé handbag. A Chloé handbag might earn her the privilege of being classed as an eccentric; if she shopped at Primark they'd feel more comfortable dismissing her as bonkers.

'I meant are you the sort of mother who refers to her son's willy as a penis?'

'I'm not any sort of mother,' Sara stated bluntly, and the words ripped at her heart. Her comment was almost too much for the ladies to compute. Sara could practically see the cogs in their minds whirring as they wondered whether she was objecting to being *labelled* as a particular type of mum. It was true that mum labelling was rarely complimentary. The presuming adjectives usually included words such as obsessive, fussy, pushy or neglectful; even alpha had become a derogatory term. Sara was perplexed. How could she know this and still long to join the club? It took a moment but then Harry's mum cottoned on to the fact that Sara didn't have any children.

'Are you trying?' she asked boldly.

Sara checked her watch. She'd known these women for about seven and a half minutes which seemed to be the required length of time people needed to have been introduced before they asked this sort of intimate question. Sara thought that she probably ought to be offended but in fact she was always delighted to have the opportunity to talk about the subject that was forever on her mind.

'Currently enduring my fourth round of IVF,' she replied frankly.

'Poor thing.'

'Oh dear.'

Both women patted her arm. She was swaddled in their sympathy and concern. In that moment she loved them with a sudden but intense love.

'After I had Lucy, I tried to conceive for nearly two years. No luck. So I had IVF and then we got twin boys. Tom and Eddie.' Lucy's mum beamed at Sara, certain she'd just delivered a message of hope.

'First round?' Sara asked.

'Yes!'

Sara stared at Lucy's mother, who was also the mother of Tom and Eddie, and she hated her. It was a cold and certain hate that sliced ruthlessly through Sara's body. She had Lucy, she didn't *need* more. Why was her IVF successful? Why weren't these things fair? Suddenly Sara wanted to throw her drink over the beaming blonde or slam her stiletto into her exposed flip-flop-shod foot. She'd have liked to have slapped her or hunted around for one of her babies to snatch him up! This woman didn't need *three* children! But, through superhuman control, Sara managed simply to say, 'If you'll excuse me, I think I've just spotted someone I know who I ought to say hello to.' Then she walked away, quickly, before they saw the angry tears brimming.

3

Margaret watched as the eighth bucket of dirty water swilled down the square stone kitchen sink, a feature of Eloise and Mark's new home. It swashed and sloshed, draining away the dirt in a wholly gratifying way. She rinsed the sink clean, wrung out the floor cloth and then peeled off her rubber gloves before she let out a deep, satisfied sigh. Ray quietly tutted and placed a mug of strong tea on the surface next to the Aga; he did this with an air that was calculated to show he was weary of watching her clean and that he disapproved. He often wearied of watching her clean long before she wearied of *doing* the cleaning. It was guilt. Good and proper. He was not a cleaner, never had been and never would be. There weren't many men of his generation that chipped in that way. He was very good with anything involving a ladder and Margaret had never in her life had to cut the grass, but Ray did little in the way of helping out around the house. He used to make the beds when that task still required the neat tucking in of sheets and blankets; that was the result of his army training as Ray was part of one of the last batches of young men called up to do National Service, a lifetime ago now. Precisely tucked sheets were the result of habit, rather than an impulse to be useful. He was proud of his symmetrical, systematic approach to bed making, but now they used a duvet so he didn't bother; there was no challenge in flicking a duvet. Still, as he'd brought Margaret a cup of tea, she decided not to be antagonistic but rather to be conciliatory.

'I'm nearly done here,' she said brightly.

'Yes, I should think so. You're too old to be on your knees scrubbing all day,' he commented gruffly.

'Thank you very much,' Margaret replied with indignation. 'I'm no such thing. I'm fifty-seven and that's not old.'

'Margaret, we've been married forty-nine years and we got married when you were twenty-one, that doesn't add up.'

She didn't dignify his comment with an answer. Forty-nine. Twenty-one. Added together those numbers were enormous. A lady shouldn't have to reveal her age. Margaret thought about it. She knew that pop star – what was her name? Angel? No. Mary? No, that's not a pop star's name. But it's something religious. She would have asked Ray but he had a bee in his bonnet about how forgetful she was at the moment so she didn't want to draw attention to another lapse. Anyway, Margaret knew that the pop star, whatever her name was, was always shouting about the fact that she was the wrong side of fifty but she could, couldn't she? It was all very well for her, with her army of nutritionists, yoga teachers and what have you. And Helen Mirren was another one always going on about her age. Yes, yes, we get it, you've said, you still look and feel hot even though you're sixty-seven! Yet some of us have to grow old; gracefully or disgracefully is our choice but we do *have* to get old. The likes of film stars seemed to believe that truth didn't apply to them, and somehow it didn't, admitted Margaret.

Margaret was not sure that she had ever been truly young. She couldn't remember feeling abandon (which surely was a privilege and proof of youth), she doubted she ever had. Marrying at twenty-one meant she'd had to grow up pretty damn sharpish. It was a few years before everyone else had caught her up and got married. Then, ironically, her friends had overtaken her. Lapped her. Margaret hadn't had Mark until much later than all her friends had had their children, so by the time she did have a baby she'd felt very old to be a new mum. And she'd been *ancient* since 1991, that was for certain. She knew the exact day she had turned ancient. She remembered it very well, no matter what Ray said about her poor memory.

Mark had come home from university for the weekend and he'd brought a young girl with him. Nice enough she was. Nicky or Vicky or maybe Lizzie. Anyway, she'd worn her hair very short, cropped close to her head, but she'd had a pretty elfin-shaped face, a bit like, oh, what was her name? Katharine Hepburn? No, not her, the other one – Audrey, Audrey Hepburn. She'd had an elfin face like hers, this girl had, so she could carry off the short hair. She'd worn dungarees, it was the fashion then. Not a very flattering fashion but then fashion rarely is. Well, Margaret had made up the spare room for this girlfriend of his, but when she'd shown the girl where she was to sleep, the girl had just laughed. Laughed straight at Margaret.

'Oh, Mrs Hamilton, I don't think we need to mess up your spare room. Who would we be kidding? Mark and I will sleep together, like we do at uni.'

That's what she'd said. No embarrassment. No shame. No tact! Smiled at Margaret. Beamed. As though she thought Margaret would be pleased that she'd have one less set of sheets to wash and iron after the weekend. As though she didn't realise Margaret was a mother, *Mark's* mother, and that she might have sensibilities or at least a say. Ray had laughed his head off when Margaret told him. He'd said, 'Isn't that what you'd have loved to have told my mother?'

'But we didn't sleep together before we were married, Ray,' Margaret had pointed out.

'Well, not for my lack of trying,' he'd chuckled.

Margaret had been forty-nine years old at the time and she'd felt one hundred and forty-nine. It wasn't even the fact that she had a son old enough to be, you know, adult. It was more that this girl was so different from anyone Margaret had ever been. Her experiences and attitude were light years away from anything the older woman might even imagine.

That was the day she'd become officially ancient.

'Eloise won't appreciate it, you know,' said Ray darkly, as he slurped on his cup of tea. Margaret wondered why he was being so tetchy. Maybe it was because it had rained all day for three days here in Dartmouth. He hadn't been able to get out to play golf; that always left him very grumpy. Even old dogs needed to stretch their legs.

'I think she will,' Margaret replied smoothly.

'No girl wants her mother-in-law interfering with her domestic arrangements.'

'Ray, I haven't employed a staff of seven or ordered curtains. I've just scrubbed the flagstone floors and washed the—' Goodness, what was the word for the look-throughs? She was always susceptible to senior moments when Ray started to get irritable. The stress passed between them like a relay baton. 'I've just washed the glass. I think Eloise will be pleased. She never has much time with three girls to look after and when she gets here she'll have all the unpacking to do. I just want her to feel settled as soon as possible.'

Ray looked at his wife and the look was one of warning. What was he worried about? she wondered. He often looked concerned nowadays; he used to be such a relaxed man. Maybe he thought she wanted this move too much. Maybe he thought it would end in tears if she couldn't remain casual.

Margaret *was* trying to remain calm, sane. Trying not to get too giddy, too overwhelmed and therefore overwhelming. But it was not easy because she couldn't remember when she'd last been this excited. She was so, so delighted that her daughter-in-law had finally agreed to move the family to Dartmouth. She was certain that Mark would have moved here years ago, given the choice, but Eloise was very London. She thought the air here was too clean to inhale. Margaret didn't blame Eloise (well, at least not openly), she realised and accepted that people had different tastes, needs and ambitions but she was glad that Eloise's tastes, needs and ambitions had finally fallen in line with her own. That was all.

'Be happy for me, Ray. To have my family close by is a dream come true.'

'They're my family too,' he said.

'I know, which is why you understand.' Margaret wanted to be placatory. She wasn't in the mood for a niggling row but, honestly, she wasn't sure he *did* understand, not exactly. Ray had been a wonderful father to Mark and, of course, he loved their granddaughters with all his heart, but it was different for him, he had other things in his life too. He had his solicitor's practice, his golf club buddies and his drinking buddies. He was happy walking to the embankment and chatting with the fishermen, he'd even experimented with a bit of watercolour painting last summer. His work and these hobbies filled his days. Margaret had never been one for hobbies. She liked to fill her days with family, that was what it was all about for her. It always had been.

'What are you doing with that bucket?' demanded Ray.

Margaret froze and focused. She followed Ray's gaze to try to work out what had caused his tone of outrage. It took a moment of intense concentration but then she realised that she'd just stacked the fire logs in the plastic bucket, when she'd meant to put them in the wicker basket that she'd bought especially for the purpose.

'Oh dear,' she mumbled, embarrassed.

'You're tired,' he pronounced. She nodded passively and then started to take the logs out of the bucket and place them carefully in the basket. 'Sit down, drink your tea. I'll do it.' His tone was softer. She let him take over because it was good that Ray got involved in preparations for Mark and, besides, he must be right that she'd been overdoing it.

'We only have Mark,' she said.

She didn't intend to say it loud enough for Ray to hear her and she didn't know if he had or hadn't, because it was not the sort of remark he'd comment on. Too emotional. Too much. Margaret would have liked more children but it wasn't to be, so she'd made much of Mark. She hadn't spoilt him, exactly, although that's what most people thought happened to an only child. No, he wasn't spoilt, not in the sense that they'd lavished expensive gifts and a private education on him, but Margaret supposed she *had* lavished her time on him. She had been a stay-at-home mum. There really wasn't any other sort in her day. Well, some women did bits for pin money – cleaning, factories, shop work, that sort of caper – but they did it around the children's school hours and no one called it a career. No one kidded themselves that they could have it all. Anyway, Margaret had been lucky that Ray earned enough for her not to have to go out to work, even for pin money. Her job was their home. And Mark.

She'd never missed a football game or a sports day. She'd picked him up from the school gate every afternoon until he was thirteen and he'd pleaded with her not to. She used to love that journey home, just the two of them. The daily ferry crossings were an adventure that they'd never tired of. They'd stay on the deck, even when the wind bit and it was raining pins. Obviously, it was best in the sunshine, sitting with their backs flat against the warm wooden slats of the bench. Margaret would point out the greedy gulls and the fishermen's lobster nets drying on the embankment. They'd breathe in the estuary air and the smell of the boat fuel with hearty delight; he chattering about his day, his triumphs and his frustrations, she soaking up every word.

They'd walked everywhere when he was very young. Margaret had only learnt to drive when Mark was a teenager, her motivation being that she could take him to and from his pals' homes, the ones who lived in the outlying villages; she didn't want him getting in a car with anyone who might have had a drink. Sometimes it had been the three of them on the walks but often it was just Mark and Margaret. It was a couple of miles up, across and down the other side of the hill, until they were at the best beach cove. A hearty walk but it was always worth it. They'd spent hours banging on buckets with plastic spades, searching for shells, getting damp with spray and then they'd warm up again by drinking tea from a flask and feasting on ham sandwiches. They listened to the waves making music. Sometimes, at night, if Margaret couldn't fall asleep, she thought of the sound of the waves breaking themselves to pieces on the shingle. Shush, shuushhh. It was comforting, like a lullaby.

They'd waited a long time for Mark. Margaret had been thirty before she became a mum. That would be classed as a young mum now, by many, but in the early seventies Margaret was seen as positively geri-atric. So when he did finally come along she'd lavished her time on him, who wouldn't have? It was natural. Besides, he was an easy boy to love. Affectionate, funny, bonny, athletic, smart. What you'd call an all-rounder. Everyone who'd ever met Mark had loved him.

But Margaret was sure she'd always loved him the most.

Eloise loved him, of course she did; Margaret knew that. She was a good wife. They were right for each other. They made one another happy, which was all that mattered. They brought up the girls very nicely indeed. It wasn't all crop tops and 'Whatever!' with their three and Margaret saw that was so often the case with her friends' grandchildren.

But a wife's love was different. Married love had conditions attached, things to be negotiated, cracks to paper over. Tempests to be navigated. Passionate highs and barren lows.

A mother's love was unconditional. Margaret could never say no to Mark. She wouldn't have been able to hold out for fifteen years knowing that he wanted to live in Dartmouth, just because she'd needed to be near a particular patisserie or handbag shop or something or other.

Mind you, Margaret wasn't going to be caught grumbling. Eloise had finally agreed to move here and for that Margaret would be eter-nally grateful. Margaret had the sense to know that a mother-in-law should never pitch herself against her daughter-in-law because, if the mother had done her job properly, the lad would always side with his wife. She just wanted to be useful to them – to help with babysitting and school runs, and she planned to do the shopping and a bit round the house. When they'd lived in London Margaret had always felt that she was too far away to be useful.

To be loved.

'I want to clap my hands with joy when I think about them arriving tomorrow,' she gushed to Ray.

'They're arriving Tuesday, not tomorrow.'

'Yes.'

'That's three days' time.'

'Yes, that's what I said. My family living here, just a ten-minute walk away, it's a dream come true!'

Ray raised his bushy, white eyebrows. He had very animated eyebrows. When they'd courted, Margaret used to think he was just like Sean Connery, in that respect. His eyebrows were smooth and dark and cocky in those days. Now it looked as though a couple of friendly, furry albino caterpillars were on the loose. Not so much debonair, more daft.

Margaret didn't know when it happened for him. Getting old. Ray's aging had been more gradual than her own; a liver spot appearing from nowhere, a click in his back when he got out of bed too suddenly, some shortness of breath when he climbed the steps in town, preferring a good book and a cuddle rather than the other. She didn't mind, though. Getting old together was what she'd expected, what she'd hoped for. What would Emily say? 'What she'd signed up for.' That was it. Getting old with Ray was what Margaret had signed up for.

'Madonna!' Margaret shouted suddenly in triumph.

'What?' Ray looked bemused.

'That's the name of the woman I was on about. The one who doesn't get old.'

'I've no idea what you are talking about, Margaret.'

'Oh keep up, Ray, keep up,' Margaret chuckled.

4

It was after ten p.m. The party had been bouncing for a record-breaking six hours and a quick glance around the carnage suggested that it wasn't likely to fold for a couple more yet. The children had been herded into the bedrooms and were more or less settled for the night, although nine p.m. had been ugly. Tearful, exhausted and jacked up on cupcakes, the kids had fought with their slightly drunken parents about the importance of cleaning their teeth or changing into pyjamas. To be frank, when challenged, none of the adults could really recall why it was so important to take off socks or comb hair; it was hard to retain adult logic after a few glasses of champers.

The younger ones were now slumbering in Eloise and Mark's bedroom; the spare duvets and sleeping bags were shoe-horned in, cemented by the guests' coats. Eloise popped her head around the door to check that everyone was OK. The toddlers were sleeping like replete cherubs, their sun-kissed limbs chubby and tangled, their breath making the air warm and sticky. It was heaven.

The older ones were shored up in Erin and Poppy's room, watching DVDs. Eloise hoped they were watching something suitable like *Gnomeo and Juliet* but feared it was more likely to be *Sex and the City 2*. She tried to check up on them but she was met with a determined barrage of about a dozen seven- to twelve-year-old faces peering through a gap where (after some persuasion) they'd allowed the bedroom door to open a few centimetres. Even her offer of popcorn had been received with a certain amount of scepticism and caution; they took the bags as though they were participating in a high-level hostage swap. Eloise had insisted that lights needed to go off 'soon', but didn't have the courage of her convictions to state exactly when 'soon' should be. She was aware that lack of sleep meant that they'd all be unbearable in the morning but she decided that the girls needed to say goodbye to their friends in style. Besides, when Eloise had envisaged this 'night to remember' she hadn't planned to remember it because she'd spent the entire evening on her landing, arguing with a bunch of tweenagers for an eternity.

Having done her duty(ish) as a responsible(ish) adult, Eloise rejoined the party. So far she hadn't managed to have a drink because every time she raised a glass she saw someone else that she needed to greet or to chat to. Not that she'd managed to say anything meaningful to anyone. There were so many beaming, familiar faces that all El was managing was 'hello' and 'wonderful to see you, thank you for coming', before someone else commandeered her attention. A quick sweep of the room confirmed that the party was clearly a huge success by anyone's standards, including her own exacting ones. The caterers had proven to be a hit (if only she'd discovered them earlier, the ones she'd used last Christmas had been a bit disappointing). Eloise had extravagantly ordered seven substantial canapés per person tonight, rather than the recommended five. Besides, there was the barbecue (Mark had insisted on the barbecue because he said that canapés were for girls – although he'd wolfed down at least a dozen Parma ham-wrapped scallops). Still, Eloise would always far rather over-cater than under-cater as she always felt she had a duty to attempt to abate the hangovers. As it was a warm night the party had spilled into the garden and Mark was now leading a break-dancing-slash-body-popping session out there. Eloise giggled as he shouted that he was 'giving it some, old school style' and she walked to the patio doors and yelled, 'There is a very real chance you'll end up in A and E before the night's out!' He grinned, fanning away her concern. 'It's a good thing the children are in bed or they would be traumatised. How is it even possible to put your leg there?' she added. Mark laughed and attempted an even more extreme manoeuvre. He knew she was secretly impressed.

It was the stage of the night where the females, having politely turned down all offers of food all afternoon and evening, had now abandoned any semblance of restraint and were swooping down on the few remaining canapés and cupcakes; they Hoovered up every last crumb like locusts. Sara and one of Eloise's neighbours were in the kitchen, whipping up cheese and pickle sandwiches, and two women from Eloise's Pilates class appeared to be trying to eat the wax fruit that was part of Poppy's greengrocer store. On the other hand, throughout the festivities, the guys had openly eaten their fill of fat barbecue burgers and sausages, as well as having drunk several beers each, so they were now full of macho instincts that they didn't quite know how to spend. When they were younger, this would be the stage of the evening when they'd hit on women; now they challenged one another to games of FIFA on the Xbox and argued about the most efficient routes to destinations that they weren't even planning on travelling to tonight.

'It's an outstanding party,' said Sara as she sidled up to Eloise and handed over a glass of champagne.

'Thank you.'

'I saw you were without.'

Eloise smiled, glad that she and Sara always looked out for each other in this and so many other ways. They clinked glasses and Eloise was about to suggest they toasted 'New Beginnings' when she caught something in Sara's expression which stopped her. There was a masked tension. Most people only saw the scarlet lipstick, but El noticed the slight lines of concern that ran like tributaries from Sara's eyes to her determined, but not quite convincing, smile. New beginnings could be deemed insensitive. So much was deemed insensitive by Sara at the moment. It was insensitive of Eloise to grumble about the amount of washing she did every week, it was insensitive of her to worry about how much she spent in supermarkets on a food shop. It was insensitive of her to say she wished she'd drowned the girls like kittens – OK, that actually *was* a bit insensitive but obviously she'd only been kidding when she'd said that. Sara hadn't got the joke. Sara rarely joked nowadays. Eloise decided to play it safe; all she said as she clinked glasses was, 'Cheers.'

'This is one of your best ever. You are certainly going out with a bang,' enthused Sara. 'Look, Maggie is minesweeping, that's always a sign of a good party.'

'Yes, and Nick is feeding Lottie strawberries from the chocolate fondue.' Eloise referred to Nick as 'the last man standing', as he was the only one of her friends who hadn't ventured down the aisle. Some of her friends had already married, divorced, remarried and divorced again but Nick had proven to be slow off the blocks. The truth was that he was a commitment phobic and an accomplished, irresistible flirt, a combination which was obviously *not* the path to blissful monogamy and a ruby wedding anniversary. El counted him among her favourite people to have fun with, but right now she fought an impulse to warn Lottie that he was an utter cad. Lottie had recently split from her partner of five years; would the re-enactment of *Tess of the D'Urbervilles* lead to a confidence-boosting dalliance or another crashing disappointment? Eloise wondered what her responsibility to her party guests was. After all, Lottie was over twenty-one. Twice, actually. But . . .

Before Eloise had time to think it through thoroughly Charlie interrupted.

'Hello, gorgeous, hello, gorgeous,' he said in a squeaky high-pitched voice; he'd been inhaling the helium from the balloons.

'Charlie, don't be such a bloody idiot. You don't know what that's doing to your body,' snapped Sara. 'And how much have you had to drink?'

'Lost count,' Charlie replied. He managed to squeak and slur at the same time, proving that men can multi-task. Eloise resisted the urge to smile at his response because Sara would definitely see it as disloyal but Charlie looked playful and relaxed, which was rare these days and wonderful to witness.

'Clearly too much,' persisted Sara. 'You know binge drinking is dire for sperm count.'

It was unfortunate that there was a freak lull in the conversation and they found themselves between music tracks when hysteria and blind panic pushed Sara's voice to a higher volume. The words 'sperm count' thundered out into the party atmosphere.

Charlie looked to his feet and then moved swiftly away. Anger and humiliation shivered through the room; it was the 'his and hers' variety – neither of them were happy. Eloise squeezed Sara's arm but Sara brushed her off.

'Well, binge drinking *is* dire for sperm count! He should be more careful,' she muttered desperately.

Eloise knew better than to point out that there was no evidence that their problem with conceiving had anything to do with Charlie's sperm count. Officially they suffered from unexplained infertility. Neither of them had anything wrong with them but, then again, neither of them knew what could be done to fix their problem. Nor did Eloise point out that since Charlie had already masturbated into a pot and this round of IVF was underway (Sara had shared all the details) there was no harm in him letting his hair down this evening anyway. And Eloise definitely did not suggest that Sara follow him in order to make up – he'd gone into the kitchen and there were a number of sharp knives in there. Eloise really didn't want her party to end in a murder most foul.

Sara avoided catching Eloise's eye. Shame and fury were welded together in a vicious threatening poison. El scrambled around for a change of subject.

'Look at Mark, he's going to pull something and I don't mean a new woman.'

Mark was attempting a head spin that he'd been quite good at, a million years ago. 'He's resolute in his determination to act his shoe size not his age. I honestly don't think he's aware that he's the wrong side of forty, although he'll feel every day of his age tomorrow. I wonder whether we'll be able to get an appointment with his chiropractor,' El joked.

Some women might have found his boyishness irritating, but Eloise never had. She was unequivocal on the matter; he was unadulterated fun and she felt lucky he was hers. She loved watching him dance, even if it was a bit scary. In a world stuffed full of people desperate to keep control, be that over themselves or other people, Mark was amazingly refreshing; she adored the way he let go. She thought it was remarkable that a man could flail his arms and legs with such a disregard as to what people might consider cool and shake his head with such passion that it looked as though there was a real danger it might just flip off, and *yet* be the sort of man who set up direct debit payments for all their bills, who took time off work to go to his daughters' sports days and nativity plays and made her feel safe and secure, no matter what. She knew he was deeper than anyone would imagine looking at him right now, all sweaty and silly. 'Let's join him, let's go and dance,' she urged Sara.

'No, I don't think so.'

'Oh, come on.' Eloise tried to take hold of Sara's hand and pull her towards the garden deck, the area that had been carved out to act as a dance floor, but Sara shook free. 'Why not? There aren't enough opportunities to dance nowadays, we shouldn't pass one up. You've often told me stories about your clubbing days. I bet you were a great dancer,' Eloise encouraged.

'Ha.' It was hard to ignore the all-consuming, overwhelming bitterness that Sara spat out with that one syllable. 'Maybe, once upon a time.'

Pausing, Eloise considered whether there was anything she could say to cheer up her friend. Sara could be very stubborn. If she was determined to have a terrible evening then she'd succeed. Mark and Eloise used to go clubbing when they'd first met but they had never been particularly hard core. They'd soon silently agreed that nightclubs were a place people went to meet other people. Once they had met each other Eloise and Mark preferred to go to the cinema, out for a meal or, if the absence of flatmates allowed, they would stay in and make love. However, Eloise had heard enough of Sara's stories to know that Sara had once been an avid clubber. Her fixation with decorum was a relatively new mania. On the surface Sara was simply a conscientious accountant, diligently auditing books and working towards the next lucrative promotion, but Eloise was privy to details about her wilder, more audacious past.

From her stories it was clear that Sara had been infinitely more adventurous than Eloise in her youth. Even though Sara had been brought up in the Home Counties and Eloise had grown up in London, it was Sara who had had a sex life from the age of thirteen, whereas Eloise didn't have sex until she went away to uni. Sara told stories about how, as a teenager, she hitched lifts along the A3 as she was desperate and determined to get to gigs in London. El had gone to gigs at that age too but her parents had insisted that she was accompanied by her two older brothers, who acted as chaperones. She'd never hitched a lift in her life and couldn't imagine ever doing so. El had seen bands like Wham! and Bananarama, Sara had seen the patron saint of disenfranchised teenagers, David Bowie. Bowie defined the progressive and independent spirit, he challenged the boundaries of rock and roll with fervour and ingenuity. Wham! produced catchy ditties that were played in department stores at Christmas. Most people would have to agree that being into Bowie was infinitely cooler than being into Wham!.

Sara revealed to Eloise that she'd smoked and drunk excessively, doing the teenage thing to the limit. She'd experimented with dozens of sexual partners, she'd tried most recreational drugs, cheated in exams, shoplifted for kicks and frequently stayed up all night at endless warehouse raves that usually only drew to a close when the police were called. Sara did all this while maintaining her plummy Home Counties accent and an inner self-confidence that she was entitled to misbehave; both attributes were invaluable every time she needed to slip under the radar when the police or parents were called. She'd had an air of enduring respectability about her that was as seductive and convincing as it was unreal. As a result, repercussions and reprisals for her mischievous behaviour glided past her as though she was Teflon coated. When Sara first relayed these stories Eloise had struggled to hide her surprise. It was hard to reconcile the old Sara with someone who freaked out when her husband sucked on a helium balloon.

Eloise had been delighted to hear that Sara had once been wonderfully exciting; she'd been impressed by these stories that suggested that Sara had a more complex – almost contradictory – character than the one currently presented to the world. Eloise had made it one of her ambitions to rediscover and unleash Sara's more daring and impetuous side. Over the last four years she had tried to somehow reconcile Sara's fixation with making a new life and living her own life. So far, Eloise had failed.

Eloise knew that the personas people cultivated in their late thirties and early forties were often light years away from the root of the person they had once been. Indeed, Eloise had endured a significantly more average adolescence than Sara and was keen to put as much distance as she could between where she was now and the middling being she had once been. Eloise had fallen deeply in love at sixteen and then (somewhat predictably) had been ditched around the time of her A levels. The ensuing crying into her pillow led to disappointing grades and her missing the opportunity to attend her preferred university. She had managed to get a place, through clearing, at Brunel, to read communication and media studies. She'd set off to uni believing she wasn't quite up to it and so worked incredibly hard to prove that she was (ostensibly to everyone else but, in truth, to herself). Long hours in the library limited the amount of excitement she'd had access to. There was not much fun to be found among the Dewey Decimal System. Eloise had worked hard enough to gain a 2:1 and, importantly, to secure decent work experience during the long holidays.

After graduating she got a job as chief gofer at an advertising agency called Q&A, a baby arm of an impressive American, big brand advertising agency. Back then she'd had vague dreams of promotion and eventually living in New York. She'd planned to wear grey Armani pencil skirts and live in a loft apartment. Even now she sometimes replayed this idea as a mental avatar game. Eloise thought that most mums probably had a harmless alternative imaginary world, to help maintain sanity.

The Q&A office was a towering building of glass, stained to primary colours; an über-modern, open-plan place, spread over six floors and in the centre of each there was something artfully playful like a ball pool, a basket ball hoop or a foosball table. These toys were introduced so that the executives could release stress and stay in touch with their inner child although, looking back, Eloise wondered whether she and her young colleagues had a clue what stress was; she was pretty certain none of them were in a hurry to grow up. Eloise soon came to the conclusion that the entire industry was a huge sport and she'd had a blast. The energy she hadn't spent at uni doing fresher week japes – pub crawls or bed hopping – was pent up. She flew like a champagne cork from a bottle. Eloise worked with intelligent, handsome, affluent, invigorating types. They conspired and connived to persuade brand managers to blow their budgets on glitzy, alluring, arty and sometimes even relevant adverts. She travelled in taxis so frequently that she'd learnt how to whistle to draw one and she had so many overseas meetings that she was awarded a BA silver card. It was a lot of work but even more fun.

Eloise had dated. All her relationships were either tediously complicated and convoluted or glorious fun but trivial. When she thought back to the years she'd worked in London she couldn't help but grin and she felt an irrepressible surge of extreme excitement. Those were days of intense hedonism when El had nothing to think of other than her career (which had been going well enough), her relationships (which were a source of amusement if not true love), her friendships (which were solid), her clothes (which were cheap – in both senses of the word but it didn't matter then) and her next night out (which was always bursting with possibility). Eloise had floated on a hazy cloud of dreamy irresponsibility.

Then, one day, she'd met Mark and she suddenly ached for something a little more permanent. It was at a party launching a new colour denim jean. He was chatting to a very young Kate Moss. *The* Kate Moss. As the advertising manager Eloise was delighted that Kate Moss had turned up at this particular party, her appearance would guarantee mentions in the diary columns of the national newspapers and create more exposure for the brand. As a woman (who had been instantly attracted to the especially good-looking guy chatting to the model), she was less elated.

But Mark was realistic and had known that Kate Moss would never be more to him than an impressive anecdote. Yet the way he'd thrown long, lingering glances Eloise's way allowed her to hope that perhaps he was interested in her. Eloise was right about both things: Mark was interested in her and Kate Moss did become an anecdote. Mark mentioned her in his speech at their wedding; he bragged he'd chosen El over Kate and had left Kate gutted. This wasn't at all factually accurate but it did raise a laugh.

The moment the supermodel yawned and her publicist led her away to be introduced to someone else, Mark and Eloise had started to walk directly towards one another. Not so much eyes meeting across a crowded room but their entire beings drawing one another across a crowded room. There was no false modesty or disingenuous behaviour, they'd wanted to be together from the off and they were prepared to take the risk and let each other know as much. They struck up a conversation, something about the vodka-run ice sculpture, then they chatted all evening, quickly finding a way to establish the fact that they were both single. At the end of the night they'd kissed passionately at Piccadilly Tube station but then gone home to their separate flats. They met up the next day, the one after that and the one after that. By the end of the week they both knew they were in love.

Easy peasy. Some things were meant to be.

Of course, there'd been rows along the way. Mark was driven nuts by the fact that Eloise was often late for things and she used to throw the occasional hissy fit when some leggy ex would pop back into their lives, but on the whole their relationship was regarded, by themselves and others, as plain sailing.

Mark's stature was impressive. As a young guy he'd worked out regularly and ambitiously, plus he played football and rowed every weekend. It had showed then and still did now. Even though he wasn't as fanatical about fitness (fanaticism demanded time he no longer had), his muscles seemed to remember the hours he'd invested pulling them taut. They'd rewarded him by holding up (despite the fact that his only regular exercise nowadays was running up and down stairs in response to the girls' constant demands for glasses of water or the retrieval of lost teddy bears after lights went out). He was still in great shape. His back remained broad and dependable; his shoulders were just as wide and willing to shore up Eloise. His body conveyed a sexy capability, he oozed a desirable reassurance so lacking in many modern men.

Sometimes, when they were out, Eloise noticed women looking at him with unadulterated appreciation. Tall, dark and handsome did tend to have that effect. She also saw disappointment burn in those women's eyes when they realised he was with her and the girls. His face was defined by high cheekbones, a narrow, straight, noble-looking nose. Somehow the length and shape suggested that life's anxieties and embarrassments slithered off him without causing him a moment's distress or concern. He had sparkly blue eyes that glistened with intelligence and humour. When they'd met, his dark, sleek hair had flopped across those sparkly eyes, ensuring that they had held her attention all the more when he brushed his hair away. His hair was shorter now, he'd had it chopped when it first began to streak with white, but his eyes still held Eloise. Theirs was a thrillingly uncomplicated relationship. There was no doubt, little drama or palaver. They were meant to be and they'd both believed it from the outset.

The tone of Eloise's London days altered subtly after she met Mark. The overwhelming hedonism was replaced with genuine passion and her career also became more crucial as they began to save for a flat together. Her friendships remained important but they were less intense. Mark was her confidant of choice and her concern with her next night out was replaced by a preoccupation with planning for the future: the wedding, their first home and baby, baby number two and three. Securing nursery and school places became far more important than reserving a table at the latest hot restaurant. Strangely, slipping off the hazy cloud of dreamy irresponsibility had suited Eloise. She liked landing with her feet very firmly on the ground. Mark, their girls and their home were everything she needed or wanted. She was fulfilled, which was rare and wonderful.

As the years had passed, Eloise's confidence had increased. El thought this was how it should be, so she found it heartbreaking to notice that Sara's confidence seemed to have seeped away. Eloise sometimes wondered whether there was a cosmic, karmic balance that simply wouldn't allow everyone to be happy all the time. What a pity. Sara still sounded like the Queen but she hadn't managed to retain the inner confidence that her stories of misadventure so clearly advertised. The birth of each one of Eloise's little girls had grounded El. They'd allowed her to expand and settle comfortably into her space in life; she felt she belonged, she had purpose and direction. On the other hand, for Sara, each month that slipped by with the bloody show stole that same chance and she seemed to shrink. It was a tragedy.

Eloise was constantly aware of her good fortune and her friend's lack of it. She felt an illogical guilt and often found herself in the position of trying to rally Sara. Eloise believed the best way to hold on to her good fortune was to share it around. She had as good as adopted Sara and Charlie, welcoming them into their family as warmly as she could. The Woddells ate at the Hamiltons' at least once a week, Eloise and Sara spoke daily, they shopped together, visited the hairdresser's together, Sara and Charlie joined the Hamiltons on family walks and even family holidays. Eloise knew that this move was going to be hard for *her* but she suspected it might be worse still for Sara. She wondered whether this was the moment that she should tell Sara how much she was going to miss her when she moved to Dartmouth. Have it said explicitly, for the avoidance of doubt. Should she present Sara with the bangle she'd bought? A silver friendship bangle with the words *laugh, love, hope, dance* engraved on the inside. Eloise decided she'd do it later. Such an excessively emotional gesture might cause Sara to become more maudlin, not less, it was hard to judge.

'So? Dancing?' Eloise asked again as she began to move towards the music, but Sara didn't follow. She backed away and then vanished. Eloise assumed she'd gone to the bathroom and comforted herself with the thought that at least she'd put clean towels and plenty of toilet roll in there before the party began. Eloise sighed; she thought it was a good hostess's duty to make sure that there was Molton Brown liquid soap and a copy of *Private Eye* in the guests' loo but she was also aware that a good hostess bothered to find out what was upsetting her guest. Although, in this case, Eloise was already aware of what was upsetting Sara and the only question was should she follow her friend and see if she could think of any new words of comfort or consolation? Had they all been said?

Suddenly Mark pulled Eloise into his arms and right on cue (mostly because Mark was in charge of the iPod) the music changed to a slow number.

'Are you dancing?' he asked but his arms were already tightly around his wife before she could answer. She could smell the beer on his lips and found it strangely attractive.

'Are you asking?'

'I'm always asking.'

'Then I'm always dancing.' They both giggled, a tiny bit self-conscious of their cheesy routine but also, secretly, quite ridiculously pleased with themselves. They repeated this daft little ditty to one another reasonably frequently. It was not unknown for Mark to whisk Eloise around the kitchen when she was in the middle of overseeing homework or just finishing up dinner. She had a phase of wondering whether *Glee* was having *too* much of an influence but then she'd noticed a pattern; a dance routine was always an announcement that his intentions were carnal.

The balmy July night and the heartfelt, melodic vocals of Duffy mooched through their bodies and they relaxed and smudged into one another. Eloise thought of these moments as the 'so worth being married' moments. Most of the time she was just married and, as careless as it might sound, she didn't really think of it at all. It just was as it was and it had been that way for a long time. Just as she was British. She was a woman. She was a mother. She was married. She didn't think about these things on a day-to-day basis, they were just part of her. However, sometimes she remembered she was British – usually when she was trying to match shoes with trousers and she was uncertain as to whether she ought to wear pumps or a little heel. Then she thought a French woman would know, an American might not care and an Italian would have decided the day before she'd needed to leave the house. As a British woman Eloise was unsure. Being married was a little bit the same. Most of the time it just *was* and she was glad about that and then, at other times, it was something she remembered and either questioned or delighted in.

When Mark had campaigned for them all to move to Dartmouth Eloise had become very aware that she was married. They'd been dashing along from paper anniversary to ivory (she'd got flowers or jewellery every year as she wasn't keen on the idea of a gift certificate, let alone anything made of elephant tusks). They were always busy taking the Tube to work, giving birth, planning holidays, managing school runs and folding washing. They divided their time between farmers' markets and dinner parties, the office and prize days without ever questioning their team, their unit. Even after Ray offered the solicitor's practice, Eloise still hadn't been certain that they'd make the move until one night, as they lay in bed together, Mark had told her he couldn't bear it any longer. Those were his words: 'I can't bear it.'

He talked about how much he missed the taste of salt on his lips, the feel of sand grits crunching in the kitchen and hallway after a family had trailed it in, following a blissful day on the beach searching rock pools and building castles; he missed that connection to the outside world, to nature. He wanted to bob on boats and hear seagulls screech. He wanted to live closer to his parents who were getting older. He wanted these things for himself, for their children, for their unit. He was passionate about it and Eloise had understood that this passion wasn't something new, impetuous or unreasonable. His desire to live in Dartmouth was a constant, unrelenting longing; he'd simply squashed his yearnings in order to accommodate hers. He must have been aware of being married every day, if married meant compromise, sacrifice and concession. And Eloise thought that it sometimes did mean exactly that.

When Eloise woke up each morning in London she wanted to punch the air. She immediately hopped on to the invisible high-speed train which dashed with unreasonable velocity through unique opportunities, retail wonders and a sense of history and of future. She was suddenly aware that every day that her husband had woken up here he'd probably sighed as he fell in step with the pacy rat race, the smog, the grime, the crime, the bustle and hustle that defined his London. He'd given her what she wanted for years and years. He would have given it to her for ever if she'd insisted but it was time for her to try to understand what he wanted.

This 'married moment', hugging and rocking to and fro in a poor attempt at dancing which was so symptomatic of being a certain age, wasn't as grandiose but it was wonderful. As Eloise melted into her husband's warmth she felt an overwhelming sense that she belonged. She belonged here in his space, whether that was in London or Dartmouth.

'Great party,' he mumbled.

'Perfect,' she sighed.

'I'm already looking forward to the debrief tonight,' he added.

This was one of the many things Eloise loved about Mark; he was a good old gossip. He really did care who looked fab, who had given into the flab, which kid had behaved most horribly (please God don't let it be one of theirs), who was heading for the divorce courts, who might have come into some money. Naturally, as a man, he didn't really 'get' everything. He didn't see the undercurrents or pick up on the nuances, and innuendo was completely lost on him. But, bless, he'd be very happy to collude and conclude as Eloise recounted and pawed over the various scenarios of domestic bliss and domestic blasts that had played out tonight.

Their swaying (more or less) in time to the music became a bit awkward. Mark tried to rest his head on top of Eloise's but as he'd had quite a bit to drink and it was getting late, neither his co-ordination nor balance was precise. Eloise felt drilled into the ground by his weight.

'El.'

'Yup?'

'Shall we go to bed?'

'What, and leave our guests?'

'I don't think they'll steal anything,' he joked. 'I don't think they'll even notice.'

He held her a fraction away from his warm body and stared into her eyes. He thought he was giving her a Jake Gyllenhaal seductive gaze but in fact he was cross-eyed with booze, so looked a bit closer to Simon Pegg. Still, she giggled and was about to agree when she was struck by a thought.

'We can't. The cast of *Annie* is asleep on our bed.'

'Oh sh—' He threw his head back and groaned. 'Do you know Erin was a bonus and Poppy was a miracle?'

'What do you mean?'

'How did we manage to make a second, let alone a third child, when our opportunities to shag are constantly being eroded?'

'Dunno, love, shall I see if there's a cupcake left instead?'

'Oh, go on, then,' said Mark with a shrug, instantly accepting the consolation prize because they were both used to doing so. Sex was lovely but it did tend to slip down the 'to do' list when life was hectic. It was somewhere beneath empty the dishwasher, set Sky Plus and read the Sunday supplements (something they managed to do by the following Friday evening, usually). Happily, it was still above alphabetising the old CDs. 'I like the chocolate ones best,' he added unnecessarily.

El knew he liked the chocolate ones, that's why there was one stashed in the fridge, saved just for him.

AUGUST

5

Eloise settled down in her new kitchen and called Sara. 'So tell me all about your holiday, then,' she encouraged excitedly; there was no need to pause and announce herself. They'd texted one another during Sara and Charlie's two-week holiday driving around Italy but hadn't managed a conversation. Mark and Eloise couldn't afford a holiday this year and so Eloise was very keen to get some vicarious pleasure from Sara's.

'Oh, it was lovely.' Sara offered up a couple of anecdotes and names of some of the tourist traps they'd visited; the Vatican, the Trevi Fountain. They'd had a pleasant holiday and Sara had really tried to relax, because that's what Dr Glover had prescribed, but she couldn't help fretting that a flight must be in some way damaging to their bodies; was it worth the risk, just for a plate of pasta and a view of the Colosseum? Did anyone really understand the effect of high altitudes? She'd found nothing helpful on the Internet. 'Have you made a final decision about the girls' schools?' asked Sara, turning to a subject she had a much keener interest in. 'School term starts next week, doesn't it?'

'Yes, it does. Time has flown since we got here.'

'You're leaving it very late.'

'I know, but you'll be relieved to hear we've made a decision. Finally. We're sending Erin and Poppy to Capcombe and Emily to the Academy in the centre of Dartmouth.'

'So much for simplifying your new life,' Sara commented. 'I thought all three girls were eligible to go to the Academy. Don't they teach children from age three to eighteen? It's on the doorstep. You should send all three of them there. It's a no-brainer.'

Sara had visited all the potential schools with the Hamiltons last May and therefore was clued-up on what each school offered. As she'd trailed around numerous draughty halls and soggy sports fields she felt entitled to give an opinion on the final decision. Eloise knew Sara was more involved with the girls' lives than other friends might be because, sadly, she didn't have any of her own children fighting for mindshare. Eloise had three, it seemed only fair to share out her embarrassment of riches when she could. Eloise had no problem with Sara being so caught up, it was impossible to have too many people loving your kids but, at the end of the day, they were Mark and Eloise's children and Eloise had to do what she thought was right for them. She made an effort to try to explain to Sara some of the nuance and reasoning behind their decision.

'Yes, you're right, they could all go to the same school but Emily went apoplectic at the thought. Ever since Erin joined her at the primary in Muswell Hill she's been looking forward to the day when she could leave her "bratty, nuisance" sisters at the breakfast table – her words, not mine – and she'd be able to walk to the big school with her friends. It's hard enough that she's had to move and she'll have to make an entirely new set of friends. I couldn't face telling her that her dream of independence might have to be shelved.'

'I think you're secretly a little bit afraid of Emily,' said Sara tutting. Eloise was sure that any parent who had done the tweenage years would sympathise but she couldn't say as much. 'Isn't Capcombe the village that's just over two miles from your home?' Sara asked.

'Yes.'

'So you'll no longer be keeping up the plan of walking to school, then? Sod the healthy, green and responsible lifestyle.'

'We are still planning on walking. At least while the weather holds up.' Eloise was pretty certain that they wouldn't be walking when the weather got harsher but she couldn't give up on the idea before she'd started. Like Sara, all of Eloise's London friends were mesmerised by the idea that she was living the dream. Other people walked to raise money for charity; Eloise was going to do it to save face.

'Really?' Sara did little to hide the disbelief in her voice. 'When you said you were going to walk the girls to school I imagined a half-mile leisurely wander through the cobbled streets to the local, practically on-the-doorstep primary school.'

'Well, yes, me too. But it will be fine.' Eloise was glad this conversation was taking place over the phone, she was certain that Sara would be able to detect the dread in her face. Two miles to Capcombe, two miles back, twice a day, not a cobbled street in sight. Not a pleasant amble, more of a risky hike along an A road (where people drove faster than they ought), followed by a mad dash along a twisty country lane and then a muddy track up the hill to the school gate. She was dreading it.

'What time will you need to get up?' Sara asked.

'Six-fifteen.'

'Ouch.'

'Quite.'

In London the girls had all gone to the same primary school which was less than a mile from their old home and yet they'd always driven there. This was not something Eloise was especially proud of. Her excuse being that straight after drop-off she'd invariably go directly to the gym (or at least a coffee bar) and, besides, Erin had cello practice three times a week; dragging the instrument along with three (sometimes reluctant) children was a little like dragging a French aristocrat to the guillotine. She now saw that maybe she'd been spoilt. The proximity of their old school and the fact that she'd driven meant that the Hamilton females had been used to staying in bed until at least 7.45 a.m.

'You must be insane, placing the girls at two separate schools and opting for a commute several times longer than the one you had in London.'

'Maybe, but I fell in love with the inconveniently located Capcombe Primary School the moment I saw it, so did the girls. It's warm and charming and the pupils seemed happy and laid-back.'

'I remember it as a bit scruffy.'

'Do you know that at Capcombe they have this tradition that every Friday the mothers take turns to make pudding for lunch?' Eloise said, doing her best to ignore Sara's slightly gloomy take.

'You'll hate that. There isn't a Patisserie Valerie round the corner, you know. You'll have to make something yourself.'

'Well, only once a term. Anyway, Margaret will make it for me. She's a great cook.'

'Whenever I think of a country school, I always imagine a traditional building,' Sara added. 'You know, with a huge shiny bell in a tower and stone archways declaring separate entrances for boys and girls.'

The school was, in fact, a big old farmhouse that was built in the nineteen thirties and had become a school sometime in the eighties. Even Eloise had to admit that it didn't look particularly special from the outside but the notable feature was that inside every single wall was painted in a different, but distinctly cheerful colour. It was very attractive.

'The atmosphere is relaxed and fun. Do you remember the kids held open the doors for us to pass through when we were being shown around and the headmaster assured us that his greatest concern was for the children to feel safe and happy and valued? What's not to love? Erin and Poppy are thrilled.'

Initially shy, when looking around last term, they'd soon un-furrowed their brows and slipped their hands out of Eloise's; swapping her protection for the art corner and playhouse. They'd had an air about them that El had recognised from the years when she'd worked in advertising. She'd loved her hustle-bustle, sexy, high-profile job but there was nothing she'd liked more than coming home on a Friday and washing the city out of her hair, ordering a pizza and snuggling up in front of the TV with Mark. The relief of not having to try quite so hard and quite so constantly was fabulous. Providing her daughters with that Friday feeling, on a Monday morning, made her feel officially successful.

'The children don't wear uniform, I love that. It gives them the opportunity to be individuals.'

'Or it gives them an excuse to pick on each other because so-and-so doesn't have the latest pair of trainers.'

'I don't think that's as important to the kids around here,' El mumbled. 'And you've got to love the fact that there's a goat tethered up in the playground.'

'Health risk,' replied Sara.

'It helps the children learn about responsibility.'

Sara simply tutted and muttered something about asking to see the books because the place didn't look solvent.

Eloise understood why Sara could be so tetchy; being in the middle of IVF was stressful, but sometimes she just wished Sara would look on the bright side of things the way she used to. Eloise missed the Sara who would scatter reassurance and compliments throughout their conversations, like friends were supposed to. Eloise needed to believe it was all going to be OK.

'So did you get as far down as Naples?' Eloise asked, deftly changing the subject.

SEPTEMBER

6

'Hello, it's only me,' Margaret called tentatively as she pushed open the back door and poked her head inside the kitchen. Margaret had knocked, but just once, very briefly and quietly. She didn't really think family should have to knock but Mark said she must. She wasn't actually expecting anyone to hear her anyway because they'd all be upstairs dashing about getting ready for school; she'd timed her visit carefully.

She started to clear the breakfast pots from the table, she scraped toast crusts into the bin, put lids back on the marmalade jars (noting that they ate an expensive brand and resolving to bring some of her own round), ran a big bowl of scalding water and started to hunt around for rubber gloves. Margaret could hear them overhead, rushing around the bedrooms, screaming for lost hair brushes or fussing about who was hogging the bathroom; the girls were always very dramatic and regularly threatened to kill one another. Margaret didn't mind the noise. In fact, this domestic clatter was music to her ears. She heard Eloise's footsteps on the stairs; she stayed at the sink, with her back to the door; this would give El a moment to compose herself when she discovered Margaret in her kitchen, which was better for both of them in the long run.

'Gosh, Margaret, you made me jump out of my skin.' Astonishment at finding her mother-in-law in her kitchen at 6.30 a.m. overrode any potential irritation Eloise might have felt.

Margaret turned and beamed at her daughter-in-law. 'Sorry, my darling, I didn't mean to startle you. I thought I'd pop by and give you a hand because Mark mentioned that this first month you've found mornings a bit of a stretch.' Margaret knew that Eloise's wish for everything to be perfect all the time meant that she was reluctant to ask for help; if you need help, you can't be perfect, or so Eloise reasoned. That's why Margaret hadn't waited to be asked but had taken her prompt from Mark instead.

'Did he now?' Momentarily, Eloise looked vexed, insulted. No doubt she interpreted Mark's comment as a judgement on her organisational skills, rather than what it was – a statement of fact. Margaret saw a rare burst of frailty and struggle exposed in her daughter-in-law's irises. She knew it was wrong of her but Margaret wanted to do a little jig when she saw that flash of vulnerability because that was her opportunity to be a real help. Her only desire was to become indispensable.

'Is Mark still in bed?' asked Margaret.

'No, he's working really hard trying to get a handle on things. He's already at the office, poor love,' said Eloise dutifully.

'On the other hand the office does give him a legitimate excuse to avoid the fractious, frantic family time,' pointed out Margaret, smiling cheekily. Eloise saw she was not on trial and returned the smile. It didn't ever take much to settle Eloise because of her deep craving for everything to be permanently OK. She put Margaret in mind of a cat, one moment content and purring, the next wary – hackles up – and then again, before you knew it, snuggled back on the mat again. They were both aware that their new close proximity was going to take some careful negotiating but both were determined to make it work.

Eloise was wearing leggings and a night dress. She had long blond curly hair that she'd carelessly scrunched up into a plastic clip. Yesterday's mascara was smudged around her eyes which gave the impression that she was either a heroin user or that she'd done several rounds in the ring with some heavyweight boxer. Margaret knew the importance of standards. She never left the house without brushing her hair, dabbing on a bit of powder and checking her boots were clean, even when she was just going for a walk in her anorak. Margaret knew Eloise had standards too. Ones she was clearly struggling to maintain. Eloise seemed to be able to read Margaret's mind because she admitted, 'I *am* a bit behind this morning.' She cast a glance around the kitchen and Margaret followed her gaze.

Normally Eloise's home was a haven; calm, ordered and clean, but right now there was something littering every surface. Margaret knew El didn't like the Formica tops but she doubted the chaos was a strategy to hide them. There were piles of old newspapers, an assortment of hair bands, books, pencils, empty sweet packets and recently purchased grocery shopping. The kitchen was littered with unfinished endeavours; a large jigsaw, sand pictures, paper doll dress designs and homework.

'I know. Other people's kitchens boast bread-making machines, juicers, toasters and espresso makers,' joked Eloise.

'Fancy a coffee?' Margaret started to rinse out the cafetière.

'I haven't really got time.' Eloise anxiously looked at her watch. Margaret started to prepare the coffee anyway, knowing Eloise wouldn't be able to resist the smell of freshly ground filter beans, especially once she found out that Margaret had brought over chocolate-covered croissants from the bakery. Now where do they keep their coffee beans? Margaret wondered, searching in the cupboards, the fridge and the washing machine until eventually she found them in a canister. Margaret's activity spurred on Eloise; she reached for the empty bread bag and put it in the bin, by way of a start.

'Who put this plate in the bin?' she asked as she delved in to retrieve a plate from the waste. 'It's Poppy's breakfast plate.' She turned to Margaret, bemused. Margaret stared back at her, equally perplexed.

'I've never seen the plate before in my life.'

'Look, and the marmalade. A full jar.' Eloise reached back into the bin again and pulled out some knives, a teaspoon and another plate. Unfortunately the second plate was broken. She stared at Margaret, baffled.

'One of the girls' idea of a joke?' Margaret suggested.

'Weird,' El muttered. She looked defeated and it was clear she hadn't the energy to pursue the mystery. She put the crockery and cutlery to one side and then folded her slim body into a wooden chair; she'd found the only one that was clear of glossy magazines and school books. 'I'm not sleeping too well,' she mumbled.

'Mark's heavy breathing?' Margaret asked. They shared a conspiratorial glance and giggled. They both knew Mark snored but he would never admit to it.

'I suppose declaring you snore is a little like coming clean about Botox or even colonic irrigation, far too human and flawed,' said Eloise loyally.

'Has he had Botox?' Margaret couldn't hide her distress.

'No.' El laughed. 'I'm just saying that I understand.'

Did that mean that Eloise had had Botox? Margaret couldn't very well ask, but it bothered her.

'It's not surprising that he sleeps so deeply, our days here in Dartmouth are extremely physical. We get up earlier than we did in London, we walk further. Why hadn't I noticed that Dartmouth is on a hill – several hills, actually? Steps, stairways, slopes and steeps are now a way of life.' Eloise was trying to strike a note that would suggest she was laughing at herself. Margaret was fully aware of the saying 'If you don't laugh you'll cry'.

'On the bright side you'll have buns of steel by Christmas.' Margaret offered this phrase as she'd heard it used on TV. She liked it, and she thought Eloise would too.

'Yes, if I can get past the stage where I simply have jelly legs that quake with fatigue. You'd think I'd sleep soundly after all that but, somewhat pitifully, the exertion simply leaves me ratty and exhausted.'

'There's bound to be a period of adjustment. You need to get used to the air and the darkness,' Margaret said carefully. She handed her daughter-in-law a mug of coffee and the croissants. 'There, I've put lots of sugar in, just the way you like it.'

'But I don't take— Thank you, Margaret.' Eloise took the mug and smiled. Galvanised, she stood up. 'OK, are you ready for the onslaught?'

Both women went upstairs and were immediately met by demands; Emily wanted help finding her homework, Erin had lost her Rubik's Cube and Poppy wanted her hair styled in a French plait. Eloise hunted down the lost bits and bobs while Margaret persuaded Poppy that a French plait was a bit ambitious at this time in the morning and she'd have to settle for a couple of bunchies instead. Once that was done Margaret ushered Poppy downstairs and found Eloise and the other two waiting.

'Wow, I love the hair, Poppy,' El gushed.

'Bunchies,' declared Poppy proudly.

Eloise beamed. 'OK, let's go, here are your snacks and bags. Let's get this show on the road. We might actually be on time today.' At the door she stopped and turned to Margaret. 'Thanks so much. You've been a treasure this morning. I couldn't have done it without you.' El blew a kiss and the girls copied her, even Emily.

Margaret thought that if she were to die that moment, she'd die a happy woman.

7

IVF was the acronym for in vitro fertilisation, the direct translation from the Latin 'in glass'. Sara knew this, because – obviously – the fertilisation took place in a lab (think test tube), not inside the mother's body. So, obviously, there was no sex involved – well, other than the thing Charlie had to do in a cubicle. Initially, Sara used to insist that he took a photo of her in there with him, now she didn't care if his prop was a grubby, dog-eared magazine with pictures of women with implausibly large boobs, as long as it did the job. Charlie used to joke that IVF was a long, hard process in more ways than one but as time passed the joke had proven to be too painfully accurate to be repeated.

First, there were the injections, then there was the egg retrieval (to freeze or not to freeze – Sara's big existential question). Once collected (retrieved, harvested, excavated – there were a number of euphemisms), the eggs were combined with sperm, left to culture and then transferred back to the woman's womb for implantation.

Simple.

Really? Sara could quote the brochure without hesitation. 'The collection of the egg takes place after the cycle has been closely moni-tored and prior to ovulation.' It sounded straightforward and sanitised; Sara had discovered that a rough translation was that there were numerous scans, hospital visits, a bout of sedation and at least twenty minutes of poking around.

The mixing it up bit? Before they realised that they had a problem with making babies Sara used to imagine that somehow it would be possible to know which particular session had led to creating the new life. Of course, she knew this couldn't always be the case, there were instances where girls and women gave birth and claimed they didn't even realise they were pregnant until they'd found themselves in Superdrug with a bag of Pampers under their arms. However, there were a huge number of women out there who swore they were aware of the exact moment fertilisation took place. Eloise was one such woman. Eloise was certain that Emily had been conceived in a hotel in Brighton, during a romantic weekend break to celebrate the welcoming of the new millennium. Sara had heard her friend talk about fireworks exploding and huge cheers beneath the hotel window; she'd had to explain to El that both of those things were to do with the dawn of the millennium and not Mark's impressive performance. Erin was conceived in Dartmouth, in the back of Mark's father's scruffy old Land Rover. Margaret and Ray had been babysitting Emily and, as a couple with a toddler and very little time to themselves, they'd both thought it was best to seize the opportunity while they could. Eloise had said it was so good that she'd almost been able to ignore the stench of the dirty crabbing buckets that Ray kept in his vehicle, almost. Poppy was the result of an inexpertly secured condom. They'd attended a boozy industry bash where Mark had impressed some important client or other; they were both high on his success and a considerable amount of champagne. El described the night of passion as one that was carefree and careless. She'd laughed when she'd said this and Sara would have laughed too, if it was her story. An unplanned-for pregnancy – some people had all the luck.

Sara had imagined that she and Charlie would conceive in a hot country while on holiday somewhere exotic and yet soulful. They'd have spent their day meditating, feeding one another kiwi fruit, pineapple and ackee and perhaps indulging in a couple's massage. They'd have made love on the beach (a private beach, this wasn't the moment to be an exhibitionist) with waves crashing in the background and the sun beating down on their bare skin. As things stood now, their baby would inherit the story that he/she was the result of an intracytoplasmic sperm injection (ICSI, between friends). Sara didn't care! She didn't care how it was done, her romantic dreams had been flushed down the loo (over and over again, every twenty-eight days for the past six years, to be precise), just please, please let it happen.

Sara was finding work slow today, which was a shame. She'd have preferred to have been busy, then time would pass faster. Really, all she wanted to do was go home, get into bed, pull the duvet over her head and wait. Wait. Wait. She didn't feel safe being out and about with crowds of people who were all prepared to trample on their grannies for a few extra centimetres of elbow room in the Tube. Plus, everyone was coughing and spluttering; it might be late summer hay-fever or it might be the first bout of autumn colds and, while there was no evidence that a cold was in any way harmful to the IVF process, Sara didn't want to risk it. She wouldn't be in work except for the fact that Charlie had more or less pushed her out the door this morning. He was certain that lying around in bed wouldn't help, and carrying on as normal was the best thing they could do. Sara was finding his common sense damned irritating.

Her thoughts were interrupted when her boss asked, 'And how are you today, Sara?'

'Fine,' she replied, with the honed British reserve that excuses dishonesty. She couldn't very well tell Jeremy that she was terrified, excited, expectant and full of dread; it was not something a managing partner of one of the big four London accounting firms expected to hear from his senior management. When he'd asked her how she was today the last thing he expected was a genuine answer.

'Busy?'

'Pleasantly so.' She smiled through the lie. She didn't want him to guess that she hadn't so much as opened a file this morning. Somehow, she had to give the impression that she was working to 100 per cent capacity but she was not stretched. Industrious but not overwhelmed. Interested but not concerned. It was never easy managing a boss but

Sara had a particularly complex relationship with Jeremy that demanded an extra bit of care. Jeremy and Sara had first met a hundred years ago when she'd been training and he was newly qualified. They'd been paired up together for a number of projects. His official role was Sara's mentor but, somewhat inevitably, considering their combined attractions (humour – his, long legs – hers, loose morals and intelligence – both of theirs), they'd became lovers. Neither of them was looking for anything serious or profound so there weren't any issues when, after a few brief months of especially acrobatic sex, they went their separate ways. Not long afterwards Jeremy had left Sara's company and gone to work for a competitor. He'd rejoined her firm last year, as her boss. It was fine. They'd both moved on. He was happily married now with two little boys and she was happily married with a fourth round of IVF treatment, so the situation hadn't been especially awkward. Just different.

'And how are you?' she asked dutifully.

'Excellent. Planning to take the afternoon off. My eldest is playing for his school.'

'Football?'

'Rugby.'

'Lovely.'

It did sound extremely lovely. Sara envied Jeremy. She envied him because not only did he have an athletic and proud-making son but he also got to sing and dance about it in the office. Sara sneaked a sideways glance at her colleague, Gillian. She was a mother of two as well but she didn't keep a silver-framed photo of her kids on her desk and she never took time off to take them to the doctor's, let alone to cheer their athletic prowess. When working in finance, drawing attention to your femininity was career suicide. Still, Sara envied Gillian just as much as she envied Jeremy. What she wouldn't do to have a baby that she had to downplay in the office, a baby to commit career suicide over!

Jeremy leant up against Sara's desk; he was almost sitting on it. Supremely confident men often invaded body space in that way. Sara imagined it was because no one ever asked them not to. He started to embellish on his sons' many skills.

Apparently Joshua was the sporty one (Olympic hopeful for 2020) and Freddie was the musical one (tutored by someone from the Royal Philharmonic Orchestra in four different instruments). Sara wondered if there was a talentless child left in London. It was weird but, despite her efforts to concentrate on his conversation, all she seemed to be aware of was the scent of his aftershave. It was woody and moist. She normally preferred something citrus; she'd got Charlie to start wearing Jo Malone's lime, basil and mandarin cologne after she'd smelt it, and loved it, on Mark. Sara suddenly had an unfathomable craving to sniff Jeremy's neck. What the hell was that about?

Hormones?

Pregnancy hormones?

It was too much to even hope for. Yet, it was all she hoped for. She reminded herself of the good stuff over and over again. The drugs had worked, the eggs had been successfully extracted, fertilised and, twelve days ago, they had been replaced and were now nestling inside her. *Cling on! Hang on!* She prayed to the itsy-bitsy cells. *I already love you!* She'd taken a progesterone dose to thicken the uterus walls and increase the chances of the embryos taking. She was hopeful and yet she was sick with fear. During the last fortnight, time had defied science; days had seemed like years, hours had seemed like months, minutes like weeks. She had to wait another three days before she could have the blood test and ultrasound that would reveal the success of the treatment and any possible pregnancy. Three days before she heard whether she might, just might, become a mum.

A nano-second after she'd allowed herself to be hopeful, an icy cold blade of fear sliced her wide open, a gash from her throat to her womb, as she reminded herself that she'd been here before. Charlie and Sara had had two IVF treatments that hadn't got this far and one that had, only for her to miscarry at six weeks. That couldn't happen again, could it? She was not that unlucky. Was she? This time she was incorporating alternative therapies, because some people believed acupuncture and head massage could work side by side with IVF treatments. She'd also done lots of positive visualisation, her diet would make Gwyneth Paltrow proud, and she'd prayed.

The success rate of IVF was approximately 20 per cent. Some thought that was horribly low, considering what a couple put themselves through both emotionally and physically; Sara's view was that those were significantly better odds than the lottery and millions of people did that every week. There were a number of factors that had to be taken into consideration when analysing the possible success or the failure of any IVF treatment. The age of the would-be mother was extremely important. It was no surprise to discover that, in general, women above forty found it a little more difficult to conceive using IVF as the ovulation rate and the quality of eggs decreased with age. This caused Sara a cold sense of dread. Of course, it was the same with compliments and wolf whistles, but it was not going to stop her trying. Anyway, she was only a smidge over forty. The cruel fact was that women who had had a normal delivery before the dreaded four-o, or even a previous successful IVF birth, had a greater chance of getting pregnant with intervention the second time. Sara found that difficult to deal with. It was a bit like a married woman taking a lover. Enough already. Just greedy.

The quality of the sperm and egg obviously affected the chances of success but the doctors had tried to reassure Charlie and Sara that they didn't have any problems with either, although this hadn't stopped Sara insisting Charlie take cold showers and eat mountains of toasted wheat germ to increase his zinc levels. The IVF centre where the treatment was done also played a part. Factors like size of the clinic, technical expertise of the team, type of equipment used, protocols for ovary stimulation, and transferring of embryos were all vital to the overall success rate. Sara and Charlie were paying for the best.

They'd done everything they could. All they could do now was hope.

'Sara, aren't you supposed to be at the audit methodology meeting with Sanders Steel?' asked Jeremy, suddenly less concerned with his son's chance of winning another rugby trophy and more concerned about his department's billable hours.

'Oh, yes. I'm on it,' said Sara, as she gathered up her bag. She suspected that both of them were aware she was rarely what could be described as 'on it' nowadays.

Having difficulties conceiving wasn't an unusual problem. Everyone had at least two close friends and a relative who were going through 'exactly the same thing', or so Sara was frequently told. People were always trying to reassure her that her situation was commonplace. She doubted them. Everywhere she looked there were women flushed with pregnancy, trailing toddlers, running their juniors to sports fixtures or shopping with teenagers. She didn't believe anyone was going through the same thing as she was, because, if they were, she wouldn't feel so lonely. And she did feel lonely.

Sara thought of Charlie as a good husband; gentle, devoted and charming. Charm was often associated with mellow old men at best or ineffectual estate agents at worst. But those associations undermined the power of the charmer. Charm was a priceless attribute to have and to spread. To charm someone meant to mesmerise, to bring someone under your spell. Charlie charmed in a real and absorbing way. His skill was particularly valuable because, as much as she hated to admit it, Sara was concerned that she was moving towards a state that was so charmless that, on occasion, she was downright rude. Her nearest and dearest understood that she was under considerable strain but this much couldn't be explained to everyone. Mr Dhar, who served in her local 7–Eleven, for example, did not know why Sara might call him a 'hopeless, just bloody hopeless little man' simply because he'd run out of HP Sauce. Charlie had realised that the ensuing exchange of sharp words meant that neither he nor Sara would be able to comfortably visit the store again, which was a pity because the next convenience store was significantly less convenient, being a further fifteen-minute walk away. Charlie had taken the initiative to visit Mr Dhar and buy their entire week's groceries from the overpriced retailer, to charm his way back into his good books. An extravagant gesture, maybe, but on the inevitable Sunday morning when they reached into the fridge and discovered that they were all out of milk and a trip to the nearest store was necessary, it was a gesture that would pay dividends. Charlie wanted to help.

So why wasn't he able to stop her feeling lonely any more?

Maybe she felt lonely because Eloise had left her, deserted her, run for the hills (literally). But Eloise had said a million times that she was just at the end of a telephone line and, even in Sara's most hysterical moments, she knew that was the case; they'd spoken at least once a day since Eloise had moved. Besides her husband and her friend, Sara had a stimulating career and two cats. She should not be lonely.

But she was. Having a baby inside her body would stop her feeling lonely. She was sure of it. *Only* that would stop her feeling lonely.

Sara hadn't believed it at first. She couldn't believe that she might be someone who didn't get what they wanted. She'd always been so in control of every aspect of her life. She had been privately educated and that did tend to place a person in the centre of a very pleasant bubble. She'd benefited from living in a beautiful home, being given a healthy allowance, foreign holidays and all the mod cons that come with a middle-class childhood; piano lessons, elocution lessons and no free time. She was a good athlete, her academic strength was maths, which always gave a girl certain kudos, and if ever she had struggled at school, her mother had done her homework for her or shipped in the most prestigious tutor to reinforce what was being taught in the classrooms. Sara had freely allowed other girls to crib her maths homework and so she had been a popular girl at school; she'd freely allowed boys access to flashes of her long legs and so she'd been a popular girl out of school too. She knew instinctively what people needed and she soon realised that giving them what they needed allowed her to retain control.

Sara had gone on the pill pretty much the day she turned sixteen. Her mother had taken her to the doctor's and when the doctor had asked if Sara was in a serious relationship her mother had sighed dramatically and pointed out that they weren't living in the Dark Ages and a young woman had every right to look after her own fertility without having to face an onslaught of intimate questions. Sara hadn't been in a serious relationship but her mother had been concerned that her luck with condoms wouldn't hold. The risk of Sara getting pregnant on the pill was less than that of her getting pregnant using condoms. End of. So Sara hadn't ever experienced a terrifying 'scare' like so many other girls; controlling her fertility to prevent herself having babies hadn't been an issue so it had never crossed her mind that she might not be able to control *having* them.

Sara had remained on the pill for the year that she'd gone out with Charlie but she'd thrown the pills away the moment they'd become Mr and Mrs. She didn't expect to fall pregnant immediately, she'd assumed it would take a few months for her body to adjust to her natural cycle but, after six months, she'd begun to wonder and after a year she'd begun to worry. They'd had all the tests. A barrage of them. They'd peed into unfeasibly small pots (harder for Sara than Charlie), they'd given blood and other bodily fluids. They'd attended stress management courses, acupuncture and homeopathic courses, they'd even tried reflexology and then cranial osteopathy.

After two and a half years they'd started IVF. Some people asked what had taken them so long to get medical help. Sara wasn't sure, so little was cut and dried when it came to an issue like this; an issue of life or no life. Part of her hadn't wanted to admit that the situation was serious enough, real enough, to demand medical intervention. While she'd been playing around with Vitex agnus castus and chaste-berry she'd told herself that the state of affairs wasn't dire; when you were flat on your back on a hospital trolley with your legs in stirrups, there was no denying that the situation was authentic and valid.

Sara gathered up her BlackBerry and a bunch of files that she knew she'd need for the meeting and dashed towards the lifts. Like many women, she often found herself literally running in heels.

It was not until she was in the lift that she noticed. There was a slimy feeling between her legs. It pulsed as though it was life. But she knew instantly that it was not. It was death. She didn't kid herself. She didn't imagine it was anything other. She felt it with an arctic, brutal certainty.

She felt the death in her gut and her arse as shock and panic turned everything to liquid. Her throat scratched with a lump of sorrow that was the size of a fist. The lump of sorrow was so huge and unpalatable that not only was she choking on it but she also felt sure it would suffocate her. She repeatedly jabbed the button to get the lift to stop at the next floor, tearing her nail low down on her finger. Eventually, the lift lumbered to a stop and she darted towards the loos. She dropped her bag and her files in the lobby, aware that people were startled and staring, probably imagining bomb scares and fire alarms, but she didn't care what they were thinking. There were tears streaming down her face and she didn't know how to stop them, didn't know if they'd ever stop, because there was blood dripping down her thighs. It was flowing so fast now that she could see it on the inside of her knees. Her baby was sitting inside her nylons and it was dead.

8

Eloise pulled the door behind her and simultaneously took in a deep breath of salty, chilly air and the view. It still startled her. *This is where I live*, she reminded herself. This quaint, lovely but unfamiliar town was her home. Every morning she was jolted by a slight feeling of surprise that this was the case, like the shock caused by static when pulling a jumper over her head, not unpleasant, but certainly disconcerting.

Dartmouth was unquestionably picturesque. Eloise was greeted by rows of two- and three-storey, white or pastel buildings which stood proudly side by side. Their multiple windows were eyes, staring out across the estuary; some winked as the sunlight landed, glinted and bounced away again. Many of the town's buildings were gathered, topsy-turvy, teetering around small cobbled alleys, like campers huddled around a fire. There were still one or two lopsided Tudor buildings, precariously standing their ground; their oak beams had compacted to a black fossil. Behind the houses there were rolling, mellow fields that were mowed by sheep and framed by hawthorn bushes.

When she turned round, there was the estuary, Dartmouth's focus, where hundreds of boats bobbed about their business. Whilst Eloise had not become any fonder of water since the move, she was fascinated by the boats. They seemed to take on individual and compelling person- alities. The yachts were gleaming and stately and put her in mind of European royalty – lean, rich and impressive. She thought of the collection of small motor boats, dinghies and day anglers as irascible teenagers looking for and offering up the promise of a quick thrill. The larger pleasure cruisers and ferries had a resigned and faithful air about them, rather like middle-aged women with charitable interests or portly old men with a work ethic; they glided back and forth, back and forth in the name of duty. Dartmouth was beautiful, Eloise knew that, but she longed for the day when she took the town's beauty for granted. Because then she'd know she belonged.

The girls bounced around her, keen to get off to school. Their enthusiasm almost countered the guilt that Eloise felt about not having taken Erin's cello with them. Capcombe Primary School didn't have a devoted music teacher, in fact, none of the local schools did. Of course, lugging the delicate instrument across dale and vale wouldn't have been feasible but Eloise constantly had to bat back the nagging concern that her daughter's musical talents were being neglected. Specialist, devoted (expensive!) music teachers were abundant in Muswell Hill. Everyone had one; they were secured about five minutes after the umbilical cord was cut.

Apparently, a Miss Cape from Kingswear taught everyone every instrument here. Or rather, she taught everyone she regarded as talented and keen enough. She visited people's homes. She'd been teaching forever, although she'd never taught Mark because she hadn't regarded him as keen enough (Margaret wouldn't speak to her for years for that). In the moment Eloise heard this she went from questioning Miss Cape's ability to specialise in all the necessary instruments, to wanting nothing more on earth than having Miss Cape teach Erin, but she had failed to muster the courage to call the teacher in case she was refused. Eloise couldn't help but think that it was so much easier when all she'd had to do was bung a load of cash at the school at the end of the term and let them sort out the lessons and exams and things. Eloise knew she had to organise something soon, it was irresponsible not to; she added it to the list of jobs she had to do.

She still hadn't informed the DVLA that she'd changed her address, she needed to register at a doctor's and find a not-too-terrifying dentist.

She needed to get a whirly bird for the garden because now she was out here – slap bang in the middle of actual green – she'd begun to feel horribly guilty every time she put on the dryer. When she'd mentioned this to Mark, he'd suggested she stayed focused and laughingly commented that her 'to do' list currently ran into hundreds of points.

'Is it really necessary to buy individual garden kits for all three girls?' he'd challenged.

'Yes. I want them to grow things from scratch. To understand and appreciate the process. Didn't we say that would be one of the benefits of being here in the countryside?'

'Did we?' Whilst trying to persuade his wife to move location Mark had thrown out endless carrots. He couldn't definitely recall every last one, maybe he had said as much. 'But chickens?' Mark pointed to the twenty-eighth 'to do'. It read, *buy chickens, etc*. It was the 'etc.' that had made him smile.

'We live in the country, Mark. I want to embrace our lifestyle choice.'

'But you don't know anything about chickens. Nor do I.'

'I can learn.'

'Don't you think you might be—'

'What?' Eloise had swiftly cut across her husband.

Mark had wanted to say, 'Don't you think you might be trying a little too hard? Setting the bar just a bit out of reach?' But when he'd looked at his wife's face he'd seen not only the determination and concentration but also the part of her that was fragile and yearning. He hadn't the heart to be discouraging. He knew her well enough to expect that she'd want an A star in country living; she was forever putting herself under pressure by trying to be practically perfect in every way. He didn't know why she bothered. He thought she was just that.

Eloise's decision to allow Emily to attend the Academy without Erin and Poppy was sanctioned as a good one when, every morning, Emily was desperate to say her goodbyes and to dash off for school. Right now, she was dancing on the spot trying to get Eloise's attention.

'Bye, Mum. See you, *children.*'

Having gained what she wanted, she couldn't resist flaunting her hard-won status as an independent senior. Eloise was relieved that the younger two didn't bite today and the goodbyes didn't degenerate into a series of taunts; instead, they completely ignored their older sister. Emily allowed Eloise to land the briefest of kisses on her forehead before she charged off. Because Emily was dashing she startled a seagull who squawked crossly, and she laughed and poked out her tongue. Eloise watched the leggy, skinny silhouette disappear around the corner and then she started to march the other two onwards in the opposite direction.

They quickly left the town behind them and reached the steeply curved road out of town. The dense hedges of privet, hawthorn and beech swelled together forming fat, impenetrable fences that flanked either side of the road. The air was scented with their fragrance overlaid with the tang of mud, grass and a hint of the autumn that would soon be upon them. It was so different from the smells of London. In London Eloise drank in petrol fumes. Who in their right mind could miss that? Maybe I'm not in my right mind, she thought.

Erin and Poppy were also hurrying in front today, but that was unusual. Normally their journeys were broken up when one or other of them decided to scamper off track because they'd seen some flower or bird or snail that absolutely demanded closer investigation – or a puddle that had to be waded through, or a story that could only be told if they stood still. Eloise usually spent the two-mile walk repeatedly urging them to 'keep up' or 'stay close'. They'd been late for school at least half a dozen times in this first month because the younger girls couldn't, for the life of them, walk in a straight line from A to B. On a good day Eloise might have described this habit as whimsical, the product of curiosity and intelligence; when she was strung out she was more likely to bawl that they lacked focus and were a bit dippy. Not that their late arrival had caused any problems. Mr Fraser, the headmaster, once caught them shuffling in after the bell had rung and simply commented that since September had given them the gift of cobalt-blue skies and silver sunshine then who could bring themselves to hurry in the mornings? Mr Fraser had encouraged Mark and Eloise to go into the school as frequently as they'd wanted this past month. Eloise had spent three mornings listening to children lisp through story books and Mark had re-felted the playhouse roof. Eloise's London school mums had *loved* that.

Eloise knew less about Emily's school. Em was fiercely guarding her independence and had gone berserk when El had suggested she might sign up for the Parents' Association.

'If you're bored then get your own life, Mum, but school is mine,' was how she so charmingly phrased her objection.

'I'm not bored,' Eloise had shouted back.

'Yeah, right.'

'Really I'm not. How could I possibly be bored when I have so much to do? I've never stopped cleaning, sorting, unpacking, painting and lugging furniture from one part of the house to the next.'

'Bor-ring!' Emily had replied emphatically.

Eloise forced herself to put her daughter's comments to the back of her mind and focused on her progress. The house was beginning to shape up as she'd hoped. Very much theirs. Or, more accurately, very much *Elle Decoration*. There were lots of clean, white walls which contrasted with the dark, scuffed wooden floors and provided a clean backdrop for her slouchy grey sofas and discreetly distressed, over-sized leather chairs. She always made sure that there was a plethora of vases of bright flowers strategically placed on the ancient, grand mantelpieces. It wasn't finished, they needed dozens of things: a rug for the master bedroom, lightshades for the girls' bedrooms, shelving just about everywhere, but Eloise wasn't sure when they'd next have time to visit IKEA and pick up these items; she wasn't even sure where the nearest IKEA was.

Eloise was beginning to know her home more intimately, though. She was becoming familiar with which of the heavy internal doors needed to be lifted a fraction so that they'd close firmly and she was charmed by the uneven wall surfaces and imperfect glass windows, all of which said heritage and worth. Slowly, but surely, the house was becoming an incredibly stylish home. Eloise often said, 'We're getting there.' The notable blights were the kitchen, which was dark, damp and pokey, and the bathrooms, which were hideously dated. Both the *en suite* and family bathroom needed to be entirely ripped out and redesigned. At the moment the girls were bathing in a brown 1970s plastic bath with a crack in it and Mark and Eloise were showering in a shower that was the size of a gym locker. The immediate problem was that Eloise was struggling to find a reliable plumber.

Margaret had made a recommendation but her man was everyone's favourite and he was busy for about the next millennia, so El had followed up three local classified ads that had been pinned to the notice board in the Flavel library. She was still waiting for one of them to call back. Another was a young guy who looked about Emily's age but didn't have her self-confidence. He'd been shaking so much when he'd come around to estimate the job that he'd twice dropped his tool bag on Eloise's toe. She'd managed to get a verbal quote out of the third chap but he wouldn't commit anything to paper. Still, he had been available to start. Desperate, Eloise was about to take him on when she'd mentioned her decision to Margaret. Margaret had reacted as though Eloise was suggesting hosting a swingers' party by way of introducing herself to the neighbours.

'Not Billy Warrell, dear. No, no, no, no!' She'd stretched the final 'no' into next week, just so El was crystal clear. 'Nobody *ever* employs Billy Warrell. He's not qualified and he's light-fingered. Everyone knows that.'

Everyone in Dartmouth. Here, as in London, people seemed to have staunch and strong views about other people. Everyone Margaret mentioned came attached to a succinct but patient explanation of character. Friends were described as 'good sorts' (her very favourite type), 'wonderful cooks' (muttered with a hint of irritation or envy) or 'well meaning' (the sense being that these people were a bit annoying or frustrating). Ray's friends were more likely to be described as 'a bit of a drinker', 'a terrible bore' or 'a rude sod'. The tradesmen and craftsmen were 'salt of the earth' or 'underqualified and light-fingered'. It had been the same in Muswell Hill. Everyone knew the *perfect* woman who absolutely *must* colour your hair and the most *wonderful* man who could invisibly hem your trousers or curtains in a flash. In fact, it had often been Eloise doing the insistent recommendations. As she breathed in the damp, fresh air and glanced around the green, lush hills she wondered whether she'd ever be in the position of recommending anything to anybody here in Dartmouth.

She dropped the girls off at school, lingering longer than necessary as she pegged up their coats, half hoping that someone would invite her for a coffee. She longed for this just as much as she dreaded it. She realised that she had to make new friends but, on the other hand, she couldn't help but secretly feel she was a little bit old for making new friends. She liked her old ones and wished they were all she needed. Plus, the women who she had to make new friends with clearly liked their old ones too, and they probably didn't want to go through the embarrassing stages of an embryonic friendship either. It was easy when you were eight; you simply shared a Curly Wurly or offered to turn the skipping rope. Most of the women Eloise met here had gone to school together. Most of their *grandmothers* had gone to school together; they were probably all related to one another if you went back far enough. Margaret was still considered a newbie and she'd moved to Dartmouth forty years ago.

Everyone Eloise had come across had been unquestioningly, unrelentingly polite and inclusive, Eloise couldn't complain. She'd been immediately accepted on to the 'pudding rota' and no one had batted an eye when she'd appeared with vats full of Angel Delight. They hadn't even pretended to believe it was an authentic mousse or asked for the recipe, which would certainly have been the London way (a complex double bluff to out the short-cut). Instead, the Capcombe mums gasped about the brilliance of going 'old school' and had all stolen a spoonful, murmuring that it brought back 'such great memories'. Eloise had been invited to coffee at least once a week, all the neighbours had dropped by and introduced themselves and the girls had been invited on a reasonable number of play dates. El made the girls accept every invitation and returned the favour within seven days – strict policy. She didn't allow any room for shyness or even personal taste. She was not as self-disciplined. She knew that she had to make small talk in order for it to ever progress into big talk but she was finding the process tricky. So far she hadn't identified a potential soul mate. No one had heard of the lemonade mixed with maple syrup and cayenne pepper diet, let alone tried it and scathingly dismissed it, no one in her new friendship pool went to the cinema, let alone was prepared to admit to an inappropriate crush on Jake Gyllenhaal, they looked positively bewildered when she referred to Illume Monogram candles and in the end she'd had to mutter an explanation which she'd found excruciating and, no doubt, they'd found patronising. Her cultural reference points were null and void.

'Hello, Eloise.'

'Hi, Arabella.' Eloise threw out her biggest, broadest beam. After a month she'd discovered that Arabella Leach was the unofficial organiser of the school and therefore a very important person to woo. She was a parent governor and appeared to be in charge not only of the pudding rota but also of the monitor rota and library volunteer rota. No doubt in December she'd be the one rallying parents to make costumes for the nativity, to bake mince pies and to decorate the school hall with holly. It was Arabella who'd asked Mark to re-felt the playhouse. Actually, she'd told him to do it, rather than asked. But in a lovely way. Eloise liked her. She brought to mind the children that appeared in Enid Blyton's mystery books. She had a no-nonsense, can-do attitude, a belief in sunny days and justice. If she was to offer Eloise lashings of ginger beer and cold tongue finger sandwiches it wouldn't come as a surprise.

Arabella was a plump lady, with a constant warm smile that revealed teeth spaced so wide that you could drive a train through them, she had a plummy voice and breasts the size of pillows. Eloise hadn't ever seen a baby actually hanging off one of the said breasts but there was always a small damp patch on her nipple or a spew stain on her shoulder because she had four children all under the age of nine. Arabella discussed whether circumcision traumatised newborns and whether a C-section ruined your birth experience. On the other hand, she held no truck with a parent allowing a child to win when playing games and she didn't care if her kids fought as she believed sibling rivalry would improve conflict resolution skills later in life. If she'd lived in London she'd most definitely be running an NCT cell. Eloise liked her willingness to come down heavily on one side of an argument or another; she only wished they could get beyond talking about their children.

'Any plans this morning?' Arabella asked as she threw out her usual generous, breezy grin.

'Does tackling the ironing basket count as a plan?'

'Hardly. Would you like to join Jackie and me for a coffee? We thought we'd pop to the Dart Café and treat ourselves to a sticky bun.'

'Sounds wonderful, I'd love to.' Perhaps over cake they might edge towards a deeper intimacy. Eloise had only said hello to Jackie but she appeared to be down-to-earth and intelligent; El would really like to get to know both of them better. But then her phone rang and interrupted her gushing acceptance. From the screen she saw that it was Sara. Eloise bowed to the inevitability. 'Oh, I'm so sorry, I'm going to have to take this.' She shrugged apologetically.

'We'll see you there, shall we?' Arabella replied. It was impossible to tell if she was offended. Some people really hated mobiles intruding. Eloise nodded in a way that she hoped conveyed her regret at the interruption and keenness to accompany them but Arabella was already halfway along the corridor, hurrying to catch up with Jackie. Eloise followed at a slower pace. She couldn't take a call with Sara while she was in the school building; the sort of things they discussed were rarely fit for infant ears, and besides, the reception was patchy – just a step in the wrong direction and the signal was lost. Eloise had had a number of calls brought to an abrupt halt recently and Sara had made her frustration known.

'Hi, Sara, how's things?'

'I – I – I've . . . ' It was difficult through the barrage of tears but Eloise made out the words, 'I've just flushed another baby down the loo.'

Disappointment threw El back against the corridor wall. She slid down it, not caring that she'd ripped the frieze about sea creatures.

'Oh, sweetheart. I'm sorry, I'm so, so sorry,' she muttered. She wondered whether her words of comfort could carry any force at a distance of 170 miles. It felt as though she might as well be 170 million miles away.

9

In between showers Margaret dashed through the damp streets and headed to the office. It was only a five-minute walk from their house but, in retrospect, she probably should have picked up a brolly. It hadn't crossed her mind. After a bright early morning, clouds had suddenly appeared from nowhere and they seemed intent on dumping a month's worth of rainfall in a day; there was a very real chance there would be another downpour before she reached the two-up, two-down town house that was the Hamiltons' solicitor's practice. Still, it was worth risking getting wet for Mark.

Margaret rang the bell and was buzzed in. She had a key and, when Ray had been at the helm, she used to let herself in without hesitation but she'd decided it was better to observe formalities, at least until Mark invited her not to do so. It was his practice now and she wanted him to know she respected it as such. She stumbled into the thin hallway and, as usual, took a moment to appreciate the small black and white Victorian tiles that paved the way into the reception and the two impressive seascape oil paintings hanging on the walls. For the first time Margaret noticed that the paintings failed to hide the fact that the wallpaper was actually quite shabby and dated. They'd hung it in 1987. She made a mental note to suggest to Mark that he might want to spruce up the place a bit – he must put his own stamp on the practice – but then she considered that no doubt Eloise already would have given much thought as to what was fashionable and welcoming in terms of wallpaper and probably had something on order. Lydia Pluckrose, the receptionist, personal assistant and all-round good sort, emerged from what had once been a front room but had long since served as the reception.

'Hello, Margaret. I saw you dashing up the street. Shall I put the kettle on?'

Lydia Pluckrose was in her late forties. She'd worked for Ray for nearly twenty years and now she was delighted to work for Mark, a man she'd known as a lad. She and Margaret had a great deal of respect for one another. They both knew how to make Ray's day better, more efficient and successful and on the occasional day when neither of them could do so they'd been in the habit of calling one another to alert and sympathise. Lydia probably did the same with Eloise now, thought Margaret.

'No tea for me. I'm just popping in, then out again. I don't want to take up too much of his time,' said Margaret.

'I think I'll make a pot anyway,' said Lydia, heading to the small out-of-sight kitchenette at the back of the office. 'I've switched the phones to answering machine so you don't need to cover the reception,' she added. 'You go straight up to see Mark. Tell him I'll bring up a cuppa.'

Mark had taken over Ray's room on the first floor. It was a reasonably big room with a magnificent view of the estuary. Even on a drizzly day like this the windows seemed to frame a work of art. Graham, the second most senior solicitor, had the opposite room which was equally spacious but lacked the view and Hugh, the most junior member of the team, was downstairs in the room opposite the reception. He had to put up with Lydia's chatter and the noise of clients clumping up and down the wooden stairs but then he was closest to the kitchen and, therefore, the biscuit box, which was a small but significant compensation in a working day.

Margaret shyly knocked on Mark's door.

'Come in.'

She tentatively pushed it open, surprised but impressed by the authority in her son's voice. 'Hello, darling.'

'Mum.' From Mark's expression it was clear that he wasn't expecting to see Margaret's face pop from behind the door; no doubt he was expecting Lydia with a cup of tea. It was unlikely he was expecting a client, not at ten past one. The people of Dartmouth had a great respect for lunch hours and didn't disturb anyone on theirs unless there was a genuine emergency. Although Margaret was an unexpected guest Mark looked delighted to see her. 'This is a lovely surprise,' he said with a grin. 'Welcome to my new powerhouse.' He opened his arms in a gesture that invited Margaret to look round. She noticed he'd made one or two changes already. There were new books and files on the shelves, there was a smart black globe on the windowsill and the computer on his desk was enormous. Ray had preferred maps and a discreet PC.

'I'm not stopping long. I know you're busy.' Margaret often started her conversations with her son with some sort of veiled apology for her presence. She was acutely aware that he was often occupied with work. Indeed, that was why she was here today. 'I was at Eloise's when you rang and said you wouldn't be able to get home for lunch because you had so much to get through, so I thought I'd bring you a sandwich.'

Mark beamed. 'Cheers, Mum. You're the best.' He held out his hand greedily. There was no ceremony between them. She'd been feeding him all his life and neither of them would expect a show of excessive manners. 'To be honest, I could've got home but I want to break the habit.'

Margaret looked confused so Mark clarified. 'When we first arrived it was a novelty that I could get home for a bowl of soup or similar every lunchtime, especially after years in London where we regularly endured twelve-hour stretches without seeing one another, but I'm not sure it's good for Eloise.'

'What do you mean? I'm sure she's delighted to see you. And a hot meal in the middle of the day is a good thing.'

'She ought to be meeting friends for lunch. We've been here nearly two months now. But as she knows I'm going to be about every lunchtime she doesn't make any other arrangements.'

'I'm not sure she has friends to meet for lunch yet,' pointed out Margaret.

'I'm know, so I'm making her go cold turkey. Tough love and all that.'

'Perhaps I should set up something with Maureen's daughter,' Margaret suggested tentatively.

'Good idea.'

'You don't think she's too old for pre-arranged play dates?'

'As long as she doesn't see it as that.'

'Anyway, she won't be meeting anyone for lunch today. Her friend Sara called this morning, in a terrible state. Eloise is driving back to London as we speak.'

'Yes, I got her message. Thanks for saying you and Dad will collect the girls from school.'

'It's no problem. We're happy to help. We can give them their tea.'

Mark nodded, but didn't add anything more. His reluctance to elaborate on the subject was quite telling. He disapproved. Margaret knew he didn't disapprove of her picking up the girls so she assumed he disapproved of Eloise dashing to London. He opened the Tupperware tub and hungrily released the sandwiches that Margaret had carefully wrapped in greaseproof paper. 'You've been a marvel, Mum. Eloise is always going on about how lucky we are that we have you. She really appreciates all you're doing to help her – us – to settle in.' Margaret blushed with pleasure. She was glad Eloise had appreciated her efforts. She was ecstatic that Mark had. It had been a careful balancing act; she wanted to do everything. If she could, she'd take the girls to school every day, clean Eloise's house, fill the freezer with home-cooked food and babysit every night. But Margaret was aware that *everything* was too much. Eloise needed something, not everything. The problem was, or rather the issue was, because it was not a problem – at least, it shouldn't be – that love knew no bounds. Margaret loved Mark and his family without limits or conditions. *Everything* was natural.

Mark looked at the ham sandwiches. 'You've cut off the crusts,' he said, not bothering to hide his bewilderment.

Margaret followed her son's gaze as it rested on the carefully prepared packed lunch. He looked quizzical and she wondered why. She'd gone to lengths to prepare his very favourite: ham sandwiches (without crusts), a carton of Ribena, a packet of Walkers salt and vinegar crisps (he actually preferred tomato flavour but they were a devil to get hold of and therefore only a very rare treat), a liquorice wheel (with a blue sweet in the centre – not pink!) and a sliced apple. He hated it when his apple went brown, so after slicing it she put it together again and wrapped it in cling film. Mark grinned. 'I think you've mixed it up with one of the kids' lunches, haven't you?'

Margaret looked at her son and then back at the lunch. His confusion was contagious. She suddenly felt dizzy and wondered what he was talking about. Which kids? What was wrong with the lunch? Why was he grinning? What was amusing? They stared at each other for a long minute and in the end Mark shrugged and started to tuck into the goodies. Margaret continued to stare at him. Something was wrong. She didn't know what, but she could feel it. Recently, over the last couple of months or so, there'd been a smudge at the side of her head. Inside her head. No one else could see it. That's what was wrong, the smudge. A patch that was covering something up. Something that she should've known and should've remembered and should just *be*.

But wasn't.

Margaret felt breathless and panicked. Which kids was Mark talking about? What was he doing sitting at his daddy's desk? He shouldn't be there. He might spill his Ribena on the important papers and Ray would be cross. She didn't want to upset Mark though. Not when things were going so nicely. Suddenly, she knew what she could do.

'Let's go and get an ice cream,' she suggested.

Mark stopped chewing on the sandwich and once again threw out a quizzical look. 'An ice cream?'

'We can get a wafer sandwich from Mr Simmons as a special treat.'

'Mum, Mr Simmons closed down his shop about twenty-five years ago. He's dead, isn't he? What are you on about?' Mark's look of confusion dissolved into one of concern. 'Are you OK, Mum? Do you want a glass of water? Should I call Dad?'

Margaret pushed past the smudge; it took a lot of effort. 'I'm fine, dear. Of course I know Mr Simmons is closed down. I was just joking about the ice cream.' She giggled nervously.

Mark was visibly relieved. 'You got me. Listen, I'm really sorry. It's great that you've stopped by but I probably should get on.'

Margaret stood up and started to make her way out of the office. She didn't want to leave Mark here as she couldn't imagine Ray would be pleased. She could only hope Mark wouldn't touch any of the important papers and mess anything up. He must be doing some work experience or something. She couldn't remember that being arranged. That damned black smudge blurred so much. Mark got up and came around the enormous desk towards her. He kissed his mother on the cheek as he walked her to the door.

'You won't mention to Eloise that I could have made it home for lunch, will you?' Mark smiled winningly at his mum.

'No, I won't mention it to Eloise,' said Margaret reassuringly.

She really couldn't have if she'd wanted to because she hadn't got a clue who Eloise was.

OCTOBER

10

Charlie was extremely keen to accept Eloise's offer to refit her bathrooms and kitchen. The next local job he'd had lined up in London had fallen through and he needed the money. Sara saw his delight and urgency and assumed that he was desperate to get away from her. She didn't blame him but she almost hated him because he *could* get away from her, whereas she was stuck inside her increasingly gloomy mind and inside her stupid, betraying, useless body.

Sara was appreciative that Eloise still called every day and patiently listened as she moaned, cried, ranted and regretted but it was obvious that even Eloise, usually so eloquent and comforting, didn't know what to say in the face of Sara's overwhelming grief. She opted to say little and Sara was grateful. Sara couldn't stand the people who told her that 'at least you know you can get pregnant' (Charlie's mother and two colleagues), or that 'You can always have another go' (many of her casual friends and her brother), or 'at least you weren't further on' (her sister-in-law all the way from Australia sent that tiding of comfort – and Charlie had agreed with her). Yes, even him. Sara couldn't believe the insensitivity. Were these people insane? At times she thought she hated them all. Including Charlie.

Was hate too strong a word? She couldn't possibly mean she hated him, could she? Because, after all, he was her husband and the man she was trying to have a baby with. But the cold fury she felt towards him was pretty similar to hate.

Something terrible had happened to Sara. Something *else* that was terrible. Recently, she had started to wonder whether she had married the wrong man. The question had exploded in her head not long after she lost the baby and now it stubbornly lingered there, day in, day out. No matter what she did to try to douse out the thought, it burned. Would another man have been able to successfully impregnate her? Was Charlie worth the loss and lack?

It was not long after she'd said as much to Eloise that El had suggested Charlie could come and do her bathrooms and kitchen. Eloise had tried to do the socially polite thing of making out that he'd be doing her a huge favour because she couldn't find anyone to do the work in Dartmouth but Sara knew there must be plumbers closer by, so all she could think was that Eloise also believed that Sara and Charlie could do with some time apart. Charlie was to stay with Eloise, Mark and the girls through the week and then return home to London at the weekends, or Sara could join them all at the weekends – once she was feeling a bit more robust.

'So that's everything,' said Charlie, as he slammed the door on his van. The familiar slide and clunk sound rang out through the empty London street. He was using his fake cheery voice again, the voice he used whenever he spoke to Sara nowadays; it was a bit like the sort of voice dentists used when they spoke to kids – no one was convinced, the big prick was still going to hurt. His cheerful tone did nothing to budge the October gloom. In fact, the tone of voice irritated Sara, but then pretty much everything irritated her at the moment. No one warned you that besides leaving you feeling lonely, gutted and listless, grief also made you mean.

Charlie pulled his wife into a hug and she allowed it; it was some small comfort to feel his solid, warm bulk. She felt fragile, like blown glass that just might shatter at any moment. As she lifted her arms, her coat swung open, revealing her grubby pyjamas. It was only 6 a.m., and Charlie was trying to get ahead of the morning rush hour. Normally she would have still been in bed and it had taken a super-human effort to get to the front door to wave him off. She knew she smelt; a tangy smell of stale sweat. She was not being as responsible as she should be with regard to bathing. It was an effort. Getting up in the morning was an effort, lifting the spoon to her mouth so that she could eat her cornflakes was an effort, going to work, catching the Tube, completing audits were all an effort. She'd somehow managed to do most of the above by operating on automatic pilot, but getting her coat dry-cleaned was a step too far.

Charlie tried to kiss her goodbye but she moved her face so that his smacker ended up on her cheek. She was aware that she hadn't cleaned her teeth yet but she wasn't sure she'd have kissed him even if she'd had Hollywood pearls as teeth. She was tired and all she wanted was for him to leave so that she could go back to bed. Of course she couldn't go back to bed, she needed to get on with her day. Another day that now required so much exertion and was devoid of hope. She didn't have a space for Charlie.

'Call me if you need anything.'

'OK.'

'Or if you get, you know, lonely.'

She nodded and didn't bother to tell him that since she'd lost the baby she'd felt so desperately alone that even when he was in the same room as she was, same bed as her, even inside her, she still felt lonely. All she could say was, 'Drive carefully. Call me when you get there.'

11

Ray and Margaret slid uncomfortably into the doctor's waiting room. Margaret discreetly wiped a plastic chair with a handkerchief before she sat down. She didn't settle right back into the chair but perched uneasily on the edge. She'd been brought up in an era when they'd told young girls they could get pregnant by sitting on loo seats and whilst she'd never quite believed that, she'd never quite disbelieved it either. She had the deepest respect for germs.

So had Ray. He'd never been keen on doctors' waiting rooms. He avoided them like the plague, in fact he thought they were where someone was most likely to catch the plague. However, despite his dislike of doctors' waiting rooms, he'd been the one who had made today's appointment. Ray didn't take a seat. Boys had never been told they'd get pregnant by sitting on loo seats, obviously. His inability to relax stemmed from something different.

He glanced suspiciously at a young mum with a toddler and a baby who were squirming in the seats opposite. Both the baby and toddler were suffering from severe colds, slimy snot shone around their noses and the dried type was evident on their scalps, their trousers, sweatshirts and their mother's coat. He thought he could see it on the wall behind where they were sitting as well, but it was hard to tell because the wall was painted snot colour. It was very depressing, someone ought to have considered that. He found himself staring at the grubby children, although it was the last thing on earth he wanted to do. He desperately cast around for something else to look at.

Margaret picked up an ancient copy of *Reader's Digest* and began to leaf through it with the air of someone who had the hope but not the conviction that something would catch her eye. 'I thought we got these on subscription. I haven't seen this copy before. Is our edition late?' she asked Ray.

'We haven't ever subscribed to *Reader's Digest*, that was your mother,' he stated neutrally, then he added slightly more darkly, 'Sick people have touched that.'

Margaret dropped the booklet instantly. 'We shouldn't be here,' she said crossly. Margaret resented Ray bossing her around. He shouldn't make doctor's appointments; that was her job. He took the car to the vet's and the cat to the garage. Those were men's jobs. Appointments at the doctor's and arranging dinner parties ought to be left to the women. This was all a waste of everyone's time; he was getting worked up pointlessly. He seemed really worried about her, which was sweet but unnecessary. He kept saying that he was concerned she was over-doing things.

She was sure they used to get the *Reader's Digest*.

Ray pulled out a Sudoku quiz book and a pen from the large pocket on his raincoat. He liked to do a Sudoku every day, he'd read some-where that doing so kept one's mind young, and he took a long walk every day too, because that was supposed to help in the same way. He glanced at his wife and felt a wave of uncomfortable nausea. Fear. He wanted to be wrong.

Margaret had never got on with Sudoku. She used to do crosswords but she didn't bother with them nowadays. She said it was because she had far more on her plate, now that Mark, Eloise and the girls lived nearby, but she'd stopped doing them over two years ago and the family had only moved to Dartmouth a few months ago.

Margaret had dressed up to come to the doctor's. She was brought up to do so. After all, the dear man had trained for many years to become a doctor and that should be respected. He certainly didn't want to have to look at more dirty or badly presented bits of people than was entirely crucial. Not that she was expecting any sort of an examination. Just a chat, Ray had said. Ask for a tonic. She had to admit that she did feel a bit out of sorts, a bit run down. The smudge was a nuisance. Maybe she *had* been overdoing it and that was why she'd become a bit slapdash and tetchy of late. But it was not something she needed to see a doctor about.

She'd put on her red trousers. Well, they weren't red exactly. How should she describe them? Pink? Brown? What was that colour in between? Never mind. She was also wearing her new pull-on. Pull-up. Pull-over. Goodness, she must be nervous about seeing the doctor because all her words were getting muddled.

'The doctor won't be long,' said the receptionist, directing her comment to the elderly couple and ignoring the harassed-looking mother with the snotty children.

'Were you next? We don't want to jump the queue,' Margaret said to the mum.

'We're being squeezed in. Probably go in after you.'

Margaret noticed Ray nodding, satisfied with that answer. He then turned to look out the window. There wasn't much to see, just the place where they parked vehicles. The vehicle park. But he was making a point, he didn't want to chat with the young mum. Men didn't strike up conversations much, thought Margaret. Mind you, when Ray had been young he'd had plenty to say for himself. Wasn't backward at coming forward and chatting up young girls then. Until he met Margaret, that was. He hadn't done any chatting up since, she was confident about that. He was not that sort. Thank God. And as he wasn't that sort she could forgive a bit of scowling and muttering when she 'chattered on', as he put it.

'Nasty colds, by the look of it,' Margaret commented.

The girl nodded. 'I've tried Calpol but they're still whiny. Tom said he has a headache.'

Margaret sucked her teeth and made a sympathetic tutting sound (quite different from Ray's simultaneous tutting sound which definitely suggested impatience rather than sympathy). 'Headache, that's nasty.'

'It's wearing,' admitted the mum. She looked frazzled. She added, 'Do you think it's, like, bad, as a parent, to welcome the times when Calpol is needed? On the one hand it means your kids are suffering, on the other it means you have a decent crack at getting five consecutive hours of sleep.'

Margaret laughed, deciding it was best to assume she was joking. The young mum smiled too, relieved that the older woman wasn't reaching for her mobile in order to call the social services. She bent forward and kissed her toddler. He pushed her away. Absorbed in a little yellow truck and a masticated bread stick, there was no room for her in his world.

'He wants me to stop kissing him.' There was sadness in her eyes. 'He's only a baby.'

'It's far too early to let go,' said Margaret sympathetically.

'Stop kissing him!' The mum shook her head in bewilderment. 'I laboured thirty-seven and a half hours to bring him into this world. He owes me the occasional cheek offered up without too much reluctance.'

'Mine is just the same. Although mine's a bit older.'

'Mark is forty-one,' said Ray.

Margaret looked confused. Really? Forty-one? It seemed like yesterday when she had first held him in her arms. 'Well, yes, older,' she admitted. 'When I go to kiss him, he pulls this face, as if he's saying, "OK, I'll endure it."'

'Endure!' screeched the younger woman. 'They have no idea what endure is, do they? I'll tell you about endure, I was ripped from—'

Ray coughed, loudly and unconvincingly. He was not comfortable with stories about births. His generation had never gone in for all that sharing. He thought it must have come over from America, about the time they'd started throwing up a McDonald's on every high street.

The woman picked up on Ray's hint and said, 'What am I thinking of? You don't want to know that.'

Margaret assumed she'd lost the thread of what she was talking about; having little ones did tend to have that effect. They'd given it a name now, 'nappy brain'. Margaret had seen it written about in magazines. In her day they'd just called it exhaustion. Same as she was suffering from now. It made you forgetful.

'I'm glad I have sons. Less to worry about. Less money spent on clothes,' the girl offered conversationally.

'Less blood spilt,' Margaret added. Ray and the young mum stared at her, neither could hide their surprise. Margaret wondered what she'd just said that had made them look so startled. Had she burped? 'I don't mean menstruation and all that, necessarily, I just mean that girls are vulnerable to more heartache,' added Margaret.

Ray turned ghostly, he'd never heard his wife say menstruation out loud and he'd have liked to have gone to his grave that way. Margaret didn't care. She was thinking about Mark. Mark had never been a worry. He was a good lad. Well behaved, always did the right thing. But, on the other hand, there were limits with boys. Margaret thought of one and shared it. 'There's no one to give you a bed bath, though, dear. That's a daughter's job. That, and bringing biscuits to dip in the tea.'

'What are we doing here?' asked the toddler who was bored of the conversation and the room.

'That's very philosophical,' said Margaret. Again, Ray gave her an odd look; a mix of warning and worry.

'He means, what is *he* doing here in the waiting room,' said Ray. 'Waiting,' he added, turning to the boy.

'To see the doctor,' clarified the mother. Margaret remembered that stage. The endless answering of questions in full and clear sentences to make yourself heard and understood. Waste of time, she thought. They give up listening to you all too soon although you never can give up the battle to make yourself heard and understood.

'Why are *you* here?' The little boy threw his question to Ray and then returned his attention to running his yellow truck around the back of an empty chair. Despite the snot, Ray melted. He'd always been good with children.

'The old trouble,' Ray joked. He couldn't imagine the child was going to get the gag but couldn't resist it anyway.

'What's that? Being ill?' asked the boy.

Ray chuckled. 'Very funny. I was going to say my wife.' The boy looked put out but Ray didn't care, he was chortling so much that his eyes had begun to water. Margaret thought it was Ray who needed to see a doctor. He might have cataracts.

'Are you here about their colds or your nerves?' Margaret asked the mum.

'Margaret!' Ray stopped chortling and stared at his wife again. He'd upgraded his glare from one of warning to one of out-and-out alarm.

'I'm only making conversation.'

'You shouldn't ask such things.'

'Why not? She might want to talk about it. It's good to talk. Like that old advert used to say.' The smiley woman hadn't taken offence but was laughing now too, as she thought Margaret was joking. 'Lots of young mothers can't cope and they just need someone to talk to,' insisted Margaret.

Despite his better judgement Ray found himself drawn in. 'How would you know? You weren't a young mum and, besides, you coped admirably.'

'Thank you, dear. But I wasn't anything special, everyone coped in those days or, at least, no one ever let on if it wasn't the case, but nowadays there are more stresses and demands. People are so much busier. Rush rush. So strangers can talk about such things. I'm sure it's OK. I read it in a magazine.' Ray shook his head in defeat and didn't add any more. 'Do you have a hankie?' Margaret asked the young mum, who looked nonplussed, but Ray understood instantly and rolled his eyes to the ceiling. 'What? I'm just asking her. She might want one. The children's noses need a wipe. I always carry a handkerchief. Cotton. Pressed. My mother taught me that. That and lots more. To chew with my mouth closed. To sit with my legs crossed at the ankles. Never to let a boy touch my—'

'Margaret!'

'Mrs Hamilton, the doctor is ready to see you now,' said the receptionist.

'Perfect timing,' muttered Ray as he directed his wife towards the doctor's room.

Margaret was baffled. The doctor was not the doctor. 'You're not Doctor Fielding,' she said to the handsome young boy who was sitting in the doctor's chair. She glanced at the door to check. It definitely said 'Dr Fielding' but this definitely wasn't him. She was certain. Dr Fielding had treated Margaret since they'd first moved to Dartmouth when Mark was a year old, he had a bushy white beard that dominated his face and while he was once handsome, his skin had now all folded in on itself and it looked like the wax that clung to those make-do wine bottle candlesticks, the ones that you came across in Spanish restaurants. This boy had smooth skin that was only interrupted by a slight shadow of whiskers; there were no lines, or broken capillaries, no brown age spots.

'I'm Doctor Fielding's son. Doctor Fielding Junior, if you like,' said the boy with a brief and professional smile. 'Dad wanted me to come and take over the practice now he's retired. That was always the plan. I've been based at Torbay for six years. Didn't you know he'd retired? I thought he'd made quite a song and dance about it.' The young doctor laughed in a way that betrayed he secretly thought his father's retirement festivities had been a little vulgar or unnecessary.

Ray was relieved that he'd decided against throwing a retirement party. He couldn't imagine his own son being so arrogant and ungrateful, but those things were tricky to manage. How did one celebrate a lifetime of work and achievement without sounding just a little smug? Besides, a party was out of the question, given the circumstances. Margaret simply wouldn't have managed.

'Yes, we did know,' said Ray. 'We sent a card and contributed to his leaving gift. I understand he wanted a leather-topped desk for his home.'

'That's right,' said the young doctor, and he flashed another smile.

'I would've thought he'd have a desk, already,' added Ray. His disapproval hung on the air. Ray was not one for over-indulgence.

'He did. He wanted a new one.'

Ray raised one eyebrow but didn't comment. Margaret stayed silent too because she couldn't remember a thing about the desk or the retirement. Dr Fielding glanced at the screen, where her entire health records were displayed, and then asked, 'So, what can I do for you?'

'I'm a bit under the weather,' Margaret replied.

'In what way?'

'Tired. Forgetful.' She paused and then reluctantly added, 'A bit tetchy.'

'Depressed?'

'No, I wouldn't say depressed.'

'Any dizziness?'

'No.'

'Coughs, colds, sore throats?'

'No.'

'Are you sleeping well?'

'Yes.'

'Eating?'

'Yes.'

'When she remembers,' chipped in Ray.

'Our family have just moved here from London. It's been a busy time. Sometimes I'm run off my feet, looking after my son and his wife and their two girls.'

'Three girls,' said Ray.

'Two and a baby,' Margaret corrected herself. 'I sometimes forget the baby.'

'Poppy's seven,' said Ray firmly.

'Not a baby,' Margaret conceded.

Throughout this exchange Ray and Margaret kept their eyes trained on the doctor, who glanced from husband to wife and back again, taking in every word. He stood up, washed his hands elaborately, then picked up a torch and shone it in Margaret's eyes. He nodded. He pulled out a wooden spatula that looked a bit like a nail file and asked Margaret to open her mouth. 'Uh huh.' He checked her blood pressure and listened to her chest. He then returned to his seat and typed rapidly but the letters on the screen were too small for Margaret or Ray to decipher. 'So just a bit run down?' he prompted.

'Exactly. I was going to buy a tonic from the butcher's, I mean the chemist. I don't really need to waste your time.' Margaret started to stand up but Ray reached out his hand and rested it on hers, anchoring her to her seat.

'There are other things, Doctor. It's not just tiredness. Or maybe it is, but she gets confused.'

'Confused?'

'I have to tell her things over and over again.'

'That's married life, my love. You should know that after all this time,' Margaret said and she risked a sprightly giggle in the hope of lifting the atmosphere.

'We got a new oven four months ago, she still can't work it. Forgets.'

The doctor didn't tell Ray to stop being so bloody naggy and leave his surgery; he nodded and typed something, as though what Ray was saying was important, which annoyed Margaret because it wasn't important, it wasn't. 'She was visiting our son last week, popping round, and she forgot where he lived.'

'He's just moved in,' she said defensively.

'Some months ago now and you go every day. How come last Thursday you forgot where they lived?'

Margaret scowled at Ray but wouldn't dignify his question with an answer. She thought it was wrong of him to wash their dirty linen in public. She should never have told him about getting lost. She wouldn't have, except that he'd come looking for her and had found her at the bandstand in the park.

There was a moment's silence and Margaret was reminded of the Cenotaph. When she was a girl, her mum used to take her to the Cenotaph in London on Remembrance Sunday, to honour her father, who had died in France just at the end of the war. She'd dress Margaret up in her best outfit and scrape her hair into ponytails that were so tight that Margaret's eyes went slitty. Margaret's mother always cried at the Cenotaph but Margaret never could. She hadn't known her dad; she'd been so young when he'd died. She'd missed him not being there because she wanted a dad, but she didn't miss the man her mum missed. So she'd never cried and her mum had always been furious that she didn't feel it more. She'd never liked silences since then so she rushed to fill this one.

'Could it be stress, Doctor?' Margaret offered.

'Do you feel stressed?'

'Sometimes.' Like now or when she said something that caused Ray to scowl. She didn't understand why Ray was always scowling at her because he never used to scowl. She'd been blessed with a husband who scattered smiles.

'Or her thyroid?' asked Ray. 'I've been reading up on her symptoms and I wondered whether it might be a thyroid problem.'

'I advise against trying to gather reliable information from the Internet,' said the young doctor with a hint of irritation. 'A lot of it is inaccurate and nearly all of it is alarmist. There is a reason we go to medical school, you know.' He made a sound that was supposed to approximate a laugh but was the sort of laugh that was calculated to show that no humour abounded. 'We can do some blood tests, if you like. I think that might be wise. Rule some things out. Anaemia, diabetes.'

'Thyroid malfunctions.'

'Yes, that too.'

'You see, sometimes she's as right as rain and other days . . . well, I don't know. I can't explain it. It's like she's not there.'

Margaret swung her head around to glare at Ray but he refused to meet her eye.

Margaret didn't mind needles, Ray hated them. For all their tough bravado, men were often more squeamish than women. He looked away as the cold steel punctured his wife's arm. She thought this whole thing was a storm in a teacup. She wasn't ill, she just needed a tonic. She'd pick one up on the way home. She needed to go into the chemist anyway because Eloise had said she wanted to pick something up for the girls and Margaret could save her a job. What was it Eloise wanted? Aspirin? Cough mixture? Vitamins? Dear me, Margaret couldn't quite remember. She decided she'd buy the lot, just in case. Eloise was so busy with the bathrooms being refitted.

Margaret questioned Eloise's judgement with regard to mixing business with pleasure. Was it ever sensible to employ a friend? What if their work or timing was shoddy? How was that to be managed? If only Eloise had exercised just the smallest amount of patience Margaret was sure that she could have got Bernie Fields to do the bathrooms and probably for a lot less than Charlie Woddell was charging. Eloise had said she'd called Bernie and that he'd been busy but Margaret doubted Eloise had mentioned that she was Margaret's daughter-in-law. If she had, Bernie would have dropped everything to squeeze her in, she was sure of it. He'd been sweet on Margaret for years, there was nothing he wouldn't do for her. Not that he'd ever actually made a move or anything silly like that. He knew Ray and Margaret were solid but every Christmas, after he'd had one or two too many in the Ship Inn, he'd always look at Margaret with those big watery eyes of his and say to Ray, 'You look after her, Ray, you've got a good one there.' Ray would then inevitably joke that Bernie could keep Margaret for the price of a pint but he was careful to put his arm around her as he said it so that they were all clear he was joking and they all knew what was what. Margaret was kicking herself. She should have rung Bernie directly. She would have, only Ray was continually saying that she had to let Eloise and Mark find their own way.

Eloise kept talking about the 'mate's rate' she'd agreed with this Charlie but even a mate's rate on a London fee card was going to cost an arm and a leg. Margaret worried about how they managed their money. They'd had no savings when they'd moved to Dartmouth, they lived from month to month, it seemed. Mark earned enough but they spent as though it was going out of fashion. Besides, any savings they might have made by employing Charlie were being eaten away (quite literally) because he was living with them. My goodness, could that man chow! Last night Margaret had noticed that he'd helped himself to a healthy-sized second portion of the boeuf bourguignon that she'd taken round. It was the Gordon Ramsay recipe, succulent, slow cooked, you needed goose fat and shallots; she liked to serve it with celeriac mash, although last night's hadn't been her best. She'd forgotten to put in the garlic – still, no one seemed to mind, least of all Charlie. After the beef he'd had a huge helping of bread-and-butter pudding and custard and he still asked for a chocolate biscuit to go with his coffee! Besides the blurring of the line between employer and employee and the fact that the man had an enormous appetite, Margaret didn't think it was a good idea that Charlie was living with them because she thought they needed to have a bit of time to themselves, as a family. To settle in and acclimatise.

'What's the matter, love? You look worried. Are you in pain? Uncomfortable?'

'I'm fine, Ray. Just thinking about Mark and Eloise and that plumber friend of theirs.'

Ray made a humph sound which clearly communicated that he thought Margaret had more to worry about than her son's bathrooms. But Margaret thought Ray was wrong. She'd be as right as rain once she'd picked up a tonic from the chemist. That and the baby milk Eloise had asked for.

NOVEMBER

12

'What do you think I should cook?' Eloise asked Charlie. She doubted he was particularly interested in the dinner party she was hosting this coming Friday, especially as it was only Tuesday, but she'd canvassed the opinions of Mark, Emily, Erin and Poppy – irrespective of their probable indifference – and saw no reason to let Charlie off the hook.

'Whatever you serve will be a hit, it always is,' replied Charlie with his broad, reassuring smile. Mark had said something similar.

'But you know I always cheat. Rationally, I realise that cooking isn't so tricky, not if it's approached in a quiet, methodical, sensible way – irrationally, it still terrifies me.'

'Have you ever cooked from scratch?' Charlie asked, leaning back on the kitchen counter. He had a great way of asking questions as though he really cared.

'Oh yes, years ago. Before we could afford foie gras doused in truffle dust from the local deli and monkfish Wellington and chocolate soufflés baked by the local caterer.' Charlie whistled, showing he was impressed. 'When I say afford, of course, I mean before I realised that it was more important to slam it on the credit card then risk giving my guests food poisoning.' Charlie chuckled and Eloise felt a bit less panicked, a bit calmer. It was a nice feeling, making someone laugh. She stood up and put the kettle on. Charlie saw this as his invitation to sit down at the kitchen table, even though he'd just got back from the builders' yard and hadn't actually done any work in the bathrooms yet this morning. 'But over the years I've lost the knack,' she added.

'Sounds like you've just lost your confidence. I bet you could take on Jamie Oliver if you put your mind to it.' Eloise smiled at the compliment but knew it was far from the truth. 'Can't Mark help?'

'He offered but it would be a debacle. He's very proficient at fish fingers, chips and beans, or anything that goes in a microwave, and he does have a notable flair for presentation.'

'Yeah, I've noticed how he always stacks the fat chips like a Jenga tower.'

'But his culinary skills are limited, and I'm keen to impress Arabella and Jackie. And their husbands too, of course,' she added as an afterthought, betraying that, frankly, the husbands mattered less.

'I could help.'

'You can cook?' Eloise passed him a mug of tea and rooted in the cupboards for biscuits.

'Don't sound so surprised. Yes, I can cook. I do a fantastic lasagne and very authentic Mexican chicken enchiladas.'

Eloise wondered why she didn't know this about Charlie and then she realised that whilst Sara and Charlie had eaten at their home about once a week for several years, the Hamiltons had only twice received a reciprocal invite. Of course, there was a very easy explanation as to why this was the case. There were five Hamiltons and only two Woddells. It always made much more sense to dine at the Hamiltons', as it was a lot less disruptive. Eloise was tempted to accept Charlie's offer but then she considered the general rule that men couldn't cook without an elaborate production; a full set design, a drum roll and loud applause would be required and Eloise didn't have time for that. She needed Charlie to concentrate on working on the bathrooms. Besides, he wouldn't be here at the weekend.

Eloise wanted to make friends, real friends here in Dartmouth. She was acutely aware that she *needed* to do so. They'd been here over four months now and she felt she still had a foot in both camps. She lived in Dartmouth, her heart was in London. She saw Arabella, Jackie and a number of other mums every day, but never managed to say more than a brief hello to them, whereas she hadn't seen Sara since the miscarriage – when Eloise had got in the car and driven at breakneck speed to London – but she talked to her on the phone, every day, for hours. If she wasn't talking to Sara, then she and Mark were hanging out with Charlie. At the weekends various other family members or London friends came to visit. The house guests sponged up all of Eloise's spare time. She'd spotted a pattern. The exhausted commuters arrived on Friday evening, they spent Saturday enviously staring at sailing boats and wolfing down fish and chips, they repeatedly sighed with longing and told Eloise how lucky she was to live in such a beautiful part of the country, but then, on Sunday afternoon, rejuvenated, they hurriedly jumped back into their cars and sped away, barely disguising their need to return to the city that offered on average twenty-seven different sandwich fillings – and that was just at their corner café. Her parents had been wonderfully appreciative guests. After their week-long visit Eloise had been sad to wave goodbye but, in all honesty, the sadness was mixed with a slight feeling of relief. Endless house guests were exhausting.

Eloise had deliberately kept this weekend free from responsibilities as tour guide and landlady. She knew she needed to commit to Dartmouth and its people more firmly and fully; throwing a dinner party for some new, local friends was a step towards that. She was conscious that the people of Dartmouth must be beginning to wonder whether she was trying to avoid them. She wouldn't want to offend anyone.

'Well, it is lovely of you to offer, Charlie, but I don't think I have a choice. I have to roll up my sleeves.'

'Don't stress, you'll be amazing as always,' said Charlie as he gave Eloise a friendly squeeze on the shoulder. 'Your new friends will fall under your spell, just like everyone else.'

Eloise spent the next few days trailing through a variety of Internet sites for ideas. She soon discovered that there were dozens of fabulous recipes to follow but that became overwhelming in itself; the extensive choice was actually one of the problems. What should she serve? How many courses were appropriate? Was champagne flaunting or fun? She didn't want to appear too flash, too London but, on the other hand, she wanted to make it clear that she valued their company and she wanted them to realise she'd made an effort. In the end she consulted Margaret.

'Has to be fish, dear. Locally sourced, of course. Go to the mongers on the embankment. You can taste the sea in every mouthful. And have you thought about oysters for a starter? Best served simply, I always think, maybe with a hot pepper sauce.'

'That would give it a contemporary twist,' Eloise agreed.

Margaret looked at her daughter-in-law blankly; she was of a generation that didn't link food with fashion. Eloise actually envied her that.

'You'll need to have a think about how to serve them.'

'Now *that* I'm fine with. Crushed ice, maybe some dried seaweed for colour. I have the special forks.'

'Of course you do, dear.'

'And Arabella's husband has a nut allergy so we have to make sure everything is nut free.'

'That's easy. Come on, let's have a look through some recipes.'

Margaret had a library of cookbooks. The entire collection of Delia's, Jamie's and Gordon's and also a large number that were not written by celebrity chefs. Her books were well-thumbed tomes. As Eloise turned the pages, plumes of flour escaped and every page had a buttery thumb print or a splash of oil to mark a culinary moment. El imagined the endless potatoes her mother-in-law had peeled, onions she'd chopped and fish she'd baked to grow Mark up. Eloise was overcome with an urge to fling her arms around Margaret and thank her but then Margaret made a crack about leaving the wine choice to Mark because 'he knows what he's doing' and Eloise wanted to knock off her block.

They settled on oysters, spiced sea bass with caramelised fennel and purple sprouting broccoli followed by apple tart with lavender cream. Margaret assured Eloise that the meal said confident and in control but not pretentious or over-trying and she offered to make the dessert. Eloise agreed readily because she was uncertain whether the local Co-op sold ready-to-roll pastry and she'd need it. Mark chose the wine. He plumped for champagne on arrival, then he picked a year 2000 Muscadet Sur Lie to be downed with the oysters and he stocked up on several bottles of a decent Chenin Blanc; finally, he opted for a Hungarian Tokay to accompany the apple tart. It took him about ten minutes to make these suggestions because he combined flair with poise. Such remarkable decisiveness balanced Eloise's unusual procrastinating. With relief and gratitude she decided to view him as her entertaining arsenal. When all was said and done, no one really cared what they were eating if they were drunk. Preparations almost complete, Eloise bribed the girls with the guarantee of a trip to the cinema the following weekend if they stayed in their bedrooms all evening and resisted the lure of wandering downstairs with a fake malady, a need for Eloise and Mark to intervene on a human rights issue, or any other excuse.

Eloise had decided to wear something in her existing wardrobe. She'd decided to do this because the King's Road was hundreds of miles away and the opportunity to browse for a new top in Seaside Fashions, a boutique that claimed to be the answer to *all* on- and offshore needs, was considerably less seductive. A glance in the window had confirmed what she already knew: they were over-promising – in fact, they were deluded. The only fashion need the store might answer was that they could furnish ladies of a certain age with something beige when they had a desire to do a spot of gardening.

It was a novelty that tonight they would be eating in the dining room as they hadn't had one in Muswell Hill. Eloise had commissioned a walnut table that seated eight to fill the room but, unfortunately, it wouldn't be ready for another two months, so they were having to make do with the old kitchen table and benches. Eloise had covered the battered table with a white tablecloth and dozens of silver candle-sticks, all of which were different shapes and sizes. The eclectic candlesticks said artisan and 'thrown together'; in fact, the collection was the result of days and days of meticulous searches through antique shops and car boot sales and then weeks of restoration and polishing. Still, the light bounced so prettily around the room that Eloise was almost certain it had been worth the effort.

'Don't let me drink too much,' she instructed Mark as she impatiently yanked off her black top with a sequin trim. A top that, just five minutes ago, she'd thought was the perfect look and now believed made her look like a desperate *Strictly Come Dancing* contestant.

'You're a big girl. You know when you've had enough.'

'Yeah, but only when I throw up.' Eloise tended to drink with nerves and, as she was petite, she'd never been able to handle her alcohol. 'You know I become indiscreet and convinced that the hilarious anec-dotes about, say, our sex life are reasonable dinner conversation.'

'You're going to struggle for conversation if that's your chosen subject,' said Mark wryly. His joke was the sort of vaguely embar-rassing joke that was thrown out when one half of a couple wanted to talk about something serious but didn't know how to open the conversation without causing hurt. Mark and Eloise had only made love a handful of times since they'd moved here. Eloise was always unpacking boxes, rearranging furniture or writing something on her damn 'to do' list. Mark was tempted to write, 'give your husband a blow job' on the list but as there were already over a hundred items, he didn't think she'd ever get that far down.

Eloise was too preoccupied with her wardrobe choice to notice his tone. 'Hey, there *are* some,' she said defensively.

'Nothing current.'

'True, but we were young once and they'd still be new stories to new friends. Anyway, my point is I *don't* want to over-share because I'm drunk.'

Mark used to delight in the fact that Eloise was a lightweight, he'd joked it made her an economical date, but Eloise feared that whilst being tipsy after half a shandy might be quite cute when you were twenty-something, it was a bit ridiculous once you were forty.

'Maybe I shouldn't drink anything tonight, that way I won't embarrass myself? That said, I'm hardly likely to impress either. I'm so nervous I'm going to have to have at least one.'

'You're worrying unnecessarily. I have every confidence tonight is going to be a huge success.'

Eloise remained unconvinced although she was grateful for his cheerleading skills. She furiously scrabbled around her wardrobe and found precisely *nothing* suitable to wear. 'I need new clothes,' she announced heatedly.

'Oh yes, what sort?' replied Mark calmly.

'I don't know, something that fits in. Something nautical. Striped, maybe? Red, white and blue.'

Mark had been dressed for thirty minutes now. He'd made an effort; he'd shaved and changed his shirt. He looked perfect. Eloise never really knew how to pull off smart casual but Mark had it nailed. He looked relaxed, in control and affluent. Eloise feared the look she'd currently hit was frazzled, wild and slutty. He'd read to Poppy and Erin and had checked that Emily really was playing Zhu Zhu Pets on her DS and not surfing the net for designer shoes while secreting their credit card under the mouse mat. A quick glance in the mirror confirmed to Eloise that she looked flustered and cross; not a bit like the hostess with the mostess. She made a conscious effort to relax her face. This dinner was *so* important to her.

'Crap! Is that the door?' Eloise glanced at the bedroom clock. 'They're early, how bloody inconsiderate. It's just gone seven, I said half past, for eight. Crap.'

Mark left her to her cursing and went to answer the door.

'It's OK, love,' he called up the stairs. 'It's not Arabella et al., it's Sara.'

Sara? Double crap.

Eloise wouldn't like to be misunderstood; Sara was a great friend and normally she'd be utterly delighted to see or hear from her any time of day or night, be that in person, phone call, text, e-mail or carrier pigeon, but not tonight. Tonight was about Eloise making new friends and Sara had never been good with Eloise making new friends; she liked to keep El to herself. Her exclusivity clause was flattering but sometimes tricky to handle. A sliver of shame crept into Eloise's gut; in all their long phone calls she'd never mentioned to Sara that Arabella and Jackie and their husbands were coming to dinner tonight. It was not that there was any definable and solid reason for keeping this info from Sara, it was just that it hadn't popped up in conversation. Sara didn't ask much about Eloise's life here. She'd had a terrible couple of months. Losing the baby had been horrific. Cruel. Unfair. El knew that her friend was struggling; it was too much to expect her to take an interest in Eloise's day-to-day goings on. Besides, on the rare occasions that she did ask how things were going, Eloise found herself walking a fine line of conversation, which wasn't exactly untruthful but certainly wasn't the entire truth either. She'd say everything was fine. She'd say she was getting there.

Somehow, she couldn't explain the vulnerability she felt when she waited at the school gate to pick up the girls. She hadn't told anyone that she still practised opening phrases and ice-breakers in the mirror whenever she was alone. She was Eloise Hamilton for goodness' sake, everyone's best friend, the girl who was never short of something to say. Eloise had sent out 219 change-of-address cards. She was popular, funny, interesting, admired.

That was her.

Who she was.

Besides, even if Sara accepted that Eloise did need friends here, in a way that she couldn't accept it in London, there was still a very real risk that she might over-share in a fashion that was likely to embarrass Jackie and Arabella. Right now, Sara didn't seem to have an awareness of what was and wasn't appropriate to air in public. There was a strong chance she might ask Arabella's husband for a sperm donation once she knew they had four kids and that therefore he was clearly very fertile. Oh God. Arabella had four kids, Jackie and Eloise had three each. Eloise knew that Sara would see that plethora as unfair. Would she feel the need to say as much?

'Surprise!' Sara popped her head around the bedroom door. She was at least beaming, which was a relief. Eloise had half expected her to be in floods again. El was sympathetic but she was just short of time right now and would have struggled to deal with tears. 'I rang Charlie this afternoon and told him to stay put, said that I'd come and see you guys. I really needed to be out of the city. I told him not to tell you. I wanted to surprise you. Did he tell you?'

'Erm, no, he didn't,' Eloise confirmed through a grimace that she hoped would pass for a grin. She silently vowed that when she was next alone with Charlie she'd tear a strip off him. He could have warned her and then they'd have pretended to Sara that he hadn't. That way Eloise could have been a bit more prepared. It was not like it would be the first secret they'd ever kept from Sara. Charlie sometimes asked El for advice on how to cheer up his wife or how to handle the latest disappointment relating to their fertility. Eloise always did her best to advise him in Sara's interests and he always ended those conversations with, 'You won't mention to Sara that we had this chat, will you? It's just between the two of us, eh?' Initially, Eloise had wondered if there was any element of disloyalty in those conversations but Charlie's confused and earnest face, begging for guidance and sympathy, always assured her that she was doing the right thing. He only wanted what was best for his wife and his marriage.

Still, Eloise might kill him for not recognising that discretion was a two-way street.

'Where is Charlie?' asked Sara.

'I'm not sure. I thought he was heading back to London. I suppose he must be in his room.' Charlie's room was in the attic; if he was up there, he'd been keeping very quiet.

'Oh well. I'll go and hunt him down in a minute,' said Sara with barely hidden indifference.

You and me both, sister, thought Eloise.

Eloise was only wearing her trousers and a bra as she hadn't settled on which top to wear yet. 'Nice look,' Sara commented, pulling her into a hug.

'Can't decide what to wear.'

'Going somewhere special?'

'We're having a dinner party. My first here.'

'Oh, you never said.' Sara looked disappointed and confused. 'I feel terrible. We can't possibly crash your dinner party. I didn't realise you'd made close friends here already.'

'Well, they're not close. Not yet. I'd like them to be,' Eloise admitted awkwardly.

'Silly me! I'm so sorry. I was imagining that tonight it would be just the four of us and the girls, with a takeaway, sitting around your open fire. Then, once the kids had scooted off to bed, we could drink too much and talk nonsense, like old times.'

'We can do that tomorrow night, I don't have anything planned then.' Eloise's tone was apologetic; she was unsure what she was apologising for exactly but she did feel an apology was in order. Sara pulled out a purple top from the open wardrobe and handed it to El. It was Calvin Klein, fitted cotton with a satin trim on the cuff, neck and waist. It was simple but sophisticated, one of Eloise's favourites and perfect for this evening. She couldn't believe she'd overlooked it. She allowed herself to feel a moment of relief. That was what friends were for. That was what she'd been missing – someone who knew her better than she knew herself. She slipped on the top.

'How many guests are you expecting?' Sara asked.

'Just two couples.'

'Well, we can't possibly force ourselves on you. I bet you haven't even got enough for eight.'

'Well, no. Not really but—'

'Charlie and I will just sit in his room and watch TV. He said you'd got him a TV in there so that he wasn't always under your feet in the family room.'

'We got him the TV because the girls were so noisy and they command the remote control,' Eloise corrected carefully. The temporary relief had already vanished. She felt as though she was on the back foot with Sara, but was unsure why that might be. When had they fallen out of step?

'Yes.' Sara smiled as though El's contradiction was confirming exactly what she had said. Eloise didn't know why Sara was making her feel so uncomfortable tonight. She couldn't bear the idea that there might be any discord between her and her old friend, especially right now when she needed every iota of confidence galvanised so that she could start to make new friends too, so she told herself that *Sara* probably wasn't making her feel uncomfortable. Eloise just *was* uncomfortable and Sara just happened to be there.

Unexpectedly.

'You don't have to sit upstairs.' El would feel terrible and certainly wouldn't be able to enjoy the dinner party if she thought her friend was hiding upstairs like some banished au pair. She was just about to add that there were some amazing restaurants in Dartmouth when Sara interrupted her.

'Well, I would like to meet your new friends! That would be wonderful. It will be so good for me to be with people who don't know all about my recent bereavement. In London, everywhere I go I get sympathetic looks and I know people mean well, but even that gets wearing.'

'Yes. Yes, of course. That's decided, then.' At the mention of the miscarriage Eloise couldn't find it in her heart to suggest the restaurant. She made a quick calculation; if she got a couple of pieces of frozen cod out of the freezer she might get away with serving those to herself and Mark. Would anyone notice that the hosts weren't eating the sea bass? Well, there wasn't any alternative. She plastered on a wide grin and asked, 'Do you want to help me shuck the oysters?'

13

Sara and Eloise found Charlie in the kitchen. He was lying on his back on the floor, with his head in the cupboard under the sink.

'What are you doing?'

'Oh hello, love, I thought it must be you at the door.' He wiggled up to a standing position and landed a kiss on Sara's forehead. She stared pointedly at the kitchen sink. It was not that she minded him working for Eloise, exactly – in fact, she was very grateful – but she didn't like the idea of him working all hours. Charlie had a tendency to run around after Eloise, he could be almost too good-natured. Charlie caught the tension in Sara's face and quickly explained, 'I noticed that there was a drip under the sink. Nothing to it. A five-minute job.'

'You should have told me that Eloise and Mark were hosting tonight.' Sara rolled her eyes with exasperation and added – more for El's benefit than his – 'We'll be in the way. I'd never have come if I thought we'd be imposing.'

The truth was Sara was secretly glad Charlie hadn't informed her that Eloise was expecting company because it would certainly have put her off coming and now she was here in the warm, higgledy-piggledy kitchen (complete with an Aga and an open fire) she realised this was exactly where she wanted and needed to be; although she sensed that Eloise wasn't exactly overjoyed to have extra guests. Eloise wasn't good with spontaneity; she liked to stick rigidly to plans and sometimes Sara felt that this was even at the detriment of pleasure. Of course, Eloise was so polite that she'd had to invite Sara to join in the dinner party but Sara could almost see her friend calculating whether there were enough veggies to go round and who should sit next to who. Sara knew that Eloise would have thought and re-thought tonight's seating plans a million times and the Woddells' presence must have screwed it up. Eloise's tendency to worry about daft details slightly irritated Sara at the moment because she had so much more to worry about. If Sara was ever pushed to find fault with Eloise, her one small criticism would be that Eloise was far too concerned with what people thought of her. Sara could just imagine how far backwards El was bending to fit in with this new Dartmouth set. In her opinion it was quite unnecessary. Eloise didn't need them. She had plenty of friends already and Sara would always be happy to come here for a country weekend.

Sara glanced around the house and thought that Eloise hadn't done her new home justice when she'd described it. Sara wondered why El hadn't wanted to expand on the full extent of its perfection. When Sara had visited Dartmouth last summer, to look at the girls' schools, they couldn't get into the house because El thought it was too much to ask the existing owners for a nose around. Sara thought this was another example of Eloise being overly concerned with what others thought; they'd already exchanged contracts, the place was just about hers. Whatever, this was the first time Sara had actually been allowed inside. Whenever Sara called, Eloise talked about the problems with the damp air making bread mould at an alarming rate or the fact she was knackered with walking up and down the town's steep slopes. She hadn't mentioned that there were window boxes at every window, bright with ochre buds that Sara couldn't name but could appreciate.

Sara had to admit that the kitchen was dated, as Eloise had said on many occasions, and a bit cramped, but the rest of the house was spacious and impressive. Eloise had filled the place with beautiful (and no doubt extremely expensive) furniture and big, shaggy floor rugs.

As they'd walked downstairs Sara had commented to Eloise that she didn't recognise much of the furniture but her question, 'Is this new?' – which was just meant to show a polite interest – had caused Eloise to blush and she'd practically gagged Sara when Mark came into earshot. Sara conceded that the potentially crass nature of so much new furniture in a listed house had been softened by piles of artfully arranged dusty books and an old piano. Their two flabby tabbies contentedly stretched in front of the open fire. Eloise had been concerned that the cats might become stressed or disorientated in the move but it seemed that they knew which side their bread was buttered on. Their purrs reverberated around the kitchen, suggesting a high level of satisfaction. Every window boasted a stunning landscape, undulating hills that held freshness and suggested possibilities and promise. The sun had set hours ago and there was a blue-blackness to the evening that seemed solid and reliable in a way that was not possible in London. London was never dark. Shop signage and lights from offices and homes disturbed 24/7. Sara had been happy to leave the brutal greyness behind her this afternoon. Somehow, out here in the country, near the sea, hills and huge sky, she felt a bit better. More alive. More vivid.

'You are not at all in the way. Not at *all*,' chipped in Mark as he threw logs on the fire. Sara smiled, grateful for his reassurance. Mark always said the right thing. As did Eloise, of course, that was why they were such a great couple, it was just that Sara always believed Mark.

'I didn't think it was important if these guys were having friends round. I thought we could go out on a date,' added Charlie with a smile that thumped Sara in the chest because it was a frail smile that managed to be at once hopeful and hopeless. She felt like a bitch. Grief and disappointment compounded to negate their marital harmony but she wished it wasn't the case.

She ignored his offer, pretending she hadn't heard it. She wished she could find it in her to boost his hope that they might have a fun Friday night out, like other couples, but she couldn't quite manage it. It was not that she wanted to be deliberately awkward and cruelly pour cold water on his optimism, it was just that whenever they were alone together they inevitably fell back into a conversation about their baby or, more accurately, their lack of baby. They had no other topic of conversation but, miserably, they never had anything new to say to one another on the subject. They couldn't change anything. There wasn't an easy solution. It was exhausting and depressing.

It was such a nuisance that Eloise had company tonight, thought Sara. While she didn't want to have another heavy discussion with Charlie, she really needed to talk to her friend. Sara found their telephone conversations inadequate. She was sometimes left feeling *more* isolated – not *less* – after one of their lengthy calls. She closed her eyes, suddenly overwhelmed with the fear that she might weep with frustration and disappointment. She had to be strong. She had to push on.

'Well, El has very kindly extended the dinner party to include us, so you'd better go and get changed,' she instructed. She was aware that her tone was a bit schoolmarmish but all her reserves were channelled into not crying and she didn't have the energy to adjust it to anything a little warmer.

'Oh, fair enough.' Charlie wiped his hands on his work jeans and looked a bit startled. 'I'll cancel my reservation at The Seahorse then, shall I?'

He was making it difficult for Sara to ignore his suggestion of going on a date. Stonily she replied, 'Yes.'

'Wow, you got a table at The Seahorse,' said Eloise. 'We haven't even tried there yet. Everyone talks about their lobster caldereta, you know. There's talk that they'll be awarded a Michelin star this year.' Eloise was genuinely enthusiastic about restaurants and wasn't aware that her comments sounded as though she was trying to tempt Sara to go out and leave her in peace.

'That sort of thing doesn't impress me much. I'd far rather stay in with friends,' Sara added firmly. She quickly turned away from Charlie, making it clear that she wouldn't appreciate it if he tried to renew his offer for them to go out alone. He understood and clomped upstairs to change for the dinner party. Mark followed him, mumbling something about checking on the girls. 'So what are you serving tonight?' Sara asked Eloise; it was only polite to show an interest.

'We're having fresh oysters to start, then sea bass and apple tart. What do you think? Sound good?'

Sara didn't really care that much, as the menu had nothing to do with her fertility, baby names or sperm count, which she thought were the only interesting topics of the day. Any day. But she knew Eloise expected a reassuring compliment so she ventured an unrevealing pleasantry, 'Sounds impressive', then she poured a couple of huge glasses of wine and fiddled with her iPod while Eloise turned her attention to the oysters.

El stood over her ancient ceramic sink that was piled high with ice chips and oysters and stared at the grainy shells, clearly a little fazed. After some moments of silence, she reached for her iPhone and finally said, 'I think I'll take a photo first.' Eloise held the view that if all else failed, turn the moment into a photo opportunity. No matter how successful or disastrous tonight might be, she'd be able to produce an arty collage of snaps of the evening and hang the results on the wall in the downstairs cloakroom. In time she'd tell herself she'd had a great night.

'Do you know anything about shucking?' she asked.

'Nope.' Sara took a big gulp of wine; it must have been a massive gulp, actually, because within moments she needed to top up. Getting blotto was the only compensation for not being pregnant but then again, if she was pregnant, she wouldn't have anything that she needed to blank out.

'I looked it up on the web, it sounds simple enough,' Eloise said, trying to buoy herself up. She reached for a tea towel and a threateningly sharp knife, then gripped an oyster firmly in the towel and tentatively inserted the knife into the edge. A sudden and determined twist caused the shell to open. With more confidence she now ran the knife along the inside of the top shell, cutting the muscle that attached the oyster to the lid. She lifted off the top shell, then slid the knife under the oyster to cut the second muscle. Mission accomplished, she let out a deep sigh of relief.

'OK, one down, about fifty-nine to go.'

'Can I do anything?' Sara asked, as she sat down at the kitchen table and reached for one of the many magazines that were piled there.

'No, no, of course not, you're the guest,' said El, as she turned back to the sink. Anything else she had to say was drowned out because she raked the ice and oysters against the ceramic sink and the kitchen sounded like a beach with waves crashing over shingle.

Sara started to read an article about a woman who was moaning on about the fact that she felt she was judged for having seven children in a world that was conscious of natural resources and everyone's personal responsibility to reduce their carbon footprint. The article incensed Sara on so many levels: A, she was not happy with the idea that anyone would reduce children to an ecologically appropriate formula; B, she'd yet to witness this world the woman in the article referred to, the one where people *were* actually taking responsibility for their carbon emissions; and C, this woman had seven children! Seven. Sara had less than zero sympathy for her. She thought she ought to happily take the verbal stick that might come with such an abundance of riches, if indeed there was any stick (which she seriously doubted). This woman had probably only written the article because she was promoting some book or fitness CD or something. Get over yourself, you stupid, spoilt cow, thought Sara. She realised that her pulse was beginning to race. She was aware that recently she was prone to bouts of emotion that really couldn't be described as anything other than rage. This sort of self-indulgent crap was just the type of thing that riled her. Once upon a time she'd have simply turned the page, shrugged and accepted the fact that everyone came at the world from a different viewpoint. Now, she had to breathe deeply to resist the temptation of picking up a dessert fork and attacking the photo of the smug, self-righteous woman; she'd really like to gouge out her eyes or, at the very least, draw a moustache and glasses on her superior face.

'Bitch,' Sara yelled. Her cuss broke the sedative rhythm of the ice and shells sloshing in the sink and cut through the mellow lounge music coming from the iPod. Her outburst startled El, who jumped and then added a curse of her own.

'Oh hell!'

'What's up?' Sara asked. It was unlike Eloise to swear (at least, not before the kids went to bed) and she wasn't reading the article, so she couldn't be incensed.

'Can you get the first aid kit? It's on that top shelf, behind you. I've cut myself.' Sara looked up and saw a thick line of blood running quite rapidly down Eloise's forearm. El was holding her hand aloft and wrapping the tea towel around the wound but there was still blood oozing, she'd clearly cut herself quite badly. The sight of the flowing blood reminded Sara of her baby running down her legs and she couldn't move. There was a blaring sound in her ears and she felt sick. All she wanted to do was lie down on the slate floor, she didn't even care that the floor was pocked with sticky marks and crumbs.

'It's OK, it's OK, don't cry. I'm OK.' Sara felt Eloise's arms around her as she pulled Sara's face into her flat belly. Sara could smell her friend's musky perfume as she grabbed tightly and started to sob. Loud, heavy, ugly sobs that wouldn't be tamed. 'Mark, Charlie, I need some help in here,' yelled Eloise. On some level Sara knew that El wanted to be released from her grip so that she could attend to her wound, but Sara couldn't let go.

She just couldn't.

14

'Hello, Margaret.'

'Hello, dear.' Margaret recognised Eloise's voice straight away but still plumped for the generic term of endearment. Sometimes she answered the phone and said, 'Hello, Emily,' and it was Poppy or Erin or even Mark. And they'd get so huffy if she mixed them up. She'd called Ray 'Frank' the other day and he'd snapped, 'Frank's your brother, Margaret, and he's been dead for seven years!' Of course Margaret knew *that*. Silly Ray to get so cross about the slip of a tongue. She told him, 'I know, Ray, and I know that Frank lived in Canada for thirty-five years before that, I'm not a bloody fool.' Still, it was easier to stay general rather than risk offending.

'I don't want to rush you, but I was wondering what time you are thinking of dropping off the tart. Or is it easiest if Mark comes to collect it? It's just that my guests will be here any minute and you know I do want to pass it off as my own.' Eloise giggled self-consciously. There was no need for her to be embarrassed with Margaret. Margaret understood her wanting to pass it off as her own, best way. Margaret would support her entirely, do everything she could. There was only one problem, she hadn't a clue what her daughter-in-law was talking about. Margaret didn't respond immediately, hoping Eloise would give her a few more clues as to what on earth she was referring to. Eloise paused and then added with rarely revealed impatience, 'So should I send Mark round? I'd come myself but I've had a bit of an accident with the oyster knife and I've unexpected guests and, oh, it's all a bit complicated and I don't really have time to explain—'

Margaret could hear the rising panic in Eloise's voice and she didn't want her to get hysterical so she jumped in and said, 'Yes, send Mark around right away.'

That was the simplest, Mark could explain.

Ten minutes later Mark walked into the sitting room where Ray and Margaret were watching *The One Show*. There was an interview with a lovely tall chap who had written a book about his family heirlooms – an extensive toggle collection, from what Margaret could gather.

The instant Margaret clapped eyes on Mark she got up out of her seat and walked towards him. She fought the temptation to hold her arms wide for an embrace. She wanted to kiss him. She always wanted to hug and kiss him whenever she saw him, she always had. This compunction hadn't gone away just because he was no longer a chubby-cheeked boy but rather a fully grown man, however, she knew that he'd think such a show was a bit much in the small sitting room on a Friday evening. Now he'd grown, kisses were the preserve of airport greetings or special occasions like birthdays and Christmas. Margaret clamped her arms to her sides and offered a different type of hug. 'Hello, dear, would you like a cup of tea?'

'No thanks, Mum, I really haven't got the time. The kids are still up and Eloise is a bit stressed out about this dinner party so I should just get straight back. I've come to collect the tart.'

'Right.' Margaret didn't like it when Mark was rude. It wasn't the way he'd been brought up. Who was he calling a tart? Jen from next door, maybe? Had she been invited to their party? Margaret was aware that Jen had had a colourful past; right now she lived with a partner – Mick, she thought he was called. There wasn't any sign of a wedding band and there had been other boyfriends before Mick. A string of them, but Margaret never thought Mark was so judgemental. Calling a lady a tart really wasn't polite. It was not as though there was a comeback, was there? No equivalent name to call a man with saggy morals, certainly not one that would cause the necessary offence. Stag or stud was a badge of honour. Margaret stared at Mark and wondered how much of her disapproval she should bother to show. She hadn't been aware that Mark and Eloise were even friendly with Jen, yet they must be if she was going to the dinner party.

'The apple tart,' he said. 'You've made an apple tart?' Mark was pulling an odd expression, a look of expectation tinged with a bit of desperation; Ray was looking panicked. They both cast nervous glances Margaret's way.

Tart. Apple tart. A bell was going off in Margaret's head. Deep, deeply buried under all sorts of other things. Thoughts like what was the name of the presenter on the television right now? She was a bonny little thing. Margaret knew she'd got one of those names that could be a boy's name or a girl's, depending on the spelling. Jo or Alex or Ashley. No, she couldn't remember. Apple tart? There was something. It was there somewhere, a thought about an apple tart. She closed her eyes tightly and really tried to concentrate. This was clearly important to Mark. It was like a nasty mosquito bite. She was aware of something, she wanted to scratch it but she wasn't sure it would help. What was it about the apple tart? Margaret remembered Emily telling her that it was only female mosquitoes that bite. She never knew that until Emily told her. She was as bright as a button, that Emily.

'You have made an apple tart, haven't you, Mum? And Eloise said something about lavender cream. She's waiting for it. We have people coming round for dinner.' Mark looked at his mother pleadingly.

'Of course, dear, it's all ready.' This was a lie. Margaret had not made an apple tart and she couldn't remember ever promising to do so. Indignant, Margaret suddenly thought that if Eloise wanted an apple tart she should make it herself. But they thought *she'd* made one. And they were waiting. The party. Waiting. Margaret felt a bit dizzy and muddled. She wasn't going to admit she'd forgotten. Ray would make a song and dance. She strode into the kitchen and looked around for something to give to Mark. The kitchen was spick and span; you could eat your food off the floor, if that was your thing. Margaret and Ray ate at about five o'clock and they'd always washed and dried up by now. As it was a Friday, a bit later on, Margaret would have a glass or two of dry white wine and Ray would have a couple of beers. They'd eat a little treat, maybe a Mars bar or a Twix. But what about now? What about this tart? There was a cheese and tomato quiche, that might do, thought Margaret. Ray had eaten a slice for tea but there was still plenty left. She quickly covered the plate with tinfoil.

'Don't forget the lavender cream, Mum. I know Eloise is looking forward to that. She said it's those extra touches that lift an expected dish into the extraordinary,' shouted Mark from the sitting room. Margaret could hear the amusement in his voice. She was pretty sure he'd be happy enough with custard but Eloise was right, if you were going to entertain, it was important to do it properly. She could hear that they'd switched channels and were just catching the last couple of minutes of news. There'd been a fire somewhere. Tragic.

Margaret stood in the doorway, unnoticed, and pretended to be watching the report showing a factory going up in smoke while she thought about lavender cream.

'What the hell is lavender cream, anyway?' Ray asked Mark. Mark shrugged and they grinned at one another.

They'd always had an easy intimacy. They liked to share a joke, many of them at Margaret's expense. A habit since Mark had been little. She didn't mind, it was just the way it was with two men in the house and one woman. She turned back to the kitchen and opened the fridge to search for the ingredients of lavender cream. The problem was she couldn't quite remember what they were. Crème fraîche and . . . oh look, she had crème fraîche. There it was. She must have bought that in especially. She reached for the tub and decanted the contents into a pretty flowered jug that had belonged to her mother. It didn't look as though it would go far. She needed to add something to bulk it out. Something had to be added, but what? Custard? Ice cream? She stared into the fridge and hoped to find inspiration. Ah, that was what she was looking for. Seeing the ingredient prompted her. Margaret reached for the jar of mayonnaise and scraped it into the jug of crème fraîche. Mayonnaise and crème fraîche, that's what made lavender cream, it was a Jamie Oliver. She briskly whisked the ingredients and was just finishing up when Mark ambled into the kitchen.

'All done.' She beamed, handing him the foiled plate and the jug. 'Have a lovely night, darling.'

'We will. I'm looking forward to this dessert.' He was already dashing for the door but turned and said, 'You're the best, Mum. Eloise is going to be thrilled. We're really grateful for your help. I don't know what we'd do without you.'

The words and sentiment were lovely but Margaret couldn't quite enjoy them the way she should. As the door banged closed, pushing back the cold autumn air, she shivered. The problem was she wasn't at all certain that was the best apple tart she'd ever made. There was something nagging, saying it was not up to her usual standard, and she certainly didn't want to let Eloise down. She turned to Ray and he read her face.

'What is it?' he asked gruffly.

'I don't know,' she replied honestly. 'I just don't know.'

15

Arabella and Patrick and Jackie and Ken arrived together. Eloise thought that maybe they'd already been to the local pub because she could smell beer on their breath when they leaned in to give her awkward double kisses on each cheek. The greetings were self-conscious because it was always a little odd to greet school-gate friends in another context. Eloise wondered whether her guests felt they needed Dutch courage before they came to the townie house to eat supper. It made no sense but the thought of them sitting in the warm boozer knocking back G&Ts while she shucked oysters, put the girls to bed, calmed Sara, chased up Margaret and set the table, seemed unfair. She wished she'd suggested that they'd all gone to a restaurant instead; they could have tried the lobster caldereta, but it wasn't the same, was it? Inviting someone to your home was a particular compliment that she wanted them to know she was paying. As she opened the door she made a big effort not to reveal the fact that she'd been firefighting and instead tried to give the impression that she was calm, cool and collected. She instantly checked out their outfits to see if hers was pitched appropriately for Dartmouth and it was a great relief to see that she'd got it about right. They'd all made an effort (the women were wearing lipstick and Eloise couldn't recall seeing either Arabella or Jackie in make-up before, and the guys had tucked their T-shirts into their trousers). So, dressed up around these parts wasn't Prada but it was a clean top with chunky jewellery, good to know.

There was a polite, expected hallway kerfuffle when coats were taken away, bottles of wine and a box of chocolates were proffered and comments were made about what a chilly evening it was.

'Come in, come in.' Eloise had run out of arms as she was clasping two bottles of wine and four large duffel coats, so she ushered everyone through to the sitting room and signalled frantically to Mark that he ought to start making introductions and offering the champagne, while she ran upstairs to ditch the coats on their bed. When she returned she found he'd failed on both counts. He hadn't asked if anyone fancied a glass of champagne, he'd asked, 'Who wants what to drink?' Ken, Patrick and Charlie had all asked for beer, the ladies had requested wine, so Eloise returned to find them quaffing the Hungarian Tokay which she'd intended to serve with the apple tart.

'That's sweet!' she cried without checking her tongue.

Arabella and Jackie both smiled. 'Oh, don't worry, we don't know much about wine either, you don't have to be embarrassed in front of us,' said Jackie kindly.

'As long as it's alcohol,' agreed Arabella, generously showing just how very un-fastidious she was by necking it with enthusiasm. Eloise quickly calculated that she could bring out the champagne at dessert, instead of the Hungarian Tokay. It was a shame, though, because if she'd known the champagne was going to be quaffed at the end of the evening, when everyone would be half cut, she might have gone for a supermarket own brand instead of Taittinger.

Eloise thought Mark hadn't handled the introductions particularly well either. Eloise had hoped to subtly let her Dartmouth friends know that the London guests were unexpected. Not that she wanted to make Sara feel less than one hundred per cent welcome, never, but nor did she want Arabella and Jackie to think that she'd needed back-up and had invited old pals for that purpose. Eloise thought it was vital that they knew she was trying to fit in here in Dartmouth and that she wasn't standing on the sidelines of the community, snidely making cracks to her old friends about the discrepancies between town and country. They'd been extremely welcoming to date but Eloise feared that the hospitality would only continue to be extended if it was clear that it was both sought after and embraced. She realised that this level of social nuance was undetectable to the average male *Homo sapiens*, so Mark had no idea how much of a gaffe he was making when he loudly joked, 'Jackie, Ken, Arabella, Patrick, meet Charlie and Sara. They're our friends from London. We invited these two to even the numbers up if debate happens to stray into territories like the rights and wrongs of fox hunting.'

Eloise stared at him in disbelief and wondered whether he was clinically insane. They didn't need to even up the numbers; they were not going into battle.

'Oh, ignore him,' added Sara, waving her hand in Mark's direction. Eloise felt an enormous sense of relief and gratitude. No one read social nuance as well as Sara did, she was clearly going to make a save. 'Really, we just came along to deliver some of the essentials that Eloise is always grumbling are just impossible to get out here. I know she just can't manage without her Guerlain Super Aqua handcream.'

Or maybe not.

Eloise's heart sank. She decided that she was going to open the champagne right away. She needed it, lots of it and quickly. Yes, clearly, they *were* going into battle.

16

Sara thought that Eloise's new friends all looked older than her London friends. The best she could say about the Dartmouth friends was that they were charmingly unaffected. No one was finished or polished the way they were in London. Everyone was damp and fizzy. Even Eloise looked slightly less groomed than she used to. The glossy-posse in London would struggle to recognise her. Eloise had often said that she'd spent the last two decades carefully training her frizzy hair into something sleek and sophisticated; clearly that was a battle she was now losing. The Greek myth of Sisyphus doomed to push a boulder up a mountain for all eternity sprang to Sara's mind.

She asked and was surprised to hear that Arabella was two years younger than Sara was herself and Jackie was *four* years younger! She really couldn't hide her shock; she didn't much try.

'It's understandable, I suppose. The weather is more extreme here and that can play havoc with skincare regimes; you have to be able to invest in really good products or rosacea is inevitable,' she said with a helpful smile.

Eloise glared at Sara hoping to silence her but Sara looked wide-eyed and innocent. She felt justified in her tactless comments because she and El often swapped beauty tips; she was just extending the courtesy to these new pals. She told herself that she hadn't done anything wrong, she was only trying to be friendly and she refused to self-scrutinise further. Besides, it really was a good tip. From what Sara could gather, Dartmouth was either basking in tremendous sunshine so everyone dashed to the beach (which did sound like fun) or it was raining (they seemed to have the full spectrum – everything from a relentless drizzle through to violent, dramatic thunderstorms). She knew this because it seemed as though they'd talked about the weather for the entire first course. Riveting. Sara did her best to stifle a yawn.

Sara pitied Eloise; she must be so bored. Eloise had always maintained that it was really important to have something to say for yourself at this sort of social event and, as a hostess, she considered it her duty to be able to effortlessly glide from one interesting subject to the next, to put people at their ease, to discover what fascinated them and to show an interest; she thought it was as important as serving good food and drink. Sara could only assume that Eloise had forgotten her own golden rule; she was distracted and had been constantly dashing in and out of the kitchen to get something for the table (that she ought to have laid before her guests arrived) or to change the dressing on her cut hand (it really was quite a nasty accident and it had only just stopped seeping blood), so had allowed the conversation to stumble in the muddy mire of lacklustre small talk.

Sara caught Eloise casting Mark a desperate look, clearly hoping that he'd somehow move the chatter on, but he was oblivious. This was primarily because he was already a bit drunk and therefore not particularly aware of the uncomfortable, faltering conversation and secondly because he depended on his wife to accomplish such social niceties as segueing seamlessly from ferocious storms to droughts in Africa and from there to tribal wars on that continent, swiftly on to gun crime back here in the UK. Those were the sorts of meaty issues Sara had come to expect at Eloise's dinner parties. Sara used to find these erudite conversations a bit competitive and exhausting but, over the years, she'd learnt how to contribute. Now she found she missed them. She longed for something, *anything*, other than this conversation about how high the flood water had risen in August 2010. So the pub was flooded and the start of the Dartmouth Royal Regatta was disrupted, whoopee do. But Eloise didn't move the conversation on tonight, she didn't throw in any elegant, subtle links to new topics. Obviously, her friend was overwhelmed. Sara didn't blame Mark for not taking the lead. He had to be interesting, probing, informed and witty all day long at work, it was understandable that he'd sometimes hang up the towel when he sat down at his own dinner table. Sara could well imagine that he was exhausted by being so bloody fascinating.

Sara hadn't always found Eloise's opinions especially well researched, to be frank. They tended to be emotive and often punctuated with examples from personal incidents or received anecdotes. Sara tried to make sure that her opinions were more considered, or at least inherited from Radio Four.

Sara had started listening to Radio Four not long after she'd got married as she'd expected they would be going to a fair number of dinner parties and similar get-togethers and she hadn't wanted to ever be at a loss for something to say. Talking about her work didn't really pull in the crowds. It was fair to say there weren't many people who wanted to talk about the finer points of accounting. Audits and financial asymmetry rarely lit anyone's fire. As it had turned out, married life hadn't been the whirl of social engagements that Sara had expected. She hadn't imagined she'd suddenly be like the most successful character in a Jane Austen novel, constantly attending lavish dinners and parties in stately homes and leaving visiting cards with Britain's most influential players, but she had expected *some* sort of change. She read about it all the time. The glossy magazines were stuffed with recipes and hints for generous at-home entertaining – what to do with your cushions and candles and what not. There were endless suggestions as to the sort of gift that was appropriate to take to a host, whether it was for a coffee morning or full-on weekend break. But, other than Eloise and Mark and one or two friends from Sara's office, Charlie and Sara hadn't really been asked to many dinner parties.

Sara blamed Charlie's job. Plumbers worked with electricians, carpenters, brickies and roofers. Generally speaking, Charlie's colleagues were not the type to say, 'Oh you and your lovely wife must come over to mine. I have a cheeky bottle of Beaune 1991 Pierre Ponnelle.

It's a light red wine, delicious with a fragrant nose of jammy fruits and toasty new oak. I've been wondering who would appreciate it the most. I'll get my wife to call yours, fix up a date.' If any of his colleagues said anything like this then they'd probably find themselves face down in the cement foundations.

Charlie had once suggested that their social life wasn't what she had hoped it would be because they spent so much of their time trying to conceive and even more time taking about it. He'd even gone so far as to say that no one, other than the marvellously patient and polite Eloise, would put up with the blow-by-blow accounts of their fertility trials. Sara had been outraged. She'd pointed out that it was the very fact that they didn't have kids that made everything so difficult. Other couples made friends at childbirth classes or the school gate. Sara hadn't spoken to him for four days after that.

Eloise's guests all knew that Charlie was doing some work for Eloise but Sara was careful to give the impression that he wasn't being paid for his efforts; she wanted them to think that he was just helping out a friend. Sara wanted Eloise's new friends to be clear that the Hamiltons and the Woddells were friends first and foremost, not employers and employees. Eloise didn't say anything to contradict her and Charlie wasn't risking saying much at all in case he got it wrong. Sara was aware that Charlie rarely said a lot nowadays. Throughout the week she got his news from Eloise and when he came home at the week-ends the silences between them had thickened to the point where they were suffocating. Charlie and Sara had yet to discuss whether they might have another go at IVF.

It terrified Sara that they couldn't even find a way into this essential conversation. They had to. They couldn't. They needed to. But when? These bleak thoughts ricocheted around her head as she stared at her wineglass. It was empty again. How could that be possible? She'd only just refilled it. She reached for the bottle of wine but Mark swooped in. For a moment Sara thought he was going to take it away or tick her off for drinking so much but, instead, he beamed broadly, winked cheerfully and topped up her glass. He'd turned to refill Jackie's glass before she could thank him. Despite Mark's reckless encouragement Sara doubted that she should be drinking so much. She thought that maybe she should have gone out with Charlie tonight after all, as being at the dinner party wasn't cheering her up or distracting her. One moment she felt consumed with intense irritation, the next she didn't even have the energy to snarl; she felt battered, decrepit.

Sometimes her longing for a family was so agonising that she thought she might actually die of sorrow. She wanted to lay her head on the table and sleep; sleep for a very, very long time. It wasn't just the drink, she was just so weary. She was disconnected from the faces swimming around her. She tried to focus, tried to stay part of the evening. She glugged back a large glass of chilled water and looked around the table.

Jackie and Ken were one of those couples who looked like one another. They were both of average height and weight, they both had light brown hair (although hers was a fraction longer than his), they both had blue eyes, ruddy faces and pierced ears (although only Ken's left ear was pierced). Sara observed that it was not just that they looked alike, but also that they looked like an awful lot of people. Middle-aged people. They seemed to want to compound the impression that they were twins because they'd selected virtually the same outfit: jeans and a white T-shirt. Hers was a plain white T-shirt with a round neck and long sleeves. Its only notable feature was that it had no notable features; it looked a lot like the sort of thermal top Sara wore under her ski kit. Clearly high fashion had flown right above her head. Ken's T-shirt had a slogan on it, which read 'Slogan T-shirts are boring'. Very droll. The most pleasant thing Sara could think of to describe them was that they looked hearty and honest, they oozed clean living. She imagined that the most dangerous thing Ken had ever done in his life was wear that supposedly witty T-shirt. Sara couldn't imagine why Eloise had invited them to her home; surely she must find them very dull.

Arabella and Patrick were opposites. She was dumpy and he was gangly. Sara had christened them Jack Sprat and his wife, and she couldn't wait to share this with Eloise. They'd always given their friends fun nicknames; well, Sara had. Sara referred to Eloise's London friends as 'The Perm', 'Little Miss Neurotic', 'The Handbag', etc. This name-calling wasn't mean, just a harmless bit of fun. A sign of affection even. Besides, all Eloise's North London friends had names like Isadora, Imelda and Iraida, so it was hard to remember who was who. In fact, Sara had a couple of names for Eloise, 'Hostess with the Mostess' was common knowledge, but she'd never shared 'Princess Perfect', which was what she called her friend to Charlie. She called Mark 'The Man', as he had a way of swaggering around the place as if he owned the planet. It wasn't arrogance, it was genuine confidence. Sara rather envied it. She hadn't confided Mark's nickname to either Eloise or Charlie.

Sara hoped that Eloise would appreciate the fact that, despite the earlier upset – when El had cut herself and all the gore and sadness of the miscarriage had come flooding back – Sara had made a sartorial effort that must offer an impressive example of how to dress for a dinner party. Just in case there was somewhere special to go this weekend Sara had packed her Joseph black twill wide-leg pants (that exuded androgynous cool) and a Rebecca Taylor ruffled silk-Jacquard camisole (it had the most adorable delicate cut-out details) and, because Sara knew it could get chilly in the country, she had the foresight to throw in a Wool and the Gang, Jolie Mimi open-knit cotton cardigan. It really was a good look, even if she said it herself. Sara had taken the time to re-apply full make-up in an effort to disguise her sobbing. Considering she'd been finding getting out of bed a struggle, she hoped that Eloise would appreciate and understand the superhuman strength it took to make such an effort. Eloise must welcome the glamour in her dining room, considering the obvious trouble she'd gone to with the food.

It was clear Eloise really was trying to establish her credentials as Hostess with the Mostess. Sara had never seen her quite so prepared to be impressed and to be impressive. She was being a bit thick with the compliments and compliance, though; Sara might have to tell her to ease up on that, it was embarrassing. There was no way Arabella was going to buy that Eloise actually *did* want to join the gang of volunteers who combed the beach and country lanes for litter every Tuesday afternoon. Yes, Sara could see it was a good thing to do, unquestionably, but 'noble'? Noble was a bit over the top. And whilst Sara was sure that Jackie did make a good pineapple upside-down cake, calling it sublime about a thousand times was just plain creepy; of course the kids at the school enjoyed having it as a dessert – juniors weren't known for their discerning palates, were they?

'How many children do you have, exactly?' Sara directed her question to Arabella. She'd lost track of Arabella's anecdotes about her kids. She must have at least three. Sara couldn't stop herself asking this question although she knew the answer would distress her. Eloise blanched and put down the broccoli. Earlier, Eloise had made Sara promise that she wouldn't think or talk about her fertility tonight. It was too much to ask that Sara wouldn't *think* about it, but she had agreed to respect her friend's desire and not openly discuss her problems. Sara told herself that she wasn't breaking her promise but simply making a polite enquiry, the way people did when they were getting to know one another. Asking about someone's children was simply civil, not leading or loaded. Besides, Sara just had to move the conversation on from the problems of parking near your home and finding a good cleaner. She could have stayed in London for those middle-class exchanges.

'Four. Two girls and two boys, very even,' said Arabella cheerfully. She beamed as she replied and then rolled her eyes playfully, as though she was surprised and exasperated by the number every time she confessed it. 'Aged nine, six, three and ten months. Quite a handful but so much fun.'

Sara knew Arabella's beam all too well. She was the Olympic gold medal mum. In polite circles five or more children suggested an inability to conquer the rudimentaries of any form of contraception; no one wanted to be thought of as thick. Five or more and you had to start writing self-indulgent, self-justifying articles like that stupid one Sara had read before dinner. Three kids might seem a pleasant, manageable number but it came with the threat of middle-child syndrome, two was respectable but a bit dull, one child was simply selfish or half-hearted and none . . . well, not having children, that was failure. Sara knew that more than anyone. Even the women who actively opted not to have children were viewed as failures by other mums, if not themselves. Four was quite definitely the number to aspire to. The Queen had four children. It was the number that suggested a particular ease and confidence with mothering, as well as a certain financial security or – at the very least – a wild abandon for rejecting anything as prosaic as money cares (because the act of parenting was so important and all-consuming). Four was heaven.

The number conjured up endless, longed-for Kodak moments. Scenes of domestic bliss splattered across Sara's cranium. She could see children gambolling along a seashore in mismatched but hand-knitted hoodies, she imagined giggling infants gathered around a large dining table, packed with jars of home-made bramble jam and freshly baked bread, and she visualised scenes of boisterous babies splashing in the bath. She followed the fantasy and thought of them as they became more passive and fell into a restful, peaceful sleep in one huge bed (having been indulged with a bedtime story and a copious amount of hugs). It was beautiful and perfect.

She hated Arabella.

'What about you, Jackie? How many children do you have?'

'Help yourselves to veggies,' interjected Eloise. Her voice was unnaturally high, betraying a note of tension.

'More wine?' Mark jumped up from his seat and started waving the bottle around as though it was a white flag. He sloshed alcohol into everyone's glass no matter what they'd replied. Mark and Eloise put Sara in mind of a couple of novice Samaritans who had a suicidal teenager on their watch. They wanted to walk her away from the edge but she wouldn't be led. Sara couldn't help herself. Any self-control she might have dredged up had been soused in alcohol and she no longer felt tethered to her promise to Eloise. Why couldn't she talk about her fertility to Eloise's new friends?

'Do you have four?' She knew that whatever Jackie replied would wound. She knew that it shouldn't matter that this plain woman who was married to a man who expressed himself through T-shirt slogans was a mother when she was not, but it did.

'Three,' Jackie said with a grin. 'And that's enough for me. I sometimes think I should have stopped when I ran out of hands,' she joked. 'Arabella is a saint. A paragon of efficiency and patience, but four? No, not for me, I'd never pull it off.'

Three not four. Four was dismissed. She could have had four but she'd chosen not to because she wasn't patient enough. Sara's knuckles were white with the pressure of gripping her knife and fork. She slowly chewed her food but couldn't swallow. Jackie detailed the sexes, names and ages of her children but Sara couldn't take it in. It didn't matter if they were called Peter, Paul and Sally or Satan, Xavier and Miss Piggy, she had an embarrassment of riches and Sara faced a drought. Sara felt Charlie prise her fingers off the cutlery. Did he think Jackie was in danger? Sara glared at him in annoyance. The table fell silent as all eyes were trained on what Charlie had hoped would be a discreet manoeuvre.

'What about you two?' asked Ken, cheerfully pulling the pin from the grenade.

'None,' Sara stated bleakly. 'No live ones.'

The table was as still as a crypt, the very air slowed and then ground to a choking halt. Sara's pain flooded on to the table and soured every mouthful of the carefully prepared meal, those still on the plates and those already digested; no one had an appetite now, everyone felt nauseous. Every face around the table settled into different expressions of horror and shame, embarrassment and, in Eloise's case, frustration. 'There were two,' Sara stuttered. 'Abigail and Ross.'

'Oh my God,' said Jackie. She pulled her napkin up to her mouth as though she was actually going to be sick.

'You lost your two children?' asked Arabella carefully.

As Sara nodded Eloise jumped in. 'No. Not children. Two miscarriages. Early miscarriages.' Sara thought adding the word *early* was particularly disloyal and unnecessary; she glared at El to communicate as much but Eloise wasn't looking at Sara, she was staring at her other guests. Eloise felt their discomfort, their twinges of uncertainty as to what to do next to paper over this social hiccup. But their smarting was minuscule in comparison to Sara's boiling grief.

'Miscarriages are very upsetting,' said Arabella gently. She leaned across the table and patted Sara's arm. 'I had one between Dorcas and George. I do sometimes think of that baby. It would be nearly eight years old now.'

'Still, there's plenty of time to try again,' added Jackie confidently and ignorantly. Sara kept her eyes on her plate, she didn't trust herself to look into Jackie's dumb, encouraging face or else she might be tempted to tell her exactly how dumb and ignorant, rather than confident and encouraging, she found her.

None of the men said a thing. Every last one of them would have liked to have started talking about the parking issues again.

'Who fancies apple tart?' asked Eloise jovially. Those who didn't know her as well as Sara did might assume she was unaffected by the conversation but Sara was fully aware of just how hard El was working to retain her happy face. Sara thought it was possible that El would like to throw the tart she was about to serve right at her, since she'd sliced through all the tedious small talk and catapulted Eloise into a deeper intimacy with her new friends. The atmosphere of her carefully prepared, precious dinner party was well and truly dampened.

No one replied straight away so Eloise was forced to push on genially. 'It's a favourite family recipe. I'm sure you'll remember it from London, Charlie.' El turned to Charlie and cast out a look which pleaded with him to fall into cahoots with her. He nodded obligingly, although he'd never eaten an apple tart made by Eloise. Sara seethed; it was typical of Charlie to be so accommodating of Eloise. It would have been funnier to hear him say that he'd rarely eaten anything home cooked of hers, even though they used to eat at the Hamiltons' a couple of times a week. Still, Sara understood that he was in a difficult position now he was working for Eloise; he could hardly upset his boss. 'I've paired it with lavender cream. Have you ever tried that, Ken? Patrick?'

Sara had often noticed that Eloise had a tendency to address most of her comments to the men in the room. Sara wondered why she courted male approval all the time, when she was so happily married to the gorgeous Mark. It was madness. Of course it might just be a harmless old habit from her advertising days; from what Sara could gather, half her job had seemed to necessitate flirting with the clients. 'It's so simple to make and very light,' she added as she started to gather up the plates from the main course. 'I won't be a minute. I'll be right back with it.'

Then she disappeared out of the room into the kitchen.

17

'Do you want to read for a few minutes?' Ray asked as he climbed into bed next to his wife.

'No, not really.'

'Don't you like your book?'

'No, not especially. I can't get into it,' replied Margaret with a sigh.

'What's it about?' he asked.

Margaret reached for the novel that had been lying by her bed for weeks and weeks now and passed it to him. From the cover she was certain that it was a thriller but, to be frank, she couldn't remember exactly what it was about. They all became a bit samey after a while. She used to read at least a book a week. The librarians at The Flavel used to say that Margaret was there as often as they were. 'This is overdue,' commented Ray.

'Is it?'

'Yes.' He sounded cross. Ray might be retired but he still had a solicitor's mind. He was a stickler for details, systems and order. Failing to return a library book in the correct time was tantamount to a criminal act in his mind.

'Not by much,' Margaret assured him.

'By a month!'

'I'll take it back tomorrow.'

He seemed mollified and pulled the duvet up around his chest. 'Maybe you'll find something that holds your interest a bit more.'

'Hmmm,' she said without committing. For a moment or two they lay silently. Margaret was wondering when he'd turn out the light. She could see a hat box on the top of the wardrobe and she idly wondered what was in it. What was kept in a hat box?

'Why don't you ever go to your reading group any more?' Ray asked suddenly. 'You used to love catching up with all your friends.'

'I do go,' said Margaret defensively.

'No, you don't,' replied Ray carefully.

'I was there just the other week. We read that one about the fossil collector.'

'Mary Anning.'

'I don't think she was there.' Margaret didn't know who Mary Anning was. 'Mary Cape was there.'

'No, Mary Anning is the fossil collector.'

'Absolutely. Mary Cape doesn't collect fossils. She teaches.'

'Music. I know.' Ray let a little sigh escape. He couldn't keep all of them in. 'That was nine months ago, Margaret.'

They fell silent for a while again. Margaret was chasing the name of the writer of the novel of the fossil-collecting book. It ran away from her, scampering through her head. Ray wound up the small bedside clock that had sat next to their bed for donkey's years. It had been a wedding present from Margaret's mother's best friend, Auntie Kathy.

'Early night will do us both good.' Ray leaned over to Margaret's side of the bed; the mattress sagged in a comfortable, familiar way. He popped a kiss on her cheek and then turned out his light. She paused for a moment before she turned out her own. The cat was in. The TV was unplugged. She knew, she'd checked it twice. Tomorrow was Saturday so she could return the library book then. The library was open until lunchtime. She'd closed the back bedroom window, put the iron away. All was fine. All was right. Except.

The smudge had been joined by a bell. And the bell kept ringing – or squeaking might be a better description. There was something nagging. Something big. She ran through her nightly check list. Ray,

Mark, Emily, Erin and Poppy were all in good health, safe and well. Just round the corner now. And Eloise too, of course. Safe and well. But there was something about Eloise that was not ideal; Margaret was sure. But what? What? She had no idea.

As she snuggled under the bedclothes Ray and Margaret began the routine they'd followed almost every night of their married lives. She cuddled into him, her arm thrown over his now sizable bulk. He'd been a slim man when they'd married. She could never have imagined he'd get so fat. She didn't mind. That sort of thing never worried her. More of him to love. They stayed in that position, two question marks pressed into one another, for about five minutes, then Margaret found Ray's body heat too much and she rolled over on to her left side. Ray was normally asleep by then and she fell to sleep within ten minutes, lulled by the sounds of his constant, slow breathing and the tick tock of their bedside clock. Their street was away from the embankment, on the edge of town and generally enveloped in silence and stillness by ten p.m. Occasionally, a daring fox could be heard rummaging through the bins but, on the whole, sleep was expected, and deep and unperturbed when it came. But not tonight. Tonight Margaret couldn't sleep.

There was the ringing in the back of her mind and now . . . what was that? Was that knocking?

18

'Mark, could you come in here and help me for a moment?' Eloise was certain that the strain was audible in her voice even though she was desperately trying to sound cheery.

Mark jumped up with an enthusiasm he normally reserved for when Apple announced they were launching a new gizmo. The kitchen wasn't generally his room of choice when they were entertaining, he liked to limit his input to pouring the alcohol but, considering Sara had just effectively urinated on the dinner party mood by announcing the deaths of her children and Eloise had clumsily tried (and failed) to put her new friends at ease by pointing out that, in fact, Sara had lost two foetuses not two babies, Mark seemed quite keen to get away from the scene of the crime.

'What the f— just happened in there?' he hiss-whispered the minute they were alone. Eloise thought it was sweet that even when under considerable strain and dealing with increased social embarrassment he tried not to swear. His restraint was a result of spending years around children who loved nothing more than to say, 'Daddy said a bad word!' or, 'Mummy, you shouldn't say that, God won't like it!'

'She's a mess, isn't she?' Eloise sighed, not certain whether she was devastated for her friend or irritated by her. 'And my supposed save probably didn't help. I certainly think I aggravated Sara more by pointing out her babies were miscarriages.'

'Yup, about as sensitive and tactful as Simon Cowell at a regional talent show. That's you.'

Eloise stared at Mark, ostensibly furious with him for being so spot on but really furious at herself. 'Look, there's nothing we can do now other than push on,' she stated, trying to sound more in control than she felt. 'There have been worse dinner parties in the history of mankind.'

'Although not in your history.'

'Thank you for that reminder. Look, we'll just keep pouring the wine and serving up food, we don't have a choice. Your mum's apple tart can mend bridges. Where is it?'

'There.' Mark pointed to the foil-wrapped quiche that Eloise had also assumed was the tart, until about a minute before calling him into the kitchen.

'No, that's a quiche. Did she give you that too? She's a treasure, we'll have that for lunch tomorrow, but where did you put the tart? Come on, Mark, I need to warm it up.'

Mark looked pale, dazed and concerned. 'That's all she gave me. That and the jug of cream.' He dashed to the fridge and pulled out the pretty jug full of lavender cream. Instinctively, he took a sniff. 'Yuk, that smells terrible.'

Eloise grabbed the jug off him and dipped her finger into the cream and then practically gagged. 'What the hell is it? Not lavender cream, that's for certain. It tastes of mayonnaise.'

'That's all she gave me. She hunted around the kitchen for ages.'

'Well, I can't serve a half-eaten quiche for pudding, especially after I've made such a big thing about serving up my own *home-baked* apple tart,' Eloise said in a hiss-whisper, not managing to hide her mounting hysteria. Even though Mark had turned away, she could see his body quivering with suppressed laughter, which was not helpful.

'Mum did seem a bit out of sorts when I went to pick up the tart. She's clearly just handed me the wrong plate.'

'Well, you'll have to go and pick up the right one.'

'Now?'

'Yes!'

'But it's after ten. They'll be in bed.'

He didn't have to say it. Eloise knew that waking up a couple of pensioners so that they could cater for her dinner party was not especially commendable, but what else could she do? 'Why would she make lavender cream with mayonnaise? Do you think she was drunk?'

'Mum? At seven fifteen in the evening? No, I don't.'

'Well, what, then? A joke?'

'I don't know.'

They fell silent, which allowed them to hear the conversation in the dining room. Not that there was any real conversation. Just Sara's heavy sobs and Arabella's well-intentioned but clearly embarrassed murmurs of, 'There, there, let it all out. That's it. A good cry always helps.' Eloise thought this was especially magnanimous of Arabella since Sara had spent the evening flinging veiled insults and criticism across the table.

'I'm sorry, love, but there's no alternative, you are going to have to run along the road to your parents' to get the tart.'

Already quite tipsy, Mark was reluctant to leave the warm house and venture out in the chilly, black night. 'Can't you just serve up some yogurts instead? Chop up some fruit?'

'No. I haven't been shopping for anything other than the dinner party. We don't even have any yogurt or decent fruit.' The couple simultaneously glanced helplessly at the fruit bowl; it offered up one blackened banana and a hair bobble. 'It will only take ten minutes. I'll suggest everyone has a coffee. I'll say we are doing it the French way, pudding last. Your parents will understand the emergency – well, Margaret will at least.'

It turned out that nobody wanted coffee but all three of the men gratefully accepted a whisky. Sara's crying was abating but she was now casting notably evil glares Eloise's way as she ran through her medical history in graphic detail. Arabella and Jackie weren't much friendlier towards the hostess. They had no way of knowing that this was the five hundredth occasion that she'd heard the details of Sara's fertility problems. El wanted to yell at them, 'Honestly, I was sympathetic on the previous four hundred and ninety-nine!' But she didn't bother, it was pretty clear that they now regarded her as a lacklustre, unsupportive friend and she couldn't imagine they'd be rushing to invite her to coffee again any time soon.

'It's not that I meant to be cruel,' Eloise mumbled, deciding to face the elephant in the room.

Sara interrupted her. 'It's just very hard for Eloise to empathise. With her three beautiful girls it's impossible for her to imagine my longing or my grief, just as it's impossible for me to imagine why Eloise might grumble about having to constantly tidy up after the girls.' Sara smiled bravely. 'I mean, that's my dream, to tidy up after a child. Pathetic, I know.' She glanced around the table, flashing her enormous doleful eyes. Even Eloise thought of Bambi.

'No, no, not pathetic at all,' Arabella and Jackie simultaneously soothed. Cast as Cruella de Vil, Eloise decided it was best to wait out Mark's return in the kitchen. There, she looked around at the debris. Pots were piled in towers in the sink, evidence of the elaborate preparations, and there were copious amounts of empty bottles lined up along the windowsill. Her hand stung, blood had seeped through the bandage; it had dried to a grubby rust colour. She probably should have gone for a stitch or two but there just hadn't been enough time. All she'd wanted was to make some friends here in Dartmouth. Was that too much to ask?

Mark came back and Eloise's heart plummeted when she saw that he was empty-handed. 'I think Dad must have eaten the pie and is not prepared to 'fess up,' Mark said with a shrug. 'They both seemed confused. I woke them up. I feel bad.'

'*You* feel bad! What am I going to tell our guests?' El snapped back. 'It's desperate in there. Sara's talking vaginal juices and sperm count. When I popped my head in the dining room Ken looked very uncomfortable and Patrick looked like he was going to pass out.'

'We'll say the girls have eaten it.' Mark's face lit up as he hit on this solution.

'But then they'll think I'm a bad mother with feral kids,' Eloise groaned.

'Alternatively you can tell them the truth and lose face.'

'Good point. I'll lie.'

As it happened, the guests didn't care too much one way or the other about the lack of pudding. They pretended to accept the excuse Eloise offered as it gave them a convenient and clearly welcome reason to leave sooner rather than later. There was a distinct sense of relief and urgency in the Hamilton hallway as the guests struggled into their coats. Their haste made the simple operation so tricky that Patrick couldn't seem to put his arm in the sleeve of his coat and in the end he just threw his jacket over his shoulders – like some sort of superhero – and bolted for the door. Eloise was not convinced or comforted by the polite calls, 'We must do this again some time' and 'Maybe you should come to us next time.'

But seeing her new friends' embarrassment was nothing compared to facing her old friend's pain. She lingered for a second in the hallway, not really wanting to confront Sara. Mark pulled his wife into a brief hug that clearly communicated in married speak that she had to bite the bullet and she had to do so alone. He called through to Charlie and suggested they went and got some air. Charlie rushed past Eloise, taking a moment to throw a sympathetic grimace her way. They understood each other; he'd been the wrong side of Sara's overly sensitive nature so many times recently.

Eloise crept back into the dining room and found Sara sitting deadly still at the table. She looked like Snow White. Dark bobbed hair, red lips and her skin was so pale that she seemed almost transparent. She was trailing her finger in a puddle of red wine that had been spilt on the tablecloth. It would stain but sponging up the mess would seem too abrupt and efficient. Eloise knew that what was needed now was kindness. She dug deeper into her reserves of patience. She suspected tonight was going to stain their friendship just as vividly as the wine would stain the cloth if she wasn't careful. Where to start?

'I think of them as babies, you know,' Sara said eventually.

'I know.' Eloise sighed, partially from relief that Sara was talking to her and partially out of pity. 'I do too. But I didn't want to mislead Arabella and Jackie. I didn't think it was fair,' she blurted.

Suddenly, Sara glared at Eloise, her anger searing. 'There's nothing fair about this, Eloise.'

El busied herself, carefully placing another log on the fire; earlier in the evening the fire was just for show but now the air really was quite icy. Eloise knew that there was no point in making a joke about the lack of pudding – or any other subject, for that matter. There was only one thought in Sara's head, there only ever was. That was the problem. They had to address it.

'Have you had any more thoughts about adopting?' Eloise asked as she folded herself into the chair next to Sara's. They'd had this conversation before, a couple of years ago. At the time neither of them really thought it would ever come to adoption, they'd talked in the abstract. Everyone heard so many success stories about IVF that it became tempting to believe that it was a foolproof treatment. Doctors took pains to remind patients that the success rate was only one in five, but everyone believed they'd be that one. Obviously, everyone couldn't be. Eloise thought it was time Sara revisited the alternatives.

'It's not easy to adopt. Our age would work against us and we'd want a baby. There are no babies up for adoption in the UK. Or at least very few.'

'Abroad, then?'

'People think it's just a case of popping into an African country and picking up a skinny tot but it doesn't work like that.'

Eloise had never thought it worked that way and she was glad it didn't and, further, she was never convinced by people who said they were desperate for a baby but baulked at the idea of adopting a *child*. What did they think those babies became? But she didn't say any of this to Sara, she never had. Instead she asked, 'Have you thought of egg donation or sperm donation? Maybe a different combination would help things develop.' Eloise stumbled over her words. There wasn't a great way to say any of this.

'Maybe it would, but we've been pregnant twice, it is possible for us to get pregnant,' Sara insisted. Her mouth was pulled into an unreasonable thin line, her lips had disappeared to nothing more than a mean red gash. She looked terrifying, ferocious and bitter. Where had El's friend gone? Where was the carefree, witty, reasonable and intelligent woman that she knew?

'Maybe you should give it up,' Eloise said finally. The words came out in a defeated tumble, running away on breath that she'd held in for months now. This was a thought so difficult to express that it seemed almost treacherous. Now she'd said as much she rushed on while her nerve still held. 'You could foster.'

'No. The constant goodbyes, I couldn't.'

'People live without children. Full and happy lives they—' Eloise wanted to tell her friend that she only had one life, that she was wasting it by longing for something she couldn't have, by focusing on nothing else at all. Eloise thought that Sara was destroying her relationship with her husband and threatening her other relationships too. She wanted to tell her that she could find other ways to be happy, if only she'd open her eyes to them. But Sara didn't allow Eloise to explain, or excuse, or even empathise or console.

'I'm going to bed,' she said stiffly.

Sara didn't actually spit on El, she didn't have to; Eloise understood the point being made. Guilt flooded through her body. After years of supporting Sara without question or limits, why had Eloise hit a threshold of patience tonight? She hated herself for hurting her friend. El placed her head on the table; she wanted to bang it up and down. How could she have gone so wrong tonight? How could she have thought impressing her new friends was more important than comforting her old one?

'Well, that was a disaster,' Eloise stated firmly.

'I wouldn't say disaster, exactly,' said Mark. El was sitting at her dressing table taking off her make-up. She'd been sitting there for half an hour, listening attentively for the front door to click, signalling Mark

161

and Charlie's return. She'd trusted he wouldn't stay out too late, that he'd understand that she'd need to talk through the night's events, and he hadn't let her down. Timings suggested Mark took Charlie for a swift pint and then they'd returned straight home. Eloise wondered whether Sara was still awake and what conversation she and Charlie might be having. They were probably agreeing that Eloise was a total bitch, she thought despairingly. El was sitting with her back to Mark but she could see him through the mirror. He looked astute and handsome. As he kissed the back of her neck she could smell the chilly, watery air and beery pub on his hair. He was delicious and it was a comfort to register he was delicious in amongst all the mess of the evening. He was hers. She had Mark and the girls. That was why she was here in Dartmouth, for her family, and these teething troubles with their new friends were worth the effort because this was what Mark wanted, she reminded herself.

But the trouble with old friends? That was altogether different.

She furiously rubbed cleanser into her face. The cold, velvety cream might be able to remove make-up and, through some modern miracle of science and rare moment of advertising truth, it might even be able to smooth out her fine lines and wrinkles, but it couldn't remove her hideous mood or smooth over the feeling of despair that was sitting in the pit of her belly.

'You remember that fairy tale about the wolf who guarded a bridge and ate the baby goats that wanted to cross the bridge?' Eloise asked Mark.

He looked bemused. 'No, I can't say that I do.'

'You do,' she insisted, although in all likelihood he probably didn't. Fairy tales were a girl thing – like eyelash curlers, men just didn't get them; they didn't have a need. 'Well, the goats' mother tricks the wolf. She cuts open his stomach, rescues her babies – they've been swallowed whole – then puts huge boulders in the wolf's stomach, sews him up and when he wakes up he can't chase after her or her babies. I feel like that wolf.'

Mark sat on the edge of the bed and started to take off his shoes and socks. He looked perplexed. 'The wolf swallowed the baby goats whole?'

'Yes.'

'Unlikely. And he wouldn't wake up, would he? Not if he'd just had open surgery.'

'It's a fairy tale.'

'Where's the happy ending?' he asked as he peeled off his shirt.

'OK, look, I think we are getting off the point,' Eloise said, trying to suppress her exasperation.

'What is your point?'

Eloise was not proud that alcohol had been her prop tonight – but she was grateful that she'd had a prop. She'd drunk nearly a bottle and therefore couldn't clearly explain her analogy.

'The point is, I feel as though I have giant rocks in my belly.' If she'd had to name them, they were disappointment, humiliation and despair.

'But you didn't try to eat anyone's babies,' said Mark gently.

'I might as well have, I don't think I could have offended Sara more.'

Mark walked towards the dressing table, put his cool hands on her shoulders and tried to squeeze out some of the tension.

'Mmm, nice,' she muttered. She wanted to encourage him because she loved his touch and didn't want the massage to stop. On the other hand, she didn't want to over-encourage him because he might think there was a chance of sex and she was too tired and upset for sex. She just wanted to talk and be hugged.

Mark read her like a book. 'Come on, get your pyjamas on and let's get to bed. It will all be better in the morning.'

'I was so determined to make an impression.'

'You did that all right,' said Mark, stifling a yawn.

'Yes, well, not the impression I wanted, obviously.' Eloise peeled off her clothes and left them in a careless heap on the floor; a puddle of herself. 'I just want to fix things,' she said, as she snuggled under Mark's arm.

'I know you do, babe. You always want to fix things. It's one of the reasons I love you, but I think this one might be out of your control.'

19

Sara lay in bed and listened to the sounds of Saturday morning in Dartmouth. They were not the same sounds as she was used to hearing in London. There she woke to cars tooting, teenagers swearing and, more often than not, an ambulance or police siren wailing in the distance. In Dartmouth, Sara was awoken by the sounds of a family. Little feet pounded up and down the stairs, chatter and whispers erupted like determined mushrooms on a moist autumn field. The girls, who had been awake for hours, had been told not to disturb Sara, so whenever they played in the stairwell below her room they whispered but, a metre away, they resumed their high-volume squabbles and squeals and so their attempt to follow instructions wasn't successful. Besides, the house was alive with the sounds of breakfast pots being clattered, the radio blaring, doors and windows being thrown open. She could hear seagulls squawking and cheery hellos being thrown out by neighbours as they passed by the Hamiltons' garden.

Last night, Sara had pretended to be asleep when Charlie came back from his walk. The last thing she'd wanted was to hear him defend Eloise, which he might very well have done. She didn't even want him to try to comfort her. She couldn't be comforted. That was the point.

Sara couldn't muster the energy to get out of bed. Eloise's spare bedroom was set up to offer her guests cosiness, combined with style and notable luxury; it was perfect in every way. Most people banished their faded linen to the spare room or opted for something cheap and cheerful (read tacky), but there was no sign of itchy nylon sheets or unattractive floral bedspreads in Eloise's guest room. Sara snuggled into a goose-down duvet; there wasn't much incentive to leave it. She cast a glance around the room. Charlie hadn't done much to make it his own. But then, men didn't tend to see a room and swear that all it needed was a couple of scented candles and some scatter cushions to make it 'theirs'. There were only three signs that revealed he'd been living here for several weeks. One, his work jacket hung on the back of the door, two, there was a stack of coins on the dressing table, and three, there was a pile of dirty washing in the corner of the room.

Sara was suddenly hit by a thought. What did Charlie do with his washing? She hadn't been doing it at the weekends when he returned home. It was possible that he'd been doing it himself; possible but not probable. Had Eloise been washing Charlie's pants and socks? The thought unsettled Sara; the intimacy of picking up laundry was strangely deep and profound. The image of Eloise bending to scoop up Charlie's underwear left Sara feeling queasy and oddly panicked. Charlie was always saying that Eloise had done everything to make him feel at home. Last night he had joked to Patrick that Eloise bought orange-flavoured Kit Kats because she knew they were his favourite biscuits – 'Better service than at home,' he'd laughed.

There was a small bunch of flowers in a vase by the bed. Eloise hadn't been expecting Sara . . .

Eloise was always so prepared, so perfect. Sara used to admire that a great deal but now she couldn't help but resent it. Eloise was smug. She had it all. Their relationship had changed.

Charlie had risen early and silently crept out of bed, suggesting he was no keener on having a tête-à-tête than Sara was. The girls were giggling in the garden, an irresistible call to action no matter how terrible Sara felt; she pulled the duvet around her body and peeked out of the window. She saw Mark, Charlie and the girls fooling around with a cricket bat and ball. They were playing French cricket, with more enthusiasm than expertise, as it happened. Still, no one seemed to care as they were obviously having a blast. The windows were at risk because Poppy slammed the bat against the ball with impressive force but an untrained aim.

It was hardly cricket weather. It was a dull, austere day. The sky was grey and looked as oppressive as an advancing tank, the hills were colourless and lifeless and the sea, which Sara could just make out in the distance, was flat and melancholy. To date it had been a bright autumn with vivid blue skies smashing up against the gold trees in an energetic, almost defiant way. There'd been nothing whatsoever misty or mellow about this season, it had been a definite tribute to summer, rather than a preparation for winter. Actually, Sara had resented the weather – it hadn't suited her mood; she thought the elements ought to have been sombre and restrained. Some small part of Sara felt gratified that today the weather gods had decided to tell it how it was, especially as she knew that from the moment she'd arrived last night, Eloise would have been planning something for them all to do today. A romp along the coastal paths or a mooch around a National Trust garden might have been on the agenda. Eloise would have been banking on another bright and vivid day to make her plan picture perfect. Sara took some satisfaction from the fact that Eloise couldn't control the weather.

Sara was about to bang on the window to get the attention of the men and children when there was a knock at her door. She knew it had to be Eloise as she could see everyone else in the garden. Sara considered pretending to still be asleep but Eloise walked in without waiting for an invite.

'Morning,' she said with a broad smile; her cheerfulness had no doubt demanded firm resolve. Eloise handed Sara a cup of tea, Earl Grey, Sara's preference. Sara took it but couldn't bring herself to say thank you. 'I'm making eggs Benedict,' Eloise said, stretching her beam an infeasible fraction wider. Eggs Benedict was Sara's breakfast of choice; she recognised that an olive branch was being shaken in her face. 'And I've called Margaret and Ray and asked them to come over. I think we could all do with a run out today. Where do you fancy going? The beach? Or maybe a bit cold for that. A walk? Or we could go to Agatha Christie's house.'

Sara felt a wave of satisfaction that Eloise's steely resolve to be cheerful needed fortification; she'd obviously invited along her in-laws to avoid being alone with Sara. And yet Sara had to admit that the message was loud and clear: Eloise was not going to allow last night's scene to intrude on their friendship. For her it was water under the bridge. Sara's head was cluttered. Her feelings towards Eloise were becoming so complicated. While part of her admired Eloise's determination to patch up and move on, part of her resented it, enormously. What if Sara didn't want to move on? What if she couldn't?

'Did you sleep well?' Eloise asked.

Sara could hardly refuse to answer. 'Yes, thank you.'

'I didn't. I spent all night hatching, and I have a plan,' Eloise gabbled. There was genuine excitement in her voice.

'For today's activities?'

'Not just that. That's part of it. I have a surprise. For you.' Eloise saw the caution in Sara's eyes but she simply smiled. 'A really good one. Come on, get up,' she urged. 'Let's go for a walk.'

'Don't you think it's a bit grim for a walk?' Sara cast a quick glance towards the window and waited for Eloise to remember she was a fair-weather walker, from London, who normally thought even a shopping trip to Islington High Street required clement weather.

Eloise walked to the window and looked outside. Her eyes flicked upwards to the bruised sky and then down towards the commotion in the garden. She smiled at the sight of her husband and children. 'It is a bit grey but it's not wet. Aren't they an astonishing contrast to the sombre landscape?' she said, nodding towards her family and letting out a contented sigh which Sara thought bordered on complacent. 'Their brightly coloured clothes and their giggly chatter defy the abounding greyness. I mean Charlie too,' she added with a beam.

Sara joined Eloise at the window and noticed for the first time that Charlie was wearing an out-of-character red woollen skull cap; he normally stuck to blacks and blues and the only hat Sara had ever seen him wear was a baseball cap. He must have bought the skull cap since he'd got here.

'Anyway, we'll go for the sort of walk that ends in a tea shop or a pub,' added Eloise, refusing to be daunted by the weather. Sara sighed and seethed because, obviously, Eloise did think she was bloody Zeus.

They needed to take two cars for the short journey to the place that was the designated beginning of the walk. Mark, Eloise, Margaret, Ray and Poppy travelled together and Sara was gratified that Emily and Erin opted to travel with her and Charlie. Eloise had been particularly excited about organising the trip out today. She'd all but skipped around the house as she'd gathered together essentials and she kept throwing Sara animated, keyed-up grins. She'd packed as though they were going for a six-week road trip, rather than a four-mile moderate stroll. She packed a map, water bottles, spare socks, a change of shoes for all of the girls, cagoules for everyone, a first aid kit, a camera, half a dozen apples and three bars of Dairy Milk. All this gear went into a rucksack that she immediately handed to Mark; he hoisted it on to his back without comment. Eloise only stopped smiling when she discovered Sara hadn't got wellies, let alone walking boots.

'You've a short memory; up until four months ago you didn't own any either,' muttered Sara.

They drove up a single track and then parked up in a tiny National Trust car park. Rather than a ticket machine there was a quaint honesty box. Eloise dropped in three pounds to cover the cost of leaving her car. Sara said she didn't have any change so Eloise added another couple of quid.

'Where are we?' asked Margaret.

'Little Dartmouth,' said Ray dryly.

'Who knew that I live in big Dartmouth?' Eloise whispered to Sara as she winked playfully. 'I've picked a route everyone can enjoy,' she added loudly and enthusiastically. 'We'll get to walk along the coast, and although it might be a bit muddy, there's nothing too arduous, lots of it is along the road or bridleways.'

Sara couldn't help thinking that Eloise's authoritative air was a bit presumptive since Eloise hadn't actually ever done this walk; she was reading from a sheet of paper that she'd printed off the Internet. Sara assumed Eloise was irritating Ray, too, when he muttered gruffly, 'I've done this walk a hundred times, Eloise, I think I'll manage.'

Eloise laughed, refusing to take offence. 'I know. I'm not implying *you* won't be able to manage. I was talking to the girls and—' Ray, who was far from his usual jovial self today, shot Eloise a cool look. Eloise stammered and then added quietly, 'Well, it was you who said she was out of sorts, a bit run down, I was only—'

Mark took Eloise's hand and started to stride down the path towards the coast before she could finish her sentence. Sara was uncertain as to what had just passed. Had Eloise been talking about Sara's health to Ray and Margaret? If so, she'd never forgive her! The two older girls scampered away, quickly overtaking their parents. Charlie fell into step with Ray and struck up a conversation about fishing and so Sara decided to walk with Margaret. Each of them held one of Poppy's small, gloved hands. They walked at Poppy-pace and so soon fell behind the others.

'Did you enjoy the party last night, dear?' asked Margaret.

Again, Sara wondered what had been said, but one look at Margaret's face eased her suspicions. Margaret's face was blank, devoid of agenda or cunning; she was simply making small talk. Sara considered telling the truth but didn't have the energy so, instead, replied neutrally, 'Eloise always puts on a good do.'

'Yes. I was going to wear my sapphire-blue dress but Ray said he wasn't feeling quite well enough for dancing and I could hardly go alone, no matter how much they begged me. It's not the done thing, being a solicitor's wife.'

Sara realised that Margaret had the wrong end of the stick; perhaps

169

there had been something that Margaret and Ray had been invited to last night, something that she thought Sara and Charlie, Eloise and Mark had attended. Sara was about to clear the matter up when she became distracted by Margaret's next comment. 'And then there was all that terrible fuss about the apple tart. Ray couldn't get to sleep after Mark's visit. Ray seemed to think it was my fault but I have no idea what they're on about and so it certainly can't be my fault, can it?'

'Were you supposed to make a tart for Eloise?' Sara asked, piecing together some of the previous evening's panic.

'No, dear. Or at least I doubt it. I've never made a tart in my life.'

'Granny, that's just not true,' said Poppy with determination. 'You *did* promise to make pudding. I heard you talk about it with Mummy.'

'Dear me, small goblins do have big ears,' said Margaret in a tone that made Poppy hang her head, abashed.

It was all a bit surreal for Sara who decided that, as they followed the coast path around to various coves, she would do well to limit the small talk to identification of flora and fauna and comments about the drizzle. Eloise continued to read aloud from her printed sheet and tried to identify Compass Cove, Ladies' Cove and Deadman's Cove. She initially declared, with real confidence, 'This is Compass Cove', but then after a few minutes she said, 'No, no. *This* is Compass Cove, the last cove was just a few rocks by comparison.' A few moments later she added with significantly less certainty, 'Or maybe this is Compass Cove – or is this one Ladies' Cove? How far do you think we've walked?' Charlie and Mark teased her as though they thought her geographical ignorance was somehow charming. Sara thought it was a bit irresponsible. If Eloise was leading the walk she ought to be more sure-footed.

After a mile or so, Margaret asked, 'No babies for you yet?'

Sara jolted because she believed the older woman had read her mind. Sara had, of course, been thinking about her longing for a baby.

'No,' she sighed wearily.

'We were late starting a family too.'

This confidence was as unexpected as it was welcome. So, whilst the sea wind buffeted their anoraks and hair, Sara told Margaret of her doomed efforts to get pregnant. Margaret was a good listener. Her passive face absorbed without shock or censure. Sara almost resented reaching Dartmouth Castle because the groups fell apart and reformed and she found herself walking next to Eloise while Margaret walked with the girls.

Eloise linked Sara's arm and asked brightly, 'Are you enjoying yourself? A brisk, bracing walk is so therapeutic, isn't it?'

Sara was irritated that Eloise assumed a couple of miles' hiking could solve her problems; Sara's distress couldn't be brushed under the carpet so she didn't reply but asked a question of her own. 'Where's this big surprise?'

'Soon. Just there.' Eloise pointed to a tiny tea shop, not much bigger than a caravan, nestled against the entrance of the castle. There were a few aluminium tables outside the shop with Loom-esque chairs scattered around them. A blackboard promised local crab sandwiches, cream teas and ice cream.

'My surprise is a fruit scone?' asked Sara.

Eloise giggled. 'Much better than that. Although they do serve lovely scones here. Come on.' She set off at such an enthusiastic speed that she almost dragged Sara towards the castle. The girls started up a chorus of protest at the thought of having to visit the ancient fortification. 'Stop whingeing, you education-averse heathens,' Eloise yelled over her shoulder. 'I'm not going to make you visit it today, although I bet it's really interesting. Do you know that the River Dart has been of great strategic importance since the twelfth century? Dartmouth's been a significant port since the Normans realised its maritime value and used it as the assembly point for the European fleets leaving for the crusades.'

'Enough,' yelled Emily.

Erin covered her ears and shouted, 'Blah blah blah blah!'

Eloise did have a tendency to see family days out as an educational opportunity. She really didn't know how to let go.

'Ice cream?' Sara offered. All three girls and Margaret lunged forward, keen to exploit the offer of a treat rather than endure a history lesson.

While Poppy investigated the box selling colourful tinfoil windmills and bags of seashells, everyone else ordered various teas, coffees, brownies, cream scones, ice creams and lemonade. Eloise encouraged indulgence and insisted that it would be her shout. Once everyone had received their order and was happily munching, Eloise asked, 'Right, are you ready for the big surprise?' She looked like a kid at Christmas with her nose pushed against a toyshop window. 'OK, well, there's a particular reason that I wanted to get us all out together today, as a family.' She glanced at Sara as she said family and then added, 'You and Charlie are like family to us.'

The girls appeared not to be concentrating on what she had to say; they were patting an enormous, particularly smelly, long-haired dog that looked as though he was wearing a dense shaggy bath mat. The pup had clearly just enjoyed a jaunt in the sea; its coat was matted into dreadlocks and it smelt of seaweed. The girls were oblivious to its unsanitary nature and fussed and petted it with enthusiasm. Eloise paused, knowing she had to wait until they were ready to listen to her.

'What breed is it?' Ray asked the owner.

'He's a silver Pastore Bergamasco.'

'Really? A shepherd of the Alps?'

'That's right.'

'A sheep dog?'

'Yes.'

'I don't think I've ever seen one like this before. He's grand.'

Ray didn't appear to have caught on to the fact that Eloise was bursting as she had something important to say. He petted the dog too, sniffed his hand and then winced at the stench. 'I might need to go and rinse my hands.'

Eloise scrabbled around in the rucksack, found some bottled water and offered it to her father-in-law.

'Seems such a waste,' he demurred. 'Mineral water to wash my hands.'

'My treat,' she said brightly. Ray hesitated and then eventually poured water on to his hands, rubbed them together, shook them and then

Margaret silently offered him an immaculate handkerchief, with which he carefully patted his hands dry. Slowly, he returned the handkerchief to Margaret and then returned his gaze to Eloise, giving her a nod that indicated she could resume.

Eloise smiled but since the table was surrounded by her nearest and dearest they all knew she was battling to hide her impatience. The pavement was cluttered with greedy seagulls. Their guttural screams creamed off everyone's attention too.

'Look, look at that bullying gull,' Poppy suddenly called out, distressed. Everyone turned to look at where she was pointing. They watched a paunchy gull waddling along the concrete path, wings spread wide to usher an intrepid sparrow away from a discarded sandwich crust that he'd been feasting on. The sparrow tugged helplessly and hopelessly at the bread but couldn't get away quickly enough. Emily stamped her foot in the hope that she'd scare away the gull. But the gull simply looked at her with hearty disdain and then gobbled up the egg sandwich crust.

'I hope there was cress on that sandwich, that would serve greedy guts right,' said Poppy crossly. She lived in a world where the worst thing that could ever happen to anyone was that they ate salad or vegetables.

Eloise breathed out deeply; she was clearly tempted to tap her teaspoon against her teacup and call the table to order.

'Right, so back to my surprise. As we all know, Sara and Charlie have been trying for a baby for some time now but, tragically, they haven't had any luck,' she said. Margaret patted Sara's hand but nobody else reacted to Eloise's opener. Where was she going with this? 'Well, last night I thought about it long and hard and I know there's something I can do to fix this.'

'You can't fix this one,' Sara muttered.

Eloise beamed and then pronounced definitively, 'Yes. Fix it. I'm going to be Sara's surrogate.'

'You're what?' Mark yelled. He jumped up, hitting his thighs on the wobbly chrome table. Tea slopped in saucers. He dropped back into his chair with a thump.

Eloise turned to him and her beam widened a fraction further. Sara could tell that she was clearly expecting to be awarded the Nobel Peace Prize. 'I'm going to be Sara's surrogate,' she repeated calmly.

Mark glared at Sara accusingly but she moved her head a fraction left to right; she was as surprised as he was.

'You are what?' he repeated.

Eloise suddenly realised that Mark might not be as excited about the idea as she'd hoped. 'I think you heard,' she said carefully, with notably less certainty.

'No, you are not,' he declared firmly.

Eloise bristled. 'You can't tell me what I can and can't do, Mark.'

'I'm your husband.'

'That doesn't mean you get to make this call.'

Everyone else remained silent but flicked their gawping eyes between the two of them. Sara was so overwhelmed by what Eloise had just offered to do and interested in Mark's reaction that she hadn't had time to think about the offer and react to it independently. A quick glance at Charlie confirmed he was also stunned.

'Actually, I bet that *legally* I do get to make a call but what I mean, Eloise, is I'm your *husband*! Of course I should have a say in this.' Mark was furious. Mystification and annoyance bubbled from every pore. He reached into his jacket pocket and fished out his iPhone. He was probably going to Google 'Is my wife allowed to become a surrogate without my say so?' Eloise and Mark used Google for their educational black holes when they were helping the girls with their homework and now it seemed its function had been expanded to moral guidance. Mark stared at the screen; it seemed both he and Google were having difficulty computing what Eloise had just said.

'This isn't something you should rush into,' said Ray calmly.

'She's my friend.' Eloise glanced Sara's way. It was the first time they'd made eye contact since she'd thrown out the offer. Sara smiled weakly although she was still uncertain as to how she wanted to respond to the idea. Eloise looked a bit disappointed.

'Just because Sara can't have a baby doesn't mean you should give her one,' added Ray evenly.

'What are you thinking?' Mark spat out the words, upset, and spittle showered down on Eloise's scone. 'You can't just have a baby and then hand it over, the way you hand over a bunch of flowers or a couple of bottles of decent wine when we go for dinner.'

'I won't be giving her a baby. It will be her eggs, Charlie's sperm.'

'Eloise!' Mark was pale. He was hoping to live his entire life without ever thinking about his pal's sperm.

'Are you having a baby, Mum?' asked Erin.

'No, darling.'

'Are you giving me away?' asked Poppy.

'No, of course not.' Eloise laughed and pulled Poppy on to her knee. She snuggled into her neck and landed generous kisses there.

'You've confused the children,' said Mark. His words hit her like a wet towel and momentary pain flickered across Eloise's face. Almost instantly she rallied.

'I've thought about it. This would be a good thing to do.' Eloise held her hands wide. Sara couldn't help but notice that it was a effective pose. She looked saintly. Martyred.

'If you want to do a charitable act start with taking muffins to the elderly neighbours,' snapped Mark.

'I don't bake.'

'No, that's true, she doesn't,' interjected Margaret. Everyone paused for a moment and considered Margaret's first contribution to the discussion. Margaret smiled at her family, seemingly unaware of the tornado brewing at the small metal table outside the tea shop.

'Eloise, I'm being serious and I forbid you to think about this again.'

'You forbid me?' Eloise was stunned. She was humiliated that her generous gift and fix-it measure had been so violently discarded.

'Yes. I forbid it,' said Mark firmly. He folded his hands across his chest.

'Which century am I living in? You can't forbid me to do anything.' Mark did look every inch the intractable Victorian gentleman who would have his way in his own home. Sara wondered how Eloise would react. The friendship between the two couples meant that they were each familiar with how the other's domestics played out. Eloise and Mark didn't fight often but when they did Mark invariably came off worse. Sara had seen him cave because Eloise got emotional and he couldn't bear to see her upset and he'd been even more accommodating since Eloise had agreed to move to Dartmouth, he had indulged her every whim. Although Sara doubted he was going to back down over this. With a low voice that communicated a cool certainty, Mark said, 'El, you can't become a surrogate just because you're bored.'

Eloise glared at him. She bit her lip, obviously trying to suppress something bordering on rage. She probably hated it that he knew her so well.

'That's not the reason I want to do this. I just can't watch Sara's agony any more.'

Sara didn't like Eloise's choice of words. *Eloise* couldn't watch *Sara's* agony. How come she always made everything about her? Sara decided to call time.

'Look,' she interrupted, 'thank you very much for the generous offer, Eloise. I know you mean well, but I don't think you've fully thought this through.'

'I have,' insisted Eloise. 'Your issue is not getting pregnant. You said that last night, it's carrying a baby full term. I could do that for you.' She looked eager and despite her husband's hostility, her daughters' embarrassment and her father-in-law's irritation she pushed on. She was either oblivious or careless.

'I might be able to go to full term, I just haven't *yet*. We can do another round of IVF.' Sara heard Charlie groan but she didn't look his way. What must he make of Eloise's idea? 'These things are really massively complicated.'

Mark pushed his chair back and strode off in the rough direction of where they'd parked the cars.

'Mark, wait!' Eloise jumped up and chased after him. She grabbed his arm but he shook her off and continued his rapid pace. She had to run alongside him to keep up.

'Would you like another cake, girls?' asked Margaret, with a broad smile. She seemed completely unflustered by the entire debacle.

'I think we ought to get moving,' said Ray brusquely. 'I'll settle up.'

'If you're sure,' mumbled Charlie.

His only contribution to the entire proceedings, Sara noted.

20

Above the car park area near the castle you could see the curtain wall and tower, all that remained of the fourteenth-century fort built by John Hawley, Mayor of Dartmouth a remarkable fourteen times, and the man who inspired Chaucer's Shipman in *The Canterbury Tales*. Margaret remembered learning all that in history class. Mrs Caterson had snapped out those facts, and many others, as Margaret and her classmates sewed neat lines of cross-stitch on the bookmarks they were making. Margaret still remembered Mrs Caterson's words bursting through the stuffy classroom that smelt of chalk and young girls' bodies. Memories clear as crystal, yet it was so long, long ago. She remembered the silky feel of the jewel-coloured embroidery threads under her fingers. She remembered the wooden desks and the cheap blinds. She remembered children playing in the playground, so clearly that she thought she could hear them.

She remembered it all just as though it was yesterday. Although nothing like yesterday because she couldn't remember yesterday. Not one bit of it. Not clearly and certainly.

There was a party.

And a pie.

Now there was going to be a baby. Or maybe not.

Time was not following a straight path any more. It was floundering around like a pebble thrown up in a wave. One moment here, the next swept away again. Hours and years, days and minutes tossed against one another. They no longer had a place. Margaret's history no longer had a place.

Immediately below the car park, to the south, was the World War II gun shelter. Margaret was just a tot during the war but the events still fascinated her generation, those who inherited the make do and mend mentality. Not so interesting to Eloise and Mark, or their girls. Two generations on. Might as well be a hundred.

Margaret didn't know why everyone was so cross with Eloise, who was obviously only trying to help her friend. What could be finer? Yet Sara and Charlie were lagging behind, silent and stony, not at all grateful. The girls were much quieter on the walk back to the cars, too. They didn't stop to investigate clumps of clover, to search hopefully for the elusive four-leafed variety, as was usually their way. Ray, the girls and Margaret walked in a silent huddle; they watched Mark and Eloise stride ahead in the distance. It was clear from their body language that they were arguing. Margaret pointed out the net-drying sheds and the fishing boats that were drawn up on to the shingle but she couldn't get the girls to be interested. Ray kept asking her if she was all right, which Margaret thought was odd because she wasn't the one longing for a baby, or trying to give one away.

'Quite well, thank you,' she snapped. She *had been* the woman longing for a baby in the past, though. She understood Sara's torment. 'Sara has been explaining this IGF business to me this morning,' said Margaret. 'Quite the ordeal I understand.' Ray didn't comment.

Margaret pondered. Of course there was none of that in her day. If a woman didn't fall she didn't go to the doctor's and expect to be fixed. She cried about it, then got on with it. Although probably never accepted it. That was a myth. It was believed that Margaret's generation accepted limits; they didn't. They grieved, like women did now, except they did it behind closed doors. The more Margaret thought about it, the more and more she liked Eloise's idea. She was a good girl, was Eloise. Well meaning. So Eloise would grow the baby but it would be Sara's. Unconventional but not impossible. Eloise would need support. She'd need someone to help her with the girls as the pregnancy progressed. Someone to cook for her, to see to it that she got the proper nutrients; vitamins and minerals were all important during pregnancy. Margaret could do that. Margaret could help. She could be invaluable. The idea excited her. She felt it pump through her head and heart. She ran to catch up with her angry son and her well-intentioned daughter-in-law.

'What are you doing, Margaret?' Ray yelled after her.

'You walk with the girls. I just want a word with Eloise and Mark,' she called back over her shoulder.

They were not too far away but even so Margaret was a bit breathless when she caught up with them. The adrenalin coursing through her body made her pulse quicken. Helping was a bit like being in love. It was urgent and positive, incapable of understanding consequences. Helping was what was left over when you reached Margaret's age, she thought. Her panting heralded her approach. Eloise nudged Mark and they both fell into a simmering silence.

Margaret squeezed in between them, linking arms, like chums.

'Silly of you to get cross, Mark,' she said.

'Is that your view, Mum?' he replied dryly.

'Eloise was only trying to help,' she added. Eloise squeezed her mother-in-law's arm, showing that she was grateful for the solidarity.

'But her suggestion was ill considered and hideously executed.' He was her own son but even Margaret couldn't help but notice that he sounded a tiny bit pompous. That was nerves and stress, the combination always made him sound a little bit haughty. Sometimes that was useful, other times it was inflammatory.

'I thought everyone would be as excited as I was,' said Eloise with a hint of petulance that didn't become her.

'You didn't think at all,' insisted Mark. 'Just because you had a spat with your mate you want to turn our lives upside down in order to make up to her.'

'That's not what—'

'What must the girls be imagining? What if they became attached to the baby? Or more likely, what if you did? What if it was born and there was something wrong with it, would Sara want to take responsibility for it then?'

'There must be lawyers that specialise in that sort of thing, mustn't there?' asked Eloise defensively but it was obvious from the look on her face that she hadn't thought it all the way through just yet.

'Oh, there are,' Margaret said encouragingly, hoping to help and soothe. 'We had a lawyer when that girl gave you to me, Mark. We didn't want her being able to get in touch any time in the future. We wanted a line drawn under it. So we made her sign a document saying as much. It was all dealt with. Very straightforward. I never looked back.'

Mark and Eloise stopped walking. They turned and stared at Margaret with frightening intensity. Margaret wondered why. Had she said something silly? She could hear Ray panting now; he was running, trying to catch up. He was red in the face. He could do with getting a bit fitter, thought Margaret.

'What did you say, Mother?' Mark never called her Mother. He said Mum. So for a minute Margaret wondered whether he was talking to her at all. Maybe not. Maybe he was talking to the other mother. Margaret looked around for her. She shouldn't be here. Margaret hadn't looked for her for many years. In the beginning she did so all the time. Throughout that first year she was constantly looking over her shoulder, so terrified the girl might pop up and snatch him back. She'd never dared leave his pram outside the butcher's, the way other mothers did. That's why they'd had to move to Dartmouth in the end. Far away from the girl. That's why there were lawyers. She was just saying as much. Wasn't she? She wasn't sure because of the smudge. The ringing was in her head again. It wouldn't go away. It was making it difficult to hear her thoughts. Everything was difficult and she was unsure. She wasn't sure what was going on.

'She's not well,' said Ray. He put his arm around Margaret and pulled her into his shoulder. 'She doesn't know what she's saying.'

'I do, dear. I was just telling Mark about the girl who gave him to us,' she insisted.

'Shush now, Margaret.' Ray pulled his wife's head towards his shoulder again. He was physically trying to gag her. She struggled to push him away. She didn't like it. She was needed here. From the look on Mark and Eloise's faces they were dealing with some very bad news. They needed her.

21

Charlie and Sara drove all three girls home but, within minutes of arriving there, it became clear that their home was the last place the girls should be. Mark was yelling at Ray, his angry voice drifting through an open window.

'Why now? Why has she told me *now*?'

Sara peered past the iron railings of the garden gate and over the short, well-kept garden. Through the window she spotted Ray. He looked shell shocked. He was sitting next to the fire, which no one had thought to light, his head in his hands, repeatedly saying, 'She's not well. She doesn't know what she's saying.'

The front door suddenly burst open causing Sara to jump; she had every right to be there but she felt like someone caught snooping. Eloise appeared, holding Margaret's hand. Margaret was weeping.

'I'm taking her home,' Eloise informed Sara. 'I'll explain everything when I get back. Later on.'

'The girls?'

Eloise glanced at her daughters; she almost looked surprised to see them clustered at the end of the garden path. 'Could you take them to the embankment? Give them fish and chips for lunch.'

'We've just eaten,' said Erin grumpily. They were usually quite happy, compliant kids but the sight of their grandmother so sorrowful had brought out the gremlins in them.

'Are you OK, Granny?' asked Poppy.

'She's fine,' Eloise replied hastily. Margaret didn't look fine. She looked confused, displaced. 'Well, if not food, why don't you go for a walk?' suggested Eloise.

'We've just been for a walk,' groaned Emily. 'I want to play on the Wii.'

That was the problem with anywhere other than London, there was nowhere to go when you were banished from the house because of family traumas. Eloise looked desperate. 'Daddy is just talking to Grandad, it's probably best you don't disturb them.' The girls could hear Daddy *talking* to Grandad. So could the rest of Dartmouth, likely as not. His chat was along the lines of, 'What in God's name made you think it was OK to hide *this* from me?'

It would be inhuman not to wonder what had been hidden. Sara tried to catch Eloise's eye but she was too distressed and distracted to find time for a gossipy catch-up.

'I need to stay with Margaret,' she said helplessly.

'We'll take the girls to Blackpool Sands,' said Charlie. His interruption startled Sara. She'd almost forgotten he was there. 'Don't worry about them. We'll look after them until teatime. Give you space to sort out—' He stumbled to a stop and shrugged as he was unsure what it was that Eloise and Mark were sorting out. Whatever it was, it was serious because Eloise simply nodded gratefully. She didn't check if they had warm, spare clothes for the girls, charged mobiles or even directions to Blackpool Sands; it was a rare moment when Eloise relinquished responsibility. She didn't so much as remember to give them a kiss on the cheek. Instead, she put her arm around Margaret and started to guide her gently along the cobbles, in the direction of her house.

The only Blackpool Sara was aware of was the one in the northwest of England that boasted an orgy of Kiss-Me-Quick hats, neon signs to dodgy nightclubs and a plethora of Elvis impersonators. That Blackpool was at the other end of the country, it would be one heck of a drive, so she assumed Charlie knew of another Blackpool. He must have been mooching around Dartmouth in these past few months, or, if not actually visiting places of interest, she guessed he'd at least chatted about them over a pint in Eloise's local. Charlie herded the children into the car with a complicated combination of bribes ('Yes, we can get an ice cream, even if you've already had one'), promises ('It will be fun, I bet the sun's shining there') and flattery ('Your mum and dad know they can depend on you to give them and your grandparents a bit of space, they know you understand that sometimes grown-ups need to sort out stuff'). Sara was impressed at his authority and calm control and was surprised to find his commanding way a bit of a turn-on. It was only when she acknowledged that she felt a swell of attraction for her husband, low in the pit of her stomach, that she realised it had been an age since she'd actively felt desire for Charlie. Desire for a baby, yes. All the time. For Charlie? Not so much. He'd become a means to an end. When they went to bed together nowadays she was often a hideous whirlwind of emotions. She wanted so much from him but she didn't always want him at all. Seeing him deal with the girls with such consideration reminded her why she wanted to be a parent with this man. He'd be a good dad. The thought comforted and sadistically whipped her at the same time.

Blackpool Sands turned out to be the nemesis of the northern Blackpool. There wasn't any sign of glitzy arcades, hectic theme parks or crowded trams. Blackpool Sands was a Blue Flag Award-winning beach, backed by evergreens and scented pines. It carried a hint of the Mediterranean. They parked up and Charlie bought buckets and spades for all three girls from the tiny beach shop. Emily rolled her eyes; the yellow plastic didn't compare to a console or even her iPod but eventually she accepted the limited entertainment options and joined her sisters building a sandcastle.

Sara and Charlie sat on the sand facing out to sea. They didn't speak. Sara's thoughts were colliding and exploding like fireworks. Was Eloise's offer for real? Could it work? No, it was madness, and yet . . . Well, it was a possibility.

'Looked like Eloise has set the cat among the pigeons with the

Hamiltons,' commented Sara, desperately trying to find a way into the conversation she needed to have.

Charlie sensed his wife's macabre excitement that Eloise was in trouble or had caused some trouble. He knew that on occasion she was pricked by jealousy; it was understandable, Eloise's life seemed so perfect and Sara was so frustrated. But he couldn't help thinking that while her envy was understandable it was also unattractive.

'Eloise has been good to us,' he reminded Sara carefully.

'I'm not saying anything other,' snapped Sara, irritated that her husband should pin his colours to Eloise. 'So, what do you think of this offer for her to be a surrogate?'

'Not now, eh, Sara.' Charlie glanced nervously at the girls.

But she couldn't stop herself. 'Do you think that's what they're arguing about?'

'I don't know.'

'I don't think it is. I think it's something to do with Margaret and Ray.'

'I'm sure we'll know soon enough.'

'It's a thought though, isn't it?'

'What?'

'The surrogacy.'

'You like the idea?'

'Yes. Maybe. I don't know.' Sara stumbled over the proposal.

Did Sara like the idea of having a baby? Yes, yes, yes, absolutely. She'd always said she'd do anything to have a baby, anything at all. The fact that they'd wiped out their savings, ruined their sex life and, to all intents and purposes, put her career on hold showed that she was prepared to try most things. But *anything*? Really? Maybe Eloise *could* fix this but did Sara *want* her to? Eloise fixing Sara again? When Sara had first moved into the Muswell Hill area Eloise was always on hand with useful tips. Tips that were too stylish for Sara to ignore but somehow irritating because no one wanted to face the fact that they were clueless when it came to interior décor (which was, after all, the new sex in most polite society). Sara used Eloise's hair stylist, tailor and dry cleaner. In the past Eloise had helped Sara write her CV, pick out outfits for interviews, and she'd even suggested which car the Woddells should buy. Now Eloise wanted to fix Sara's agony of dealing with failed IVF treatment. Eloise was the person Sara owed the most to. Was it healthy to owe one person so much? Why was it that Eloise was the person Sara owed the most to and ought to be most grateful to yet she was the person Sara liked the least right now?

Sara hated herself for thinking this. For even allowing the idea to swill around her head long enough to form as a firm thought. It wasn't right. It wasn't decent. But the truth was, when Sara looked at the wall in her house that had eight black-and-white photos of her family, cradled in ornate gold frames, instead of thinking, 'Wow, that was such a great tip from Eloise, that feature wall makes the entire room', she seethed. Of course she could just take down the photos, but they did look great. It wasn't that she hated Eloise's idea, she just wished she'd come up with it first. Sara hated needing Eloise. No one wanted to admit to feeling jealous; a bleak and low emotion. But jealousy crept like mould, it oozed and reproduced. It suffocated. Sara told herself that she wasn't jealous, no, it was not that. Perhaps resentful. She could reconcile herself to feeling resentment towards Eloise; that wasn't quite so low and evil. It was just that Eloise was so unaware of all she had. And it fell into her lap, thought Sara with indignation.

Considering Sara had started to resent Eloise giving tips on interior décor, could she stand it if Eloise gave her the thing she wanted most in the world? Was a baby something she wanted as a gift from Eloise?

22

'Do you want to talk about it?'
   'No, not really.'
'I think we should.'

Mark didn't respond. As the silence stretched between them Eloise wondered whether he had actually fallen asleep. It was pitch-black and, besides, he was on his side, rolled away from her; there was no way for her to tell that his eyes were wide open. She moved closer to him and wrapped her arm around him. He didn't stir but now she could tell, from the pattern of his breathing, that he was still awake. 'Mark?'

'What?'

'What are you thinking?'

'I don't know.'

She paused and then tried, 'What are you feeling?'

'Eloise, I really don't know.' He spat out his words like gunfire. Shocked, Eloise rolled away from him and stared at the ceiling; she fully expected to see a physical embodiment of his pain, maybe splinters in the paintwork.

'It doesn't change anything,' she added carefully.

'Yes, it does.'

'No, it doesn't. Well, at least it doesn't have to.'

'They're not my flesh and blood. They're not the girls' flesh and blood.'

'What does that matter? They love you. They love the girls. They couldn't love you more.'

'They should have told me before,' muttered Mark.

'Maybe,' Eloise admitted.

'How would you feel if your mum rang from Portugal and said, "Oh, by the way, I've been meaning to tell you something. You're adopted"?'

'I'd be very confused,' admitted Eloise. El couldn't imagine how devastating such an announcement would be and she knew she wasn't even as close to her parents as Mark was to his. 'Scared, hurt, angry.'

Mark nodded. He was wounded, alone, lost. He didn't dare say these words aloud, not even to his wife. He felt he was less of a man than the man he had been just this morning because he didn't know who he was any more. This morning he'd known. He had built everything on a lie.

'They should have told me before or not at all.'

Maybe, thought Eloise, but this time she didn't say anything. She had a horrible feeling that this was all her fault. If she hadn't suggested being a surrogate for Sara, Margaret would never have mentioned the adoption. Eloise desperately hoped Mark hadn't made the same connection.

'Margaret is ill.' Eloise mused on the other lightning strike that had hit today.

'And they hadn't seen fit to mention that to us, either,' spat Mark, not able to sympathise because he was drowning.

'Mark, they just didn't want to worry us.' Was she on medication? Eloise wondered. Something that made her forgetful. Would that explain the apple tart and disgusting lavender cream? Thinking about it, there had been a number of times that Margaret had muddled up a name or an appointment time. Eloise had just assumed they were examples of run-of-the-mill senior moments.

'You know, I only became a solicitor to make my dad proud. To be like him. It hasn't ever come easy to me. He has the right sort of mind. A tidy mind. I've always had to work so hard at it. I've often wondered why it wasn't more natural.'

'But you are a good solicitor, a great one.'

'I don't look like them.'

'Well, no.' Eloise wondered whether she ought to add that he was significantly better-looking. She decided not to. She knew Mark was wondering who he looked like.

'You are the spit of your mum,' he muttered.

'Well, yes,' Eloise admitted. This wasn't a fact she'd ever given much thought to. Mark glared at Eloise. She felt guilty for having such uncomplicated parentage.

Eloise slipped her hand under the duvet and slowly ran it up and down Mark's thigh. This was her way of suggesting sex. Mark, like most men, found sex a comfort and as she was all out of words she hoped this would be welcomed.

Instead of responding by rolling towards her, Mark reached for her hand and carefully but deliberately moved it away. 'I'm really tired, actually. Just not in the mood.'

'Of course.'

Eloise knew that she shouldn't take the rebuff personally. But she did. She decided that she wouldn't bring up the subject again, not until Mark did. He'd know when he was ready to talk.

23

Eloise was alone in the house. The girls were at school, Mark was at work and Charlie was at the builders' yard. Her solitude was firm and overwhelming. She envied the others their sense of purpose; she wished she had somewhere she ought to be or something that she had to do. Being busy was defining. You didn't have to be a pioneering astronaut or a scientist working on the cure for cancer (although obviously they were good things to be), for some it was enough to be the woman that other women turned to for an emotional crutch if they discovered their husband was having an affair, or – less dramatically – if they wanted advice on what to wear for a particular event. Eloise was that woman. The turn-to woman. Or at least she had been.

She could, of course, wash the inside windows. For days now the autumn afternoon sunlight had been showing her up to be slovenly but that chore didn't appeal. She played with the idea of visiting Margaret and Ray but then she remembered that they'd mentioned they were going for a drive to Torbay this morning and they hadn't invited her along. She didn't know if she was thrilled they hadn't invited her along because they'd assumed she had something better to do with her time or whether she was gutted because, in fact, she hadn't. Eloise called her parents but got the answering machine. She didn't leave a message. She called once a week on a Sunday evening; they'd worry that something was wrong if she left a message on a weekday morning. Eloise was a chatterbox and needed noise to validate her existence;

she turned on the radio, accepting it could only offer her a poor substitute for company, but beggars couldn't be choosers. The radio was tuned to a local station that at 5 p.m. pumped out old pop tracks that Eloise once believed spoke to her and her alone; 5 p.m. was the time she usually listened while making tea for the girls or if she wasn't actively listening, then at least the pop music offered a suitable backdrop to their chaos. She was surprised to discover that at this time in the morning considerably more contemporary pop was playing; bands she couldn't confidently name but had heard Emily singing along to.

Modern music intimidated Eloise. She found it too blatant. Eloise was not a prude but she really doubted the need for motherfucker this and motherfucker that in song lyrics. It was awkward if the girls were listening. Even with the 'ucker' bit blanked out by the radio producers she found it embarrassing; the girls were not daft, they knew the blanked word had to rhyme with 'she's a real looker' or 'so den I took her'. She found herself in the strange position of longing for them to assume that the lyric was 'she's a hot motherhooker'. But the girls weren't listening right now, they were safely at school and so Eloise gave the music more attention than she had in the past. She didn't halt at her first reaction (embarrassment), she moved beyond that and tried to understand why it might be popular.

It was sexy. It was throbbing. She felt it in the parts of her body that she was usually only aware of when she was doing her pelvic floor exercises (which she did regularly whenever she hit a red traffic light and had a few moments to kill; she'd given birth three times, the old school way, the area needed all the help it could get). Before she knew it Eloise found she was tapping her toes, then wiggling her hips. She pouted at her own reflection in the shiny toaster. She pulled the face that Mark described as her 'going out face', an expression that she never actually wore in public but one that she secretly thought made her look most like a supermodel. Or maybe, nowadays, a catalogue model. Within moments, Eloise was dancing around the kitchen. It felt good to thrash her limbs about in a disordered way. She nodded her head, backwards, rather than forwards or side to side because a long time ago she'd been told backwards was the cool way to nod her head. She let it out, she let it go. The tension, the responsibility, the maturity that was demanded of her nowadays, all slipped away and she simply regressed for ten minutes. El was the type of dancer who had always been noted for her enthusiasm rather than her ability but in the privacy of her own kitchen that really couldn't matter less. She danced with tremendous, mesmerising abandon until she began to get a bit damp around her hairline, until she was breathless, and she *loved* it.

Eloise tucked her T-shirt into her bra, the way she'd seen the girls on music videos wear theirs, and she tugged her tracksuit bottoms down so that the edge of her knickers was revealed at her hips. She didn't think too carefully about the reality of her look – her knickers were wash-faded and her tracksuit had yogurt on the thigh, although in her mind she was wearing a crushed velvet designer tracksuit, maybe in a startling orange or cerise. The only jewellery she was wearing was her wedding band; in her mind she was bedecked with bling. Just for a moment Eloise believed she had a honed stomach that glistened with the exertion and she was still twenty-two and really *hot*. Actually, she decided to give herself licence to imagine she was significantly hotter than she had been at twenty-two, than she'd *ever* been. Why the hell not? She waved her arms around in the air, not the way she danced in her youth but the way the sexy motherfuckers did in the videos, or at least in an approximation of how they danced now. It was all shrugging shoulders, little fingers and thumbs turned out with the other fingers curled in, knees bent and all the time with the nodding.

It wasn't until he coughed for a second time that she realised Charlie was in the kitchen.

'Jeez, Charlie, you gave me the fright of my life.' Eloise slammed her hand down on the radio control panel, silencing it. She breathed heavily, chest up and down, up and down as she tried to regain control. 'That was quite a work-out,' she gasped.

'Nice look.' He was staring at her stomach, not honed and glistening, but not bad, not considering her age and three children and the fact that since they'd moved here she'd been indulging in more portions of fish and chips than was sensible. Eloise laughed at her own silliness. She unknotted her T-shirt and hiked up her tracksuit bottoms with efficiency.

'Fancy a cuppa?'

'Don't let me stop you.' Charlie smiled, a slow teasing smile.

Eloise could handle it from him; he was like a family member. She knew he was completely within his rights to take the mick. She must have looked ridiculous. As she filled the kettle she commented, 'I was just mucking around.'

'You looked pretty serious. You looked pretty good.'

'Nice of you to say so but I was just playing. You know, like kids play at being grown up. I play at being a kid.'

Charlie didn't reply, he didn't say a thing while she made the tea. They sat at the breakfast table together; hot, strong tea steaming between them. She was trying hard not to acknowledge that instead of the patent teasing she'd been expecting there was a flush of embarrassment growing between them, some sort of tautness in the air. 'Sorry that you had to witness that undignified display of optimism over good sense. Thank God it was you and not Arabella or Jackie who caught me prancing around my kitchen at nine fifteen in the morning. It's not that I'm vain and painful, I'm simply deluded,' Eloise added with a grin. Charlie still didn't say anything so, to fill the silence, Eloise rattled on. 'You must think I'm barmy, rocking out in my kitchen to bands that my kids own. What can I say? I like to get breathless and excited, still. The thing is, the breathlessness happens a damn sight quicker nowadays.' She laughed. Eloise always laughed at herself to break tension.

Charlie finally found his voice. 'Don't be daft, you're in great shape . . .'

'If you add *for your age*, I swear I'll throw this scalding tea over you.' Charlie ducked playfully. 'I know I'm not a total horror but that's good luck rather than good management. I have my skinny mother to thank for my fast metabolism but she's also responsible for my curly hair, so it's swings and roundabouts.'

Eloise wondered whether that was the conversation closed, whether Charlie would now take his tea upstairs and start banging around in the bathroom. Part of her wanted him to do that, she needed to see some progress in the bathroom, but part of her was glad of the company and didn't mind if he lingered.

'When I rock around the kitchen my music of choice is Springsteen,' confessed Charlie with an embarrassed shrug.

'No way!'

'Way.'

'Where is Bruce Springsteen now?' Eloise wondered aloud as she sipped her tea.

'Well, when he's not in my kitchen, I imagine he's rocking out to middle-aged ladies in Madison Square Garden, no doubt doing rock-and-roll hall-of-fame stuff.'

'Bet you can taste the HRT in the air.'

'Hey, not everyone can be as cool as you, digging da rap and hip hop homey girl,' Charlie said with an accent that was a poor approximation of Kanye West's or Jay-Z's.

'Not at all. If I was choosing, I'd dance around my kitchen pretending to be Nicole Kidman singing to Ewan McGregor, like in *Moulin Rouge*.'

'Oh yes, I remember you had that Moulin Rouge party for one of your birthdays.'

'That was a great party. All the men in black tie.'

'All the women dressed like sluts.'

'Everyone was happy!'

Charlie and Eloise chuckled and then fell silent again. Eloise was thinking about music and parties. She really ought to have a party here in Dartmouth but not now. Not on the back of Margaret's bombshell. Maybe at Christmas or on New Year's Eve.

'Do you miss it?' asked Charlie.

'What?'

'London?'

Eloise didn't know how to answer, at least not immediately. She did miss London, had done so for months, but she had worked so hard at suppressing her feelings of loss and longing that she didn't know how to pull them to the fore now she'd (finally) been directly asked. She knew that it would be unhelpful to allow the raw craving to spill on to her kitchen floor; what was the point of admitting to her feelings of displacement and fears of difference here in Dartmouth? She needed to find a way to package up her response in a more acceptable form, otherwise Charlie might feel uncomfortable and Eloise hated making people feel uncomfortable.

'Oh, yes, a bit, naturally. But I worry about so many other things nowadays,' she joked.

'Like?'

'OK, in no particular order, you asked. Landfills, gun violence – home and abroad – war, paedophiles, my mother-in-law's bombshell that Mark is adopted.' Eloise counted her worries on her fingers, swapped hands and continued. 'Whether I picked the right schools for my daughters, whether my daughters will pick the right men to marry, whether our home insurance really would cover us if our house burnt down following a freak strike of lightning or similar . . . need I go on?'

'Have you always been such a worrier? I mean, you present a very calm, cool and collected exterior.'

Again Eloise side-stepped the question. 'I used to worry about whether I'd ever convincingly straighten my massively curly hair and whether I kissed properly. I still worry about my hair on days when I can't find my straighteners. Not so much about the kissing. I think I've got that nailed. Although, seriously, is that progress? Is that enough progress?' Charlie was laughing now. Eloise was pleased with herself, Charlie didn't do much laughing nowadays; it was good to see. 'What about you, Charlie? What do you worry about?'

'Just two things. Getting old and Sara.'

'Right.' Sara's name, here in the kitchen, somehow dampened their spirits. Her pain travelled like an aggressive virus. It lingered in the air.

'I do want it, as much as she does.' Charlie didn't need to say what *it* was. Eloise dignified this admission with silence. After a few minutes Charlie mused, 'I thought I was born to be wild.' Eloise couldn't imagine that masturbating into a pot every couple of months was anyone's definition of wild.

'Emily would say they were born to *get* wild, rather than *be*,' said Eloise gently. 'I'm always tempted to correct their grammar.'

Charlie smiled again, as she'd hoped he would. 'That's the thing about getting older, you become a stickler.'

'Yes, I find myself saying things like "in my day", which even I can see is just a little bit boring. Of course, if ever I was in any doubt as to how boring I'm becoming there's always Emily on hand to confirm it.' Charlie laughed again. 'But consider the alternative to aging.'

'Death. Right.'

'And I am aware that there are positives.'

'Name them,' Charlie challenged.

'No pressure to wear fashions that don't suit – I can wear stained tracksuit bottoms at the breakfast table in front of a bloke and not have to worry about it. I get excited when my mail order deliveries arrive. I'll never have to worry about trying to make anyone fall in love with me again, which really was exhausting. I get great pleasure from growing tomatoes from seeds.' Eloise stood up and rinsed her mug under the tap to indicate that she had to get on. She didn't really have to get on but she'd hate for Charlie or anyone to gather how little she was actually required. She decided she'd take a walk to the library and pick out a new novel to read. Charlie got the hint too.

'I need to pop out again and buy some self-levelling compound.'

'Right.' Eloise had no idea what self-levelling compound was but nodded authoritatively anyway.

'You're fun, Eloise.'

'Cheers, Charlie. But don't you mean funny?'

'No, no, I really don't.'

24

'Charlie is refusing to try for another round of IVF,' Sara stated bluntly the moment Eloise picked up the phone.

'Why?' Eloise asked.

'I don't know. Maybe it's the expense or my reaction to the drugs. Maybe he's given up hope or maybe he's a selfish fucker.'

'Oh, Sara. I'm certain that's not the case.' Eloise gently tried to calm and comfort her friend.

'Are you?'

Sara knew she probably needed to take a deep breath; to breathe in some semblance of rationale, but her chest hurt so much, she couldn't. She'd been to the doctor about her shallow breathing and the pains in her chest. She'd been told they were symptoms of panic.

Sara imagined Eloise in her smart hallway and the vision caused her chest to tighten a fraction further; as though a screw was being turned. Eloise would be sitting on the stylish but fake (sorry, neo-!) Georgian chair, right next to the mirrored table where the antique ivory Bakelite telephone nestled; at least one of the girls would be hanging around, trying to eavesdrop or get her attention. Eloise was always in demand. From where she'd be sitting she would be able to see into her kitchen. Charlie was probably in there right now, doing something domestic and fun with the other girls. Maybe he'd be preparing a satsuma for Poppy because, while she was capable of peeling and segmenting her own fruit, she swore they tasted better when someone else did it for her. On Sara's last visit to the Hamiltons, she'd noticed that she and Charlie were the only ones in the household who continued to indulge Poppy in this way. OK, Sara knew that time was a precious commodity to Eloise, especially now she was spending so many hours with Margaret at her various doctors' appointments, but if it was Sara's daughter who wanted her fruit segmenting, she'd damn well do it. Sara wouldn't try and reconcile the selfish fucker with a man who segmented a child's fruit. It was too much.

She stayed silent for a moment or two. Other than the sound of heartbreak there was nothing to be heard.

'What did Mark make of your offer?' asked Sara. Even though they hadn't discussed Eloise's offer to be a surrogate since it had been made – two weeks ago – both women immediately knew what she was talking about, without her having to be explicit. Sara hadn't wanted to discuss the offer until she was certain she was comfortable with taking it further; or, more honestly, until she was certain she was out of options and had no other choice. As Sara had been exclusively focused on the situation from her point of view, she hadn't wondered why Eloise hadn't broached the subject again. Until now.

Sara thought that, most probably, Eloise was coming up against resistance from Mark. He'd made his feelings pretty clear in the castle car park. As far as feedback went, 'no', 'absolutely not' and 'over my dead body' were basically impossible to misinterpret.

'Oh, he's got a lot to think about at the moment, we haven't had much time to discuss it in detail. I know he understands how important this is to you, but—'

Sara cut Eloise off. 'I don't think anyone can really understand.'

'I thought he'd want it. I thought he'd support me or at least rationally discuss it.' Sara didn't hear the confusion and hurt in Eloise's tone, she had too much of both emotions already. Eloise pushed on. She knew she had to be straight with Sara. 'I think I could have talked him round.' Sara wanted this so much that she missed the tense Eloise had used. It was true that the Hamiltons were rarely diametrically opposed on anything. 'But then Margaret dropped her bombshell that Mark's adopted. Then Ray tried to explain her actions by declaring she's ill. Seriously ill. Nothing's been the same since. It's not the right time. I can't even imagine when the right time will be. I'm so sorry.'

Sara finally heard Eloise.

She understood that Eloise was withdrawing the offer.

Another dead end.

It had been nothing more than an enormously flamboyant gesture! She'd probably never had any intention of following through! Sara felt icy resentment sneak through her body. It took everything she had not to scream at Eloise and, instead, to ask, 'So what is dementia, exactly?'

Eloise sighed. 'A progressive disorder that affects how a brain works and in particular the ability to remember, think and reason. That's what the consultant said. Easy words that somehow don't cover the confusion, the grief.'

'The inconvenience.'

'What do you mean?'

'Well, it's not quite the family life you imagined in Dartmouth, is it?' Sara commented.

'No,' Eloise admitted. 'But it *is* family life, a.k.a. responsibility. Don't get me wrong, the doctors have been very sympathetic and kind. They explained that memory problems can have many underlying causes, including some physical illnesses. Side-effects of medication, stress, tiredness, depression.'

'These possibilities have all been considered?'

'And ruled out. It's strange to find myself in the position of longing for someone I love to be diagnosed as stressed or depressed.'

'So what exactly do you have to expect?'

'It's tricky to be specific, apparently. Making a diagnosis of dementia and confirming which type someone has can be very difficult, particularly in the early stages. It takes some time and lots of tests. Each person experiences dementia in their own way and their condition will progress at a different rate. That's what they said. The doctors put me in mind of a headmaster justifying a child's poor exam results; kindly meant but not a comfort, not in the cold light of day.'

'But the neurologist did a brain scan and that will be emphatic, right? Those results will tell them what you need to know.'

'More than we want to know. Then we'll have to think about managing Margaret's care.'

'Can't Ray cope?'

'In the short term, with our help. But after that? In the long term? Ray won't be able to feed her, dress her, take her to the loo. God, it's too terrible to think about. We've been told to expect this sort of deterioration but I can't imagine it. I can't believe it.'

'How's Mark?'

'Oh, you know.'

'Worried about Margaret.'

'Of course. And furious with her and disappointed in her and lost without her. He's vulnerable.'

'Will he look for his real mother?' asked Sara with a bluntness that Eloise admired but at the same time shied away from.

'Margaret *is* his real mother.'

'You know what I mean.'

'Oh God, Sara, we haven't thought that far ahead. There's so much going on. It's overwhelming. Totally overwhelming. So I'm sure you can see why I can't possibly – I mean – I'm sorry, but—'

'I get it. You can't be a surrogate. Let's drop it, eh,' said Sara curtly.

25

'How's it going?' Eloise placed a mug of sweet, strong tea on the only surface that she could find – the floor. Charlie was lying on his back fiddling with something under the whirlpool spa bath that was yet to be plumbed in. The room smelt of wood shavings and his aftershave, which was the same as Mark's, and whilst this was pleasant Eloise wished the room smelt of sweat and toil. 'How's it going?' was client code for 'Will this be ready for Christmas?' Eloise had been using the same code for a couple of weeks now; today the longing was tinged with something a little more abrupt and resentful. Glancing around the bathroom, she could answer her own question; you didn't need to be a trained plumber to know that there wasn't a hope in hell of this room being finished by Christmas. Least not this Christmas.

It had taken ten weeks to get this far. To date, Charlie had pulled out the ugly brown suite, pulled up the hideous, cheap lino and chiselled away at the wall tiles (which, when loosened, had brought down half of the partition wall, which then had to be fixed). He did these tasks well. He worked with care and precision, he didn't mark Eloise's hall walls as he carried debris out of the house, and none of the children had punctured their feet with discarded rusty nails. So far so good. Charlie had made the room square again. He'd re-plastered the wall so Eloise was now staring at what looked like the inside of a grocery box, beige and flat, but that wasn't the look she'd been going for. Eloise *really* wanted the bathrooms finished. She knew they should be the least of her concerns but living with the chaos of unplumbed bathroom suites littering the house couldn't be overestimated. Ray and the mums from school kept making jokes about some people favouring the industrial look as an interior design choice but Eloise was pretty sure that the industrial look wasn't supposed to mean piles of tiles stacked precariously in towers in the bedrooms and bags of cement blocking the hall entrance.

She'd imagined the ultimate designer bathroom. Obscene luxury where she would literally feel her cares float away. A modern, white suite, with clean lines and no fuss. Eloise was adamant that a stylish home could be defined by the presence of white sheets and towels, white loo roll and white bathroom suites; anything else was tacky. Her mother had taught her that colours were for walls and children's clothes. She'd chosen dark purple mosaic tiles for the surrounds and large, grey slate tiles for the floors. She had clusters of candles on stand-by and the brand-new fluffy towels, with as much bounce as a trampoline, were patiently hibernating in the airing cupboard, just waiting for their moment. When Eloise looked at the far-from-finished bathroom she tried not to despair and scream, 'When oh when!' Instead, she tried to see it as a blank canvas, a place where transformation was imminent. Eloise told herself that it was progress that the bath was now upstairs and awaiting plumbing. For the past four weeks it had been stored in the sitting room.

'Yeah, we'll be done for Christmas,' said Charlie, with a confident grin, as he wiggled into a sitting position. Eloise wondered if he was lying to her or just to himself. He reached for his cuppa. 'Any biscuits?'

As Eloise ran downstairs, rummaged through the kitchen cabinets, retrieved a bag of Hobnobs and then scampered back to rejoin Charlie in the bathroom, she cursed her reflex to be eternally polite, the world's best hostess. Mark had pointed out that the constant tea breaks were counterproductive, considering Eloise ended most of her days lying in bed hiss-whispering, 'Just when *do* you think he'll be finished?'

Charlie had said that the gutting and reconstruction of the family bathroom would take six to eight weeks, as long as Eloise was single-minded in deciding which tiles and suites she wanted and as long as cash flow wasn't a problem. He went on (at some length) about indecisive clients of his who had more money than sense and had often caused delays in the work because they'd changed their minds about fixtures and fittings several times over. He also pointed out that he'd had a number of clients who, when it came to stumping up cash, said their bank accounts needed thirty days' notice. He'd named and shamed these people he grumbled about, some of whom Eloise knew well, as they were mums at the girls' old school. They were contacts Charlie had made at her dining table. He retold the stories with such derision that Eloise had been determined that she would be decisive and solvent, the best sort of client. Eloise and Mark had paid Charlie several thousand pounds up-front and Eloise had ordered the tiles and suites the day he'd agreed to the job. No one had to point it out – she knew she was a people pleaser.

Yet there'd been delays.

Initially it had been agreed that Charlie would revamp the family bathroom, the *en suite*, the kitchen and the tiny downstairs cloakroom. He'd started with the family bathroom because that had the highest traffic, and he hadn't got beyond there. At this rate Charlie might still be living with the Hamiltons when Emily graduated. The thing that had been bothering Eloise was that even though Charlie did live with them, he still somehow managed not to start work at 8 a.m., as agreed. Practically every day he took advantage of the time she spent walking the younger two girls to school to slip out of the house and vanish. He'd arrive back any time between ten and noon and deliver some complicated explanation as to his whereabouts, often to do with the mysterious black hole that was the builders' yard. Apparently, in builders' yards, time deformed and followed the rules of another dimension. Five minutes became two hours.

Last night, while lying in bed, Mark had suggested that Charlie was stringing out this job for as long as possible because he didn't want to go home to Sara.

'That's a terrible thing to say,' gasped Eloise.

'Maybe, but that doesn't make it untrue.'

The thought terrified Eloise. 'I don't want to adopt a fully grown man and I couldn't bear sharing the *en suite* with the girls indefinitely. Besides, Sara *needs* Charlie at home,' she pointed out.

'No doubt. Ironic, since you invited him to do the work because you believed Sara needed Charlie to be away from home.' Mark had yawned and added, 'You shouldn't get involved in other people's marriages. It's not like we haven't got enough on our plates.' The sting of the words was not abated by the fact that he'd pecked his wife on the cheek before he'd turned out the bedside light.

Eloise didn't want to be involved in their marriage, she wanted to take a bath, and she believed that one might lead to the other. Maybe Mark's theory that Charlie didn't want to go home to Sara was horribly accurate. After all, whilst Eloise did not sign up to the 1950s good wife brigade (she didn't believe Sara ought to greet Charlie with a pair of warmed slippers and an inch of whisky on the rocks whenever he came home), she did think Sara needed to welcome him to *some* extent. Independently, Charlie and Sara had confided in Eloise that the welcome Charlie was most likely to receive when returning home at weekends was Sara throwing his slippers or drink at him. Charlie had communicated as much through hints and sardonic jokes; Sara had given Eloise a word-for-word account of every squabble. Their rows had reached a new intensity since Charlie had refused to try another round of IVF.

Truthfully, Eloise was desperate to regain control of the situation but she was floundering. She was aware that Mark probably thought she was petty to be concerned with the bathroom décor right now, considering everything else, but Eloise was focusing on the bathroom project because it *should* be manageable. It *should* be within her control and nothing else was anywhere near manageable. Eloise felt like a spinning top. It was all she could do to think five minutes into the future. For the first time in her life planning and plotting and preparing seemed not only redundant but taunting. Who could have prepared for the events of the last few months?

There'd been too much to deal with. Moving home, Sara's ongoing and failing attempts at IVF treatment, Mark's furious reaction to finding out that he was adopted and that his parents had kept it from him all these years, Margaret's terrible diagnosis, not to mention all the necessary preparations for Christmas. The children were rehearsing for their nativity plays and needed to be run to and from school, there was the extra Christmas shopping and cooking, she had to write cards, wrap gifts, hang tinsel . . . the list seemed endless. She knew it was wrong but Eloise had quietly sighed with relief when her parents had said they'd like to stay in Portugal this Christmas. Two less people to worry about. Eloise had so wanted the girls' first Christmas in Dartmouth to be perfect. Now, she'd lowered her expectations. Now, her hope was that they'd avoid actual bloodshed.

Yes, there was so much going on. Except in her bathrooms. They were a place of calm and serenity. Some might say inertia.

To date, Eloise had been as sympathetic as she could be with regard to Charlie's delaying tactics. She was prepared to walk a tightrope between her two friends as they struggled to recover peace in their marriage. She was aware that her home was being used as a haven. Or maybe not exactly a haven – not considering the number of cold, impenetrable silences that had littered the stairway and sitting room of late – but at least if not a haven, then a hide-out. However, some of the mystery as to why progress in the bathrooms had been so slow had been revealed today and Eloise's patience was being tested to the limit.

Eloise had seen Erin and Poppy safely into their classrooms, and was planning on heading straight to Margaret and Ray's house to see if there was anything they needed from the shops, when she'd paused – just for a moment – to pat the school goat. She'd started chatting to Bernadette Walton, Becky and Tim's mother, and, despite her best intentions, Eloise couldn't resist a bit of a grumble about the fact that she feared her plumber might never leave, although she'd been careful not to mention him by name.

'Oh, goodness, don't I know what you mean!' said Bernadette.

'I've had months of the same with Billy Warrell. I was tearing my hair out but then last month I found a new guy. He's been a marvel. Didn't need much from him. A new basin in the downstairs loo and a bit of tiling, but he turns up every morning, does a good couple of hours of work for me, then cleans up and clears out because, as you probably know, I do a bit of child minding and it's not easy to have a plumber in the house once the little ones arrive. Too many potential hazards. But this chap is so flexible and reliable. I can't recommend him highly enough. I can give you his number if you like.'

'Oh no, honestly. I couldn't sack my guy,' Eloise said. She really couldn't, even if she wanted to.

'Think about it. He's almost finished up at mine now, there wasn't much to it.' Bernadette paused and looked momentarily concerned. 'Although I understand he's pricing up Lucinda Pickering's kitchen now. I think that will be a big job, but maybe he could fit you in around that.'

'No, honestly I—'

'I'll text you his number.' Bernadette wouldn't take no for an answer and within a moment she'd pulled out her phone and composed a text to Eloise at a speed that a fourteen year old would be proud of. An instant later Eloise's phone buzzed in her pocket. Out of courtesy, she'd checked the message.

She could not believe it.

'Is your plumber called Charlie?' she asked, incredulous.

'Yes.' Bernadette beamed. 'Do you know him? I bet you do. He's quite dishy.' Bernadette smiled and then set off down the lane. She threw a cheery wave over her shoulder and yelled, 'Call him.'

Eloise was left with two thoughts tumbling around her head. One, how remarkable it was that people still said 'dishy' nowadays, and two, would it be an overreaction to punch Charlie out cold? Eloise had steamed all the way home.

No one liked being taken advantage of. Eloise was good natured. She gave people the benefit of the doubt. She tried to be decent. Decent mattered to her. Kind was a bonus. She strived for kind but if she fell short and just landed at decent, then she was OK with that. If Eloise was on your team, there was nothing, nothing at all, she wouldn't do for you.

Charlie was married to Eloise's good friend, they'd known each other for five years, he was her husband's great pal; just one of those factors alone would have meant that Eloise was on Charlie's team. All three meant that she was prepared to go in goal, wave a couple of pompoms for him, and even dress up as the mascot! Hadn't she just offered to carry a baby for them, for God's sake? The very least she'd expect in return was a bit of commitment to her bathroom plumbing. Was it too much to ask?

Loyalty.

Loyalty was intricately woven into the fabric of decency. The weft to the weave. Loyalty was the backbone of every army and the mechanism of every school playground. Loyalty was important. Sometimes it was even more important than reason or logic. Loyalty, of sorts, was the thing that guaranteed grumpy old aunts weren't ignored at Christmas but invited into homes where they might just be a bit less grumpy. Loyalty was what allowed saggy, familiar bottoms to win over pert ones (which they often did but fidelity didn't get the publicity infidelity did). Loyalty was all.

There was no question, it was disloyal of Charlie to be retiling Bernadette Walton's downstairs loo when he was supposed to be re-vamping Eloise's bathroom!

Eloise considered a way into the conversation as she sat on the floor, next to Charlie, back up against the unplumbed bath. She didn't want to tower over him, nailing home the point that she was the client, the boss, and he worked for her; she wanted to be sensitive. Side by side they had the same view. A view of the porcelain loo, incongruously standing in the hall, waiting to be plumbed in, sparkling, free from its box. It was an oddly intimate view.

'Charlie, at the school gate today I got talking to one of the mums and I heard something that, frankly, I'm concerned about.'

Charlie took a long slurp of his tea; his green eyes twinkled over the top of the mug. He hazarded a guess. 'Competitive stuff? You don't need to get worked up about that crap. Erin and Poppy are bright girls and very popular, from what I can tell,' he said firmly.

Eloise momentarily basked in the compliment, losing focus. She had to visibly shake herself and remember what it was she needed to discuss with him. 'No, it was nothing to do with the girls, something altogether different. Bernadette Walton told me you've been doing some work for her.'

'Has she got a problem with it?' He looked agitated, ready to leap up, grab his tool kit and dash out of the bathroom. Everything about him suggested white knight on a steed rescuing a damsel. Somehow his demeanour reminded Eloise of the very first time she'd met him in her Muswell Hill kitchen, when he'd come to their rescue by fixing their boiler.

'No, *she* doesn't have a problem with it,' Eloise said, placing a restraining hand on his arm. 'I do.'

Charlie turned to Eloise, confusion flooding out of his eyes. 'Why?'

'Because you are supposed to be working for me,' she said flatly.

'Jealous?'

'Stop being daft. Charlie, you can't be in two places at once and you are supposed to be doing my bathrooms.'

'I am.'

'Well, yes, but . . .' Eloise faltered. How could she say he wasn't working hard and fast enough without causing offence? 'Every hour you spend on her cloakroom is an hour less on my bathrooms.'

'We never agreed exact hours.'

'No, but you know I'm in a hurry.'

'We never said this work had to be exclusive.'

'But it's a big job. I thought it was understood—'

'We don't actually have a contract.'

Charlie held eye contact throughout the exchange. His twinkling green eyes, which Eloise thought she knew as well as her own brother's, had a flinty edge to them that she'd noticed before. There was no contract because they were *friends*. Eloise thought about what Charlie was saying for a moment and in that moment the hardness she thought she saw in his eyes vanished and she was left thinking she'd imagined it, especially when it was replaced by eyes that were clearly begging for understanding.

'The thing is, Eloise, the extra cash came in useful. The cost of the IVF is crippling.'

Eloise felt embarrassed. 'Of course.'

'We're in, well, a bit of trouble.'

'Financially?'

He lowered his head and nodded.

'But we paid you in advance,' Eloise pointed out gently.

'I already owed most of what you paid me. All of it, actually, and a bit more. There's none left. I had to take Bernadette's work to earn some cash to buy materials for yours.'

'Oh.' Eloise had no idea what to say. Charlie and Sara lived well. They lived the way Eloise and Mark did. A life full of occasions and treats. She'd had no idea they were stretched. 'I see.' She didn't, but what else could she say? She patted his arm, offering the sort of comfort she might offer a baby that was fretful for a nap.

'Sara doesn't know the extent of our problem. Not exactly. I don't want to worry her. Financial pressure is the last thing she needs but we're getting towards Christmas.'

Eloise weighed up the situation. Charlie didn't seem to think he'd done anything wrong by working on Bernadette's cloakroom or by pricing up Lucinda's kitchen. Maybe he hadn't. Perhaps she hadn't been clear about her terms and needs. She had so much going on right now that she wasn't sure she was doing anything very well at all. It was probably all down to her poor communication. The irritation and sense of betrayal that had churned inside her as she'd walked home from school began to abate.

'OK, I see. Well, no biggie but, to be clear, moving forward, I'd really prefer it if you only worked for us.' Eloise couldn't bring herself to say 'you must' or even 'if you only worked for *me*'. It sounded too imperial. She was hampered by the English middle-class impulse to be overly polite. 'At least until this first bathroom is done. I mean, if there's a problem with cash flow, then we could . . .' Eloise trailed off. She wasn't sure what she could do. She didn't feel comfortable offering more money on top of the amount they'd already paid since he hadn't spent that on the materials for their job. Eloise stared into Charlie's eyes trying to decipher what he was thinking.

'I get it, you want me exclusively,' he said.

'Yes.'

'You don't want me working for anyone else.'

'Well, no, there's a time issue.' Eloise held his gaze, hoping he'd understand her point.

'You want me to yourself.'

Eloise didn't see it coming. She really didn't. Suddenly, Charlie's lips were on hers, he firmly and expertly put his hand on her head and pulled her to him. She'd be lying if she didn't admit it was a good kiss; firm, confident, practised, yet, despite that, it was the worst kiss of her life. She pushed him away with more violence than was strictly necessary.

'What the fu—'

Eloise scrambled to her feet and leapt to the open doorway. She turned back to Charlie, almost as though she needed to check what had actually happened. She watched him slowly stand up, saunter towards her and smile. It was an arrogant smile. Almost a leer.

'Don't worry, I won't tell Mark or Sara. It can be our secret.' He stretched out a hand and put it on the side of her ribs. His thumb nestled against the slight curve of her breast. She was paralysed with shock. He was . . . he was . . . he was touching her up! She jumped backwards, banging her foot against his tool box and nearly tripping over. 'Steady, you don't want an accident,' he added.

'Why did you do that?'

'Because you wanted me to.'

'No, no, I didn't.'

'Yes, you did. You know we'd be good together. I've seen you watching me. For a long time now, Eloise. A long time. Isn't that why you invited me to do this job? What are you waiting for?'

She didn't answer him. Instead, she ran out of the room, down the stairs and out of the front door, without even stopping to pick up her bag. She needed air.

26

Christmas was such a lovely time of year, thought Margaret. Dartmouth looked at its best in the winter. No noisy, dishevelled tourists dropping litter or wearing garish, floral cagoules to interrupt its majestic beauty. On a good day, Dartmouth glistened. Truly, it did. There were the silver-cobbled streets that sparkled whenever the stones were wet and there was the weak morning sun, low but determined in the December sky, reflecting light all the way across the frosty fields, gleaming as far as the eye could see, and there were the shiny boats bobbing and mooching in the – the – the home thing.

Margaret's stomach started to churn and she felt sweat creep on her neck. What was that word? Damn it. Where had that word gone? The word for the home of boats, near the edge of land, still in the sea. Blast it. It annoyed her! Upset her! She told herself the word would come to her. Eventually. Although it might not. Less of the words were coming to her nowadays. They stayed away. Lost in a blackness. In the cloud. She must not let it distress her. What was she thinking about before? Oh yes, the weather.

There was sometimes snow in Dartmouth. Not lots of it, like in Scotland and the north, not enough to be inconvenient or destructive. Margaret had always thought northern snow was like women in the north; powerful and dramatic but a bit of a handful. And southern snow was like southern-county women; pretty and manageable, never too much trouble. Margaret had been born in north

Yorkshire but lived in Dartmouth and was no longer sure what sort of woman she was.

Of course there were wet days, when the rain simply relentlessly poured, running down the hills in muddy, land-based trajectories. Days when the sea and the sky both looked bruised and angry. But even so, Margaret loved Christmas time.

Ray and Margaret always bought their tree from the tree farm in Capton, always had. Ray would strap it to the top of the car and they'd drive carefully home along the windy, wiggly roads that were flanked by mud mounds and bare, prickly bushes. Once home, they'd build a fire and enjoy a glass of champagne as they dressed the tree. Margaret liked to play the old soundtracks; it was law that Bing Crosby had to be dreaming of a white Christmas as she pulled out the box of decorations from the back of the wardrobe and began to decorate.

Normally, this ritual was her very favourite of all the possible Christmas-time rituals. She'd feel a bubble of excitement erupt in her stomach every time she unwrapped an ornament, carefully releasing it from its cradle of tissue. Most people of their generation dressed their tree with large tartan bows, red and gold tinsel and lots of those little wooden ornaments; tasteful, uniform. Not Margaret and Ray. Margaret had bought two enormous silver baubles on their honeymoon and she'd collected special trinkets every year since. One each. First, there were two a year, then finally – thankfully – three. The hand-picked ornaments were imbued with meaning and personality. They were treasured. A glass cat, Santa on a scooter, a hand-knitted heart. An ornament each, year after year, they'd built up the tree's wardrobe and when Eloise had come along, Margaret had started to buy one for her too, and then the girls. They needed a big tree now and still it was packed full. Brimming with small tokens of care and thoughtfulness.

Habitually, as Margaret un-swaddled each cherished toy, she'd say to Ray, 'We bought this one in Bath, Ray. When Mark was eight', or 'Remember this one! We bought it in Canada, and stowed it away until Christmas, now that was a trip!' Ray would smile politely, pretending to take an interest but not seeing anything other than a slightly tatty toy for the tree. To Margaret, the ornaments were like old diaries or photo albums; potent, splendid and proof that they'd lived, made memories and had fun.

But not this year.

This year Ray and Margaret had bought the tree as usual; in fact, it was nicer than usual because Emily, Erin and Poppy had gone along to the tree farm too. They'd ran around in the rain, gulping in the smell of spruce. Ray had splashed out and gone for a six-footer; whether this was to abate their excitement or to prolong it, it wasn't clear. When they'd returned home, they'd lit the fire, put on the music, popped the champers and then they'd all turned to Margaret; excitement gleaming in the girls' eyes, expectancy waiting, more patiently, in Ray's face.

And, suddenly, she could not remember what it was they were waiting for.

She offered cake and poured glasses of milk, but she could see that they were not satisfied. Their excitement turned to frustration as the moments ticked by. Margaret could feel the spiky impatience in the room, needling her, but she didn't know what they wanted from her. She began to feel upset as she remembered that people were often bothered or irritated by her nowadays, she was never certain what it was she'd done to discourage or annoy. Margaret stared at her granddaughters, wanting to please them, but not sure how to. After a while Ray had gone out of the room and then returned huffing and puffing, carrying a huge box. It was full of tree ornaments, tinsel and sparkling lights. The girls pounced on the box, like a litter of playful kittens, scrabbling to pick up one bauble after another, unwrapping them, holding them to the light, lavishing praise and whoops of pleasure on them, which Margaret realised meant that the other people in the room remembered the trinkets and valued them in some way. A way that was no longer available to her. She didn't recognise any of them. All she saw was a haphazard box of dated junk.

'We should throw this lot out and buy fresh,' Margaret said firmly.

Four heads turned to her like startled synchronised swimmers. Their faces displayed a range of not especially festive emotions, from shock to outrage. 'No way! We love your tree, Granny,' declared Erin. 'It's the nicest, funnest tree ever. Anyway, this one is mine. So you can't throw it out. You made it for me last year, look.'

Erin held out a four-inch handmade ragdoll for Margaret to inspect. The doll had clearly been modelled on the girl as it boasted raggedy, long hair, jeans covering coltish legs and a pink roll-neck jumper, pink being Erin's favourite colour last year. This year she preferred purple. The only indication that this was a Christmas decoration was the fact that the doll wore a tiny elf-size Santa hat and was carrying a knitted gift. It was well made. Margaret recognised the stitching as her own; she had every reason to believe that she had made the doll but no memory of doing so. Margaret could remember Erin's favourite colour but not this box of ornaments, it didn't make sense.

Margaret tried to concentrate. She wanted to fight the black hole. Close it up, not sink into it. She'd slowly unwrapped a golden robin with a red glitter breast and a glass mince pie hung on a red string. Nothing stirred. Nothing. She felt Ray's eyes on her. The worst of this whole business was that she knew there was something wrong. They'd told her; Ray and the doctors and Mark and Eloise had told her that she was ill. Sometimes she didn't believe them. She felt fine. She was sure of things.

And sometimes she thought they were right. She was ill. Very, very sick.

Margaret sat in blackness. It felt like someone was gagging her and someone else had pulled a hood over her eyes as well; she was left with nothing but brutal pitch-darkness. Black holes were scattered through her head and now, also, her heart. Because it was in her head that she stored it all and it was in her heart that she was able to cherish it further. In her heart she gave facts depth and meaning, gave memories weight and order and sorted experiences into the good and the bad and the ugly. If Margaret could have remembered the baubles when they wanted her to she would've known for sure that she'd often anticipated, then celebrated, Christmas in the past. Without the memories, she wasn't so sure. Had Christmas ever happened for her? Ray watched as she unwrapped a glittery, purple Cinderella-type slipper, about two inches long, not very Christmassy, but certainly glam.

'That was the first one you bought Eloise,' he said gruffly. Margaret looked at the sparkling ornament and fought ferociously, prayed desperately, for something to flicker, to trigger. Nothing. Emptiness, bleached blanks. The gaps pounded through her head, taunting her for lacking. Lacking.

'Bugger!' she'd yelled as she flung the trinket at the wall. It smashed, satisfyingly, and small shards splattered across the sitting room. The girls had looked surprised rather than afraid. 'We should throw this lot out, and get some more!' she'd said angrily. Better to be cross than tearful.

The hardest thing was that now, today, it was all clear. Margaret remembered it all. She could remember the ornaments charged with history and love and she could remember forgetting them and dumping them in the bin, an action fuelled by spiteful self-doubt, confusion and self-loathing. They'd since bought some tartan bows and wooden ornaments; the new ornaments taunted Margaret with their uniform cheerfulness. But then again, soon she'd forget them, too. Most likely.

Margaret and Ray had eaten mince pies at the pub as usual, washed down with mulled cider. It had been a lovely evening although Margaret hadn't been able to remember anyone's names, but she thought there was no point in grumbling, no point in drawing attention. She'd sat by the fire, it was electric now, not a real one. She didn't know when they'd changed it. They went to church for the Christmas concert on the nineteenth, it was beautiful, she said some prayers. She wondered if He was listening. She didn't know. In fact, she only knew they'd gone to church because it was in the book.

There were three of them now in their marriage: Margaret, Ray and the book. Margaret knew she was making a joke when she used that line. Someone else had once said something like it. It was a great scandal, they were very famous. Possibly Margaret Thatcher? She was not sure.

Ray had bought the book. It was a large blue thing with lines and he wrote down their life in the book. He asked Margaret to write down things too. She did so, when she remembered. It wasn't a diary. It was a series of lists. The first list was the list of people they'd bought presents for this Christmas and what they'd bought them exactly. Margaret had always kept this sort of list so that she could avoid making the mistake of buying anyone a similar gift two years in a row and so she always bought the right sort of Brazil nuts for the vicar, he liked a particular brand. She thought most people probably had a Christmas gift list. It was not odd. It was not diseased. Then, customarily, Margaret would hide the gifts around the house, because the girls (and even Ray) were not above mooching round in the hope of discovering what they might get. She'd bring them out on Christmas Eve and wrap them as she sat in front of the fire, taking care to add big fat, exuberant ribbons. This year, Margaret had started to buy presents, as usual. She'd spotted a beautiful stationery set for Erin, covered in pictures of kittens drawn in that Manga style. Just Erin's thing! When she'd shown her purchase to Ray, he'd looked horrified.

'Don't you think she'll like it? I think it's perfect,' Margaret had insisted.

He went to the sideboard and slowly, reluctantly, pulled out two identical sets of stationery that she'd already purchased that week. So Ray had accompanied Margaret Christmas shopping this year, and he wrote the list, and wrapped the gifts and labelled them immediately; they didn't hide them in the house, couldn't risk not finding them on Christmas Eve when they needed to. They had enough on.

Ray had taken to constantly carrying around the big, blue book that held their life. Besides the gift list there were lists about who had called on the telephone and who had popped by the house. He wrote down what Margaret had eaten for breakfast, lunch and tea in case she forgot. He wrote down when she bathed and what she'd done with the morning for the same reason; did she dust, wash her hair, visit the opticians? Margaret didn't mind, not really. At first she thought he was playing silly buggers and it was unnecessary, intrusive, but now she'd come to see that it was a help, the book. Before the book she'd done daft things like eat six eggs in a day because she fancied an egg so she'd made two boiled ones for breakfast and two poached for lunch, then two boiled ones again at tea time. She'd been very gassy that day. Ray had been out fishing with Mark. Margaret thought it was Mark or maybe it was Frank, her brother. Ray and Frank had become very close recently.

The book said they'd bought, written, addressed and posted Christmas cards, although Ray was circumspect about how many reached the correct people. Margaret got muddled with the names of some of the recipients. Was Mary's husband called Harry or Henry? And was Wendy's son called Fred, or was that the dog? Margaret told herself it didn't matter; people would think she'd been on the sherry.

Margaret looked at the little girl sitting next to her trying to knit with needles almost the size of her body. Pretty little thing but she couldn't quite place her. Maybe she was Ray's secretary's daughter. Margaret didn't mind doing a bit of babysitting to help out. This child was no trouble at all.

'I do a lovely Christmas lunch even if I say so myself,' she told Poppy.

Poppy nodded but didn't look up from her knitting; it wasn't an easy skill to master and she had no room for chitchat with her granny, she had to focus.

'Most people lack imagination when it comes to Christmas food, too hampered by tradition to think of producing something people actually want to eat, but I like to surprise every year. Last year we started with English onion soup made with sage and cheddar. Soup gets a bad press, always associated with invalids, but it can be delicious. Do you like soup?' Poppy nodded and Margaret carried on. 'Onions meant we had a sorbet course, next. My son, he's about your age, skipped the starter and moved straight to the palate cleaner. Throughout January he told everyone who would listen to him that he'd had ice cream for a starter on Christmas Day.' Margaret chuckled to herself at the memory.

Poppy wished her grandad was paying more attention and that he'd interrupt, she hated it when her granny went on like this.

'I do like turkey, but people get a bit sick of it by the time they reach the twenty-fifth. So many opportunities to eat it before then. It's often on the menu in restaurants in December and Ray often has it at the office do. I always try to do something different for Ray and Mark, my mother and stepfather. My mum and Edgar have come to us every year since we married and whilst they aren't lavish with their praise, they always hand back empty plates and what bigger compliment is there?'

Poppy shrugged.

'So, I was thinking of pheasant this year, Ray. What do you think? And maybe pork, too, with crackling and roast apples, seasoned carefully. People sometimes over-do it with the thyme and parsley.'

Ray lowered his paper and stared at Margaret. He always took his time when he answered her nowadays. He often had to climb over his impatience and suppress his disappointment until he could find a suitable response.

'I thought we talked about Christmas lunch.'

Had they? Well, yes, Margaret imagined they had talked about Christmas lunch, but she wasn't aware that they'd decided on anything. Or if they had, what it was, exactly. She looked at the blue book lying on the dining-room table, and considered reaching for it. She should have checked it before she'd said anything to Ray. Had they agreed a menu? Margaret tried to bluff it out. 'I saw a recipe. Something in one of the lovely free magazines that you get with the papers on a Sunday. They suggested rum and raisin sauce rather than gravy. And sprouts, of course, but with almonds to make them a bit special and carrots baked in citrus juice, a twist on the traditional.'

'We're eating at Mark and Eloise's. We've talked about this.'

Oh. Right. Margaret felt the blackness and the humiliation swell up all around her again. She might drown in it. Mark had a place of his own? Where? When did he leave home? She wanted to ask Ray but she sensed it would bother him. She was supposed to know. She laid her head on the sofa back and closed her eyes so that the tears couldn't eke down her face. Margaret thought that people shouldn't cry at Christmas, it spoilt it for everyone.

27

When Sara arrived at Eloise's on Christmas Eve, she was greeted with the smell of mince pies and mulled wine. Eloise was especially attentive; she threw around hugs and compliments with the same extravagance as she'd thrown around the glitter and tinsel. Eloise's home looked like a movie set version of how a house should look at Christmas; every room was drowning in garlands of holly and ivy which Eloise had picked and threaded herself. That said, the abundance and lavishness was exactly the right side of tasteful and the Christmas decorations were all white or silver which provided a stylish contrast to the fresh greenery. Sara was torn between admiring Eloise enormously and really being quite fed up of the perfection. She thought Eloise was even keener to impress than usual; a little more on edge than usual. Sara supposed she was bound to be stressed by the Christmas preparations as she was hosting lunch, but she couldn't bring herself to feel especially sympathetic – after all, wasn't this Eloise's dream? Everyone's dream? Hosting a huge family lunch on Christmas Day. There was no real reason for Eloise to get uptight. She'd offered to host.

Well, as good as.

Sara had to admit, at least to herself, that Eloise hadn't actually invited her and Charlie to lunch. The two families usually spent Boxing Day together, but not Christmas Day; however, Sara pointed out that things had been different when they'd lived around the corner from one another. Now the Hamiltons had moved miles away Sara couldn't really be expected to make the long journey to Dartmouth just for one day, and as Charlie was already there, it just made sense for her to join them for the entire holiday weekend. Eloise hadn't agreed to Sara's offer quite as enthusiastically as Sara had expected. Normally, Eloise was too polite to so much as hint at her own desires if they in any way conflicted with those of a stranger she bumped into on a street, let alone a friend. So Sara was surprised when Eloise said carefully, 'You know we'd understand if you wanted to spend Christmas alone together. I mean, you don't see much of each other at the moment and there won't be much privacy at ours. You mustn't feel you have to come. We'd understand.'

Sara and Charlie had no need for privacy at the moment. Since Charlie had vetoed the possibility of continuing with IVF Sara hadn't had the desire to share a pizza with him, let alone share a bed. Going to bed ought to be the easiest part; wasn't that, after all, what it was all about? But sex with Charlie seemed so dishonest at the moment. She certainly didn't want to be alone with him for four long days. Just the two of them rattling around their home, she couldn't think of anything more depressing. What would the point of that be, if they weren't trying for a baby?

'But we always spend Boxing Day at yours,' Sara had argued.

'Yes, I know, but I'm just saying we wouldn't be offended if you don't want to this year.'

'Of course we want to, Eloise.'

'Oh.'

'That's settled, then.'

'I guess.'

Sara had heard the reluctance in Eloise's voice, but wasn't prepared to acknowledge it, let alone examine it. Sara needed to be in Dartmouth, around Eloise, Mark and the girls, she *needed* it. Sometimes she thought being with them was the only thing that kept her sane, certainly the only thing that made her happy. When she was with the girls she remembered why she put herself through the years of treatments and disappointments; with them she could clearly imagine what it might be like for her one day. It was complex, though, because whilst being with Eloise's family gave Sara hope and pleasure, it sometimes felt like someone was pounding her with nasty, sharp stones. She pushed these emotions to the very depth of her being because few people were big enough to admit to jealousy. Jealousy was so base and pointless and dark.

Anyway, there was something else now that gave her hope and pleasure. Someone else. Sara had a plan, a direction, a resource, and that was something. The idea came to her not long after Eloise had offered to be a surrogate. Sara thought it was her only answer, the only way. She hadn't had the time or opportunity to talk to Eloise about her plan yet. It was not something she could comfortably spill over the phone. She thought it would be easier to explain in person but now she was here, in amongst all this tinsel and goodwill, she wasn't so sure it would be. She wasn't certain whether Eloise would understand. Maybe she would, maybe she wouldn't. She had a different perspective. Their paths might appear to be running alongside one another but Sara was lurching up and down brutal terrain, she had to overcome sheer hurdles and avoid falling into snake pits; Eloise was strolling through a sunlit forest, a forest that was overflowing with pots of gold, unicorns, fairies and fluffy animals.

Ultimately, as harsh as it sounded, Sara had decided that she didn't really care if she had to sacrifice her friend's approval or confidence over this matter, not if it came to the wire. It would be regrettable to have a secret from Eloise but worth it. Sara had a plan and that was all that counted. At last, for the first time in months and months, years, actually, she was going to be in control. *She* was. Not a doctor, or Charlie's hapless sperm or God. Sara. The relief was enormous. So enormous that joy was beginning to sneak back into her life. Not in abundance, but there was a crack of light coming through the heavy dark curtains; a glimmer of hope. Her plan had given her a new whiff of possibility and a definite sense of control; she wasn't sure if she could risk exposing these tentative buds to Eloise's scrutiny.

It wouldn't be easy to achieve but then anything worth having demanded a certain amount of effort. Whatever it took. She'd always said as much. Sara wasn't rushing into this, she wasn't mad, she realised that she needed to think about it all very, very carefully. Being in Dartmouth over Christmas would give her time to do just that before she made her final move. Because once it was done, it was done. Irreversible.

Last year Sara had missed all the parties at work because she'd been in the middle of a round of IVF. Drinking until she couldn't walk home, let alone remember the way home, was out of the question but this year that alternative had seemed very appealing. Sara had made up for her previous abstemious behaviour and it had been like the old days. She'd been quite the party animal.

Or rather, she and Jeremy had been quite the party animals together, to be accurate.

They'd shared four long, boozy client lunches that had lingered on into the afternoon. On the third and fourth the clients had left before they had. Jeremy had insisted that instead of shuffling back to the office, to do a bad impression of being sober enough to work, they were better off staying put. At first all they'd talked about was their clients and the lunch that they'd just enjoyed. Then they'd talked about their plans for the Christmas hols, the new exhibition on at the Portrait Gallery and the latest movies showing in the cinema but soon the professional boundaries dissolved at the bottom of a wine glass and they'd started to light-heartedly speculate on which client was looking for love, who was crushing on whom at the office, who was bored at home and not getting enough. They hadn't talked about his wife and they hadn't talked about Charlie, at least not until Sara had glanced out of the restaurant window into the pitch-black, late afternoon. It was raining, but the seasonally dressed shop windows twinkled, suggesting to Sara that maybe the party could go on.

'I probably should be going,' she'd announced in a way that clearly communicated her reluctance.

'Hubby waiting for you?' asked Jeremy.

'No, actually. He's working away.' Sara had pulled her gaze to meet his. Her look was at once challenging and inviting. A subtle expression that she was sure wouldn't be lost on him.

'Then what's the rush?'

'I should get back to the office.' It was a token suggestion and they'd both known it.

Jeremy shook his head. 'You'd do more harm than good to your career returning to the office now in this state, you'd probably lose your clients' millions down the back of a filing cabinet or something. Stay, have another,' he'd urged.

'You're the boss,' said Sara, flashing a grateful smile. 'Shall we have liqueurs?'

She'd pronounced it 'lick yours', it was an old joke that they'd shared when they'd dated. He'd say, 'Shall we lick yours?' and she'd reply, 'Yes, let's, and I'm all for coffee.' Pronounced, 'I'm all fuck off-ie'. Even now Sara thought you probably had to be there to think this exchange genuinely funny. It was a moment of impulse that made her throw the old line at him; suddenly she'd wanted to see if he'd remembered any of it. Any of the good times they'd had. She'd drunk a G&T, a glass of champers and the best part of a bottle of red at lunch; he'd matched her glass for glass. She wondered whether he, too, could recall the crazy nights of irresponsibility, their carelessness, their sexiness, the throwaway youth that they'd spent sumptuously. Did he recollect the late nights drinking and dancing in sleazy dives, entire Sundays lost in bed? When they'd dated, their relationship had been as much fun as candyfloss, and the same substance, too. That had been the attraction. They'd been hot, hedonistic, insolent, indolent, wild and wilful. Young. Did he remember any of it or was it all school league tables, organised childcare programmes and anxiety about nutritious school lunches now? Sara wouldn't have blamed him if that was the case, she'd have understood. After all, wasn't that her ultimate aim? But she hadn't wanted it to be so for him, not right at that moment. She needed him to be thinking about something different.

'Yes, let's, and I'm all for coffee,' he'd replied, without skipping a beat.

Sara had lowered her eyes, concentrating on pouring the very last of the wine into his glass, and delighted in the feeling of adrenalin pumping around her gut and chest. Not hurtling. Not bouncing around her body as it did when she peed on a stick and there was the hope that she might be a mum, but adrenalin was notably there. Gathering.

Breathing in deeply, she'd flicked her eyes back towards Jeremy, just to check, and was rewarded with what she'd hoped for. Jeremy had been staring right back at her. His big brown eyes, fuzzy with alcohol and lust. This confirmed what Sara had always known, a wedding ring didn't fence in the lust, it didn't fence out the predators; it was simply a warning for those who were the type to listen to warnings.

'A whisky on the rocks?' he'd asked.

It was the drink she used to indulge in way back when. Way back when she sometimes smoked cigars and drank hard stuff to show the boys she was flint and that they could fuck her without any consequences. Truthfully, she hadn't drunk whisky for years; it fouled her mood and left her with a stinking hangover, but something stopped Sara from admitting as much to Jeremy. She didn't want to draw attention to the symptoms that showed she was waltzing towards middle age; she didn't want to admit defeat.

'If you'll join me.'

Jeremy had signalled for the waiter, who was attentive and returned with a couple of doubles in a blink of the eye. No doubt he could smell a generous tip as drunks and their cash were easily parted. As Sara sipped, she took a moment to study Jeremy. Really study. Of course she saw him in the office, almost every day, but she wanted to appraise him outside the work context. Size up the man in the expensive, luxurious restaurant. What did people see when they saw this man? What did other women see? Jeremy was not in as good a shape as Charlie was. His desk job and extensive, extended executive lunches had led to an inevitable fleshy overhang on his waistband. Other women might notice that, and the fact that his hair was greying, his face was wrinkling, but

Sara remembered when he was hard bodied, young and full of fun, so the spare inch, the greying hair, the lines didn't matter to her. Sara had become aware that Jeremy was staring at her too. He'd already checked out her boobs and arse almost the moment she'd sat down to lunch – he was a man, it was what they did. He was staring at her in a different way. Not with longing or lust alone (although that was there, that was tangible); he was looking at her in a way that somehow communicated that he was depending on the fact that she wouldn't see his pinchable inch around his waistline and his grey sideburns. Sara realised he needed her to see him as he had been when they were an item. Not a tired dad of two but a Jack-the-lad. As she'd taken another sip of her whisky, and it scorched its way down her throat, she'd decided that she could do that. She could see him as he wanted to be seen.

Eloise brought Sara back to the here and now when she asked, 'So is everyone ready to sit down? Lunch is served.' Her tone was slightly harassed. Her high-pitched voice betrayed that she wasn't particularly confident with what she was about to dish up. 'I hope it's all right,' she added. Sara noticed that Eloise's self-effacing stance guaranteed a round of compliments and assurances.

'It will be delicious.'

'I'm looking forward to it.'

Sara added her own reassurance. 'Lunch will be a triumph. Marks and Spencer are so reliable.' She knew it wasn't the nicest of compliments but, really, Eloise was asking for it with all that simpering.

'There's no seating plan, sit where you like,' suggested Mark, as he took a place at the end of the table. His parents sat either side of him, Poppy scrabbled to be seated between Margaret and Erin. Sara found herself between Ray and Emily and Charlie was between Erin and Eloise. The moment they all settled, Eloise jumped up and said, 'Charlie should swap with Margaret.'

Her tone was insistent and cut through the cries to pull crackers and chatter about which of the three girls had eaten the most chocolate orange that morning.

'We're all right where we are,' said Mark. He looked a bit exasperated and Sara wondered whether he ever found Eloise's controlling ways a bit much.

'All the guys together,' Eloise insisted.

'I'm good, thanks,' said Charlie. 'Happy next to you and the beautiful Erin. You girls do look wonderful today.' The girls were all dressed in red; Poppy in a pretty dress with a purple velvet trim, Erin and Emily in jeans and sparkly tops. Sara imagined Eloise had thought through their sartorial elegance.

'But I'd like to sit next to Margaret,' said Eloise. She sounded a bit whiny and desperate; Sara wondered how much champagne she'd drank since they'd got back from church that morning. Sara assumed that Eloise wanted to be close to Margaret in case she got confused but Eloise was making a scene and no one needed that, everyone wanted to get on with carving the turkey. 'Margaret, would you like to sit with me?' Eloise asked.

Margaret looked up from her plate; she was already wearing a paper hat, which had slipped over her right eye. She seemed to be considering the request for a moment. The table fell silent, waiting for her reply and a resolution. Finally she said, 'Who are you, dear?'

Ray and Mark look crestfallen, the girls giggled and Eloise looked almost as lost as Margaret.

'I'll get the cranberry sauce,' she said, with a sigh of defeat.

'I'll help you,' said Charlie and he was up on his feet in an instant.

'No, it's fine, I'm fine,' insisted Eloise.

'You take too much on. You've done all the cooking already. Let me help you carry it in from the kitchen at the very least,' he added, laying a solicitous hand on her arm. Eloise pulled away suddenly and her jerky movement knocked over Emily's glass of coke. For a moment everyone stared at the coke spreading across the pristine white cloth and several napkins. Sara thought there was a real danger Eloise might cry. She could only imagine what effort Eloise had put into laying the table. 'I'll get something to mop that up,' said Charlie. He dashed past Eloise, giving her shoulder a quick, comforting squeeze.

Eloise shrugged and accepted his offer with ungraceful reluctance.

Sara wasn't Charlie's biggest fan at the moment but even she thought Eloise could be a bit more grateful; he was only trying to help. Sara rolled her eyes, in order to communicate generally, rather than to anyone in particular, that her friend really was a control freak. She really did have issues.

JANUARY

28

'So back to work tomorrow. Back to normal for me.' Mark's right hand slithered under the covers and towards Eloise. He deftly unfastened the top two buttons of her pjs. He wasn't subtle, he didn't have to be; years of loving familiarity gave him a certain amount of licence, yet Eloise was a bit surprised; it was the first time he'd made an amorous move since the day he'd discovered he was adopted. She was delighted that he was hoping for a bit of last-day-of-the-holidays sex. Did this mean he was feeling a little happier? A bit more relaxed?

Last-day-of-the-holidays sex was not an unreasonable hope. Eloise subscribed to the theory that Christmas and birthdays were the bare minimum, even for married couples, however, she seriously doubted she could summon the energy. Her body ached with tiredness. For weeks now Eloise had thrown all her energy into creating the perfect Christmas for her family and friends. She'd made sure they had everything from advent candles and calendars to thoughtful stockings and superb surprises. She'd wanted to observe every tradition, from putting a sixpence in the pudding to swimming in the sea on Boxing Day, therefore she was exhausted and she wondered whether holiday sex was the one tradition she might have to forgo.

It had been a long and gruelling holiday and if that was an oxymoron then it was one Eloise was sure every mother understood. Christmas was never a carefree time. The most reasonable hope was that the turkey was cooked right through and that there were no out-and-out family rows. This much Eloise had achieved, which was tantamount to a miracle considering she'd had to balance the happiness of three little girls, two spiky friends, one old lady with dementia, one grieving ex-solicitor and a closed-down husband. Eloise would have preferred twelve lords a-leaping or five gold rings any day.

Today she'd got up at 6 a.m. to finally wave off Sara. Then she'd stripped the tree, packed away all the decorations, chopped up the tree and burnt it on the fire (whilst the girls toasted teacakes and drank hot chocolate). She tidied the entire house and then popped round to Ray and Margaret's, to wash and blow dry Margaret's hair, giving Ray a chance to go to the pub for an hour. There was no doubt that looking after Margaret was becoming a huge physical and emotional strain. One moment she seemed in rude health, willing to chat about which Dulux colour Eloise should paint on the wall in the dining room (Gentle Fawn or Mellow Mocha?), the next, she seemed so vulnerable and helpless, incapable of remembering if she'd even seen the doctor that morning. The hardest part was knowing that things were only going to get worse. For everyone.

Eloise wanted to make the most of the last afternoon before Mark returned to work so had suggested they all went for a four-mile walk along the coastal paths. The girls had also wanted to make the most of the afternoon but the issue was that Eloise and her daughters disagreed as to how that might be achieved. Emily thought making the most meant going round to her friend's house, Erin thought it meant reaching the next level on her new DS game and Poppy thought it meant watching back-to-back episodes of *Wizards of Waverly Place*. It took Eloise over an hour to persuade them that a family walk was a good thing, by which time Mark had been caught up on a work telephone call and couldn't join them. Eloise had questioned her own sanity as she and the girls stumbled through the dark afternoon alone.

Eloise glanced at her husband lying next to her; he looked equally exhausted. He might not have concerned himself with making paper chains, gift tags, centrepieces, chocolate logs and mince pies, but he had worries enough of his own: the new practice, Margaret's health, the adoption . . . she acknowledged that it was hardly startling that making time for one another had slipped down the list of priorities.

Eloise knew that Mark was hurting, he'd been hurting since Margaret had blurted out that he was adopted, and yet he'd side-stepped every attempt she'd made to discuss the matter. Since that first night she'd twice asked if he wanted to talk about it, and he'd firmly replied in the negative. She hadn't pushed things. She was hoping he was still processing the fact that he was adopted, but she knew there was a chance he was simply blanking it. Eloise privately believed Mark's silence on the matter to be unnatural and unhelpful. Mark had always found talking easier after they'd been physically close, but as the only intimacy they'd managed for months was when they'd banged heads while manhandling the enormous Christmas tree through the hallway, it wasn't a surprise that he hadn't found a way into conversation. Eloise decided to push her fatigue to one side; they should make love right now. She'd get into the mood once they started, she always did.

Eloise grabbed Mark's hand and brought it to her lips. She kissed it passionately and then she laid another smacker directly on his lips. He responded urgently and, even though his breath smelt of Stilton and port, Eloise found she was suddenly quite wrapped up in the moment.

'Mummeeeeee!' The cry came through the wall.

'It's Poppy.' Eloise broke away from the kiss. 'She hasn't slept well since the *Dr Who* special on Christmas Day.' El scrambled out of bed as Mark fell back on the pillow and accepted that his chances of love-making had just been significantly reduced, probably eradicated along with the Daleks and the Weeping Angels.

It took Eloise fifteen minutes to resettle Poppy. When she came back into the room she couldn't swallow her yawn; it was so big that she couldn't even hide it behind her hand very effectively. Mark knew her well enough to understand that they'd missed the moment and nookie was unlikely.

'Too tired?' he asked sympathetically.

'To be honest, yes.'

The 6 a.m. start had taken its toll. The originally agreed three-day visit had turned into nine days. Nine days! Having house guests for nine days wasn't easy at the best of times and these were so far from the best times. Eloise shouldn't have allowed them to stay that long but somehow she'd found she wasn't able to get her point across, not without stirring up the hornet's nest. When she'd tentatively suggested that she could pack something nice for them to eat on the journey back to London, Charlie had said that there wasn't any point in him driving all the way back to London, just to have to turn round to come back again to work on their house, and Sara had added that the sea air was lifting her spirits. They pertinently pointed out that there wasn't anything they needed to go home for so Eloise found it impossible to ask outright for them to leave. It felt akin to asking political asylum seekers to pack their bags and return to some despot-ruled wasteland.

At least Sara hadn't been quite as glum as she had been in November, or indeed quite as glum as Eloise had expected. There were times, good half-hour stretches, when Sara seemed genuinely buoyant, very much like her old self, although Eloise couldn't figure out exactly why. It was clear that Charlie wasn't the source of her renewed optimism; they'd barely spoken to one another, which Eloise found excruciating. Friends' domestics played out at close range were never fun but they were particularly awkward if you suspected you were part of the cause.

Charlie had kissed her!

It blew her mind and not in a good way. Her best friend's husband had kissed her. Why? Why would he do that and would he try to do it again? Charlie's kiss was unexpected and unwanted. Ever since it had happened, Eloise had gone over and over in her mind as to what she might have done to prompt it. Was it an impulsive mistake or a pledge of deep longing?

Eloise *really* needed the bathroom finishing. It was no longer just a style issue. She wanted Charlie to leave. She wanted her home back and time alone with her family. Charlie's presence was a tangible strain. She was fed up with making extra meals and washing extra sheets but, more importantly, she was exhausted by his barely disguised flirtatious ways. The problem was that Charlie wasn't behaving like someone steeped in regret, having acted on a daft impulse. He was acting like someone who believed he was part of a secret society; an *exciting* secret society. Even though Charlie hadn't explicitly referred to the incident throughout the seasonal break he'd made a point of throwing her knowing smiles and he frequently touched her more often than she thought was necessary or normal. His actions weren't blatant; he was simply solicitous to the point of slimy and considerate in a way that suggested she was colluding in an intimacy.

Eloise had studiously tried to avoid being alone with him, to stop the possibility of a repeat incident. She'd turned Poppy and Margaret into unwitting chaperones as she Velcroed one or the other to her side at all times. On the plus side, Poppy had loved the attention and Mark and Ray were both very grateful for Eloise's devotion to Margaret. Still, it had largely been to no avail because as hard as Eloise worked to avoid Charlie, he seemed to work equally vigorously to manoeuvre opportunities for private moments together.

Whenever Eloise said she was going for a walk Charlie said he felt like stretching his legs too, then she had to think of an excuse as to why she no longer wanted to go anywhere. If she said she was popping to the Flavel centre, he offered to carry her library books. She always seemed to be bumping into him in the supermarket; what was he doing lurking in the cereal aisle when she prepared all his meals? Eloise could give up fresh air and reread old books in order to avoid him but giving up eating was a step too far! The Christmas break had been fraught with potential misunderstanding. Eloise had unthinkingly hung mistletoe throughout the house but then yanked it all down again after she'd met Charlie in the hallway and he'd lingered conspicuously. It was like an elaborate game of chess; he moved closer, she headed in the opposite direction. She was concerned that she was being cornered.

It was Eloise's New Year's resolution to be firmer with Charlie. Yesterday teatime she'd sat down with him and they'd drawn up a timetable for the remaining work. Or rather, Eloise had drawn up a timetable and Charlie had made daft comments throughout about there being 'no rush' and how great it was that they 'could spend time together'. It took all Eloise's energy to keep him focused but eventually he'd promised he'd have everything finished by Easter. Eloise wanted to believe the assurances but privately doubted whether this target was likely to be achieved and anyway Easter seemed a long way off. Could she keep a lid on this situation for that long? Eloise wondered whether she should just cut her losses and sack Charlie, deal with the raised eyebrows and questions. But, no matter what excuse she could come up with, sacking Charlie would certainly mean the end of her friendship with Sara; dead, cremated, ashes scattered.

Eloise was surprised that Sara, with her finely tuned radar, hadn't already picked up on the fact that Eloise had been jumpy and uncomfortable over Christmas. Mark didn't have a radar, finely tuned or otherwise. He'd only guess his best mate fancied his wife if there was a written statement. But should Eloise have kept it a secret? Until now she'd never kept anything from him that she considered significant (secrets about how much she spent on a piece of furniture or a birthday gift didn't count). Mark and Eloise had met sixteen years ago, and since then she'd never kissed another man, never *looked* at another man. Popular belief was that fidelity was as dead as a dodo and about as relevant as Betamax video recordings, but Eloise disagreed. She liked being so single minded and sure. Eloise knew it wasn't a welcome kiss or a sought-after kiss and that was enough for her, but would Mark draw the same conclusion if he knew about it? Charlie was Mark's best friend, living in his home, currently earning a living through Mark; all that considered, no doubt Mark would see Charlie trying to snog Eloise as an act of betrayal, rather than an indiscreet transgression.

The last thing Mark needed right now was more disruption, duplicity and disappointment, more firm ground sliding from under him. He was so obviously struggling. He felt that his mum and dad had betrayed him; a mum who was suffering with a degenerative disease to boot. Eloise didn't want to add to his burden. She didn't dare mention that Charlie had done work for other people or that he'd spent the money they'd advanced for their project to pay off old debts. All of this would simply worry Mark or cause a row. And doubly so for the kiss! Eloise blushed everytime she thought of it. She kept telling herself the kiss wasn't significant. Least said, soonest mended was applicable here. Better to bury the incident. Ignore it. Let it die quietly.

Yet, she had thought of the kiss; its very strangeness was somehow captivating. Fascinating.

Quite definitely wrong, yes.

But in a deep, dark recess, buried so deeply it would never see the light, Eloise felt a tiny spark of pride that a man wanted her in that way. Charlie wanted her in *that* way. It had been so long since someone had fancied her. She wasn't even sure Mark fancied her any more. She was sure he loved her. But did he still desire her? She wasn't certain. More often than not it seemed he could take it or leave it. For years now they'd been effective, productive partners. Carefully raising and guiding their children, conscientiously welcoming and entertaining their friends, consistently and successfully working in the office and at home to provide a good life, an affluent, valuable and useful life.

They'd forgotten about sex.

About desire.

And lust.

Not that Eloise felt any of this for Charlie, but now she wondered whether he felt it for her. That thought alone was enough to make her . . . unsettled. Curious. Which, in turn, made her awkward, verging on frosty. There was a definite tension between them. Not sexual tension. Surely not that. But when Charlie walked into a room it was as though all the air was forced out and somehow she couldn't quite breathe properly. She felt his presence. Even the spaces between them suddenly became solid so that they seemed to be uncomfortably squeezed closer to one another.

Eloise was certain that Charlie could feel the tension too. More, that *he* wanted there to be a tension. He wanted there to be something between them. He was enjoying her discomfort because it was a reaction of sorts and any reaction was encouraging. He knew she hadn't mentioned the kiss to Mark because he knew that he'd have been kicked out by now if she had, perhaps with a bloody nose. By remaining silent Eloise had been complicit and so the kiss – however regrettable, however unwanted, however *nothing* – had become *something*. Charlie's kiss sat between Mark and Eloise. Her deception, though well intentioned, stained and strained.

Eloise couldn't relax in her own home. She reasoned that all she could possibly do was try to pretend the whole embarrassing episode had never happened. A faulty solution, no doubt, but her only option.

'I'm shattered too,' Mark said, swiftly pulling the duvet up around his shoulders.

Again, Eloise didn't know whether she was grateful for, or worried about, the speed and ease with which her husband accepted her tiredness as a valid reason for skipping sex. It was such a familiar excuse and both of them had made it with alarming regularity for some months now. Getting his teeth into the new practice had meant long hours at the office and he'd had to commute to London at least every other week to attend to a new and valuable client which neither of them had anticipated. Tomorrow, Mark would have to get up at five to be on time for the nine-thirty meeting in London. Eloise was realistic; they were no longer able to have all-night sessions and still go to work with a bouncy step. Frankly, they were no longer able to have a quickie and still go to work with a bouncy step.

Eloise would like to think that the Christmas break had left Mark rested and ready to heartily take on the New Year but she had her doubts. Despite her determined effort to provide Mark and the girls with the most fantastic Christmas ever, she thought that he was coming out of the festive period feeling a bit heavier; both in terms of the physical weight he was carrying (having indulged in too much eating and drinking) and in terms of the emotional weight he was carrying (having spent too much time in a confined space with his nearest and dearest). It was a maddening thought. Eloise had followed every glossy guide that promised the ideal Yule time but scented acorns burning in the fireplace, handmade crackers, colour-coordinated gift wrap and even a New Year's party for all their new neighbours and friends somehow hadn't added up to a perfect holiday. As ever, Eloise looked to Mark for reassurance and praise.

'Did you have a nice break?' she asked.

'Really great. You're the Christmas Fairy. No one does it better.'

'Thank you.'

'The girls liked all their pressies,' Mark mumbled sleepily.

'I'm not sure about the wisdom of a drum kit for Emily.'

'She loves it.'

'Yes. But do the neighbours?'

'Probably not.'

'Still.'

'Not our problem.'

'Least not yet.'

'Dad was really touched by those antique nautical maps you sourced on eBay.'

'They did look good framed, didn't they? I think your mum liked the Cath Kidston sewing basket, too.'

Mark made a harrumph sound and rolled on to his back and stared at the ceiling. 'Who can tell?' he mumbled. Eloise could hear anger in his voice. And maybe pain.

'You did well this holiday, angel.' She put her hand on his thigh and squeezed. Should she reconsider her decision as to whether or not they ought to make love? Mark was certainly in need of a bit of one-to-one TLC. The sort that was bigger than finding a sixpence in the Christmas pudding or even finding the box set of the entire series of *The Sopranos* under the tree.

'I don't know what you mean,' Mark said stiffly. His remoteness suggested that he knew exactly what she meant but was still finding it too distressing to talk about.

'Well, it was the first big family event since, you know, the news,' she said hesitantly.

'The news that I'm adopted?'

'Yes.'

'The first big event since I discovered that my parents, who are not my parents, have been lying to me for my entire life,' he said bitterly.

'They *are* your parents, Mark,' Eloise replied carefully.

'Are they?' He sounded lost.

Eloise kissed his shoulder and shuffled closer to him, so that her boob was squashed up against his arm. She hoped this was an encouraging gesture or at least a comforting one; she had very small boobs so she had to be extremely close. She hoped her message was loud and clear. 'I'm here for you. I'll listen to you.' She started to run her fingers over his chest. She wanted to soothe him, move closer to him.

'Early start for me in the morning,' Mark said and then he rolled over, turned out the light and the conversation.

Eloise lay awake staring at the ceiling long after Mark had fallen to sleep. She couldn't relax and her numerous worries swirled around her head, threatening to drown her. Tiredness gnawed at her skull and eyelids like a hungry monster. As the minutes and hours ticked by Eloise's worries about Mark, Margaret, Charlie and the bathrooms were replaced with the concern that she couldn't get to sleep and therefore she'd start tomorrow – the last day of the girls' school holidays – feeling shattered. Good mothers didn't do that, she reminded herself critically. She felt dried out and worn out; she decided she needed a refreshing glass of water to help her sleep. Dartmouth water was delicious, it was always cold and it didn't feel slimy on the roof of her mouth. Eloise lay pinned to her bed wondering whether she could turn on the bedside light and risk waking Mark or whether she should try to get down the stairs and into the kitchen without doing so. She was still not absolutely sure-footed in her new home. She didn't know every nook and cranny or the depth of every creaking stair. Eloise had made Mark ditch the electric alarm clock in favour of a more traditional wind up one as it looked better with the eighteenth-century French boudoir effect that she'd tried to achieve in the bedroom – however, right now she wished there was a glaring red glow of something distinctly twenty-first century to light her way. The blackness around her was intense and complete but it was velvety rather than cold, so not threatening, just disconcerting. After lying still for what seemed like hours, Eloise remembered that there was a last slice of Christmas cake in the kitchen and that provided enough motivation for her to negotiate the pitch-dark stairs.

She slowly inched down, keeping her hand on the banister at all times, giving her eyes time to adjust. She slid into the kitchen, closed the door behind her and only then did she turn on a light.

'Jeez, Charlie, you gave me a fright.'

'Sorry, didn't mean to.' Charlie was sitting at the breakfast table, facing the door that Eloise had just walked through. He'd been sitting in darkness, other than the small glow from a hand-held torch. He switched the torch off and grinned. He had a mug of tea in front of him and a plate with half a slice of toast on it. An open jam jar, the butter dish and a used knife were scattered across the table. There was a half-empty bottle of red, too. A midnight feast. He looked quite at home. He was bare-chested, in fact, he was only wearing a pair of boxers; his legs were spread wide under the table.

Eloise's hand shot up to the neck of her pjs. She quickly fastened the two buttons Mark had loosened earlier. Then she nervously tucked her hair behind her ear. Charlie watched and smiled at Eloise's obvious embarrassment.

'Don't go to any trouble on my account. You look gorgeous.'

'Don't be daft, Charlie,' she muttered dismissively. She didn't know what else to say. She wasn't rearranging her hair to look more attractive for him, was that what he thought? She always fiddled with her hair when she was nervous. That was all. The silence sat between them, thick with misunderstanding and tension. 'I just came down for a glass of water,' Eloise said, finally. She wanted to add that she hadn't known he was here but it seemed childish.

'Can't sleep?'

'Just thirsty.'

'Something playing on your conscience?'

Eloise stared at him and weighed up the situation. She guessed he was a bit drunk. He'd probably sat up later than was wise, drinking more than was good for him. The tea and toast were to sober him up. It was obvious that, unlike Mark, Charlie was keen to talk. He had something he wanted to say. Damn.

'There's nothing on my conscience at all,' she said sternly.

'No guilt?' He paused. 'No regret?'

Eloise thought she should probably just go back to bed. Turn round and leave him to whatever it was he was thinking. She didn't want a conversation with her friend's husband – her husband's friend – about guilt and regret, not at ten past four in the morning, not ever.

But this was her home.

Wearily, Eloise acknowledged to herself that she'd been feeling like a stranger in her home for almost a month now. Suddenly, she felt a wave of intense irritation that this was the case. These were important months; she ought to be settling her family, not walking on eggshells around Charlie and Sara too, come to that. Eloise began to reconsider whether she should put herself through the inconvenience of sacking Charlie and getting him to move out. Finding another plumber – someone who didn't have an unsuitable crush on her – might be a good idea. Yes, it would be better in the long run. She didn't have to tell Mark the real reason for firing Charlie; she could just say she wanted their place to themselves. Or she could mention the other clients, the squandered advance. Surely those alone were sackable offences. But she couldn't sack him right now. Not when he was sitting in his underwear, it just wasn't professional. It was weird. She decided to do it first thing in the morning.

'I'm just going to get my water and then I'll be out of your way,' Eloise said curtly.

'Oh don't be like that, Ellie. We need to talk.'

Eloise walked to the sink, picked up a glass from the draining board and then filled it. 'No, we don't,' she replied carefully.

'Yeah, we do. You know we do.' He sounded determined. 'Please sit down just for a moment. There's something I have to say.'

Eloise wondered whether he wanted to apologise. Get it all in the open and then move on. A wave of relief swept through her body. That would be brilliant. She wouldn't need to fire him then. She wouldn't need to find another plumber. Her bathrooms would be completed by Easter.

Eloise pulled out a chair, not next to his and not opposite, either, but at a distance that she hoped said 'distance'. 'What is it you want to say?'

'About the other week. When I kissed you in the bathroom.'

'It doesn't matter.' She stared at her hands, she really didn't know where else to look. The kitchen clock's usually discreet tick suddenly sounded like Big Ben.

'It *does* matter,' insisted Charlie.

'It didn't mean anything.' Eloise thought it was wise to get in her pre-emptive blow. Set the record straight. Make sure they understood one another. It had been years since she'd had this sort of conversation and she was out of practice. She knew she sounded abrupt and clumsy. There had been a time when she'd known the words to use when she wanted to captivate, flirt or move a guy right on by, but she couldn't seem to find the suitable tone any more. Her throat was dry and gritty. She could feel the tension in the air again, smell it. Taste it. She didn't want there to be anything between them, but there was. Undeniably.

'Look, you know more than anyone that Sara and I have been under a lot of strain for quite some time now,' said Charlie.

'Well, yes,' Eloise admitted. This wasn't the opener she wanted from him. She didn't want to hear about problems between him and Sara, it was one step away from 'my wife doesn't understand me'. She tried to put him back on track. 'Things are difficult, obviously. But they'll get better.'

'When?'

'Well, when she has . . .' Eloise faltered. She couldn't insult Charlie by saying things would get better once Sara had a baby. They both knew she might never have a baby. What sort of sentence was she handing him? 'They will get better,' she said, less definitively.

'I don't think so. It's not just the baby, although that's massive. She doesn't seem even to like me any more. I don't earn enough for her. I'm not clever enough for her. All we do is row and scream at one another or ignore each other altogether. You must have seen as much this holiday.' Charlie sighed dramatically. 'I'm at the end of the line with Sara.'

'No, no, you don't mean that.' Panicked, she reached out and squeezed Charlie's arm. She suddenly understood. They had money problems and fertility problems. They'd been rowing. He was desperate and confused. *That* was why he'd kissed her.

'I think I'm in love with you, Ellie. *That*'s why I kissed you.'

The word love slapped her in the face. It was the last word she expected to hear in the kitchen, among the tea towels and stacks of washing-up – well, at least, the last word from his lips. It affected her more than she could have imagined. It was a big word. Love. The biggest.

Years ago, when passion was all, there had been various men who'd said they loved her, so Eloise knew that the scary thing about the introduction of the subject of love was that there was no set pattern to the course of the events that followed. However, the word definitely had the power of alchemy – change was guaranteed, but a change for better or worse could not be predicted. Eloise thought that was surprising. Love should simply be universally good, but it wasn't. Not if it was unwanted or misplaced. Some men and boys had meant it when they'd said they loved her and she'd believed them – but still, a happy ever after was not guaranteed. Some didn't mean it and yet she'd wanted to believe them; those stories had a definite leaning towards heartbreak. Some meant it but she hadn't been convinced, which led to the most bitter of exchanges. One or two, the real time wasters, hadn't meant it and she hadn't believed them. Eloise wasn't sure which category Charlie fell into. It hardly mattered; now he'd put the word on the table there would, undoubtedly, be trouble ahead. Eloise desperately wondered how she could head this off.

Men didn't like women to tell them that they were wrong. Plus, they didn't listen to a woman who told them that they couldn't love her. But the thing they liked least of all was when a woman told them that she didn't love them back.

Hell.

'Don't call me Ellie. I've never liked it.'

'Is that all you have to say?'

It was all she could think of.

Suddenly, Charlie jumped up from his chair and knelt down next to Eloise. In an instant he was all over her. His lips were on her face and neck, his hands were grabbing her waist, her arse and then the back of her head, he was trying to pull her lips towards his. His firm, determined hands caressed her boobs through her thin pyjamas. It was a fraction in time but it seemed to go on for ever. She pushed him away but he pulled her closer towards him and he was stronger. It felt like she was tangled in one of those cruel and probably illegal animal traps that she'd seen on the hills; the more she struggled the tighter she was held.

'What the fuck is going on?'

Charlie and Eloise sprang apart from one another and they both turned to face Mark. He was standing, in his suit, with his laptop in his hand, ready for his crack-of-dawn commute to London.

'This isn't what it looked like.' As she heard the cliché she'd muttered, Eloise realised just how impotent and insulting it was. Charlie said nothing. There was an instant where both Mark and Eloise found themselves staring at Charlie's boxer shorts; they watched his hard-on deflate. There were loads of other things in the room, two sleepy cats, a plethora of kitchen gadgets, a fruit bowl overflowing with sweet satsumas, but, because Charlie was only wearing his boxers, his failing hard-on seemed to command the most attention. Mark strode through the kitchen towards Charlie, punched him, once, hard. Then he left.

He walked right out the door.

29

'Hello, it's only me, Eloise and the girls. Emily, Erin and Poppy,' Eloise called as she tentatively pushed open the back door and poked her head inside Margaret's kitchen.

The heavy, wooden door creaked like an old arthritic man getting out of a chair and the early morning winter daylight slithered across the tiled floors, illuminating the abandoned breakfast table. Eloise routinely said her name and the children's names to help Margaret. It was thoughtful but pointless. Margaret might hold on to the names, she might not. The girls charged into the house, briefly hugged their granny and then started making demands. Emily wanted to know where her grandfather was; apparently he'd promised he'd drive her somewhere. She had Christmas money that was burning a hole in her pocket and she wanted to go and spend it before the new school term started tomorrow. Erin walked directly into the sitting room and put on the telly.

'Why don't you have any decent channels, Granny?' she moaned.

'Dear me, everyone says I'm the forgetful one but I swear you ask that every time you come here,' replied Margaret. She turned her attention to Poppy. 'You're a good girl, aren't you? But then, you all were, when you were so young. So willing to be loved. It's so easy to love young things.'

The eldest two grandchildren looked a bit huffy but didn't challenge Margaret. They were getting used to her saying odd things. Her lack of tact was sometimes hilarious and when it was hurtful they just tried to ignore her. Triumphant, Poppy went into the dining room to dig out her granny's miniature china tea set.

'My father bought that for me,' Margaret told Eloise, not for the first time. 'I never let anyone play with it, other than my best friend Mabel and this other little girl who is visiting now.' Eloise nodded; she was distracted, so didn't bother to point out that the 'other little girl' was Margaret's granddaughter.

'Where's Ray?' she asked instead.

'Oh, he's gone to the erm . . .'

Eloise reached for the big blue book that was lying on the breakfast table. She flicked through it and then read the latest entry. 'He's just popped to the shops. He won't be long. He's going to be home in time to take you to the doctor's,' she informed Margaret.

'That's it. Shall I make us a cup of tea, dear?'

'Yes, yes, tea would be lovely.'

As Margaret made the tea she felt anxious for Eloise. Margaret knew that people thought she was the unwell one but actually Margaret thought it was Eloise they should be worrying about. She looked like she was at death's door this morning and she hadn't been quite herself all Christmas. No matter how much tinsel she'd strewn around the house, she couldn't hide that. Margaret would have liked to offer her daughter-in-law something stronger than tea to drink but decided against it because Eloise would think she was confused, offering spirits early in the morning. Margaret didn't feel confused, she felt concerned. Eloise had trouble spelt out across her face.

Margaret faltered as she made the tea, she couldn't remember what went in tea, other than the tea bag and the hot water. Eloise saw her hesitation but said nothing; she simply went to the fridge and got out some milk. Margaret appreciated Eloise not making a fuss. She and Ray were forever wasting time looking for things she'd misplaced; her purse, keys, her glasses. Sometimes she forgot what they were looking for while they were looking for it. Margaret would shout out, 'Here we are, darling, my locket!' and he'd growl back, 'We're looking for your watch, Margaret.' Not that he was a bad man. Or a bad-tempered man. He was neither. He'd always been good to Margaret. A good husband. He was simply an angry man. Disappointed. Margaret knew Mark was angry too. With her. And disappointed with her. Ray said she shouldn't have told Mark about the girl that gave him to them. But if not now, when? Margaret wondered.

Never?

Maybe.

The women sat down at the kitchen table and sipped their tea. 'I need the number of your plumber, Margaret. Who was it you mentioned? Someone Fields? Bernie Fields?'

Margaret nodded but knew she couldn't help Eloise. Telephone numbers were in a book. If Eloise found the book, she was welcome to the number, but she'd have to do it herself. Matching names and numbers was beyond Margaret now. That had sunk deep into the blackness.

'What happened to your plumber? Has he died?' Margaret asked.

'No. Why would you think that?'

'There was a window cleaner who fell off his ladder and killed himself. Terrible business, it was. He was doing next door's windows, not mine, but it was awful. I heard him yell and then the thud. The thud was sickening. I remember his shoulder and neck didn't seem to be in the right place. Well, they weren't, his neck was broken. And the blood stained the path for weeks. Horrid.'

Eloise looked shocked. 'My God. When was this?'

'The twenty-second of July 1976.'

'Oh.' Eloise wondered, not for the first time, how Margaret's memories worked right now. Some things that had happened years ago were clear and accessible, but there were days when she couldn't remember if she'd had breakfast an hour after doing so. 'Well, my plumber isn't dead,' she explained carefully. Then, more ruefully, she added, 'More is the pity, but it's not working out. I've asked him to go.'

'I said all along that it never works, mixing business and friendships.'

'Yes, well, you were right.'

'Doomed.'

'Thank you, Margaret, for your insight.'

'Gone, has he?'

'He stores his van in someone's garage. That someone is still visiting his wife's rellies in Yarmouth. They aren't expected back until about eight p.m. tonight, so he won't be able to get his van until then, but he's leaving the moment he has it.' Eloise paused and pinched the top of her nose. Margaret knew that trick; it was to stem tears. Eloise sighed and continued, 'Not a moment too soon, either. Not as far as I'm concerned. Do you mind if the girls and I hang out here today, Margaret?'

'That Sara is trouble,' said Margaret, as she dipped a biscuit into Eloise's tea and then ate it. Eloise didn't grumble about the intimacy.

'Sara? No, Sara's not the problem.'

'Yes, yes, she is,' Margaret insisted firmly.

Eloise leaned closer to Margaret and whispered so that the girls, who were in the sitting room, couldn't overhear their conversation. 'It's Charlie, actually. He's, well, it's all a bit embarrassing, he's developed an unsuitable crush on me. It's all got a bit out of hand.'

'I knew all along that Sara was dangerous.'

'Charlie,' corrected Eloise. 'It's Charlie that's—' Eloise suddenly broke off and then stared at Margaret for the longest time. Margaret could see she was searching for something in her face or eyes. Wisdom, or the keys perhaps. Eventually, Eloise sighed and said, 'We'd better get you dressed, eh? If you are off to the doctor's, you'll need to get sorted.'

'I am dressed, silly girl. I always dress up for the doctor's,' replied Margaret.

She was wearing her new pink towelling bath robe that Ray had bought her for Christmas, sequined flip-flops that were purchased for her last holiday to Spain and the hat Margaret had picked up for Irene Cooper's youngest boy's wedding.

'It's not quite suitable, Margaret,' said Eloise gently.

'Really? Is it the hat? I know the wedding was in 2002, but I thought it'd do as it's navy, and navy is such a marvellous colour. It never dates. I don't think anyone would call it unfashionable.'

Eloise patted her mother-in-law's hand. 'It's lovely, but it might get spoilt in the drizzle,' she said kindly. 'Come on, let's see if we can find anything else.'

30

Sara's plan was fully formed. She'd been mulling it over and she was confident that it would work, at least the first part of it, the sex part. That was always the easy bit. The second part, the pregnancy part, well, that was in the lap of the gods.

She'd been texting Jeremy over the holidays. Not incessantly but consistently. The texts had not been at all professional. She was banking on the fact that however much of a family man he liked to appear to be in the office, it was unlikely he could display the same exuberance to his wife and kids for the entire holiday break. Her texts had been fun, flirty and forward. Via the phone she'd been more dangerous and dirty than she might have dared face to face. Jeremy had always texted back within a few minutes of receiving one, the tone of his messages mirroring hers. Sara wondered how people managed illicit affairs before the invention of the mobile. It must have been so frustrating and taken *ages*. In her texts she'd subtly and not-so-subtly conveyed the fact that she was currently satisfied enough with her husband to never entertain leaving him, but dissatisfied enough with the bedroom action to consider supplementing it elsewhere. She'd never breathed a word about babies.

Now, she had to move things along. She'd called Jeremy's PA and said she was sorry but she wouldn't be returning to work today, she was sick. The PA sympathised and commented that loads of people had a bug and that it was going around. This was the standard thing to say. Sara knew the assistant would be rolling her eyes and the moment she was off the phone she'd tell everyone who'd listen that there was nothing wrong with Sara, other than a huge dose of can't-be-arsed, that she was probably just hung over. Sara was depending on her indiscretion.

Within minutes Sara's phone beeped to say she had a text. It was from Jeremy:

Ill in bed? x

In bed x

They'd taken to signing off their messages with an 'x'. Sara had started it, he'd followed instantly. In many industries that would mean nothing. In advertising, journalism or publishing, directives from the managing directors were signed off with three kisses and a smiley face, but in accountancy people were not so casual. The 'x' was charged.

Hope you are wrapped up warm x

No, actually, don't like wearing much when I have high temperature! x

You're saying you're hot? x

Are you saying I'm not? x

I wouldn't dare! xx

She waited. He needed the fun of the chase. After two minutes he sent another text.

Drink lots of soup x

I need someone to spoon it to me x

Isn't your husband around to help? x

No. Am alone. He's away for week. Anyway not sure about soup. I
find champagne is way more medicinal xx

Sara pressed send and then waited again. It was agonising. She knew
she was playing with fire, Jeremy was her boss and she'd as good as
told him she wasn't ill after all, she'd told him she was near naked and
she'd practically issued a gold-embossed invite for him to join her in
bed, with a bottle of champagne. It wasn't subtle. Sara was betting a
lot on the fact that he'd had a dreary Christmas break and there was
nothing urgent in his in-box. After a Jurassic age, her phone beeped
again. She snatched it up.

Sounds fun x

Could be x

Again Sara felt the wait between responses was probably contravening
some human right or other, it was so painful. She knew he'd be
weighing things up, deciding how far he dared transgress. Sara's heart
was beating at a rate that possibly would qualify her for a doctor's
note.

What are you saying? x

I think you know x

Spell it out for me x

Where's your imagination? x

Trampled beneath a mountain of boring responsibilities x

Sara wanted to punch the air. She was right, he was bored and randy, a perfect combination for her needs. She took a deep breath and then sent one last text.

Come to me x

Half an hour later, the door bell rang.

31

Eloise couldn't forget Mark's face as he'd punched Charlie and probably never would. His expression wasn't one of anger or hate – as might be expected – that she could have coped with; his face was tattooed with hurt. He'd looked injured, wounded. In that instant, the residue of excitement that Eloise had felt at being desired by another man vanished – exploded, exposing the feeling as ephemeral and meaningless. Mark stormed out of the house and didn't so much as glance back as she desperately called out that she could explain the situation; that she knew it looked bad but she could explain. He'd simply got in his car and driven away, presumably to the station. Their marriage might be in tatters but he had the commuter train to catch, a meeting to attend, a chargeable client to deal with. Eloise knew how seriously Mark took his work; normally she loved this about him, but today she wished he was a little more irresponsible. Returning to the kitchen, Eloise found that Charlie had at least the decency to look ashamed.

'Get dressed and get packed, Charlie. I don't care about your money troubles. I don't care about your fertility troubles. I don't care that you've just said you love me. I love my husband. All I care about is him. Now get out of my house.' It was so easy to say in the end. Eloise wondered why she hadn't said it earlier.

Charlie offered absolutely no resistance; he just muttered something about not being able to get his van until later that evening, it was locked in Arabella's brother's garage. Eloise realised, if there had been any doubt, his reaction to her request to get the hell out of her life put him firmly in the category of men who said they loved her but didn't mean it. The time wasters.

Eloise had run upstairs and locked herself in the bedroom. She called Mark but, as she'd half expected, it rang through to his voice-mail. She hung up without leaving a message, regretted it and called again.

'Seriously, Mark, you have to believe me, Charlie just pounced on me. Come home. Please. I need you here. We need to sort this out. It meant nothing. It was just a kiss.' She hung up and immediately doubted the wisdom of leaving such a message.

'It meant nothing' meant *something* happened, even if it was a some-thing that wasn't important to her. 'It meant nothing' was what sorry-arsed, low-life adulterers said after they'd slept with someone they shouldn't have. 'It was just a kiss' implied she agreed to the kiss, she was part of it, which in a dry, factual way she supposed she was, but in the true sense of being part of a kiss she was nowhere near the scene of the crime. Oh God, this was silly. She just wanted him to pick up his phone. Why wouldn't he just pick up his bloody phone and let her explain? He was being so pig-headed! Comfortably aware of her innocence, Eloise momentarily failed to see just how bad it looked but then she remembered his face. Hurt was scalded there.

Eloise had spent the next three hours regularly pressing redial but Mark had switched off his phone – or perhaps he'd left it in the car as he'd got on the train to London or, perhaps, he'd thrown it away so that she couldn't reach him. Eloise believed that was the sort of thing Mark might do if he was angry enough. He'd enjoy imagining some other commuter picking up the phone and then listening to her apolo-getic messages. Eloise began to think that the situation was beyond embarrassing. It was actually a bit terrifying. She repeatedly told herself that Mark would believe her, once they'd had a chance to talk. Wouldn't he? He *knew* her. She was his wife, for goodness' sake.

His face. The sorrow.

Her breath caught in her chest. Eloise realised now that she should've told him about the first kiss. She shouldn't have allowed this situation to gather momentum. It was all her fault. After all, she'd been the one who'd invited Charlie into their home. She hadn't consulted Mark before she made the offer; she'd relied on his easy-going nature and assumed he wouldn't mind Charlie crashing at theirs. But who could have guessed that this would happen? After all those years of friendship. She hadn't seen it coming, she really hadn't. Eloise had felt ridiculously tired, having spent most of the night staring at the ceiling and the next part grappling with Charlie and chasing Mark (at least emotionally) so inevitably, sleep eventually overwhelmed her. At 9 a.m. she'd been woken up by the girls banging on her bedroom door, demanding to know why it was locked and what she'd planned to entertain them that day.

After breakfast Eloise had taken the girls to Ray and Margaret's, reasoning that at least there she'd be some practical help to someone. She'd figured she could hide from her own problems by swapping responsibilities with Ray and so she'd suggested that Ray entertain the girls while she took Margaret to the doctor's. A change was as good as a rest and both she and Ray needed a rest.

The doctor had no good news for them. An official diagnosis of Alzheimer's doesn't come with any good news. There were treatments that could slow down the deterioration and help people to cope with it, even understand it, but there was nothing to cure it. Eloise sensed that Margaret's GP felt out of his depth, especially as Margaret was often uncharacteristically rude to him. He was a sympathetic, well-meaning man who had been subjected to some of Margaret's most ferocious attacks because she sometimes thought he was an impostor who had (for reasons unspecified but insidious) 'done away' with her old doctor. Last week she'd spat on his floor. On other occasions, she'd believed he *was* his father, the beloved doctor she'd known for years, and on those visits she flirted with Dr Fielding Junior in a most unsubtle manner. She flashed her legs and constantly touched his arm. She'd once suggested that they could go and drink cocktails together. Eloise was unsure which mood the doctor found most tricky to deal with but she hated both because she knew Margaret had never been either a sulk or a flirt and both of these impostor personas were villainous symptoms.

The care available for Alzheimer's largely depended on where in the country a person happened to be. The Hamiltons had discovered that, depending on where you lived, you might be diagnosed and treated by a consultant geriatrician (a doctor who specialised in conditions that affected older people), or a consultant psychogeriatrician (a doctor specialising in older people's mental health problems), or a neurologist (a doctor who specialised in conditions that affected the nervous system), or a general psychiatrist. Over the months, Mark and Ray had taken Margaret to all of the above; the result was always the same. Some worn-out, good-hearted professional told them that Margaret had a disease that was degenerative and that there wasn't a cure.

Today Dr Fielding had some test results back from the consultant psychogeriatrician. The results confirmed that Margaret was a stage-five Alzheimer's, a 'moderate or mid-stage', where there was 'moderately severe cognitive decline'. The word moderate was thrown around the doctor's small, neat office; it bounced off the walls like a ball. Eloise looked at the box of tissues on the desk, the posters on the wall that urged people to follow healthy diets and the piles of rubber gloves stacked near the sink; she was searching for an understanding of the word 'moderate', especially when it was combined with the word 'severe'. What did that mean? Experience had shown it meant noticeable gaps in memory and a lessened ability to reason, besides which Margaret was beginning to need help with day-to-day activities. The doctor confirmed that was exactly what 'moderately severe cognitive decline' meant.

'At this stage, those with Alzheimer's may be unable to recall their own address or telephone number or which school they once went to,' he said. He held his hands in front of him, fingertips meeting; he put Eloise in mind of a pastor or a politician delivering a sermon or a lecture which, frankly, she didn't find very reassuring at all.

'I went to St David's Primary School,' chipped in Margaret with a defiance Eloise couldn't help but admire. Eloise felt a surge of hope that perhaps Margaret wasn't stage five yet, maybe she was stage four, but hope was shredded when she added, 'And then I went to The Royal Ballet School, on a scholarship.'

'She didn't.' Eloise flashed an apologetic grimace at the doctor. He shrugged. He understood; it was to be expected. Margaret's dashed hope to enter The Royal Ballet School was a well-known family story. Eloise reminded her mother-in-law of the facts. 'You applied there, Margaret, but, sadly, you didn't get a place so you went to secretarial school instead. Then you met Ray, so it all worked out for the best in the end.'

Eloise squeezed her hand, a gesture which was meant to comfort Eloise as much as Margaret. Eloise wanted to believe it had all worked out for the best. They'd adopted Mark, given him a loving home, they were a happy family. It was all great. Well, at least up until the part where Margaret had got Alzheimer's. Wasn't this all anyone ever wanted to believe about loved ones? Everyone clung to the hope that wherever they'd ended up, whatever they'd endured, there was nothing to regret and there was only a sense of fate and it all being OK. Eloise wondered if this was the ultimate hope we all harboured for ourselves? Looking at Margaret now, dazed and disconcerted, believing that it was all for the best was a tough sell.

'Don't be so rude,' Margaret snapped at her daughter-in-law. 'I *did* get a place at the ballet school. I was a very good dancer. *Very* good.' Eloise sighed, gave up and allowed the doctor to return to his list.

'A sufferer of Alzheimer's may become confused about where they are or what day it is or they may have trouble with less challenging mental arithmetic, such as counting backwards from forty by subtracting fours, or even backwards from twenty by twos.'

'Well, *I* might struggle with that,' Eloise joked lamely. Her joke was inappropriate and the doctor's face clearly told her as much. She began to hate him. She didn't know why she was beginning to see the doctor as an enemy, he'd never been anything other than polite and professional, but someone had to be hated when such bad news was being delivered.

'Quite,' he said civilly, humouring Eloise but simultaneously writing her off as some hairbrained, ditsy, artsy type.

Margaret had always been good with numbers, mental arithmetic was one of her fortes; dancing, playing the piano and baking were the others. Eloise couldn't bear the idea of testing her maths right now, just in case she'd lost that skill, but she made a mental note not to ask Margaret to help with Emily's homework any more as Emily's grades were bad enough as it was. 'They may need help choosing proper clothing for the season or the occasion.' The doctor looked up from the list he was reading. 'Are any of these familiar?'

'Yes.' Eloise sighed. 'Pretty much all of them.'

'The good news is she is still likely to remember significant details about herself and her family.' Like Mark being adopted. 'And at this stage most Alzheimer's patients still do not require assistance with eating or using the toilet.'

That was the good news.

Margaret and Eloise left the doctor's feeling bleak and shattered. The moment they were outside the overly centrally heated doctor's practice, they were whipped by a bitterly cold January wind. Eloise buttoned up Margaret's coat; it was unnecessary to do so, as Margaret could still manage buttons perfectly well, but Eloise wanted to do something to protect her. Eloise felt her eyes prick. She told herself that the wind must be the cause, or maybe it was the fact that she hadn't had enough sleep last night, or maybe it was because her husband was under the impression that she was having a fling with his best friend; whatever the reason, fat tears began to slip down her cheeks. She tried to rub them away with the back of her hand before Margaret noticed them but they were relentless.

Margaret rooted in her black leather handbag and produced a grubby handkerchief. She dabbed at Eloise's face and then fastened her daughter-in-law's coat. The gesture caused Eloise to weep more.

'There, there, no need for tears, Eloise. No need.'

And now Eloise knew for certain why she was crying, she was crying for Margaret.

'You called me Eloise,' she said, through a sob.

'Yes, dear. Well, that's your name. Pretty name, too, I've always thought. Shall we go home and have a cup of tea?'

32

Things hadn't turned out exactly as Sara had planned but ultimately she got the end result she wanted, so she didn't concern herself too much with the variation on the details. More alcohol was involved than she'd anticipated – he really had needed to get quite drunk before he could do the deed – and there was way more talking than she'd imagined. She hadn't factored in any talking. He'd insisted on telling her about his own wife's infidelity. She hadn't seen *that* coming. She'd had no idea. He'd never mentioned it before. Not a hint. It was clear that this was his main motivation for being there with her; he wanted to even up the score. Sara didn't care.

It wasn't an angry fuck. It wasn't a passionate union. It was actually quite mechanical. Maybe even a little bit sad. He kept most of his clothes on. She'd gently pushed him back on the bed and started to unfasten his trousers. He hadn't stopped her. She'd been wearing a flimsy red nightdress. It was short and silky. Not much effort was required before it fell off her shoulders and revealed her breasts but he didn't seem to notice. Sara was just beginning to wonder whether she'd even get what she needed when something raw took over. Darwin's theories all dropped into place and the fittest, most ruthless animal was rewarded.

Sara had hoped the spirit might have been a little more playful. She cast her mind back to the years when she and Eloise had shared excited stories about how Eloise's children had been conceived and Sara had held such great hopes as to how her own might be. She did wonder whether this was a grim start but then she rallied. There wasn't room for sentiment. How could this be a bad start? It was just perfunctory, like mixing it all up in a glass in a laboratory. Technically, it felt good. It was good sex. Sara thought it was a bit like drinking a long, cold drink on a very hot day, exactly what she needed. She wasn't looking for a grand love affair. She didn't need more than this. Despite how it might look on the outside, Sara wanted Charlie. He'd be the daddy. Once she was pregnant they'd get back to the place they used to be. They'd become the people they used to enjoy being.

They would be happy again.

33

Eloise and Margaret returned to the Hamilton Seniors' warm and cosy home and, despite the fact that the girls had each received about a million new toys over Christmas, they opted to spend the rest of the afternoon playing the old faithful, Monopoly. Eloise had loved Monopoly as a child, providing she'd won, and that was the universal truth of Monopoly; everyone loved it, providing they won, but no one liked it much if they didn't. Losing at Monopoly seemed so much more personal than losing at, say, Cluedo or Top Trumps or even chess, which was ridiculous because those games required an element of skill and Monopoly was largely luck. Maybe that was the issue; no one liked to think they were unlucky.

The girls played ruthlessly and greedily. They bought up anything they landed on. Ray played fairly and with decorum; he wouldn't strike deals or create alliances that would sink another player but, then again, nor would he allow people to forgo debts if they owed him, not even Poppy. Margaret had a good afternoon, she followed the game pretty well and rolled a higher proportion of double sixes than would be expected so she seemed to be forever passing Go and collecting two hundred pounds. She had no trouble counting out her moves or remembering which pile was Chance and which was Community Chest. This was enough to sustain Eloise through an afternoon where her husband refused to take her calls. She left four more messages on his voicemail but finally admitted to herself that there were a limited number of ways of saying 'It wasn't what you think. Call me, I can explain.'

The light began to fade, so Ray drew the curtains on Dartmouth's depth and darkness and switched on electric lights to keep everyone cheerful. By four o'clock Margaret owned hotels on Mayfair and Park Lane so no one else had any money left.

'I guess I'm just very lucky,' she said as she clapped her hands. Eloise didn't know if Margaret was aware she sounded stoical or whether she'd temporarily forgotten that she was dying, but Eloise wanted to hug her, hold her so tightly that they were both safe. She resisted, because doing so might have unsettled Margaret and the girls. Instead, she simply beamed back. 'Now, does anyone fancy tea and crumpets? Perhaps a slice of Victoria sponge?' added Margaret.

'I'll do it, Margaret,' Ray and Eloise chorused in unison.

'No, I'll be fine. The girls can help.'

With only the minimum amount of resistance the girls stood up and followed their grandmother into the kitchen to provide whatever assistance they could manage.

'Blind leading the blind,' mumbled Ray, as he sat back in the high-backed chair that was known as his, but despite his grumbling Eloise could tell he was delighted. A peaceful afternoon such as this, without any mishaps or disasters, was to be treasured.

At eight-thirty Eloise and the girls walked home. The house was in darkness, which was a mixed blessing. On the one hand it meant that at least Charlie had cleared off but, on the other, Mark wasn't home. Eloise hadn't *expected* him to be there but she'd *hoped* he might be. This was so silly. The kiss was nothing. She wanted to explain, apologise and move on.

Spending the afternoon with her family and just her family had been a delight, despite reeling from the consequences of the traumatic row and despite Margaret's failing health. Eloise began to see what she'd been shutting out since she'd arrived in Dartmouth and maybe for a long time before that. Not intentionally, of course, but quite certainly. She was always dashing around. Looking after Sara and feeding Charlie or trying to make new friends or stay in touch with old ones. Eloise had a reputation for generosity and hospitality in terms of her physical and emotional resources. She was the woman people called if they needed someone to look after their kids, if they'd had a row with their husband and craved a chat or if they were getting married and wanted an opinion on the seating plan. Eloise was always available. But how generous was she with her time in her own home? With her own family? What about their needs? What about hers? For the first time Eloise gave some serious consideration as to why she was often too tired to make love with her husband when she had the energy to clear rubbish from the beach and sew fifteen pairs of angel wings on to costumes for the school nativity play. When did her priorities become so warped? Of course those things were important, certainly, but not as important as simply being with her family. How had she forgotten that? As soon as Mark came home she'd tell him that she was going to re-prioritise. She was going to calm down. She'd settle into Dartmouth by simply settling, rather than rushing.

Eloise bathed Poppy and then Erin and Emily bathed themselves while she read to Poppy. The half finished bathroom haunted her. *How could Charlie have been so stupid?* The suite was plumbed in but the tiling wasn't done. Eloise thought she might just tackle that herself, for her family. The girls finally fell to sleep, each resisting because tomorrow would bring school and, however much school was enjoyed, it was never going to be favourably compared to being at home.

Eloise couldn't sleep. She sat in the kitchen, waiting for her husband to return.

34

'Well, wasn't that a lovely day, Margaret?' Ray called through from the kitchen. 'It is so nice to spend a bit of time with Eloise and the girls without those ghastly hanger-on friends of theirs. Missed Mark, of course, but a chap has to work.'

Margaret didn't reply but Ray was becoming used to that. Sometimes they held completely normal conversations that were sequential and even informative. At other times she got the place or person skewed in her head, and sometimes she just remained totally silent. Ray could never work out if in those cases her silence was a result of the fact that she was processing the day or because she simply didn't have a clue what was going on and had decided that the best way to disguise this fact was just remaining mute.

Occasionally, she was silent simply because she'd fallen asleep in the chair.

Ray popped his head back around the sitting-room door. Margaret was awake. She was sitting side-on to him but he could see she had her eyes wide open and was staring at the TV. She was watching some awful soap opera. She'd never had any interest in soaps until about two years ago, when she'd suddenly developed an obsessive interest in all of them: *Coronation Street*, *EastEnders*, *Hollyoaks*, *Emmerdale*. Ray didn't know whether to sigh or chuckle when later he identified the fact that soap watching was one of Margaret's first symptoms of dementia. What did that say about modern TV? It seemed to him that she took some sort of comfort in the characters' lives, perhaps because they were even more traumatic and haphazard than her own or perhaps, simply, because they were consistently beamed into her sitting room on a regular basis and she was able to keep track in a way that had started to elude her in reality.

Ray liked the silences the least. He didn't really mind the occasions that she skewed something in her mind, at least not when they were alone. Of course it was frustrating in public because people saw her disease for what it was then. They saw it stripping her, eroding her and he hated that. He hated Margaret being exposed. But at home, if she forgot who he was and talked to him as though he were Mark or even Frank, her younger, late half-brother, he found those conversations quite edifying and enlightening. She was often completely lucid, as though she was right there in 1956 or 1989 or whenever. It allowed him to catch up a bit. Catch up on the parts of her life that he'd missed because her memories dated back to before they'd met, obviously. He also caught up on the parts that he'd missed because he'd been at work and she'd managed most of Mark's upbringing on her own, as was the norm in those days. Hearing what his wife and son used to get up to when he was in the office was like being given a second chance, of sorts.

Ray hadn't understood it, not completely, not in his core. He hadn't quite comprehended just how much Margaret loved Mark until he'd been privy to some of her recollections. Of course, they *both* loved their son more than anything in the world, and had from the day he'd arrived, the way right-minded parents do, but a mother's love, well, that was something extra again. He'd had no idea. The stories she told! The details she could recall! It was fascinating. When Ray remembered Mark's childhood, he remembered a few very pleasant years visiting castles and paddling or sailing in the sea. It had been marvellous, idyllic. But the memories were all a bit vague. Margaret remembered it clearly as though it were yesterday. She could bring it back to life for both of them. She could sometimes recall which jumper Mark had been wearing on a particular family occasion, like a birthday or boating trip, and what little toy he'd bought in a particular National Trust shop attached to some castle they'd visited. She recalled which parts he'd played in all his school productions, when he lost his teeth and the funny things he used to say. Ray had completely forgotten that Mark had gone through a stage of impersonating Michael Crawford's Frank Spencer from *Some Mothers Do 'Ave 'Em*. That used to have them in stitches. Until Margaret became ill, they hadn't spent much time reminiscing; there'd been no need, they were still moving forward.

Ray had, on occasion, started to wonder whether they should have adopted more children. Margaret had so much love to give. She could have spread it round a bit more. She'd never asked for more children but did she yearn for more? It was an odd thing for Ray to allow to shuffle around his head. He wasn't one for regrets or 'what ifs', he'd always been far too rooted in the practicalities of the here and now to glance back over his shoulder. He'd always been a happy man, content with his life choices, and had no need to reconsider or reassess. But lately he'd started to wonder if there was anything, anything at all, that he could have done to make Margaret's life any better. Because if there had been, he would have wanted to do it. He really would have.

'The girls were fun today, weren't they? Not too scrappy.' Ray knew that Margaret liked talking about the grandchildren, it was her favourite subject. 'Emily's growing up to be very bonny, I think. Of course I'm biased. I think they're all delightful. But she definitely has a more contented glow about her recently. I think she's truly enjoying her time at the Academy. Don't you?'

Ray had found his family an enormous comfort today. Today they'd allowed him to believe that Alzheimer's didn't have to ruin his life. It often felt like the disease was the end of his world because it was the end of Margaret's – which was the same thing, in his mind. Eloise was a marvel. He'd been dreading the trip to the doctor's. The appointments were so harrowing and this one, coming straight after Christmas, had been something he'd been feeling especially anxious about. Ray Hamilton was no coward. He'd face full on whatever it was he had to face. He was not the sort of man who buried his head in the sand. Not usually, but he'd been grateful today when Eloise had taken Margaret to the doctor's and come back with a version of events that he knew had been edited. He was aware that his daughter-in-law was protecting him to some extent but just this once he allowed that. He was kind to himself. He wasn't avoiding, he was galvanising. He was aware that it was going to be a long journey and he'd be able to reserve his own strength by sharing the load.

Mark was lucky to have Eloise. They all were. Of course, she concerned herself with things that bemused his generation; shopping and brands and 'statement foods' in expensive restaurants (whatever the hell that meant), but she had a good heart. And she was surprisingly practical, which was not what you'd imagine when you saw her ooh-ing and ah-ing over something like a bit of slate shaped as a heart with the word *home* written on it. Today Eloise had suggested Ray pin up a note near the door reminding Margaret of the things she needed to check before she left the house: remember to lock up, take your keys and put on warm clothing, that sort of thing. And she was right about making sure the home was well lit and that there were no obvious hazards. Good idea to suggest fixing the loose carpet in the hall and to remove the locks from the bathroom and loo so that Margaret couldn't lock herself in again, like she had last week.

Eloise was good at wallpapering over cracks, smoothing ruffled feathers, which was an estimable skill. She was doing her best to fix things between Mark and Margaret. That one was a struggle, though. Irrationally, Mark seemed to be angrier with his mother than he was with his father, even though they'd both colluded to keep the truth from him all these years. Perhaps it was because Margaret was the one who'd blurted out the truth or perhaps it was because she was unwell. Dying. And really Mark was furious about that; it was possible that he was subconsciously displacing his emotions. Or perhaps it was simply because Mark loved Margaret more than he loved Ray. Finding out Margaret wasn't biologically his mother must be more of a blow than finding out Ray wasn't biologically his father. Ray didn't know. It was all too much. Ray thought he needed to sit down with his son and have a man-to-man. Get it all said and out in the open. He was fed up of Mark's barbed comments and sneaky digs about honesty, especially since he refused to actually discuss the situation in an adult way. It wasn't good enough. Ray resolved to call Lydia in the morning and make an appointment to see Mark in the office. That way Mark couldn't say he was too busy to talk, which was what he'd mumbled on every occasion when Ray had tried to broach the subject. Ray thought he owed Eloise this much, it was clear that Mark's unhappiness was a strain. She tried so hard to make everything right. They could all take a leaf out of her book.

It wasn't tricky; all he had to do was sit Mark down, apologise for the deception and tell him how it was. They couldn't have loved him more. That was the fact of the matter. He was their all. It just needed saying.

Ray was feeling buoyant. He'd had a good day and he had a plan. He stirred the powdered chocolate into the hot milk. He was feeling so jaunty that he spooned an extra tablespoon into each cup and then, with a flourish, he squirted that ghastly squirting cream that Margaret had recently taken a fancy to. He called through, 'I have a treat for you, Margaret.'

Bright and breezy he carried the tray into the sitting room. Margaret was still watching the soap. She hadn't moved. She didn't turn to him when he set down the tray and yet Ray knew that she was perfectly aware of his presence. There was something about her stance that suggested she was studiously avoiding his eye. Then he smelt it. Acidic and familiar. Undeniable. Urine. Ray looked at his wife, dressed in beige slacks and a chocolate-brown roll-neck jumper that Eloise had picked out this morning; she looked elegant and almost serene. She was wearing pearl earrings and even a touch of lipstick. Had she reapplied her make-up at some point today? She looked beautiful.

But she was sitting in her own pee and didn't even seem to know it.

35

Sara's big concern, her only concern, was would it be enough? She'd hoped he'd stay all day. Ideally, she'd wanted to have two or even three rounds, to increase her chances. Was that even possible at their ages? Maybe not. Anyway, it wasn't to be. After the first unthinking, drunken session he'd become increasingly maudlin and started to go on and on about his wife and family again. It was clear that she wasn't going to benefit from a repeat performance. She supposed an element of regret was always a potential hazard. She'd been as reassuring as she could be. She'd promised him that his wife and family would never know, that what they'd done meant nothing, that he shouldn't really give it another thought. She was as sympathetic as she could be whilst remaining horizontal with her legs discreetly propped above head height. Luckily, he didn't notice her lack of animation; she didn't want him to suspect that she was after more than a quick tumble. It was only after he'd left that Sara could lie with her feet blatantly propped on the headboard, which she did for over two hours.

Would it be enough? She wasn't sure. She'd done everything she could. She'd pinpointed the date she was most likely to be fertile. There were helpful kits that assisted with that, kits that had been part of her life for five years now but had yet to help bring her dream to fruition. Would it be different this time? Please God, it would be. Sara concentrated very hard and tried to imagine cells splitting and reproducing. She laid the flat of her hand on her belly and prayed. Then she spent the rest of the day in bed reading the latest Costa novel winner. She felt totally composed and tranquil. She was certain that what she'd done wasn't wrong. How could it be wrong when it felt so right? She'd bathed in a feeling of peace and optimism for the first time in a desperately long time.

At 6 p.m. she stripped the bed and put on fresh sheets.

36

It was nearly midnight when Eloise finally heard the car pull up outside. She was wired on coffee but hadn't had a drop of alcohol as she needed a clear head to negotiate these choppy waters. She still had no idea what Mark was thinking. She could only hope that years of trust and honesty would give him the faith he needed to believe in her. From the kitchen window she could see Mark at the wheel. He paused, sank his head into his hands and rubbed his eyes. He looked wrecked. Even worse than she'd imagined he might. Worn, deflated and simply very, very sad. Eloise's heart contracted. She wanted to rush out to him and throw her arms around him but something held her back. Instinctively, she knew that he had to come to her in his own time. Five minutes passed. Seven, nine, the kitchen clock taunted her. It was ten minutes before finally he got out of the car and came into the house.

Mark was carrying a huge bouquet of white roses, Eloise's favourite flowers; they weren't easy to find in the middle of winter. She breathed in their scent and the sign that it was all going to be OK. He hovered in the kitchen doorway holding the flowers out in front of him, like a schoolboy offering his mate a bite of his apple. He looked handsome and sheepish and uncertain and determined. The mix of emotions shooting across his face made him appear vulnerable and adorable. Eloise knew she wasn't having a fling with Charlie and she knew she didn't want one. She decided that her absolute clarity on the matter would have to buoy them both up for a while, until Mark learned to trust her again, until Mark felt confident again. This was a glitch. It was not part of their history, Eloise wouldn't let it be. Love, real and absolute love, allowed her to feel confident.

'Did you get my messages?' she asked.

'Yes. Late this afternoon. I didn't turn my phone on until then.'

'Right.' Eloise was aware of her own breathing. It was shallow and faster than comfortable. 'And do you believe me? It was not what it looked like. He came on to me. I'm innocent. Nothing happened.'

Eloise knew that she sounded frighteningly like a nineteenth-century tragic heroine but she felt entitled to be a bit melodramatic under the circumstances.

'Yes. I believe you.' Mark was close to tears. Eloise had never seen Mark cry. Not once. Not through happiness or grief. He hadn't cried when the girls were born, or when he'd heard he was adopted, or even when Margaret was diagnosed with Alzheimer's. He was old-school English. Stiff upper lip. An internaliser. He'd never bought into the new man vogue that gave guys permission to cry at animated movies. She did not want to be the one to make him cry.

Eloise swept the flowers into one arm and him into the other and she kissed him. His lips, cold from the night air, fitted hers, hot from the warmth of the kitchen. He kissed her back. Carefully at first, eyes open and staring at one another. It was like a first kiss. Unexpected. Unsure. Unknown. Clearly well received. Mark's confidence grew and he started to kiss Eloise with determination and intention. His kiss became vigorous, sensual and overpowering. It was nothing like Charlie's childish and desperate fumble that had taken place in this very room this morning. Her husband kissed her as though he was concentrating, something they sometimes forgot to do because of their cluttered lives, chock-a-block with endless chores and errands. For too long they had been settling for affectionate but thoughtless pecks on the cheek. This kiss was deep and focused, startling and interesting. All the things Mark and Eloise were to one another, all the things they'd taken for granted.

'Your hair is wet,' mumbled Eloise through the kissing.

'I went swimming in the sea,' he muttered, not wanting to talk, just wanting to kiss.

'In this weather! You're mad.' Eloise broke away momentarily and started to worry about hypothermia.

'Possibly. I haven't skinny dipped since I was a teenager but I just needed to, you know . . .'

'Get back to nature?' Eloise threw out the cliché doubtfully.

'Not exactly.'

'Sober up?' She could vaguely smell the faint hint of alcohol on his breath. He shouldn't have driven.

'That was part of it. I just wanted to . . .' He stumbled.

'Feel something?' she asked with more thought.

'Yes.'

Eloise was tempted to ask him what specifically was it that he'd wanted to feel when he'd plunged into the icy sea? Young, clean, renewed, challenged, scared? What was he facing down? Mark was a man who did his best to hide what he was feeling but any of these emotions were possible, he had a right to them all. Eloise decided this wasn't the moment for a chat but instead she started to kiss him again. They kissed for ever. He moved on from her lips. He kissed her neck, sending shivers erupting through her body, he kissed her jaw, her cheeks and her eyelids and he whispered in her ears telling her he loved her and she told him that she knew, she knew. They lost track of time and just roved. Being together was all; the misunderstandings, the silences, the fear, the embarrassment dissolved away. Eloise couldn't think of anything other than Mark's kisses.

That was until he picked her up and carried her to the kitchen table.

'I can't believe we haven't christened this room,' he said. His voice was husky with longing and lust. Eloise had never felt as appreciated and attractive, or at least not for a long time. A complex ball of emotion threatened to choke her; relief, gratitude and pure, unadulterated lust. Overwhelmed, she took refuge in banter.

'We haven't christened any rooms in the house, other than our bedroom.' She didn't add that they'd only done that a couple of times. Quickies. Auto-pilot sex.

'Well, there's a challenge,' said Mark, beaming. His smile lifted her heart, cleared her head and caused flutters between her legs. He gently pushed her back on to the table.

Afterwards, they talked. Mark asked Eloise to tell him exactly what had happened with Charlie, and she did so, including the first kiss in the bathroom. She laid out the facts as calmly and coolly as she could.

'I was nothing more than a sympathetic pair of ears for Charlie and because he's so stressed out about baby making and finances he's inflated our relationship from friendship to something more. It was nothing in reality. A brief infatuation. Everyone makes mistakes.'

'They do,' groaned Mark. 'I thought –' he coughed as he choked on his words – 'I thought I was losing you. I just couldn't stand that, El. Not considering everything with my mum and the adoption. If I lost you and the girls . . .' Mark sounded panicked.

'Shushhh. It's OK.' She kissed him again, to calm him down. They were in bed now, because whilst the kitchen table was fun and liberating it was also a bit cold and uncomfortable, so the second time they made love (second!), they did it in the comfort of their bed, between the White Company duvet and sheets. Eloise was lying on her side, head propped up on one elbow. Mark was flat on his back, staring at the ceiling but drinking in every word she offered up. They'd lit the fire in their bedroom; it was only the second time they'd bothered to do this and the warmth and the smell of burning logs swaddled them. Eloise couldn't think why they didn't light the fire every night, she couldn't think why they didn't make love every night. It was heaven.

'Are you angry?' she asked.

'Not with you,' he muttered. 'Certainly not.'

'With him?'

'I'm so sorry, Eloise. I should have trusted you. I should never have left this morning. We have to stop seeing Charlie and Sara. You know that, don't you?'

Eloise had expected Mark to ask this of her, she understood why it was necessary but she wished it wasn't. 'Cutting Sara off is going to be hard. She's one of my closest friends. Possibly my closest,' sighed Eloise. She wished there was another way.

'No, she's not. Your friendship is all one way. What does she do for you?'

'Friendship is not about what's done for you.'

'OK, then what is it about?'

'Having fun together, making memories together and what you do for them.'

'Well, I accept you'd do anything for her.' The surrogacy offer pounded around both their heads. 'But when did she last make you laugh, or arrange a night out or even ask you how you are?'

Put so starkly Eloise was forced to face the bleak facts. 'Well, she's been going through a bad time,' she muttered half-heartedly. Even she could see that things had become unbalanced, untenable.

'So have we. I don't want anything more to do with them.'

'What should I tell Sara?'

'Nothing.' Mark looked worn out with the subject. 'Let's not talk about them any more.'

Eloise allowed the silence to wash over her. She decided Mark was right. She had to let the friendship go. They could do without the hassle. It would be very difficult to try to get past this incident with Charlie, why bother? Instead, what Eloise needed to do was to focus on her family.

'How are you, Mark?' she asked.

'How am I?' He seemed confused by the question.

'Yes. How are *you*? Really? We've never talked about your mum or the adoption. You've pushed me away.'

'I know.'

'It's not healthy.'

'I know. I'm sorry.'

'Don't apologise. Just tell me what you are thinking. Let's tackle it.'

'You want to fix me now?'

'Is that so bad?' She put her hand on his chest. She could feel his heart beating. 'Look, even if I can't fix this one, I'd like at least to be part of the mess,' she said with a smile.

Mark was silent for a few more minutes and then he said, 'It feels like I've lost everything. I don't know who I am any more. I don't know where I came from. I don't know where the girls came from.'

'You're overreacting. They came from me, from you. That hasn't changed.'

Eloise's hand was still resting on his chest. She could feel his heart-beat speeding up. His anguish hung around in the air they were breathing. She moved her hand to his face and started to stroke his cheekbone. It was damp. Eloise froze as she registered that her husband was sobbing silently. Then a strange sound escaped from him. Something between a howl and a groan. The sound of misery and loss. It cracked the air as he cried, 'Everything has changed.'

FEBRUARY

37

Ray stood on a small wooden stool and reached up to the top of the wardrobe. He had made the stool in woodwork class when he was a lad of about eleven years old. It was well put together. Mark had taken proud ownership of the stool when he was a toddler, once he'd understood that his dad had crafted it. Now Mark was concerned whether the old stool could take Ray's weight. Mark looked on anxiously but knew better than to offer help. Mark was more or less constantly anxious about his parents at the moment. His parents, Eloise and the girls. He found he was riddled with a vague feeling of fretfulness when he saw his mother and father walk through the cobbled streets, which were made treacherous with regular February frosts. He constantly warned the girls to take extra care when they were messing about on the boats or even crossing the road. He'd taken Eloise's car in for a service even though it wasn't due for months; he wanted the car to be in prime condition as she drove around the twisty, narrow roads. Mark was waiting for something bad to happen.

Something else bad to happen.

Eloise wanted him to see a counsellor. It was obvious to her that his anxiety was a result of receiving the unforeseen news that he was adopted and then fast on the heels of that, the confirmed diagnosis that Margaret had Alzheimer's. He'd endured a seismic shift in his world and he was struggling to find a sure footing again. Mark refused point blank to see a counsellor on the grounds that he'd never liked

Woody Allen's films. However, he had at least talked to Ray and Margaret and he'd told them he'd like to try to trace his birth mother and even his birth father, if that was at all possible. Ray swallowed the news with a dignified and understanding nod of the head. If he felt rejected or in any way inadequate, he did not show it. Instead he offered to dig out the few bits that had come with Mark, in a hope that they might find a trail. Margaret said she'd put the kettle on and that she'd always liked playing 'Hunt the Thimble'.

Eloise had wanted Mark to face his feelings but she hadn't *necessarily* wanted him to trace his birth family, not that she had a problem with him doing so – she knew it had to be his decision and all she wanted was for him to be happy. She pledged her support either way, although she was desperately hoping that if they did track down his birth mother she would be at least one twentieth as wonderful as Margaret. The idea of inheriting a trickier mother-in-law, after all these years of marriage, wasn't something Eloise relished.

Secretly, Eloise had started to torture herself with 'what if' moments; none of them were particularly positive. She didn't find herself pondering What if his birth mum has won the lottery and wanted to give us a couple of million? Instead she found her mind rammed with thoughts such as what if this woman doesn't want contact? Will Mark then be left feeling rejected again? What if she's no longer alive or Mark can't find her? Will the search go on and on and on like some bad art house movie? What if she's in need of financial support and expects our help? Or worse, what if his other mother is ill too and needs running to the doctor's or hospital every five minutes? What if she was an alcoholic? Eloise wondered whether she had the necessary resources for a stranger. Eloise could even see problems if the woman was overjoyed that Mark had tracked her down. What if she wanted to spend too much time with them? Eloise had only just begun to reap the benefits of spending time with her family and not using every weekend as a platform to showcase her hosting skills. The past weeks had been peaceful and she wasn't sure whether she was ready to relinquish them. Eloise managed to keep her concerns in check. She tried to pour caution but not cold water.

'Deciding to trace a relative has to be one of the most life-changing decisions anyone ever makes,' she had said, as conversationally as possible, one night as they were watching *Merlin* on TV with the girls. The storyline had happily offered her a segue into the very difficult topic.

'Yes, I realise that,' Mark had commented. The girls were unaware of the conversation taking place above their heads and kept their eyes glued to the screen. Emily and Erin both had a crush on King Arthur although Poppy thought Merlin was the nicest. Their youthful, barely understood longings were enough to keep them occupied.

'The outcome is unknown and the journey will be an emotional rollercoaster.' Eloise had read that in a self-help book; she'd hoped it sounded like her own advice.

'Are you saying you don't want me to look for them?'

'No. No, of course not. I just want you to be sure about your reasons for doing so. It might be exciting and fulfilling but it might also be frustrating and disappointing. I just want you to be prepared,' Eloise had warned carefully.

But Mark was determined, which was why they were now in Ray and Margaret's bedroom watching Ray precariously balance on the wooden stool.

Ray handed down the small box of keepsakes; Mark noticed that his father's hand was shaking. He wondered whether he was dizzy because he'd been standing up on a stool or whether there was another reason.

The box didn't reveal much. Eloise leaned over Mark's shoulder but there wasn't a letter written by his birth mother, a tearful confession explaining her particular circumstances, begging for his understanding and including a forwarding address in case of the eventuality that he ever wanted to meet up for a coffee. That would have been too much to ask. Of course, a letter like that would also have been too much for Ray and Margaret to hide.

'There's not much to go on. Sorry to disappoint,' said Ray. 'We don't even have your original birth certificate.'

'What was I called before?'

'Mark. You came as Mark. Mark Antony, she called you. The social worker said she picked the name because of Antony and Cleopatra. She'd probably seen the Burton/Taylor film, I imagine. We kept her choice because it seemed the proper thing to do.'

Eloise glanced at Mark and wondered again whether this was the right move. He had parents who had lived their life doing the proper thing, wasn't that enough? Mark's face was impassive; only a twitch at the side of his mouth gave away the fact that he was working damned hard to stay impassive.

'The first step is to make sure we have as much information about your origins as possible,' said Ray. Eloise had heard him use this tone of voice in the past on many occasions, on the telephone when he'd been talking to clients. No doubt he found it reassuring to retreat into the rigidity of the law. 'We need to get hold of a copy of your original birth certificate, which will contain identifying information about your birth mother and birth father, if it was ever recorded. As you were adopted before the twelfth of November 1975 and we don't know your surname at birth, we'll need to apply to the Registrar General for access to birth records.' Eloise was sure that Mark must be comforted by the fact that his father constantly referred to what they had to do as a team. 'I've already made some inquiries and I'm told that you'll also need to meet with an adoption advisor. They become a sort of intermediary between us and the Registrar General. Meeting with an adoption advisor is required because, prior to the twelfth of November 1975, promises of lifelong confidentiality were given to birth parents. At that time it was understood the adoption order would mean that all legal ties to the birth family were severed and that there would be no further contact.' Ray didn't wait for Mark to respond to his words, he coughed and then returned to the box. 'There's no real information in this box at all. Just things with sentimental value.' He pawed over the contents.

There was a thin, mass-produced cream blanket with a yellow ribbon trim, a dated but immaculate blue cotton Babygro and a photo. Ray picked out each item, one by one, and handed them to Mark. Mark couldn't take his eyes off his father's hands. Eloise wondered whether this was because he didn't want to look into his father's face or because when he'd clasped the cream blanket Mark's hand had brushed up against Ray's; a hand marked with age spots, that felt like the grease-proof paper Margaret used to line cake tins when she was baking. Hands that had lifted him into the air, tied his shoe laces and fastened his buttons, hands that had taught Mark to skim a stone, and make a catapult, hands that fastened his cufflinks on his wedding day when Mark had been too jittery to do so himself.

'Your mother knitted all your blankets,' said Ray. 'But she couldn't bring herself to throw this out because it came with you. We never wanted to wipe out your past.' Ray paused, awkward. Aware that they had ignored Mark's past whether that had been their intention or not. 'We simply wanted to give you a future.'

'Have you got the box out?'

Ray, Mark and Eloise all jumped at the sound of Margaret's voice. They'd decided to tackle this operation while she'd been dozing on the chair in the sitting room. No one was sure how she'd take it, as no one was ever sure of anything about Margaret nowadays. She was now taking some medication that was supposed to help but didn't always. Yesterday she threw a pineapple at the greengrocer's head because she'd thought he'd cheated her when weighing out mushrooms. Eloise had tried to defuse the situation by making jokes about the fact that Margaret had missed her vocation and should have trained for the 1968 Olympics, she'd have had a chance in the shot put. The greengrocer, who was new to Dartmouth (he had moved here just four years ago), didn't see the funny side and said the 'crazy old bat' was banned from his shop.

Ray, Mark and Eloise stared at Margaret warily, trying to judge her state of mind. She moved towards the bed where the box lay open. She took the blanket off Mark and buried her face in it. 'I think this came from the hospital,' she said thoughtfully. Margaret addressed her comment to Mark. 'It has that air about it, doesn't it? An institutional air. But I'm not sure. They didn't tell us much.' She sighed. 'We didn't ask much. I do know that she was eighteen. She was supposed to be going to university. So must have been a bright girl. Cambridge, wasn't it, Ray?'

Ray nodded. 'It was never confirmed. They didn't want to give out that sort of detail but the social worker was so impressed that she let it slip. It wasn't the norm, you see.'

'Cambridge?' Eloise couldn't help but be impressed too. 'Maybe she'd read the play, then, rather than seen the film. Shakespeare rather than Hollywood.'

Ray looked surprised at Eloise's suggestion. He'd clearly never thought of that.

'Maybe,' he admitted now.

'I used to like imagining her at Cambridge,' added Margaret. 'I imagined her as having long, dark, flowing hair, dashing through the arches, rushing to her lectures.' Margaret paused and looked at Mark. 'Dark hair, like yours, I thought. I always imagined her very happy in amongst those gowns and books because I wanted her to be happy, Mark. You understand, don't you? You see, she'd made us so happy. That girl made me the happiest woman in the world.'

'We don't know for definite, of course. She may never have gone to university,' said Ray, refusing to get caught up in the potential romanticism.

'I like to think she did,' said Margaret firmly. The family fell silent. They were all looking at the flimsy baby blanket. Margaret stroked the tiny Babygro, it wasn't much bigger than an adult's hand. She turned to Mark and almost giggled. Eloise knew she must be marvelling at the fact that a tiny baby could grow into such a big guy; it was a fact that surprised every mother. Eloise suddenly thought of Margaret's cook books, she imagined the endless meals her mother-in-law had cooked to grow this man.

'I do know something, though, son,' said Margaret, breaking the contemplative silence.

'What's that?'

'She loved you very much. I've always been so certain of that because look, she took this photo the day you were first born. Look, it's dated.' Margaret handed the photo to Mark, and Eloise peeked at it from over his shoulder. Baby Mark was lying in just a towelling nappy on a mattress. His eyes were wide open and he was staring at whoever had taken the shot. He looked like most small babies in photographs, wrinkly and startled. He looked healthy, bigger than average. His hair was the only truly notable feature; black and thick even then and perhaps there was something about the shape of his lips that was familiar too. Her girls had inherited his lips but, oddly, not his hair colour. Eloise had thought that gene would dominate her blondness but in fact the three girls were all fair. 'I knew from this photo how much she loved you. You see, she's taken a photo of you as near naked as she dared. I think she was trying to drink you up. Absorb every last bit of you while she could. And look here –' Margaret pointed to the edge of the snap – 'this photo has been part of a set. In those days we used to get photos printed in shops and they often did the same image in pairs or even fours. So you could give one to relatives and such. Can you see, this has been cut with a pair of scissors? Along this edge. I think that she kept the same image. I've always imagined she kept it in her purse.'

'You don't know that,' said Ray grumpily.

'No, but I do know that she gave us a copy of this photo, no matter what she did with the other one. She loved you so much, Mark, that she gave us this photo of you before we knew you, so even those few weeks could be ours too. Do you understand what I'm saying? She was generous enough to gift us everything. I always thought that showed her to be something special.'

Mark didn't comment. It was a lot to take in. He was dealing with an overwhelming rush of gratitude, whereas for months he'd been swamped by feelings of frustration and anger. Suddenly, he was grateful to the woman who gave birth to him, whoever she was, wherever she might be. And he was grateful to his mum and dad, who clearly loved him, had always loved him, and always would. The resentment, that they had kept his adoption a secret, receded fractionally. He understood that they had done what they thought was best at the time. The terror that his mum was disappearing still tore at his gut but he was grateful that she was lucid right now. He was so, so appreciative that, on top of everything she'd already given him, she'd given him this story too.

38

Eloise found that severing her intimate friendship with Sara was considerably easier than she'd feared. Eloise had no idea how she should tell Sara that it would no longer be possible to have daily telephone calls that might last over an hour, that she would not be available to scoot down the motorway whenever she was needed to comfort or console and that Sara and Charlie would no longer be welcome to join the Hamiltons for festivities and holidays. She wondered whether she ought to slowly retract, simply send texts and emails for a while, rather than making any direct contact. This would allow the friendship to cool to tepid and ultimately freeze over altogether. Or should she call and say she was going to be out of action for a while as she concentrated on Margaret's health care? It wouldn't be an absolute lie but then it probably wouldn't be a powerful enough excuse to put off Sara; she was very determined about commanding attention if she needed it. It didn't cross Eloise's mind that she should tell Sara about Charlie's hideously inappropriate behaviour. Eloise was not the sort of woman who'd get any pleasure from breaking another woman's heart. As it happened, Eloise didn't have to do any severing. Three days after Charlie left the Hamiltons with a bloody nose, Sara called Eloise.

Eloise was sitting in the Dart Café with Arabella and Jackie enjoying the long overdue but oft-talked-about cup of coffee and sticky bun. Eloise liked the Dart Café very much. She and the girls were in the habit of going there on Friday evenings, after school, to sit on the mismatched chairs and eat fish-finger sandwiches accompanied by a bowl of fries. Arabella and Jackie had witnessed Eloise's patience and dedication with Margaret and they'd seen that the Woddells had visited the Hamiltons over Christmas, so they'd concluded that Eloise couldn't possibly be a total bitch, despite the impression she'd given at the disastrous dinner party. They were experienced enough to understand that even the most decent people lost patience and perspective occasionally. Although Eloise had never considered it, Arabella and Jackie were also very keen to extend their friendship circle and so were delighted when the buoyant Hamiltons moved into the town. They'd opted not to race to a hasty judgement after the dinner party but instead decided to spend a bit more time with Eloise and try to get to know her, if she'd let them. They'd been pleased when, after the Christmas holidays, she'd called Arabella and suggested a lift share to school and then called Jackie and suggested a date for coffee.

The women had spent the morning discussing whether it might be possible to organise a pony-trek along the beaches in the early spring for children and adults. Eloise knew her girls would love that. Their lessons in London hadn't tested their skills beyond gently trotting around Hampstead Heath under close supervision. Eloise resisted offering to organise the entire project but enthusiastically signed up to participate.

When Eloise saw Sara's number flash on her mobile her heart had sunk to the bottom of her Hunter wellies.

'I'm so sorry, I do have to take this, but order me another coffee, it won't take long,' Eloise had said as she'd left the table, pulled on her coat and headed outside. She'd wanted to pledge her commitment to the coffee date but she couldn't ignore Sara.

It was chilly outside the steamy café. Eloise rocked from the balls of her feet to her heels in an attempt to encourage circulation.

'Hello, Eloise.'

'Hi, Sara.' Eloise didn't know what tone of voice she ought to try to hit. Jovial, as though there was nothing wrong? Or serious? Because, after all, Charlie had left her home with a bloody nose and some sort of explanation was likely to be required. She'd tried to keep her tone neutral and waited to hear what Sara had to say.

'I thought I'd better call.'

'Right.' What did Sara know? What was she thinking?

'Charlie told me what happened.'

'He told you?'

'About the accident with Erin opening the door into his face and your somewhat unsympathetic reaction.' Sara had paused over the word unsympathetic, letting her disapproval be felt. Eloise bristled as the charge fell at her feet; but she had to stay silent and try to piece together the fictitious story. 'It could have been broken,' Sara added shortly. 'I realise it was an accident, but I do think you should have offered to take Charlie to hospital and I really don't think you should have allowed him to drive all the way back to London.'

'Well, he's old enough to make his own decisions,' replied Eloise, through gritted teeth. So, Charlie had gone home and spouted a load of lies, well, what had she expected? He was unlikely to have returned to his wife and admitted to declaring undying love for Eloise. 'Is it broken?' Eloise had asked, actually hoping it was.

'No. But considering everything, I'm sure you can see why he had to resign from your job. I think we both know that you were becoming a little too demanding. I remember that time I came to yours for dinner, way back in November, and he was working on your kitchen sink although it was past seven in the evening.' Eloise wanted to interrupt and point out that she hadn't asked Charlie to fiddle with the faucet but she decided not to bother. What was the point of dripping just a bit of truth into the fabrication Charlie had constructed? 'I don't *blame* you, Eloise. I know you are extremely house proud' – Sara made the charge that someone was house proud sound akin to accusing them of having a particularly nasty venereal disease – 'but you have to see the arrangement was becoming untenable.'

'Yes, I do see that now,' muttered Eloise. That much she could agree with.

'There was such tension at Christmas.' Eloise sighed. Yes, she had to admit that was also certainly true. Sara carried on. 'Living in someone else's house, no matter how lovely that someone else is, is so difficult. And I missed him.' Eloise certainly hadn't noticed that. 'He just had to get out. Get home. I'm sure you'll be a bit cross because you won't find anyone else who could do such a marvellous job at such a great price but I'm fully depending on the strength of our friendship to see us through this muddle.'

Eloise was almost swept along. She almost believed that Erin had injured Charlie, that she'd been unsympathetic, then demanding and finally argumentative so, really, Charlie had no alternative but to resign and return to his loving wife. If she almost believed it, no wonder Sara had bought it hook, line and sinker.

Eloise seethed for a few moments and then she recognised that Charlie had inadvertently done her a favour. His version of the dissolving of their relationship at least provided an explanation for a cooling off of their relationship. She could simply capitulate to the lie presented before her and she wouldn't have to say Mark had demanded that they split; she was off the hook.

'Charlie's found work locally now. You may not be seeing as much of us as usual. We're going to be very, very busy. I'm sure you under-stand,' added Sara with finality.

Eloise returned to the café and ordered a second cake.

'Treating yourself?' asked Arabella.

'Yes.'

'For shock or celebrating good news?' asked Jackie, with concerned interest, glancing at the telephone still cradled in Eloise's hand.

'Bit of both,' replied Eloise as she crammed the carrot cake into her mouth and sank into its sweetness.

JULY

39

Eloise could hardly believe she'd lived in Dartmouth for a year now; on the other hand, she could no longer remember – with absolute clarity – living in London. She couldn't quite recall the smell of dust and heat in an underground station, blasting like a dragon's roar when a train pulled into the station. She couldn't precisely remember the exact sound of the traffic thundering, honking and screeching as busy people rushed from A to B, correctly confident of their importance. She couldn't even entirely recall her havens; the glittering windows of the King's Road, the cool serenity in the deeply impressive halls of the National Gallery or the sweet-smelling patisseries in Soho. The aromas and the breeze of the air conditioning eluded her. She had different sounds and sights to indulge in now.

Eloise had learnt to enjoy mellow, rolling hills, peach sunsets and lush green fields. Her ears expected to hear seagulls squawking and boats chugging, she actively listened out for the toot toot of the steam train that nowadays did nothing other than ferry tourists but was a hangover from times of more strenuous industry; she set her watch by it. Eloise and her family had found a new rhythm. They spent their free days crabbing, fishing or paddling and in the evenings they walked to the local pub. All five of them; the girls ate salt and vinegar crisps and drank coke, Eloise and Mark tried real ales and they all played dominoes. Sometimes Ray and Margaret joined them. Their local had stood for nearly eight hundred years and Eloise always felt prickles of excitement scamper up her spine when she thought of the stories packed within the timbers which had once belonged on a merchant ship. The wooden floor boards were steeped in history, dripped in alcohol. She appreciated the low beams, the open fire and lead-framed windows, it was picture perfect. The brass horseshoes that hung on the wall and the plastic dustpan and brush that were tucked behind the bar weren't quite so picture perfect but they were frank. Sometimes Mark and Eloise visited the local arty cinema that showed films a month or so after their release date, sometimes they went to a restaurant, Eloise had finally tried the lobster caldereta at The Seahorse. It was sublime.

On Saturday mornings they often followed bridle paths across the fields and hills and found themselves in the outlying villages where they commented on the candyfloss-coloured houses. They passed small garages, which only had one petrol pump but always sold colourful, tinfoil windmills and plastic buckets and spades. The garages didn't sell alpine car fresheners. The people of Dartmouth were more likely to simply wind down the car window. They stopped off in pubs that advertised real ales, fine wine and great food on blackboards and invariably had a pack of dogs tied up outside. They tried the pub grub which was frequently adventurous and of a good standard and was occasionally disappointing, in which case they settled for a bowl of fat, steaming chips smothered in ketchup. Eloise had become familiar with the twisty roads, the way a woman knew the contours of her own body (a bulge here, a bump there). She knew where the dry-stone walling was tumbling down and while she still regarded the endless walls of hedges with wonder, she no longer saw the high banks of foliage as sinister fences, shutting something out, trapping something in. She no longer felt a sense of claustrophobia. She just saw brambles punctuated by wild flowers and butterflies.

The girls were tanned as they spent most of their time out of doors, combing beaches and scrambling on boats. Eloise was taking swimming lessons at the local pool. Poppy regularly picked cowslips (which she believed to be fairy parasols), buttercups and bluebells. She put some in a vase next to her bed and pressed others between the simple wooden flower press that Ray had made for her. They all played tennis in the courts in the centre of town and had done since February. They played if it was windy or lashing with rain; Erin said it was great training for Wimbledon's centre court. One morning last May, Eloise woke up, looked out the window. Another lovely day, she thought. It took her until she was eating her toast in the kitchen to realise the importance of the placid observation; she'd arrived. She belonged. She was taking it for granted.

Eloise was so utterly confident in her new surroundings that she'd made the decision to spend a week of the summer school holidays visiting her brother and sister-in-law in London, while Mark stayed in Dartmouth working. She wanted to catch up with old friends and take the girls to museums. Since moving to Dartmouth Eloise had avoided going back to London, only visiting when Sara had called on her to do so last year. She'd been concerned that the longings she was taking care to tame would be stirred once again if she returned. She'd gone cold turkey, the way she might have with an ex-lover, best not to be seen at all in case she felt tempted back or simply full of helpless yearning. But now Eloise felt confident that Dartmouth was her home and so she was pretty sure she could holiday in London and be a tourist; enjoy its treats without becoming depressed that she'd stepped outside. She wanted to test herself. Besides, most excitingly, if she went to London she could have her hair coloured by her fabulous and dramatic Russian stylist. Eloise had tried to resist the cliché of disparaging provincial hairdressers but, truthfully, she really hadn't found anyone who was prepared to apply three different shades of blond streaks and she'd had to settle for a less sophisticated block colour.

The girls were giggly and excited when they saw their Aunt Fran and Uncle Ed and some of their old friends. The Hamilton women spent a few wonderful days spoiling themselves. Eloise wanted to buy a new outfit for Jackie's birthday party. She thought she needed to go to Westfield and the King's Road. She'd allocated a day for shopping but Emily wanted to forage in the massive fashion stores on Oxford

Street too, and the younger two were still interested in visiting a Build-a-Bear shop. Remarkably, they managed to do everything at the cost of a few blisters (and quite some sterling!). They all agreed that YO! Sushi was great fun, as was hanging around Covent Garden watching people pretend to be statues or eat fire. Eloise had never spent time doing any of these things in London. In the past she'd carelessly dismissed these activities as tourist traps, now she found it was fun to be ensnared along with millions of other willing-to-be-pleased, jostling visitors. Was she a tourist now, she wondered? Born and bred a Londoner she no longer lived there. She hadn't lived there for a year. A calendar year equated to a couple of decades in London, as things moved so quickly. Something that was 'in' and 'a must have' late one night might be over by the time you'd eaten your cornflakes the next day. Indeed, that's what she'd always loved about London; she believed that people packed more in, did more, saw more, felt more, thought more. Lived more. But did she still believe that?

Eloise and Fran decided to go to the cinema in Leicester Square one evening, leaving Ed in charge of six kids. They watched a chick-flick which was not thought provoking (well, at least not beyond the thought, 'I wonder where she bought that dress?'), but all the same, the film provided a great night's entertainment. They were planning on taking advantage of the warm summer evening by wandering through the streets looking for a place to eat a late supper but both women sensed a storm in the air and knew that if it rained, taxis would be gold dust later, so they decided to hop in a cab straight away.

'We can have a sandwich at home,' mumbled Fran, sleepily leaning her head against the cab window and closing her eyes.

The cab slowly mooched along Regent Street, one of Eloise's all-time favourite roads. Its grandiose breadth was a reminder of London's former glory days and its huge, gleaming retail windows, boasting a treasure trove of affordable fashion and virtuoso design, were a testament to its current brilliance. The heavens opened as Eloise and Fran had predicted but the street, traffic and shop lights still shimmered like jewellery. Eloise looked out of the window and saw crowds that she recognised, that she used to be part of. There were several groups of young girls stumbling in impractically high fashion shoes; they giggled and clung to their friends, offering each other imperfect support as they wedged their scantily clad bodies under shared umbrellas. She'd been a stumbling girl, dashing to a pub or to a club, hoping that by the time she left she'd be hanging on to the arm of some guy or other.

She watched a stylish twenty-something couple leave a smart restaurant, the young woman sheltered under the restaurant's canopy as the boyfriend efficiently hailed a cab. He opened the door for her and she dashed into the car, kicking up rain water in her wake as she flashed her boyfriend an appreciative and lustful glance. Eloise was reminded of her early dates with Mark; she'd been that young woman. And she'd been that young mother, the one looking harassed and fretful as she dashed towards the Tube pushing a sleeping baby in a buggy, even though it was way past the time a child should be in its own bed. The mother was still at the stage where she thought she could do anything she did before her baby was born. She couldn't. And, in a few months, exhaustion would tell her as much; she'd stop trying to visit late-night experimental art exhibitions with her baby and, instead, choose to pay for a sitter or stay at home and watch a box set of an American TV show. Eloise wished she could wind down the window and tell the woman to cut herself some slack. Eloise spotted another woman, one in her late thirties or early forties, perhaps; carefully, expensively preserved so that it was difficult to be accurate. That woman was grasping a theatre programme. No doubt, she was regretting the fact that she'd eaten a box of chocolates *and* an ice cream during the show. Eloise had certainly been that woman! She watched as the theatre goer linked her arm through her husband's. He had his hands in his pockets and his head down against the rain, he was laughing at something she'd said. It was easier to walk that way in the rain, rather than he with his arm thrown around her shoulders and she with her arm thrown around his waist. Eloise was pretty sure that tonight, when they got home, they'd talk about whether or not they were too tired to have sex and whatever they decided would hardly matter because they knew they loved each other. She could tell by the way they were laughing.

And now Eloise was this woman; the one in the cab observing, the one who'd left London behind because her husband wanted to do so. London was her birthplace, her country's capital city and her world. Yet now, quite definitely, Eloise felt it was all OK. London was still here, in all its vibrancy and vitality. She could visit whenever she wanted; she could go to criminally expensive cinemas, she could amble along the high streets and be amazed at the length of the skirts this season (so long! so short!), here she could buy sushi, Kalamata olives, rogan josh curry or smoked scamorza cheese at midnight, if the mood took her. But in London she couldn't walk along dramatic rugged coastal paths. She couldn't feel the wind in her hair and the salt and sand stick to her skin. During the cab journey home Eloise finally and firmly accepted that being a tourist in London – an appreciative, awe-struck tourist – was OK. It was certainly better than being a jaded or complacent inhabitant. She realised that London still belonged to her, even though she no longer lived there, and she found the fact very reassuring.

On the last day of the holiday Eloise left the girls with Ed and Fran, so that she could visit the hair salon in peace. The plan was for the girls to go on the London Eye and visit the aquarium. They had done both of these activities before but Poppy swore she couldn't remember and the other two were compliant enough as they were well aware that a day out with their aunt would be packed with sweet treats and trivial trinkets.

Settling back into the leather-backed chair Eloise eagerly anticipated a couple of hours drinking herbal tea and reading the sort of gossipy magazines that Mark fondly referred to as her comics. She breathed in the chemical smell of hair colourants the way other women might Hoover up the aroma of fresh bread. She felt calm, relaxed and cheerful.

Eloise heard her voice before she saw her. The woman was asking for a trim. She was being very pleasant and giggly with the receptionist as she tried to negotiate being squeezed in for an appointment tomorrow. It was her breeziness that Eloise failed to recognise, it threw her and she had to take a second glance. 'Sara?'

Eloise could hardly believe her eyes. There she was, her old friend, larger than life. Literally.

40

'You're having a baby.'

Sara laughed as she always laughed at the marvellous and delightful thought that she was indeed pregnant and she laughed at Eloise's surprise, which was worn with open affection all over her face. How else, in that split second of time, should she respond?

'Yes, yes, that or I really have been overdoing it with the pies,' Sara joked as she tried to gather her thoughts.

Sara's bump was ripe and obvious. She'd had the perfect pregnancy with no morning sickness, unnecessary bloating, skin tagging or stretch marks. She hadn't been plagued with any worries about diabetes or blood pressure – either high or low. Whenever she visited her midwife the midwife beamed and called her a dream expectant mum. Sara wore her bump loud and proud; the pregnancy flowed out of her belly but did not cling to her upper arms or her backside. The other women in her prenatal class sighed enviously as Sara's hair grew thick and lustrous, her skin cleared and became creamy and spotless and her eyes glistened; they seemed to be lit by an internal light that shined unstintingly. But the other women couldn't hold their resentment because Sara was the happiest mum-to-be imaginable. She never grumbled about feeling tired or hot or sore or large. She actually liked to catch her ballooning reflection in shop windows or mirrors.

Sara and Eloise paused for a moment as the instinctual, breathless excitement at bumping into an old friend was immediately tempered by their recent history, or, rather more accurately, their lack of it. Eloise was awash with an intuitive euphoria at the fact that Sara was pregnant. At last, at last! Hang up the bunting, let the tickertape shower down and crack open the champers! She wanted to throw her arms around her old friend. She wanted to run her hands over the taut bump and lean in and kiss it. She wanted to lavish the little being with love and greetings of delight.

And she also wanted to slap Sara. How could Sara have kept this from her?

Sara saw at once the mix of emotions that were passing through Eloise's mind. She, too, was in turmoil. Following the conversation about the abrupt end of Charlie's contract with the Hamiltons, Sara hadn't really been expecting to see Eloise ever again. There had been times when she had missed Eloise, of course, she was only human. They'd once had such fun together and when the fun stopped they had at least been bound by misery, even if it was all Sara's misery. Eloise had been a good friend throughout the IVF years, Sara could never say anything other. Sara remembered a time, after the second failed IVF, when Eloise had been a particular godsend. Sara had taken sick leave from work, as she just couldn't get back into the stride of things. She struggled to see the point in carrying on with her day-to-day concerns that, by comparison to failed IVF, just seemed utterly futile. Eloise had visited and had found Sara languishing in bed, not bothering to wash, or dress or clean her teeth, not bothering to do anything but allow Radio Four to chunter on in the background. Eloise had snapped off the radio and instead put on *Now That's What I Call Music 77*. She insisted Sara listen to something cheerful. 'I'd be depressed if I listened to nothing other than doom and gloom all day. Go and have a bath.'

Sara had bathed and while she was doing so Eloise had cleared away the discarded mugs that had puddles of tea and mould inside them. She had stripped the bed and put the sheets in the wash. She'd cleared out the rotting fruit and salad from the fridge and then she'd gone to the corner shop and bought fresh replacements as well as chocolate and a couple of glossy magazines. When Sara finally emerged from the bathroom, Eloise had sat with her on the sofa as she sobbed for her lost baby. Sara did this every day for a week and Eloise held her hand. Then Eloise had picked out Sara's clothes and escorted her back to work. Sara remembered this incident and countless similar ones when Eloise had demonstrated exceptional kindness and generosity.

It wasn't all one way, though, Sara reminded herself, irrationally irritated by Eloise's generosity, even though it was Sara recalling Eloise's most glorious moments. Sara had always believed that Eloise rather liked having a friend who didn't fall into one of the usual categories. Sara was useful to Eloise. Eloise was free to tell Sara stories about the girls' triumphs and Sara would celebrate them, rather than try to trump them, the way friends with children of their own so often did. Eloise could furiously blow off steam over school-ground cruelties and Sara would call the playground minxes 'little bitches' with a refreshing honesty that Eloise's mother-friends dared not risk. Eloise's university friends had scattered when they reached their thirties. They were hilarious fun to catch up with from time to time, but they all had their own corners of the UK to rule nowadays. Her old work friends were brilliant, almost too dazzling. Sara sometimes wondered whether Eloise regretted her decision to give up her career, whether she was aware that her ex-colleagues occasionally gossiped about it, questioned it. Sara and Eloise had never competed on the same stage and there must have been some compensation in that.

Naturally, there'd been times during this pregnancy when Sara had been tempted to call Eloise. She'd wanted to share the excitement of the first scan picture, she'd wanted to endlessly discuss names, she'd wanted advice on what to pack in her hospital bag. Sara knew Eloise would have been the perfect person to indulge her this way, but she had not called.

Being pregnant was everything Sara had ever dreamed it would be and more. The blue line on the pee stick was Willy Wonka's golden wrapper, it was the lottery ticket with winning numbers, it was her passport into the life she'd always wanted. Sara felt delight surge back into every cell of her body. At times she felt as though she might implode with happiness. The pregnancy had given her the confidence to cut her losses, start afresh. She didn't need to complicate her life with trying to rescue a friendship with the Hamiltons. It had become a difficult, uneven friendship; sometimes she thought of it as stale, bordering on toxic. Yet here was Eloise, standing in front of Sara, beaming that wide, accepting smile that Eloise had a copyright on. A smile that embodied an olive branch. Eloise was expecting to be welcomed and warmly received. Sara had always found Eloise's buoyancy difficult to challenge. Eloise wasn't even fazed by the tinfoil packs dancing around her head. Most women would have pretended not to see Sara waddle into the salon; they would have shrunk behind their over-read copy of *Closer*, but not Eloise. Eloise called out to Sara, reached out to her. It was touching.

'I simply can't believe it!' she gushed. 'You're pregnant!' She actually clapped her hands. 'It really is a dream come true. I want to hear *everything*. I want to know *all* about this pregnancy minute by minute.'

If Eloise felt any resentment that Sara hadn't called to tell her the news, she buried it immediately. She was all about the thrill of it. The joy of it. She wouldn't have dreamt of pouring cold water by grumbling. Her effervescent mood once again enchanted Sara, like it always had. Sara felt herself wanting to giggle and natter with Eloise, she wanted to share her most amazing and intimate moments. Eloise always knew exactly what to say, exactly what Sara wanted to hear. Against her better judgement, after much gushing and chuckling, after a lavish sprinkling of compliments about how Sara was radiant, positively blooming (sincerely given, warmly received), Sara agreed to meet Eloise for a celebratory dinner that evening.

She couldn't not, it was the only way to stop Eloise repeatedly shouting, 'Ohmygod. Ohmygod. I'm so thrilled. I'm *so thrilled* for you.'

41

Eloise was not naturally secretive; it went against her grain. She was a chatty and effusive person who had a tendency to over-talk and over-explain so she felt distinctly uncomfortable when she'd mumbled, vaguely, to her sister-in-law about meeting 'friends' for dinner rather than offering up any detail. The issue was Mark had asked her not to see the Woddells again and she was expressly going against his wishes. She veered from feeling outraged that he'd given her this directive – after all, hadn't Emmeline Pankhurst fought ferociously so women had an equal say? – to believing that, in fact, Mark was completely within his rights. Whenever she thought of Charlie standing almost naked in her kitchen as she and Mark watched his hard-on deflate, she wanted the floor to open up and swallow her.

Mark had once asked, 'When he kissed you, did you like it? Even a little bit?' She'd missed a beat before she'd replied. She'd been searching for a way to be as honest as possible. She hadn't liked *Charlie* kissing her especially but she had liked the fact *someone* wanted to kiss her. Eloise realised that Mark misinterpreted the missed beat; he thought it was a confession of something he'd have to learn to ignore. The only way he could deal with the situation was to cut the Woddells out of their lives. And, on balance, Eloise had been happy to cut them out too. It would have been impossible to have carried on as they were. She'd tried to behave normally at

Christmas and it had felt like collusion, as though she was betraying Sara by sharing a secret with Charlie. So she'd had to let Sara go. Sad Sara. Sara who had become obsessive, a little neurotic and depressive.

But the Sara who she'd met this morning wasn't that woman at all. Sara was now buoyant and alive. She had a rare quality about her; she combined expectancy with fulfilment. It struck Eloise that as she'd done her years of cheering, consoling and comforting, she wanted some of the fun stuff now, some of the celebrating. Most of Eloise's friends had stopped having babies; they'd gone through that phase and were now worrying about school places. Eloise missed the gurgles, the cuddles and the developmental milestones. She'd always loved babies; that was one of the reasons she'd been so sympathetic to Sara's plight. She got it. She got why a woman might become myopic and desperate because of her desire to have a baby. Eloise thought she might have been the same if she hadn't been lucky enough to have Emily, Erin and Poppy. Nowadays, Eloise spent a lot of time cleaning up after Margaret. It was impossible not to notice that some of the necessary care was similar to that of looking after a baby. Margaret had to be watched constantly in case she got herself into trouble with electric appliances or the gas rings. There was also the occasional bathroom accident and the odd tantrum to deal with. Eloise didn't mind doing her share of the practical, messy caring. She'd found that she was good at it. Quite a few people had said she'd missed her vocation, that she was a natural nurse. Eloise doubted that. She was certain she wouldn't have the generosity to attend to a stranger's needs with such care, but on the days when Margaret was lucid and laughing they were so close and Eloise wanted to help her as much as she could.

It would be nice to be welcoming in a baby, though. It would provide balance because, at the back of her mind, no matter how much she tried to hide from the fact, her time with Margaret was all about goodbyes.

Eloise sent Sara a text saying she'd secured a dinner reservation at the sort of restaurant that was so trendy it was actually terrifying. Eloise assumed they must have lucked out and picked up someone else's cancellation because she never really expected to get a table; she'd tried on a whim. Luck must be on their side! The place she'd selected was reputed to be the most expesive restaurant in London. Eloise didn't know if that was actually true, there was some seriously tough competition for that particular honour, how could anyone measure? But it was fair to say that it was the sort of restaurant that only Russian Mafia and those with expense accounts visited. Eating at this sort of place unequivocally said celebration.

Eloise was the first to arrive and was shown to the table. She briefly panicked that Sara might fail to turn up. Their relationship had become so complex and maybe Sara simply didn't need the hassle of unpicking her way through it. Ignorant of Mark's veto, Sara thought that the Woddells had dumped the Hamiltons because Charlie was fed up with working for Eloise, but even that version of events had its own set of consequences. When Sara had called last January, she'd spoken as though she expected them all to remain civil, if not actively friendly. She must have been expecting Eloise to stay in touch to some extent, perhaps she envisaged that they'd swap the odd text or e-mail, but Eloise hadn't. She had her reasons but she couldn't explain them, not without causing more hurt and upset. Eloise worried that Sara must have felt offended and confused that she'd been cut out of the Hamilton world so suddenly. El had briefly wondered why Sara had accepted the new status so quickly and thoroughly; now it was all clear. Sara must have found out she was pregnant right around that time. Such news would have been more than enough to wipe the Hamiltons from her mind.

Eloise sat, straight backed, on one of the vibrant and unique hand-painted Julie Verhoeven chairs that the restaurant website made such a fuss about; she waited patiently for Sara. The room was swathed in various shades of luxurious gold; the palette and the towering ceilings created an ambience of a Renaissance court. On the walls there hung huge, ever-changing screens, with various video exhibitions from young, emerging artists whom the restaurant wished to support. Tonight's exhibition was of cityscapes. Paris, Eloise guessed; if she'd correctly placed the numerous bountiful fountains, elegant gas lamp-posts, impressive cream buildings, and flanking wide avenues. Paris, lovely, she mused.

Eloise spotted Sara approaching, she threaded through the tables making jokes with other diners about the size of her bump. Eloise jumped up and leaned in to kiss her.

'Wow, you really do look gorgeous, Sara,' she said enthusiastically. She was always quick with the compliments and she was always absolutely sincere, but as compliments weren't generally freely given in the land of the stiff upper lip her effusiveness was often mistrusted. Eloise held Sara at arm's length so she could have another good look at her, bump and all. She kept her hands on Sara's elbows; many Londoners air kissed and dismissed but Eloise never had.

'You look great too!' Sara gushed. She now had it in her heart to be equally magnanimous.

Eloise smiled; it was a smile that revealed genuine pleasure and relief. Obviously she enjoyed receiving a compliment, who didn't? But her pleasure was mostly derived from the fact that Sara was giving every sign of having re-entered the land of the living. Eloise couldn't remember the last time she'd received a compliment from Sara.

Eloise was wearing a purple pleated skirt; the colour and style were both very fashionable and she was confident about this because she'd read as much in a magazine yesterday, just before she'd shopped for Jackie's party. There weren't many people who could pull off the pleats. Pleats created booty where there was an ironing board but, on Eloise, the skirt looked fresh and sophisticated. She'd teamed it with a raspberry cashmere jumper and she was wearing beautiful purple patent leather killer heels that weren't going to be much use to her in Dartmouth but she didn't care; they were irresistible and had called to her from the shop window. Eloise saw Sara clock her new clobber. 'I had a splurge,' she confessed with a cheerful grin and a careless shrug.

The women sat down. A waitress appeared at their table. She was clearly a model-in-waiting, so beautiful she was almost intimidating.

'I'm Angel English and I'm your host for this evening. Do let me know if I can do anything at all to make your evening more pleasurable,' she said, as though they were in California and could genuinely expect good service. A few moments were lost as Angel took their drinks order and then brought them a small bowl of olives. The women remained silent using the hustle and bustle to organise their thoughts. Once they'd settled Eloise said, 'So, you're pregnant!' She was stating the obvious but neither of them were likely to get bored of the news.

'Yes.' Sara beamed so widely that Eloise really thought her friend's face might split. They both giggled as the unbearable tension, created over years of longing, began to seep away. It was mind-blowing.

Eloise continued, 'It's such wonderful news. It's amazing. It's—'

'Shocking?'

'Well, surprising. I mean, the last time we talked about it, Charlie was so against another round of IVF. When did he change his mind?' Eloise looked at the size of Sara's bump with a practised eye and tried to guess how far on Sara was.

'It's not an IVF baby. It's natural. It's a miracle.'

'Oh. My. God.' This time Eloise gave in to a sea of emotion; tears threatened, in fact, they spilt, unequivocal tears of joy. She jumped up from her seat and started squealing, she flung her arms around Sara in a display that was so full of passion that she knocked over her glass of water. Judging by the flock of waiters who instantly surrounded their table, oozing concern and mild irritation, it was obvious that her actions were probably the most uncool display to ever have taken place on this hallowed ground. 'I just can't believe it! I just can't. I mean, you do read about it, though, don't you? Just when a couple gives up hope, a miracle happens.'

'I hadn't given up hope,' Sara stated calmly, interrupting Eloise's jabbering.

'No, well, of course not. But it was, erm, looking difficult.' Eloise was choosing her words carefully; she was used to doing so around Sara. 'OK, OK, tell me everything. What was Charlie's reaction when you first told him?' Eloise knew she had to ask.

'Delighted, of course.'

'Of course.' Eloise hurried on, 'And how far along are you? What's the due date?'

'I'm thirty weeks along which means I'm due on the twenty-seventh of September.'

'But there might be some room for manoeuvre, yes? I mean, two weeks either way. Doctors do that calculation that doesn't seem to have anything to do with when you actually might have had sex,' said Eloise with a laugh. Over the years a number of her friends had said the same. They'd either endured long pregnancies because the midwife had insisted they go ten days past the due date or had been caught by surprise, two weeks before they were expecting the baby to arrive.

'I am due on the twenty-seventh,' said Sara firmly.

'Well, yes, they do get it right more often than not,' said Eloise, doing a U-turn, quite prepared to accept anything Sara said because she wanted everything about this evening to run smoothly and pleasantly.

'I know the exact the day I conceived.'

'You do! I did!' squealed Eloise, loving the fact that they'd fallen back into an easy intimacy.

'I know. I remember you saying. The millennium, the car seat and the corporate dinner.' Sara counted the conceptions on her fingers. 'But mine is less about a romantic notion about – you know – a sensation, although that's part of it, obviously. Mine's a bit more practical. We went without sex for months after I lost the last baby.'

'I see.' Eloise's mood sobered a fraction at the mention of the last miscarriage.

'There's only one date it could possibly have been. So, I guess it's pretty clear cut.'

'Right.'

'We've had sex since, obviously,' Sara added as an afterthought.

Eloise didn't quite know how to respond and so offered, 'My goodness.'

'Goes to show, eh? This one is meant to be.'

'Absolutely.'

'It was that day Charlie left yours, actually.'

'Oh, right.' Eloise suddenly wanted a drink. She wished Sara hadn't told her this. Now, she saw the pregnancy in a slightly different light. It was a wonderful miracle, of course, but now a grubby thought crept into Eloise's head; She couldn't help but think the conception might have come from something less pure than the simple desire for a baby or the love between Charlie and Sara. She briefly wondered whether Charlie had arrived home angry, rejected or humiliated. Did he have sex with Sara to make himself feel better, to feel more desirable, after Eloise's rebuff, or was it to feel more secure in case his attempted indiscretion with Eloise was ever revealed? Either way, it seemed a bit sullied and desperate.

Eloise glanced at Sara. She was glowing; rosy cheeked, sparkly eyed and clearly deliriously happy. Eloise took a deep breath. What did it matter? Not at all. It did not matter if this baby was conceived in less than ideal circumstances. It was a baby! Besides, if Mark could have been privy to Eloise's thoughts on the matter (which he really couldn't be!) then he'd have laughed out loud. He'd have said she had an inflated sense of her own importance. He was good at bringing her back down to earth if she got carried away. He would have pointed out that there was nothing more natural than a couple rushing back into one another's arms or, in this case, rushing back into bed after they'd been through a rough patch. Hadn't the Hamiltons done exactly that? It was survival, animalistic, erotic, even. If Eloise had played a part in this at all it was to show Charlie how much he loved Sara and how important it was that he was at her side. This conception was nothing to do with Charlie's anger, rejection or humiliation, it was all about reaffirmation, love and verification. Eloise smiled to herself, much more comfortable with that version of events. The baby was a wonderful miracle. Full stop.

Eloise started to giggle. She was overwhelmed about how wonderful this news was. 'God, I want to drink champagne. I'm going to order a glass, you can have a sip.'

The women ordered their food without looking at the prices. Sara chose a starter of beetroot salad with gingerbread and fig and vinegar sorbet and made it clear that this was because beetroot was a great source of nutrients, including magnesium, sodium, potassium and vitamin C, all of which the baby would welcome with open arms. They discussed Sara's food choices at length; Eloise indulged her in doing so because they knew this was a club that Sara had been longing to join. The club where women were painful to eat with.

'You should avoid the oysters.'

'Not just because they bring back traumatic memories of your terrible dinner party.'

'I meant because pregnant women shouldn't eat oysters.'

'Right. For my main I'll have organic salmon.'

'Oh yes, it comes with fennel and bok choy, very nutritious.'

'I'll ask the waiter to tell the chef to hold the white wine broth. Normally, I would've picked the roast lamb fillet, but it comes with peanut and tandoori sauce, and everyone knows that feeding a foetus peanuts is tantamount to homicide,' said Sara.

Eloise laughed indulgently.

The evening passed in a flash of bonhomie. It was just like old times, the very old times. Before baby longing choked and smothered them. Laughter was frequent and unfettered, the conversation was lively and unguarded. Eloise got over her issue of drinking alone and knocked back three glasses of champagne as Sara talked about the baby. They talked about names (Sara was undecided, she currently liked Fifi for a girl and Denzil for a boy; Eloise was practised enough with pregnant women to know that she mustn't pass comment, although she was relieved when Sara said, 'Maybe I should wait. Some people believe you can't decide until you see the baby'). They chatted about Sara's plans for decorating the nursery (white, white, white) and what sort of birth she wanted (a water birth, minimal intervention, lots of candles burning and Ella Fitzgerald crooning in the background). Eloise suggested some websites that sold great nursery furniture and she gently suggested that birth plans might be the biggest con since the round dice.

'And how much leave do you get?' Eloise asked. 'I imagine you want to take as much time as you possibly can, paid or unpaid. Every moment is so precious.'

'Absolutely. I might not even go back.'

Eloise was surprised to hear this. She knew that Charlie always described Sara's salary as 'very useful for extras' – code for 'keeps us afloat'. But she didn't pass comment, it wasn't her business. Loads of couples decided to manage on less money so one of the parents could stay home with the offspring; Eloise had. It wasn't always easy but for her it was always the right choice.

'Good for you.' Eloise took another gulp of the champagne that probably should only be sipped. She loved the woozy feeling that resulted from the fact that the champagne was spreading through her body. She felt free and floaty, full of possibility and fun.

'Besides, I won't miss it. Things are really difficult at work at the moment,' added Sara carefully.

'Because you're feeling tired?'

'No, not just that. Do you remember me telling you about Jeremy Hudson?'

'Yeah, of course. Isn't he the guy you dated when you first started training as an accountant? The one who is your boss now,' Eloise said, then elaborated, 'The guy with the big—'

'Heart?' suggested Sara with a wink. Both women burst into indecorous fits of laughter because having a big heart wasn't what Jeremy was known for. 'Yeah, him. Well, he's been really funny about my maternity leave. My pregnancy in general, in fact.'

'Funny in what way?' asked Eloise, trying to focus on the conversation which had clearly taken a slightly more serious turn.

'Oh, it's nothing really. But it's turned into something. I'd told HR that the baby was due on October the twenty-seventh.'

'A month later, why?'

'Because I was up for a promotion but I had to lead a particular project to get it and I knew that in reality I wouldn't be able to see that project through to the end but, if I admitted as much, I wouldn't have had a shot. But then I was asked to fly on a business trip and I had to come clean about my dates because the flight would've been risky. I tried to make out it was a simple slip but no one really bought it. I mean, considering how much I've been longing for this baby, I'm unlikely to make a mistake about my due date. Jeremy got really arsey about my lying. He said I'd got the promotion under false pretences.'

'But they can't not give you a promotion because you are pregnant, it's illegal.'

'Correct, but if I'm not going to be around at a critical time of the project they can legally overlook me without any fuss.'

'Tricky.'

'Yes. So now Jeremy is being very nasty.'

'Nasty, how?'

'Oh, stupid things,' replied Sara, clearly not prepared to go into details. 'He said it was a matter worthy of a formal warning of misconduct. So the whole silly incident has gone on my records.' For the first time that evening Sara's delight looked fractured.

'My God, it sounds like he has an agenda. Maybe he just didn't like you being pregnant. Some bosses are like that in the city, aren't they?' Eloise wanted to be firmly on Sara's side so she vociferously voiced her outrage. 'You should make a claim of sexual harassment.'

Sara laughed. 'Don't you mean sexual discrimination?'

'Oh, yes. Yes, I do. I'd better stop drinking.'

'I don't want to make a fuss. I could do without the hassle. Only a few more months and I'll be out of there. You know what, we might go and visit Charlie's sister in Australia. Have a break for a few weeks, maybe even a month, it's such a long way you have to make it worthwhile. We've never been and we used to always talk about it.'

'Wow, you're full of surprises.' Again, Eloise wondered where the money for such a trip would come from but knew it wasn't any of her business. There was a time when they might have discussed that aspect of the trip but a six-month break in a friendship has an impact. Instead, Eloise started to talk about the pros and cons of Bugaboo strollers versus Quinny.

They both ate pudding; Sara pointed out that she was eating for two and Eloise generously refrained from pointing out that an expectant mother actually only needed roughly 300 calories more. No one wanted to hear that as they tucked into *croquant chocolat* with vanilla parfait and almond cream.

The evening went on longer than Eloise had expected. Besides the baby, they talked about the girls, Dartmouth and Margaret. Eloise found she could chat more freely about Dartmouth to Sara now, without risking Sara feeling resentful. Sara even asked after Arabella and Jackie and refrained from making any barbed asides. She was sympathetic about Margaret's deterioration. The only subject Eloise struggled with was when Sara asked, 'And how's Mark dealing with the news he's adopted? He was really cut up about it at first, wasn't he?'

'Well, understandably.'

'Absolutely.'

Eloise didn't want to say any more. She felt that it was somehow disloyal. Mark's search for his birth parents and his relationship with Ray and Margaret were his business and deeply private. Eloise didn't really want to go into details over mint tea. She turned the subject by sharing her top tip that frozen cabbage leaves could soothe nipples if breast-feeding got painful. It was enough to make Sara screech with laughter.

'You're laughing now but you'll thank me later,' giggled Eloise.

The evening rushed by on angel wings, as happy times do. Eloise delighted in remembering what easy company Sara could be and she was glad that they had happened to bump into one another at the hair salon. It was only when they were gathering their coats from the unfeasibly beautiful girl at the cloakroom that Eloise began to wonder what next? She knew that she wanted to be part of this baby's life, part of Sara's life. Surely the silly incident with Charlie could be stepped over. Eloise knew she needed to call Mark, tell him she'd bumped into Sara and that had led to a great night out. He was angry with Charlie, not Sara, so he'd understand that Eloise wanted to reignite the friendship. He'd support her. She was sure of it.

42

Eloise left the restaurant feeling pleasantly drunk and full; full of delicious food but – so much more importantly – full of a sense of pure undiluted happiness. She took a deep breath and allowed the stirring London night to seep into her bones. She couldn't face the inevitable smell of McDonald's on the late Tube so she treated herself to a cab. She whistled one down and smiled to herself as she noticed that her confident whistle not only stopped traffic but turned heads. Yay, the girl's still got it! She settled in the back of the cab, efficiently gave her brother's address, and then avoided the cabbie's eye in the mirror by staring out of the window. As a Londoner (even an ex one) El knew the code which gave the cabbie the hint as to whether you wanted to philosophise and put the world to rights or whether you wanted the benefit of their silence on your journey. Tourists always felt compelled to make conversation.

Eloise called Mark. He picked up after just three rings. He'd clearly been waiting for her to ring. 'Hi, love.' His voice was a mix of pleasure and fatigue. He stifled a yawn.

'You're up late. I thought you'd be trying to get some early nights as we're all out of your hair. Get some sleep in the bank.'

'I miss you and the girls and I can't sleep, it's too hot. I think there's going to be a storm.'

'Were you online?' Eloise wasn't accusing her husband of watching porn; she'd almost be relieved if he had been. Eloise's guess was that

323

Mark would have spent the night online continuing his search for his birth mother. A search that was proving to be more complex than anyone had imagined; it absorbed most of Mark's spare time and mindshare as progress was slow and faulty.

He had discovered that he was born Mark Antony *Fletcher*. When he announced this, Eloise wondered was Mark Fletcher any better or worse than Mark Hamilton? Was he any different at all? She grappled with this question and finally reached the private decision that she thought Mark Hamilton had the edge but she would have been OK with becoming Eloise Fletcher if that had been what was on offer. Eloise didn't think there was much in a name. The value lay in a heart, in a head. But, for fun, she tried out the new name for size. Emily Fletcher. Erin Fletcher. Poppy Fletcher. It appeared that Fletcher was a name that worked well enough with all their Christian names. Not that she was suggesting they change their names. She was just playing, investigating his other identity. It was impossible not to.

His mother had been called Julie Anne Fletcher, his father's details were not recorded on his original birth certificate. Julie Anne Fletcher was born on 24 May 1955.

'A Gemini,' Mark had commented, shaking his head. 'Split personality.' He'd sighed as though that explained a lot. Eloise had been surprised. She wasn't aware that Mark had any knowledge about Zodiac signs, let alone faith in them. Was he so desperate to give his mystery mum a personality that he'd fallen back on nonsense and superstition? A nano-second's thought and Eloise realised, yes, he quite probably was.

Surprisingly for a solicitor, Mark hadn't approached his search in a very methodical way. At least not initially. He'd decided to pursue Margaret's romanticised view of Julie Fletcher's future. He'd sent letters to every college in Oxford and Cambridge to see if they had records of a Julie Fletcher going up in 1972 or thereabouts. Secretaries from nearly every institution wrote back, which was a testament of their impeccable manners, but sadly none of them had a record of a woman of that name attending around that time. Mark was crushed. He'd wanted to believe that this girl who had given him up had done so because she was at least going on to enjoy an illustrious career. Eloise suggested he try other universities but Mark seemed wedded to the idea that his birth mother would only have attended one or other of the nation's two finest universities. Eloise privately doubted this was the case – none of their children's current school results suggested they came from genius stock – but she couldn't bring herself to say as much. Mark flailed around without a strategy. He read articles in the *Daily Mail* about whether tracing birth parents was a human right. Eloise knew he was desperate; Mark was normally a *Guardian* reader. He read blogs and joined chat rooms where people undergoing similar searches swapped suggestions on how to manage the endeavour and traded stories on how their reunions had panned out. Some of the stories were positive, some were disastrous. Eloise held her breath.

For weeks Mark had messed around with free sites that claimed to help people find someone else through social networks. Again, Eloise had felt concerned.

'It might feel like an easy route but you might find the process running out of your control. Facebook and Friends Reunited offer a chance of an immediate contact point but even if you did find her that way, can you imagine the pressure she'd feel to respond as soon as she'd received your message?'

'What do you suggest that I do? Find her and then not get in touch?'

'No, of course not, but maybe a letter would allow her to have more time to think through the implications and prepare for contact. Besides, Mark, honey, what tweet is going to be the correct tweet to reach your mother? Tonally, how can you even attempt that?'

'You're right, it's a ludicrous approach.' He'd typed something into his computer and then tutted. 'That wouldn't work. Too needy, and there are seven characters to spare.' Eloise leaned over his shoulder and read: *Man, 40, looking 4 birth mother in order to return cream mass-produced blanket. Please fill void left by other mother, who has lost mind.*

'You could add "6ftGSOH", but there'd be no room for spaces.'

'Very clever.'

El had wrapped her arms around her husband and suggested that they went to bed.

After three months of endless letter writing and staring at confusing sites that often gave contradictory advice and always wanted credit card details, Ray persuaded Mark that he had to take a more considered and uniform approach to the search if he was serious about it. They pulled together the scant information they had about Julie Fletcher; it wasn't much. They knew her name (although it might have changed if she'd since married), they knew her age and the fact that her last known city of residence was Birmingham (a city with a population just shy of a million). They had no idea if she'd ever been known by a nickname, where she went to school or what her last known address was. Nor did they know the names of any of her relatives or previous or current employers. The adoption agencies that helped with searches such as these suggested this extra information would be helpful. Mark found this patronising and irritating. Obviously, if you knew where someone worked, they weren't missing, were they?

Ray and Margaret had adopted Mark privately, so lawyers had been involved but not adoption agencies. Information was limited. Ray was able to provide the name of the court where the adoption order was made but nothing more than that. Mark contacted the court but was disappointed to discover that a flood in the basement in 2007 had destroyed the records that might have held some background information such as his mother's last known address. If they'd had a last known address, the next step would have been the electoral registers. Although many people move, it was clearly worthwhile checking out old addresses to see whether the person was still living there or if a neighbour remembered them. Hitting a dead end, Mark had written to the local authority that undertook his supervision pending the adoption; he was hoping they might hold some details on file. He was waiting to hear back.

'I registered with two adoption contact registers today. Both adopted adults and birth relatives can register a wish for contact.'

'Oh yes.' Eloise had learnt to hold her voice in the most neutral tone possible whenever they talked about the adoption.

'And if a link is made, the adopted adult is sent the birth relative's contact details, then it's down to the adopted adult.'

'And what about the birth relative? Can they contact the person they gave up?'

'The birth relative will only be notified that a link has been made and their name and address have been sent to the adopted adult.'

'Sounds very sensible. You never know, she might have registered.' Eloise felt she had no alternative other than to try to sound optimistic, but looking out the window at the enormous crowds in London made her feel desperate. Even with Big Brother watching through satellite navigation and four million CCTV cameras monitoring our movements round the clock, Eloise knew that people who wanted to go missing and stay missing could do so. She thought the task Mark had set himself – the desire he harboured – had similar odds to finding a needle in a haystack.

As though Mark was reading her thoughts, he admitted, 'Some people record a wish for no contact.'

'Oh. What else have you been doing?'

'Well, following the flood in the kitchen earlier this week, I got Bernie Fields to go round to my parents'. He's fitted some sort of clever device on to all the taps which only lets out a limited amount of water, in case Mum forgets to turn them off again. And while he was at it he put a temperature control in too so she can't scald herself. You know, he wouldn't take a penny.'

'That was good of him.'

'People are being good. Very understanding.' Mark had hated trawling around their friends and neighbours repeatedly explaining that Margaret had Alzheimer's and what that meant exactly, but it had been a worthwhile activity. People had to know why, if their door was unlocked, she might wander into their kitchen and make herself a sandwich or why she might totally ignore someone she had known for years, blank them, even possibly run from them. 'Did you do anything special with your last day of holiday?'

This was Eloise's opportunity. She should just say, 'Well, actually yes. You'll never guess who I bumped into', but something made her hesitate. Mark had a lot on his plate at the moment. Quite naturally he was still unsettled by the search for his birth mother and caring for Margaret was becoming increasingly exhausting. Would he be OK with her bringing Sara and Charlie back into their lives so suddenly? He was bound to point out that they'd been doing OK without them for the past six months. Eloise decided it wasn't a conversation to have on the phone. She'd mention it when she got back to Dartmouth. Face to face. That was much better.

'The girls have been playing tourist and I've been to the hairdresser's. We've all had a great day. We miss you.'

'Home tomorrow.'

'How's Margaret been today?'

'Oh, it's not been a very good day for her. She bit Dad and accused him of using whores.'

'Oh.' Sometimes they could laugh at these outbursts and other times they simply couldn't.

43

Margaret was very pleased to have Eloise and the girls home. Margaret and Eloise were walking the girls to play tennis on the public courts. They strolled arm in arm along the harbour, the girls flitted around them; trailing behind, running ahead or dawdling by their sides. When Margaret looked for them she never seemed to see the same girl twice. This could worry her. Today she was not worried because they were with Eloise and Eloise knew what all three looked like and always arrived at the place she intended with the right number of daughters. Margaret felt safe with Eloise. Margaret knew the girls were going to play tennis because they were all carrying tennis bats. The plan was for her and Eloise to watch them for most of the afternoon and, while they were doing so, they'd have a cup of tea and a cake. Margaret knew about the tea and cake because Eloise had explained it very carefully. She'd also said that they might take a walk around the small public gardens. Margaret liked the gardens which were crawling with cheerful golden flowers, she forgot which sort. There was a bandstand, although probably no music. The canvas of the empty deck chairs flapped in the breeze.

Eloise was good at explaining things. She stood completely still, looked directly at Margaret, and calmly, factually, described what was going to happen. Margaret now found she couldn't understand as much as she'd have liked to if the person who was talking to her didn't look at her. She needed to get clues from their faces. Eloise didn't tell Margaret the whole day at once, she told her about something just as they were about to do it, which Margaret appreciated. It helped. Margaret also couldn't always understand what was being said if the TV or radio was on in the background. She didn't know where to listen and that became alarming. She also didn't like it when they told her plans for tomorrow or next week or further ahead than that even. It made her cross and tired. It was too far. Too long.

It was a warm day today. The sun fell on Margaret's shoulders and the tips of her ears. She wanted to eat an ice stick rather than eat cake. Everyone was quiet, busy with their own thoughts; Margaret had been thinking for a very long time about how to start a conversation. Sometimes she forgot how to do that nowadays and after some effort she remembered.

'Did you have a nice time in Kenya?' she asked Eloise.

'London,' replied Eloise, gently squeezing the hand that Margaret had linked through Eloise's arm. Margaret didn't think it any sort of response at all. Unless London was the new fashionable word for 'marvellous'. But then it could just as easily mean 'awful'. Margaret found this new lingo that young ones used too confusing. Emily practically spoke in code. She said something was 'bad' or 'wicked' when she meant it was exciting and something that was desirable could at once be 'cool' or 'hot'. Eloise must have seen Margaret's confusion because she stopped, looked at Margaret and said gently, 'I'd love to go to Kenya one day but this holiday we went to London.'

'Your father and I got engaged in Kenya.'

'You and Ray have visited Kenya, that's right,' said Eloise and then she started walking again. Margaret wished she wouldn't call her daddy Ray, it was very cold. Eloise added something else that was a bit confusing, 'You and Ray got engaged in Whitby, I think, Margaret. Prince William and Kate Middleton got engaged in Kenya. I bet that's what you are thinking about.'

Margaret didn't like to contradict Eloise, it might embarrass her. Margaret hated it when everyone told her the opposite of what she knew, so she asked something else altogether. 'Did you have a nice time in Kenya?'

'This isn't one of your good days, Granny,' said the littlest one, taking hold of Margaret's free hand. 'Mummy said you might be a bit muddled today because we've unsettled you by going away. You need routine. You've missed us. But don't worry, we're back now.'

Margaret looked across the estuary to the bank of green trees. The massive trees were bowing to the sea, showing due respect. Margaret thought that was a good idea. It was never wise to underestimate the sea. She turned to the sea and bowed down low too. They all stared at her except for the little one who copied her.

'We went to London,' shouted the middle one, from a distance of a few metres. Her mother scowled at her. Margaret tried to think what her name might be. She was delighted when she remembered. It was Eric. Eric was some paces in front of Margaret but she was always eavesdropping. 'You remember London, don't you? We used to live there. You used to visit.'

'We went to the Tower to see the crown jewels!' Margaret said excitedly. She suddenly remembered, with great clarity, being in a dark room, on an escalator, moving past a row of glistening crowns, golden orbs, an ampulla and spoons.

'That's right,' Eric said, smiling.

'I've been reading up about dementia, Granny,' said Emily. Emily was the oldest one. She was about to become a woman. Yes, that would happen any day now before her parents knew it. Before they expected it and almost certainly before they wanted it.

'Have you, dear? Funny the things they teach you in school nowadays. Do you like algebra? You get that from me. I was always very good at algebra.'

'Algebra is different from dementia, Granny, you have the word muddled and, anyway, it's very unlikely that I've inherited a genetic gift from you since you adopted my daddy.'

Margaret was surprised. 'Did I, darling?'

'Yes, you did.'

'I think that is a secret,' whispered Margaret.

'It was, until you told us,' said Emily.

'Mark has never been a worry and now I worry about him all the time,' mused Margaret.

'Do you, Margaret?' asked Eloise. She was almost glad to hear it. It was so normal for a mother to worry.

'I told him because I thought he might need a reserve. I wish I hadn't told him. Or I'd told him before, a long time ago. I just did what I thought was best at the time.'

'That's all anyone can do,' said Eloise, squeezing her hand again.

'He's so angry at me.'

'He won't stay angry for ever.'

'Look at that beautiful basket of flowers hanging from the lamppost,' Margaret said. 'The way the foliage tumbles looks like a bridesmaid's skirt.' The females all looked at the baskets lining the street and could see what Margaret saw.

'So I read on the Internet that it's a good idea to spend quality time together creating a life history book for you,' continued Emily.

'A what?'

'A book with your personal history in it. It'll be fun. It will give us all the opportunity to explore your memories and learn more about our family history.'

Eric interrupted. 'Dad will love that,' she said, rolling her eyes. Her long plaits fell down her tanned back, her sharp shoulder blades stuck out, oozing athleticism and good health.

Emily cast her sister a withering look and carried on. 'A life history book is also a really useful tool later on.'

'Later on?'

'So we, and you, remember how wonderful you are when you are being less wonderful, when you're biting Grandad, for instance. And carers know you as a person, not just a nuisance.'

'Emily!' Eloise sounded cross but Margaret thought it was a marvellous idea.

'What fun!'

'I knew you'd think so.' Emily turned to her mother and flashed a triumphant smile. Eloise looked quite pale. Margaret didn't doubt Eloise wished the girls were a little more careful and reflective when they spoke to her. Subtle. But Margaret liked the way they told it how it was. It helped her hold on to how it was.

It was important that she knew.

'Thank you, by the way,' added Emily.

'For what?' asked Margaret.

'For adopting Daddy. I think it was a nice thing to do. He's very lucky.'

'You're welcome, darling, it really was my pleasure.'

SEPTEMBER

44

Eloise wondered whether, if Mark wasn't so caught up in his search for his birth mother and, to a lesser extent, his work, he would suspect she was having an affair. It felt like an affair. For two months now Eloise had made secret, exciting phone calls, she'd had two covert rendezvous which were enormous fun and she was constantly sending texts, gifts and little thoughtful cards to someone else.

To Sara.

Somehow Eloise had not found the right moment to tell Mark that she'd bumped into Sara in London; that they'd had a night out and had rekindled their friendship. She had tried. She'd tried the very first evening she'd returned from London.

They'd packed the kids off to bed and then sat together in the garden, enjoying a cold glass of wine and watching the late sunset. The sun sank behind the horizon, the wide sky blazed with pink and scarlet light, the birds sang one another to sleep and lazy bumble bees hovered low in the long grass, gorged and exhausted by a hot day spent popping from one flower to the next. Eloise had noticed that the grass needed a cut and she thought she might attempt it in the morning or she might leave it a little longer until Ray became exasperated with it, then he'd drag out the lawn mower. Eloise knew that Mark wouldn't notice the untidy lawn until the grass was waist high. There had been just enough of a breeze for it to be pleasant. Eloise had glanced around the garden, reacquainting herself with the abundance of pretty bobbing snapdragons, the colourful pin cushion protea, the numerous rose bushes and the bright phlox. Her country garden had blossomed in her absence. Indeed, it was almost over ripe. The pungent scent of the ample flowers hung in the air; the borders seemed so full they were almost fleshy. There was a sense that any moment now the plump flowers would spill and their petals would cascade. Eloise had long since noticed that nature had a way of pushing its way into Dartmouth's homes; weeds seeped through garden walls, damp penetrated linen cupboards, the sea air climbed into her hair. She breathed in the countryside, surprised to realise that she felt more connected to the world here in Dartmouth, surrounded by earth and water, than she had in London, surrounded by theatres and shops. It was the perfect British summer evening; peaceful and romantic. Eloise had thought that they had a good chance of ending up making love that evening.

In fact, they'd ended up sleeping with their backs to one another in a grumpy silence.

'So, who did you catch up with in London?' Mark had asked conversationally.

'Loads of people. It was brilliant seeing everyone, Maggie, Nick, and Lottie. Some of the school mums.'

'Did visiting make you hanker to return?' Mark had tried to sound jokey but he'd placed so much emphasis on the word hanker that he'd sounded as though he was auditioning for a Broadway musical. There was genuine concern behind his question and Eloise knew as much.

'Do you know something? The trip was good for me. It confirmed the fact that I no longer miss London – at least, not in a way that makes my heart ache or pound. It's all there, all going on without me, but somehow that's OK now.'

'Really?'

'Yes. I know that there are twenty-somethings running in heels and thirty-something new mums attending baby massage classes, but I've done it all.'

It had been hers but now it belonged to others. It hadn't vanished; she simply no longer accessed it. That was enough. She had a different world now. It was no less and no more, it was different and it was hers.

'That's so good to hear, love. So good.' Mark couldn't hide the relief in his voice. He was aware that he'd coerced Eloise into living in Dartmouth. At the time, he'd firmly believed it was the best thing for their family but there'd been so much unanticipated aggravation this past year that the move had turned out to be a lot harder than he'd imagined: his mother's Alzheimer's, the news about his adoption, the Woddells. It had been tough. Thinking about the Woddells prompted Mark to add, 'So you didn't bump into Sara and Charlie. Well, that's a relief. I was concerned that you might, what with you staying just around the corner with Ed and Fran. I mean, that's a headache we could really do without.'

Eloise sipped her wine and avoided Mark's gaze. 'Why do you say that?' She'd tried to keep her voice neutral.

'They were so much trouble, weren't they.'

It wasn't a question and so Eloise struggled to phrase a rebuttal. She noticed one of the tea lights had blown out and she played with the idea of going back into the kitchen to root out the matches. Instead, she pushed on with the conversation about the Woddells. 'Well, were they really so much trouble? Wasn't the whole incident as much trouble as we allowed it to be? After all, no genuine harm was done.' Eloise took another sip of her wine, though this time it was much more of a gulp.

Mark didn't comment directly but added, 'I've never understood why you clung so tightly to your friendship with Sara. She didn't fit into any of the friendship patterns.'

'What do you mean, friendship patterns?' Eloise became aware her wine glass needed to be refilled; was it hot? It was certainly uncomfortable.

'Well, you have friends from university, friends from work and your mum friends. You collect people from important parts of your life—'

'I collect them?' Eloise bristled. She thought his comment made her sound like some sort of friendship megalomaniac; a pathological egotist. 'I don't collect friends, I *make* friends.'

'Of course, that's what I meant.' Mark had squeezed his wife's leg affectionately. It was an odd thing that, after they had spent a bit of time apart, they always needed a few hours to settle back into one another's company. Somehow, despite hopes to the contrary, they could vaguely irritate one another when all they wanted to do was ingratiate. It was frustrating. 'You're a great friend, El, and friends help us define and remember the times that are important to us. I'm just saying I never really understood where Sara fitted into that model. Sara was the friendly plumber's wife but you seemed to imbue her with so much more importance than a casual acquaintance.'

'You were the one who first invited them to our home.' They'd both found Sara compelling and entertaining once upon a time, Mark had just forgotten.

'I wish I hadn't.'

'Why say this now? For five years you never said a word.'

'I did. I used to ask why you had to invite them to lunch *every* Sunday.'

'And I explained that if we didn't invite them, I wasn't sure who would have.'

'And that was our problem because . . . ?' Mark left the sentence unfinished. A challenge.

This was not the way Eloise needed the conversation to go. She felt fractious and thwarted. 'Sara was lonely.'

'She must have had other friends?'

'I don't know if she did have, at least not close ones.'

'Don't you think that was odd?'

'Not really. They were new to the area.'

'Why did they move to Muswell Hill in the first place?'

'Catchment area. The primary schools were great around there, as you know.'

'But they don't have kids.'

Eloise had realised they were at another crossroads. This was her opportunity to say, 'Well, funny you should say that, but she *is* expecting now, as a matter of fact.' But she had paused. She'd glanced at Mark who was scowling at the apricot sunset, not allowing its beauty to warm him. This wasn't the moment. So all Eloise had muttered in reply was, 'Sara was always a planner.'

Eloise was aware that she'd deliberately put her friend in the past tense. It was a tiny duplicitous moment, a split second, but decisive. She could not find a way to bring Sara back into their present.

'I don't even know why we are talking about them. I'm going to bed,' said Mark suddenly. Eloise knew he really was in a huff because he'd left half a glass of wine untouched and it was a Guigal Condrieu 2008, from Rhône, one of his favourites and not cheap.

Eloise couldn't explain it to Mark. He would not have understood that she found Sara's pregnancy irresistible, that she had wanted it for almost as long as Sara had. Admittedly, she hadn't longed for it the same way as Sara had; Eloise's was a solid, reliable wish, Sara's longing had been almost demonic in its intensity. Eloise had loved being pregnant and she loved being a mum. It was the most over-powering, awesome experience she'd ever had; it devoured her days. She had so much to say about being a mum that she remained relatively silent on the matter; she feared once she started she might never stop and she'd just ramble on and on, like the magic porridge pot in the fairy tale that constantly produced food. Eloise had found that being a mum was a clashing combination of contrasting emotions. Elation, worry, contentment, frustration, awe, dread and delight. Eloise liked other people's children too. Not indiscriminately; she didn't fall into the camp (that seemed like a cult to her) that believed every child was an angel and could do no wrong. She'd met enough kids to understand that they were simply young people; some good, some less so. She knew that Hitler was once a child and doubted very much that he had been a pleasant one. However, she did believe that with each child came hope. Hope and opportunity. Children were the result of all that had gone by but they were an embodiment of the imminent. There was renewed aspiration and possibility in every one of them. She wanted to welcome Sara's longed-for baby.

Besides, whatever Mark thought about how and why Eloise had made friends with Sara, the fact was she *had* made friends with her. Eloise believed friendship was a type of shared altruism, a complex and considerate exercise in cooperation and dependability. Eloise was a good friend and that was defining, Mark had been right about that much at least. She had invested five years in her friendship with Sara; Over that time they'd shared experiences: delicious meals, fun (or sometimes exhausting) day outings with the girls, weekends camping (rain or shine), frivolous shopping trips and countless bottles of wine. They'd also shared some low-key secrets, mostly about how much Eloise had spent on clothes or furniture, sometimes stuff about covering grey or effectively removing upper lip hair. This Eloise believed led to an unqualified tolerance, commitment and backing.

Now, when Sara finally had the one thing she'd long since dreamed of, the icing on the cake would be having someone to share the experience with. Eloise didn't doubt that Charlie would be embracing his role as expectant dad but a girlfriend, at a time like this, was vital. Eloise was determined that their next shared experience was to be Sara's pregnancy, the biggest, most exciting experience she could imagine. How could she opt out of that? If being part of it meant that she and Sara had to share a bigger secret, then so be it.

Eloise had called Sara just ten minutes after Mark had left for work, the day after Eloise and the girls had returned from London. Neither woman had cared that Sara was in the office.

'So, you are resisting finding out the baby's sex?'

'I am, although my guess is I'm carrying a boy.'

'I agree. You've a neat, upfront bump. I wore the girls everywhere: on my bum, arms, thighs . . .'. Eloise slipped into self-deprecating humour, she was confident enough to laugh at herself.

'None of it matters though, does it?'

'No, not really,' admitted Eloise.

'As long as it's healthy,' both women chorused, the mantra of parents-to-be worldwide.

They'd quickly fallen back into the habit of talking every day.

'How are you feeling?'

'Amazing. Baby kicked all night.'

'Are you tired, then?'

'No. Well, no more than normal.'

'So exhausted?'

'Yes,' Sara laughed. 'I fell asleep on the Tube again.'

'Today?'

'Fat but good fat. I've grown so large that I'm invisible. It allows me to arrive late and leave the office early, which I'm taking full advantage of.'

Eloise loved to hear the contentment and joy in Sara's voice ooze down the telephone. El managed to get to London twice. She didn't take the girls, even though she knew they'd have liked to see their 'Auntie' Sara. It wouldn't be fair to ask them to keep a secret from their dad. On the first trip Eloise helped pick out the pram. They chose a trendy Bugaboo Bee Stroller with a cheerful yellow sun canopy. On her second visit, Eloise took Sara to Rigby and Peller for a maternity bra fitting; she insisted it was a rite of passage. It was a deeply intimate experience discovering you had 36FF boobs when you were used to a more moderate 34B; both women had screeched and howled with laughter and excitement. They were drawn towards an extravagant Cherry Blush nursing bra, which was marketed as the 'innovative nursing bra for the modern and fashion-conscious breast-feeding mother'.

'Look, it has a soft foam cup which will disguise the feeding pads,' pointed out Eloise. 'That's clever.'

Sara fingered the delicate cotton lining with longing. 'It's really expensive. I probably should just nip to Mothercare.'

'And it has a Kwik Klip strap system that allows you to do the drop cup thing one-handed, so you can hold the baby securely in the other.' El caressed the carefully constructed garment. 'I love the lace overlay and the little satin bows. It's gorgeous. They didn't make maternity wear like this when I had my girls,' she added temptingly.

They bought four. And matching knickers.

Sara never called Eloise's landline by unwritten, silent agreement. Sara always politely asked after Mark and Eloise was always careful to ask after Charlie too; both women assured the other that their husbands were well. Sara went as far as telling Eloise that Charlie sent his love but neither woman suggested they get together as a foursome. Eloise was aware that Sara must sense that Mark was unhappy with their friendship and her thoughts were confirmed when one day Sara finally brought up the subject.

'Mark doesn't know we talk, does he?'

Eloise was evasive. 'What makes you think that?'

'Am I a guilty secret? What will you do when I have the baby?' Sara joked.

'Don't be daft.' Eloise deftly changed the subject. 'He's just very caught up with the adoption process.'

'How's that going?'

'Slowly. Hey, I was reading this article recently which suggested breast-feeding should be maintained for a year. That's a hell of an ask! I managed six months with two of mine and only three months with Poppy.'

Sara allowed the conversation to be moved on. But it was a good question. What would Eloise do when Sara's baby was born? El wondered how much longer she could keep her friendship under wraps. The other week she'd bought a hand-knitted monkey in yellow and white; it was so cute she couldn't stop herself. Mark had found the toy in among the shopping and innocently asked, 'Who's this for?'

Eloise had blushed, snatched it from him with unnecessary violence and replied, 'No one in particular, I just liked it. I'm going to put it in the present cupboard.'

She didn't like heaping lie upon lie. What would she do when the baby was born? A baby she was already half in love with. A baby she was prepared to fall entirely in love with. How could she hide that?

45

Sara had been worrying about false labour. She'd read everything she could to prepare her for the moment of birth (or, more accurately, to prepare her for the several hours of birth) but because she'd had so many false conceptions she was irrationally worried that she'd experience false labour too. She didn't want to get it wrong and look foolish. She knew that in real labour contractions ought to be regular and follow a predictable pattern. Contractions would become progressively closer, longer, and stronger. That's what all the books said. In false labour, contractions were irregular and unpredictable; she'd bought a new stopwatch so that she wouldn't make a mistake with the timings. She wanted it all to go perfectly. She imagined that she'd be stoical, not silent – like the Scientologists – but preferably not swearing like a sailor either.

Sara found she was surprisingly nervous when she asked Charlie, 'Do you want to be at the birth? You know, in the actual room.'

'Absolutely.'

'Oh, I'm glad. I wondered if you'd want to go back to the old school way of doing it. You know, impatiently pacing the hospital corridor, cigar in pocket.'

'No, absolutely not. I know I can't actually do the pushing but I want to do everything I can to support you. We're in this together, aren't we?' Charlie was almost surprised to discover that he wanted this baby just as much as Sara did. True, he'd given up hope of them

346

ever having a baby before she had and, true, he'd almost given up on them as a couple, but that didn't mean he wasn't aware of just how wonderful things had turned out. How lucky he was. Now, he was embarrassed about how he'd behaved with Eloise. What had he been thinking? Of course he wasn't in love with her, he never had been, but things with Sara had become almost untenable; Eloise had seemed an attractive alternative, an escape. He wanted to put that all behind him. All he wanted was whatever made Sara happy. Seeing her so joyful over the past nine months had been amazing; he'd forgotten she could be fun, mischievous and simply good to be around. He'd do anything at all to maintain that. Sara hadn't replied but gave him a big smacker of a kiss.

When it came to it, Sara was surprised to find there was no room for mistake. She felt her first contraction on Tuesday at teatime – remarkably, her exact due date. Each contraction started in the lower back and then radiated around to the front, deep in the groin. She made a cup of herbal tea. In the time that she drank it she experienced just one more contraction. Eighteen minutes apart. She called her midwife who advised her to stay in the comfort of her home until the contractions reached five-minute intervals. She called Charlie who'd just gone to the supermarket. He dashed home, arriving ashen and sweaty, groceries spilling at his feet. The contractions continued all night. Sara discovered that changing position, rubbing her belly, drinking warm drinks, walking round the house did not offer her any relief. At nine the following morning the contractions were seven minutes apart and Charlie decided he couldn't bear it any longer, even if Sara could. He picked up her hospital bag and they set off, buzzing with a mixture of disbelief, apprehension and excitement.

'Try to stay calm and focused,' he said.

'Did you just read that in the baby manual?' asked Sara. She was puffing now, trying not to scrunch her face in agony, but it was difficult as the contractions were becoming powerful.

'Yes,' admitted Charlie. 'Remember you *can* do the job that lies ahead. Women have been bringing babies into the world for thousands of years.' He stopped talking, doubting that he was comforting her much. Instead, he leaned close and kissed her forehead.

'OK, let's go and do this thing.'

46

Margaret understood. She and Eloise would not be picking up the girls from school today. It was already arranged that the middle one was going on a play date and now Eloise had made arrangements for Poppy to go to Arabella's too. Because Eloise was going to London. London, how lovely!

Ray had gone fishing. All day. It said so in the book. Eloise had sighed when she'd read that, she'd seemed perturbed and in a hurry. She kept looking at Margaret and asking, 'Are you sure you'll be all right, here on your own all day?' Margaret told her she would be but Eloise continued to look doubtful. She'd called Ray to see if he could come home earlier but she couldn't reach him, there was no signal, and she'd sighed again. 'And I couldn't get hold of Arabella directly, either, but I've left a message at the school to say that I won't be collecting and to send Poppy with Arabella.' Margaret nodded but neither woman held much hope that this information would stay in her head.

Margaret wrote Poppy's name on her hand to help her remember because they'd called her after a flower, rather than giving her a person's name, and so it could cause Margaret some confusion sometimes.

Eloise made Margaret roast beef sandwiches, she cut up an apple and opened a packet of chocolate biscuits and took out two, hesitated, took out a third. She put these things on a plate and attached a yellow sticky note which read, *Eat this between 12.30 and 1 p.m.* She left three glasses of squash made up on the counter and put a yellow sticky note on each glass, too: *10 a.m., lunch, 2.30 p.m.* It made Margaret think of *Alice Through the Looking Glass. Margaret Through the Looking Glass,* she thought. There were instructions on how to make a cup of tea pinned to the wall. On a good day, Margaret might not need any of these prompts, but on a bad day she couldn't remember whether she'd eaten or not and even if she did want to eat she might cry with annoyance as she'd forgotten how to open a bag of crisps. Eloise felt grateful that today had every sign of being a good day.

'I'll tell Jen from next door to look in on you before lunch.' Eloise wrote that in the book in case Margaret didn't recognise Jen when she knocked. The sitting room felt gloomy as the window was already pitted with rain. 'It doesn't look as though it's a very nice day, you should stay in. Ray will be back at four p.m.' Eloise wrote all of that in the book too. Eloise showed Margaret *again* that she was number 3 on speed dial. Number 1 was Ray's mobile, number 2 was Mark and Eloise's home number, number 3 was Eloise's mobile, number 4 was Mark's office number and number 5 was Mark's mobile. It was all written down there on the list. And the list was pinned on to the wall near the phone. Margaret knew that she was not allowed to take down any of the lists that were pinned around the house because if she did she'd forget where she'd put them, which ruined everything.

Eloise kissed Margaret on the cheek and then sped off in her car. Very fast. London, how lovely!

Margaret managed extremely well. Jen visited. Came, was recognised, and went. Margaret switched on the television and the radio. She didn't remember to turn either off but she did remember to eat her lunch and to drink her fluids. Most importantly, she remembered that Eloise had trusted her to pick up Poppy after school. She knew she must go to Poppy at 2.30 p.m. because there was a note with that time written on it and Margaret had written Poppy's name on her hand just to be sure. Margaret was thrilled that Eloise had trusted her with this task. She was determined she'd get it right. It had been a long time since they'd let her do any childcare on her own.

Poppy was due out of school at 3.15 p.m. Margaret often collected the girls with Eloise. The walk did her good. She knew the way. She'd roved these parts a million times since she was a young woman. The middle one was going on a play date and Margaret knew she mustn't try to stop that. There had been that one time when Margaret had hit Arabella with her handbag because she saw Arabella in the street with the girls and she'd thought she was stealing them. Margaret was fiercely protective of her girls. Now, Eloise always took care to explain if someone else was picking one of them up, to avoid that sort of incident happening again.

Margaret had a large cotton bag. She checked the list near the door and made sure everything she needed went into the bag. She had keys so she could get back in the house when she brought Poppy home and she had a moving telephone. She had also packed a biscuit for Poppy, just as she used to for Mark when she'd picked him up from school. She had packed a bucket and spade. She was wearing shoes, she had a coat. Margaret was doing very well. She was enormously pleased with herself when she remembered to pack the bedside lamp. It got dusky by tea time now and you should never go out in the dark without a bedside lamp. Wonderful! All organised!

Poppy was delighted to see her granny at the school gate, especially when she was immediately offered a chocolate biscuit. Erin gave them a wave but then ran off on her play date. The woman who stole the girls from time to time approached Margaret.

'Hello, Margaret, how are you today?'

Margaret thought the woman with the large breasts and gappy teeth should call her Mrs Hamilton as she'd never been invited to do otherwise. The world was too casual.

'I'm fine, thank you, Mrs . . .' Margaret couldn't make her point about the correct way to address someone because she didn't know what this woman was called. Addressing her just as Mrs sounded impertinent and Margaret felt foolish. Damn.

'Where's Eloise?' The gappy woman looked around.

'Down the hill in the car. Waiting for us.' Margaret knew she was telling a deliberate lie but she was pretty sure that if she said she was on her own Mrs Gappy would spoil their fun. Margaret was quite pleased with herself for pulling off a lie. The pleasure at doing so sent warmth through her belly. Margaret sometimes felt wet and warm when she went to the loo in her chair or bed but this warmth was the good sort, it was inside her heart. 'Now, if you'll excuse me, we have to get along,' she said and then, as an afterthought, she sternly added, 'You make sure you return the other one. We need all three.'

Margaret had decided to take Poppy to the little coastal cove that she and Mark used to visit when he was a boy. They'd have to walk and it was quite a distance, but she thought it was best to tell Poppy that it wasn't. They set off down the road towards the coast. Hedges quickly gave way to a simple wire fence that penned sheep off the road but soon all signs of man fell away and they were left with nothing other than a narrow foot track and rolling, rabbit-cropped fields. Margaret paused at a stile, partly so that she could get her breath back, discreetly, but also to drink in the view, so familiar and yet so unknown. The quality of light, the infinite variety of greens in the trees and fields, meant that everyone was offered a new masterpiece every day. As it happened, Margaret and Poppy were offered the masterpiece twice as Margaret inadvertently walked them in a circle.

'Haven't we been this way?' asked Poppy.

'I don't think so.' Actually, the green fields dramatically bumping up against sheer drops to the sandy beaches did seem familiar, as did the flora and fauna, but the windy bridle paths seemed alien. Had Margaret seen that terracotta, thatched cottage before? The one that was snuggled on the hill at a distance of about two miles?

The late afternoon was growing chilly and the clouds were swelling up from the sea. Poppy was beginning to feel cold and there was drizzle in the air. Grey, British drizzle that left everything feeling saggy. Her socks kept falling down her skinny legs and she wasn't wearing the right sort of shoes for this long walk. She was in her new pumps that weren't a brilliant fit anyway, as she had very narrow feet, and it was hard to find snug shoes. In the shoe shop Poppy had sworn to her mum that they fitted beautifully because they had pink glittery stars on the sides and, frankly, Poppy was prepared to put up with a bit of slipping for pink glittery stars. The pumps were caked in mud now. Poppy couldn't see the stars and she had a terrible sinking feeling that they'd never shine quite as brightly as they had that morning. The mud had oozed in at her ankle and her foot kept sliding in the shoe, she'd have a blister if they didn't get to wherever they were going soon. They trudged over endless rough meadows that all looked the same and might even be the same. Poppy thought they should have stayed on the path but Granny had said they were taking a short cut. They were deep in the countryside now, far away from any electric lights; the soft, dark rounds of the tree tops and bushes could just be made out against the bruised sky.

'Shall we ring Grandad and get him to bring the car?' Poppy asked. There were fine droplets of rainwater hanging around her hair line, on her eyelashes and cheekbones; she looked luminous, like a mermaid.

'Not far now,' said Margaret, although she wasn't sure. She could see the sea, hear it, smell it, but she didn't know how to get down to the little cove that she and Mark had so often enjoyed together. Margaret stood at the sheer edge and peered over; the wind was getting some bite behind it now and her coat flapped around her body like an untethered sail. It was frustrating because she knew this place she was looking for was there, just below her, and she knew Poppy would love it. But she couldn't get to it. There was a path but it wasn't the right one. The path she could see was too steep. There was another, gentler path. Somewhere.

'I think we should just go home and watch TV,' suggested Poppy miserably. She was shivering and beginning to doubt her granny would ever find the small strip of sand that sat next to the dark sea. Even if she did, would it be worth it? Would there be somewhere that sold ice creams? Poppy didn't think so. If the place was this difficult to find, it was unlikely that an ice-cream van would reach it. 'Let's just go,' she moaned.

Margaret, who was also feeling weary, suddenly became incensed.

Didn't this child know how much planning she'd had to do? What an opportunity this was? Didn't she understand that Margaret might not be allowed to do this again? Ever again! They were always stopping her from doing things. Blocking her. Thwarting her.

'Lazy cow,' snapped Margaret nastily. 'You'll get fat, fat, fat. Like that child-thief woman.'

Poppy gasped. No one had ever called her a cow. Well, except for Emily, who had once but she'd been really sorry afterwards and had given Poppy two Lego Minifigures to make up. Granny didn't even own any Lego Minifigures. No adult had ever said anything so mean. Granny reminded Poppy of Gollum in *Lord of the Rings*; terrifying.

'Down that way, is it?' Poppy pointed her skinny arm towards the steep, narrow path. Tears were stinging in her eyes but she didn't want her granny to see her hurt, so she dashed off towards the windy, precarious walkway.

47

By the time Eloise arrived at the hospital Sara was a mother. She had crossed over the line. Finally. Fabulously. Charlie rang as Eloise pulled into the car park. He sounded delighted, delirious. 'It's a boy. A boy. Totally healthy. Perfect. We've got a boy.' Eloise thought she heard tears in his voice and so she forgave him for the ancient tonsil-tickling incident and simply squealed with unadulterated joy. Eloise rushed through the endless corridors of grey lino and pushed her way through heavy swing doors until she finally arrived in the maternity wing. She knew she'd arrived because pink and blue balloons bobbed on ribbons tied to the reception desk and there was a smell of roses and lilies in the air, almost dousing the smell of industrial-strength disinfectant. Eloise told the nurse on the reception desk that she was Sara's sister because she knew morning visiting hours were over.

'I've just driven four and a bit hours to get here.'

'Missed the action by "the bit",' commented the nurse. 'He was born just seventeen minutes ago. Already back on the ward. Number sixteen. Go ahead. I'm sure your sister is desperate to see you.' The nurse looked Eloise up and down and Eloise knew she was trying to reconcile Sara's height and dark, poker-straight hair with Eloise's petite frame and blond curls.

'Half-sister,' mumbled Eloise, sure she'd been rumbled.

Eloise dumped the armful of gifts she'd brought on the end of the bed and swept Sara into a huge congratulatory hug. She grinned at Charlie over Sara's shoulder. The grin said everything was forgiven and forgotten. Everything was OK again. New life fixed things. Charlie beamed back, relieved, and then stepped forward to receive his congratulatory hug. It was brief as Eloise's eyes landed on the magnetic bundle in the Perspex bassinet. Sara gave Eloise the nod and El scooped him into her arms. He was sleeping and it would probably be wisest if they'd left him to it, but their combined overwhelming sense of euphoria meant there was no chance of that. He was swaddled and there wasn't much to see of him other than his little pink face and shock of thick, dark hair.

'He's gorgeous,' Eloise cooed appreciatively. Eloise liked the weight of the baby in her arms. He fitted comfortably and she held him confidently, cupping his head gently in her hand.

'He's got rugby player's thighs,' said Charlie. The pride and delight resounded around the ward. 'Go on, unwrap him. Check them out.'

Sara swept aside the copious number of gifts Eloise had delivered so that Eloise could carefully lie the baby down. El undid the swaddling and gasped. 'He's perfect!' she said, taking in his deliciously cute belly, perfect little arms and hands, his stocky legs and tiny feet. She swooped down and planted kisses all over him. Her lips dissolved on his warm and smooth skin; it felt as though she was diving into a pool of feathers. She took a quick snap with her phone and then, fretting that he'd catch a chill, she efficiently retied his swaddling. 'What are you going to call him?'

'Cooper,' Charlie and Sara chorused together.

'That's great. Very strong and unusual. Unusual is good.'

Sara closed her eyes and put her head back on the pillow. Eloise thought that might be serenity and fulfilment or it might be plain old exhaustion. 'You don't want that thing that I have that when they get to school there are about five kids in the class with the same name. There's another Poppy in Poppy's class and it's the smallest school imaginable. There are at least three Emilys in Emily's year group. It's annoying because hers is shortened to Em or she's known as Emily H, as though she were one of the Spice Girls.'

'I still have to call quite a few people and tell them the news,' said Charlie. 'I can't use my mobile in here.' He glanced at Cooper, clearly reluctant to leave the room and miss even a second of being with him. Then he turned to Sara with equal tenderness. 'You'll be OK with Eloise to keep you company, won't you?'

'Of course. Go on. I want everyone to know as soon as possible. Then come straight back and give me word for word accounts as to what people said.' Sara smiled.

As Charlie left the ward the midwife entered and came directly to Sara's bed. With an air of efficiency she pulled the thin nylon curtain around the bed to create the semblance of privacy.

'Can I have a quick word?' she asked.

'I'll go,' said Eloise immediately.

'No, stay,' instructed Sara. 'Is it about Cooper's blood group?' The midwife nodded her head, once. 'He's rhesus positive, isn't he?'

The midwife nodded again. 'And you are rhesus negative, so you'll need an anti-D jab, just to look after any future babies. The sooner the better.'

'Why wasn't that picked up?' demanded Eloise crossly. 'You should have known there was a risk of the rhesus factor and given her those jabs throughout the pregnancy or at least as soon as the baby was born. How could that have been missed?'

The nurse kept her gaze away from Eloise and didn't answer the question. 'I'll go and get the jab.'

'That's so incompetent,' muttered Eloise and then, aware that she sounded stressy, she thought to add, 'I mean, there's nothing to worry about, Sara. It's an easy fix, I'm just a bit cross because it's so simple to avoid.' She patted Sara's arm reassuringly.

Like many mums, Eloise had also had to have the anti-D jab after she'd given birth to Emily, so she was quite clued up on the subject. It was a standard procedure in many hospitals to combat the rhesus factor which occurred when the blood of anyone who was rhesus negative came into contact with rhesus positive blood. If that happened, the rhesus negative blood reacted to the rhesus positive blood as 'foreign' and developed antibodies to kill off the rhesus positive cells. Some of Cooper's rhesus positive blood might have got into Sara's circulation during birth. It wasn't unheard of. If it had, her body would be currently producing antibodies that would stay in her blood and, if she became pregnant again, problems might arise. Another baby with Cooper's blood group would be at risk of anaemia, jaundice or even brain damage. Fortunately, the rhesus factor problems were preventable. The anti-D jab destroyed any rhesus positive cells that might have got into the bloodstream, which meant no more antibodies would be produced.

'They should have known that as Charlie is rhesus positive there was a chance the baby would be too,' said Eloise irritably. 'They did check Charlie's blood group, didn't they?' Despite being aware that really she ought to remain calm and cheery, she was fretful; Sara was considerably more poised.

'It's not their fault. Charlie is rhesus negative, they wouldn't have anticipated any risk,' Sara said matter-of-factly.

'But Cooper is positive.' Eloise didn't understand. She was pretty good at biology and there was only one way that could be the case. She glanced at Sara for confirmation.

Sara nodded. 'Yes.'

Eloise could hardly bring herself to say the words. 'Charlie isn't the father?'

'That's right.'

'You never said.' Eloise tried to compute the information. What was being said to her? 'You had a sperm donor? Well, they should still have had records, they should have known—'

'No sperm donor.'

Eloise couldn't hide from the facts any longer. 'An affair?'

Sara shrugged. 'If you like.'

'With who?'

'Who do you think?'

Eloise was too stunned to cope with a guessing game. Charlie wasn't Cooper's father.

She was glad she was sitting down holding the baby or else she might have dropped him, she was so stunned. She was sitting on a hard plastic visitor's chair and suddenly she became aware of how excruciatingly uncomfortable it was. She felt clammy and a bit light headed too. Eloise had only spent ten minutes with Charlie since she'd arrived at the hospital. He'd clearly been trying to keep out of her way. Eloise didn't think it was necessary for him to do so. She'd forgiven him, it was forgotten. Besides, the Charlie who'd tried it on so many months ago was not the man El met in the hospital ward. The man in the hospital was a proud and delighted father, a strong and dependable husband, a focused and impressive man. He'd become all that because he was a father. Only he wasn't.

The nurse reappeared and gently gave Sara the jab. Eloise noticed that the midwife kept her eyes lowered and when Charlie popped his head around the curtain and asked 'What's going on? What was the injection for?', she simply answered, 'Routine.' Eloise wondered how many times the covering of parentage occurred. She wondered how the nurse had trained herself not to pass judgement. Was she immune?

Eloise didn't say a word. She gazed at the sleeping bundle. Tired after his ordeal of making an entrance into the world. She tried to make sense of everything she had just heard but it was difficult. When Charlie had been dispatched for the second time – this time to get chocolate from the visitors' shop – Eloise said, 'He's Jeremy's, isn't he?' Suddenly it made sense. 'That's why you tried to fudge your due date at work. Presumably there was a risk that Jeremy might have put two and two together and come up with four.'

'Isn't it more of a case of one and one together make three?'

'Sara!'

'Calm down, Poirot. We ought to get you a moustache,' said Sara.

'Sara! How can you joke?'

'Why shouldn't I joke? I've never been happier.' Sara turned to Eloise and she beamed. Brilliantly.

The baby stirred in Eloise's arms and started to mew. On auto pilot, Eloise passed him to his mother who unbuttoned her nightdress and released her enormous boob. She guided her nipple into the baby's mouth and murmured, 'That's right, isn't it, Cooper? Never been happier, have I, little man?'

'You, maybe, but what about Charlie?' Eloise glanced at the door. She was concerned Charlie would return any minute.

'Charlie is the daddy. He'll be the best daddy there is. I've seen how wonderful he is with your girls. Patient, kind and thoughtful. It's fine.'

Eloise gasped, surprised that Sara seemed incapable of grasping the enormity of the situation. Sara's calm and reserve made Eloise begin to doubt her own sanity. Was she making a fuss? Was this OK? She shook her head slightly, confused by the sounds of a hospital trolley, other mums and dads chatting on the ward, someone's baby crying. She couldn't think clearly.

'But he knows that Emily, Erin and Poppy aren't his. It's different.'

'I don't know why you are being so excitable, it was your idea.'

'My idea?' Eloise asked, aghast.

'Yes, you offered to be a surrogate.'

'A surrogate, not a . . .' Eloise felt faint. She felt blood rushing to her ears. Had she caused this?

'He made a donation, that's all.'

'Does Jeremy know the baby is his?'

'No. Why would I want him to know?' Sara stroked Cooper's cheek with her index finger. The gesture, though small, was infinitely tender.

'But there will be consequences,' Eloise stuttered. She was terrified for Sara, for Charlie and Cooper. This was such a mess. So poorly thought through. Why couldn't Sara see as much? Eloise had always known that Sara's desire for a baby was all-consuming; now she understood it was overwhelming. 'Think of Mark.'

'What does Mark have to do with it?' snapped Sara. Her serenity momentarily interrupted.

'Think of the way he's manically trying to find his birth mother.'

'This is different. I am Cooper's mother.'

'What if Cooper ever wants to find his birth father?'

'He won't know that Charlie isn't his natural father. Will he?' Eloise could not fail to hear the icy steel in Sara's voice; the veiled bullying, the barely contained aggression. 'He'll never know,' she repeated firmly. 'Not unless you decide to spoil everything, unless you decide to cause trouble. But you won't do that, will you, Eloise? Because you like things to be nice. And this is nice now. It's perfect.'

Sara glanced down at her son and her face relaxed once again. She exuded contentment. Eloise was reminded of what she'd always believed; there was hope and opportunity in every new soul. Children were the product of all that had passed, but they were an embodiment of the future.

'Do you know how lonely I've been? How sad? But now I feel complete. I'm a different woman. I'm a better woman. I'll be a fantastic mother, Eloise. You can't doubt that, and Charlie will be a brilliant dad. Does it matter if Cooper isn't biologically Charlie's? We're a family. Just a happy family. You're the last person to want to ruin that.'

Eloise couldn't decide if Sara was demented or inspired. 'Why did you tell me?'

Sara seemed to consider the question for a long time. Eventually, she said, 'I wanted you to know.'

Eloise bit her tongue. It was true she did like things to turn out well. She did like life to run smoothly and happily for everyone. That was why she put so much effort into canapés and selecting comfortable bedding for her guests, that was why she put so much thought into Margaret's health care. She did like to plan to make people's lives as comfortable as possible, but this plan of Sara's wasn't the same at all. It was selfish and it was a disaster waiting to happen. Wasn't it?

Could Sara hide Cooper's parentage for a lifetime? The instant Eloise asked herself the question she thought yes, of course she could. People did it all the time.

Was it wrong? Would anyone get hurt? Whose rights were being buggered with here? Charlie's? Cooper's? Jeremy's? Jeremy's wife and sons'?

She didn't know. All she knew was that Sara was playing God and that couldn't be right.

'I think I'm going to go now,' Eloise muttered.

'Uh huh.' Sara didn't look up from Cooper's face. She was gazing at her son, nestled tightly into her, in a way that suggested confidence, buoyancy, self-belief and faith. Suddenly Eloise realised that Sara didn't care if she'd shocked Eloise or over-burdened her. She didn't care if she was in the room or not. Eloise wondered whether Sara cared that, for months, Eloise had been carefully hand-picking thoughtful and individual gifts to welcome this baby and congratulate the parents, that she had left Margaret on her own today, that she had had to make complicated childcare arrangements for her own children and that she had driven for over four hours to be here.

Somehow Eloise doubted it. Sara didn't care about any of this because all she cared about was Cooper.

Eloise stood up, took one last look at the baby and started to walk away. She thought Sara hadn't even registered as much until Sara said, 'Come on, Eloise, admit it. You like a secret if it's yours.'

'What do you mean?'

'I know all about you and Charlie. I know you kissed my husband.'

Eloise thought she'd been shoved over. She felt the sting of surprise just as though she'd fallen and grazed her knees. 'I did not. I – I – he told you?'

'Enjoy it?'

'No. It wasn't like that. I didn't want him to . . .'

Sara finally looked up from Cooper's tiny face and shock of dark hair. 'Not even for a split second?'

'No. I . . .' Eloise wanted to tell Sara to go to hell, tell her she was wrong, but she couldn't find the words that would be convincing and accurate enough. Had she wanted him, even for a fraction of a second? Sara read her mind.

'Doesn't that muddy your perfection? That split second detonates everything. My point is, Eloise, no one's perfect.'

48

Margaret stared in the direction the angry child had stormed off in. She couldn't remember what she'd said but she knew she'd hurt her little girl and she needed to say sorry.

She heard the scream first and then the thuds and the clattering of jagged stones tumbling down the steep and twisting path. She could see little flashes of skinny arms and legs tumbling. Margaret thought that Poppy was doing a cartwheel or a forward roll. Not a very good one, she wasn't tucking in her limbs like she'd been taught, and she wasn't pointing her toes. But it was down a steep hill, practically a cliff, so doing a cartwheel couldn't be easy. It took a moment listening to the silence for Margaret to consider whether Poppy ought to be doing a cartwheel here. Was that what she'd been doing?

'Poppy. Poppy. I'm sorry,' she said into the damp shadows. Poppy didn't reply. 'Don't sulk, my baby. You know I say things I don't mean. Let's forget about the cove. It's too dark now anyway, the tide will be coming in. Let's go home, like you said.' Still Poppy wouldn't reply.

Margaret knew how effective sulking could be. She regularly didn't speak to – oh, what was he called? The man she was married to. She ignored him because he'd said or done something to make her angry. But then she'd forget. Forget what had made her angry and that she was ignoring him. But Poppy wasn't a sulker, she wouldn't sulk for this long, she got bored too easily. Poppy couldn't even play a successful game of hide and seek because she couldn't bear how long it took people to find her; not that anyone ever wanted to play hide-and-seek with Margaret any more.

Margaret looked out to the sea; a wall of rain was gathering threateningly. Not just drizzle but a full-on deluge. There were minutes and minutes of silence. Margaret wasn't sure how many exactly. Five? Twenty-five? Fear started to trickle down Margaret's spine; it dribbled and oozed into every pore. Or maybe that was the rain. It was falling solidly now; wetting her ears, her shoulders, her thighs. Margaret peered down the path but it was so dim and gloomy, she couldn't see much. She certainly couldn't see Poppy's little blond head and she should be able to see that much, shouldn't she?

Margaret started to weep silently. She understood Poppy had gone.

What to do? What to do? She would have known once and it tortured her that she no longer did. She sat down on the ground because her legs were aching after the long walk here. The ground yielded slightly as it was sodden. She felt the wind sneak between the buttons on her coat, up her sleeves and down her neck. The wind could get anywhere, like fear. Margaret couldn't remember what Poppy was wearing. Trousers or a skirt? Was Poppy cold? Margaret used to volunteer with St someone's ambulance, she'd been a first-aider. Yes. She'd helped people. With choking and falls and banged heads. She knew what to do in an emergency. Or at least she used to. Before. Now she was useless. Margaret's uselessness overwhelmed her. She felt it creeping up her body, covering her feet, legs and now her stomach. She sank into a deep pit of uselessness, it clogged and stifled like quicksand. Her uselessness – the solid weight of her inability to understand this, to help with this – made her want to be sick. She couldn't move at all. She decided to lie here on the grass while Poppy was lying down there, on the very edge. That was all that could be done.

Margaret lay down and the rain drilled into her. She lay with her cheek on the wet grass. Her nose was only a few inches away from a fat black slug that had popped its odious body up from underground in response to the pitter-patter of the rain. If Poppy was lying near a slug she'd hate it, thought Margaret. Poppy was terrified of slugs.

So lying on the ground wasn't enough. It was wrong. She had to *do* something. She had to push away her uselessness and find a way past the bells and the dark smudgy clouds. She had to leap over the holes in her head and not fall down them. Margaret sat up; her back ached. She wiped her eyes and snotty nose on her sleeve. She waited and noticed her eyes had adjusted to the dusky light somewhat. It wasn't pitch-black but the rain had come in from the sea and it was heavy now. Crying didn't help. Margaret saw black when she was scared. She had to try not to be scared and then it wouldn't be as dark.

Margaret started to shuffle on her bottom down the steep path, following blindly in the direction Poppy had sped. She didn't dare stand up because she might trip. Staying close to the ground seemed safest. She could smell the wet grass and mud and sheep droppings; she put her hands in it, it was soft. Then there was something hard. Rock, stones, some of them slipped from beneath her touch, rolled away. Far away down there into the sea. Some of the sharp things cut into her skin or stung but she kept moving down, edging down towards Poppy. Because Poppy was all that mattered. Margaret knew that much. Quite certainly she knew that much.

Slowly, bit by bit, Margaret edged down the extremely steep hill. The seat of her trousers quickly become sopping and slimy with mud, she could smell nettles and her own sweat. The air seemed broad and endless. Sea air. She knew she was very close to the sheer edge and the terrible blackness that followed that. How close was Poppy? It was taking forever and Margaret didn't have that long but she didn't dare hurry. She might fall too. Not that she cared about herself; stupid, stupid old woman, but Poppy mattered and if Margaret fell too, no one would find them.

She kicked her flesh first. Nudged a limb with her toe.

'Poppy, Poppy! It's Granny, can you hear me?' Margaret scrambled closer. Thanking God that Poppy hadn't rolled a few more feet. She'd have been in the icy water by now because the tide had brought that threat close. Margaret stroked her granddaughter's body, checking all the pieces were there. They were, but there was a lot of red water coming from her head and her arm was twisted oddly. Broken. Margaret knew it was broken. She remembered that was what a broken arm was like, swollen and pointing the wrong way. She should support the injured arm. But what else? There was red water from her head and she wasn't talking. Margaret remembered what she had to say. 'Can you hear me? Can you hear me? Open your eyes.' Margaret gently shook Poppy's shoulders. She opened Poppy's airway by tilting her head. There was a word she needed. She needed to shout it very loud, through the silence, the darkness, the despair and the rain. It was to bring people. Why couldn't she remember the damned word! Margaret wanted to cry again but stopped herself. If she cried, things went black. If things went black, she'd forget what she was trying to do. She must not forget Poppy.

She put her cheek close to Poppy's mouth; looked and listened but couldn't be sure. She gently put her hand on the little girl's chest. Her hard baby chest that had many years to go before it would swell and turn into a woman's. That must happen. This couldn't be a stop. Margaret knew that more than anything in the world all she wanted was to feel movement in this baby chest. Was there? She couldn't tell; the wind and rain swept around her, moving the grass and earth and air. It wasn't clear.

What was the bloody word? 'Here! Here!' she yelled and then, at last, she remembered. 'Help! Help!' She shouted it so loud that her voice cracked but she didn't care. She shouted on. She'd shout until she shattered. 'Heeeeelp!' She shouted it with every iota of strength that came from being a mother and a grandmother. 'Help my Poppy!'

The words echoed out on to the drenched land. No one answered. No one was coming.

Margaret needed to go and get help. She had to find someone. But if she left she might forget Poppy. The thought stabbed her. It was the most horrific piece of knowledge that Margaret had ever possessed. If she went she might forget why she'd left, who she should return to.

She might let Poppy down. Again. This was all her fault in the first place. She had to keep her eyes on Poppy to remember her, to hold on to her. But it was cold and she was pouring out the red water; Margaret knew Poppy had to do some holding on of her own.

49

Eloise was not a fan of tea served in plastic or polystyrene cups. In an ideal world she'd have everyone stop for formal tea drinking at 4 p.m. No matter what they were doing, they would pause to indulge in a quaint tradition; a reviving beverage. The tea would be served in a fine bone-china cup with a saucer. There'd be a strainer and milk and lemon as options.

But she accepted that she didn't live in an ideal world, not always, no matter how hard she tried.

Tea from a machine, served in a plastic cup, was an integral part of twenty-first-century life. Besides, wrapping her hands around a scalding cup of tea, no matter how hideous the packaging or even taste, was comforting and reassuring and exactly what Eloise needed right now.

Eloise sat in the grim visitors' room and wondered, what was her responsibility here? How much did she owe to Cooper? To Charlie? Even to Jeremy, who she had never met but had occasionally heard Sara mention over the years? Eloise took her responsibilities very seriously, she always had. It was because of her responsibility as a mother that she'd given up her dream of working as an advertising exec in New York; Eloise had long since lived with the fact that she would never wear Armani business suits and live in a loft apartment. It was because of her responsibility to Margaret and Ray that she had so fully embraced Margaret's care.

Responsibility *and* love in both cases. It was an utterly compelling combination.

Eloise knew she was just at the beginning of the journey with Margaret. Her illness had not manifested in too many debilitating physical symptoms yet but Eloise had read enough and talked to enough health-care specialists to know that there was a lot that they would yet have to face. A lot that they would lose. Brutally, Alzheimer's disease had no survivors. The disease gnawed away at a person's brain cells causing memory loss, erratic behaviour, including – in some cases – stunning aggression and even hallucinations and then loss of body functions. With excruciating thoroughness the disease hammered down cruel blow after blow and stole a person's identity, her ability to maintain relationships, to reason, eat, talk, walk and even find her way home. Eloise knew that they were going to lose Margaret a thousand times before the disease finally took her; lose her physically and emotionally. There was no hiding from it. The thought made Eloise sigh so deeply that it was as though she'd blown all the air out of the room.

And Eloise felt enormous love and responsibility towards Mark, naturally. Poor lost Mark. Even thinking of him caused something to snag in her chest. He was so blatantly struggling and floundering at the moment. Somehow focusing on the search for his birth mother had provided him with a legitimate way of avoiding the fact that he was losing Margaret. It was as though he was trying to replace his mother before she'd even gone. Was it a futile hope that he'd somehow be protected from the enormous pain that was waiting in the shadows, ready to pounce on him, ready to smother him? Eloise had never known a man who loved his mother as much as Mark. When she'd met him she'd been nervous that Mark and Margaret's relationship was so intense that she'd never be able to find her place between them. It was her own mother who told her to be brave, to push on, and to have faith.

'A boy who loves his mother that much has to make a good husband,' she'd said. Eloise's mum didn't go in for big emotional talks that often, it wasn't her style. So Eloise had listened to this rare piece of advice.

The unyielding chair offered no comfort. Someone ought to think about that sort of thing when designing visitors' rooms in hospitals. She wriggled uncomfortably and as she did so something slipped into place. Suddenly, it was clear. Crystal.

She had no room for any more responsibilities.

'Sod them,' she thought. Actually, she realised she'd said it aloud when the old man sitting in the chair next to hers turned round, startled. Sod Sara and Charlie. This was not her responsibility, not her mess. Leave them to it.

Eloise stood up, flung her plastic cup – still half full of tasteless tea – in the bin and walked away. It was liberating.

50

Margaret's dad arrived and she was so, so very pleased to see him. There were bigger words than pleased, Margaret knew that, but they had burst out of her head or sunk somewhere deep and they were no longer hers to use, so she settled for pleased. There had been many, many times during Margaret's life when she'd wanted him to turn up, to pick her up and cheer her up, but never as much as today. He found them lying in despair, under the ominous, dense and engorged clouds that were being buffeted by the intensifying wind. The rain was slicing into her body at right angles now. Angry little needles were being thrown at her. She leaned right over Poppy to shelter the little girl from the worst of the downpour but they were still both soaked through to their underwear. Margaret could smell sick, earth and nettles. She wondered whether she'd been buried alive. But then she saw her dad. He was striding towards them. Not running. But walking quickly, purposefully. He didn't lose his footing on the steep narrow path but seemed to negotiate it effortlessly; he was in big boots. Relief and delight flowed through Margaret's body, fusing. She didn't even care that he was wearing his army uniform, although she'd always hated it because the army had stolen him.

He knelt down beside her, pulled out a handkerchief, wiped her tears and then told her to blow her nose. He held the handkerchief while she did so, like you do with a child, and then he put it back in his pocket; he wasn't squeamish about her germs because he was family. 'So what's going on here, then?' he asked.

'I can't move her.' Margaret felt the tears rise in her chest again. Rocks of anguish and panic. 'I can't climb back up, it's too steep, but we can't stay here.'

'That's true, the tide's coming in quickly, you'll both drown,' said her father flatly. He had a northern accent, her father. Margaret hadn't known that. She liked it. It sounded capable and calm. Straightforward and dependable. He sounded a lot like the man she had married.

'I don't know what to do,' Margaret groaned. 'She has opened her eyes and she's spoken to me.' Margaret's tone suggested all she was doing was giving her father the facts of the situation, rather than a genuine reason for hope.

'Well, that's good news.' He sounded very positive and Margaret immediately felt slightly better. It *was* good news, he was right. Poppy was conscious.

But then she remembered.

'There's all this red water.'

'That's blood, that is, Margaret, and you need to stop that flowing,' said her dad. Margaret looked about her for something to help with that task. She tipped the contents of the cotton bag on to the ground: bucket and spade, keys, bedside lamp, phone.

'Granny, call someone,' whispered Poppy.

'I would, angel, but there's no connection.' Margaret had tried this already. She'd pressed the number 3, over and over again, but there'd been no answer. There was nothing in the bag that could help. Her hands flew to her chest in despair, which was when she touched the silky scarf she was wearing. It was a long, thin, fashion scarf that Eloise had bought her for a token on Mother's Day, some years back. It didn't do much by way of keeping a person warm but it would make a perfect bandage. Margaret pulled the handkerchief out of her father's pocket again and folded it into a rectangle; she carefully placed it over the black and sticky bit of Poppy's head. Then she gently wrapped the scarf tightly around the wound. Poppy smiled, as Margaret said authoritatively, 'It's all going to be fine, Poppy. You'll see. I'm here and I'll look after you.' There was sick around Poppy's mouth because once she'd woken up she'd thrown up. Shock, Margaret knew. Shock. She wiped it away.

'That's it, put your coat around her,' said Margaret's dad. Margaret could hear the approval and pride in his voice. He was impressed with his daughter. She was doing a good job.

'I should have thought of that earlier. The coat. Keeping her warm is good for shock. But I'm useless. I have this thing in my brain. A hungry monster that eats my brain,' she explained to her daddy. She hoped he would hug her and swathe her in sympathy and understanding. Instead, he stayed firm and focused, but Margaret didn't mind that either.

'We haven't got time to talk about that right now, Margaret. You're going to need to get going.' Margaret's dad looked out at the sea and it was true, it was getting ever closer. How close did it come? Could they get trapped?

'Do you think it's OK to move her? What if there's something wrong on the inside?'

'I don't see there's much choice, Margaret. It's getting very cold.'

'And if I leave her, I'll forget her.'

'Maybe.'

'I'm going to strap up her arm first,' said Margaret, suddenly confident.

'Are you?'

'Yes, like I learned at the St someone's.' Margaret picked up the cotton bag and swiftly ripped it along one seam, then she fashioned it into a sling to support Poppy's arm. 'Try and keep it still,' she instructed.

'Blimey, I bet you were a smashing Girl Guide,' said Margaret's dad. He was oozing pride now, Margaret could see it in his face, and although everything was terrible, him being with them made it a bit less so.

'Can you stand up, Poppy? Do you think you can walk?'

Poppy shook her head. 'My ankle is hurting so much.' The little girl started to cry. Margaret had no idea where an ankle was but she knew it must be bad.

Margaret turned to her dad. 'I can't carry her on my own,' she said, wearily shaking her head. 'She's only a slip of a thing but I can't carry her on my own.'

'You're not on your own, Margaret. I'm going to carry her with you,' said Margaret's dad. 'We'll get to somewhere where there's a signal and you can call someone on that new-fangled phone of yours. Look over there. That's the path you wanted.'

Margaret looked to where her father was pointing and she saw the path she and Mark used to take, the one that weaved gently rather than fell steeply. Yes, yes, she could manage that path. She had to. 'Pick up the phone, Margaret, and don't lose it,' continued her dad. 'Come on. Chin up. Remember, we never leave a man behind, Margaret. Never.'

51

'Who are you thinking of as godparents?' Charlie asked as he carefully sat down on the bed next to Sara. Sara was feeding Cooper, again. Charlie chuckled. Cooper was the hungriest little man anyone could imagine! He placed his finger near the baby's palm and Cooper curled his tiny fingers around Charlie's. Charlie gasped as though the baby had just grasped his heart. Which, in a way, he had.

'Not Eloise and Mark, if that's what you are worrying about.'

'No?'

'No. I think we should pick family. How about your sister?'

Charlie was delighted and surprised in equal measures. 'But she's in Australia.'

'We could go and visit them. I've been playing with the idea for a while now. I know you've always wanted to go. We could have the christening out there.'

'Really?' Charlie was thrilled. It was true that ever since his sister had moved to Australia five years ago he'd longed to visit. He'd missed her. He'd like to see where she lived and meet her Aussie husband. Sara and Charlie hadn't been able to make their wedding; they couldn't afford to go over because they were in the middle of an expensive round of IVF and, even if they had been able to pull the money together, Sara was nervous that the long flight might muck up her cycle. There had been a thousand similar sacrifices along the way. Charlie didn't mind now, it had all been worth it. They had everything they needed or wanted now. But Charlie's sister had really resented his no-show. She'd been hurt. If they had Cooper christened out there she'd be delighted. Naturally, Charlie wanted to see Sydney Harbour Bridge, the wineries and loll on the beaches, but now, more than any of that, he wanted to show off Cooper.

His amazing son, who was perfect in every way.

Sara was right, he was really strong and good-looking, way more impressive than the other kids in the ward. Charlie didn't want to be harsh, they were all cute, of course, but his son, his son was magnificent. He'd known he was a fighter from day one. A miracle. Against the odds, this one, and look at him. Wonderful. They were going to play ball, they were going to travel, to read, to fish – like he and his dad had. And he was going to do the small stuff too. He was going to teach this kid how to tie his shoe laces, hold a pencil and zap aliens in video games.

'Thank you for our little boy, Sara,' said Charlie. It didn't cover it.

'You're welcome.'

He was going to be the best dad there was.

52

Ray had arrived home a little later than expected because traffic on the Bridge Road was virtually at a standstill. He'd been resigned to this being the case the moment the first rain dropped. Everything ground to a virtual halt as the roads were too narrow for speed during downpours. He'd decided not to call Margaret and tell her he'd be late because if she was alone when the phone rang, it startled her and, anyway, she probably wouldn't remember he'd called. He rang Eloise, who was the lynchpin for Margaret's care, but, unusually, her phone was switched off. When he'd found the house in darkness he'd initially assumed Margaret must be with Eloise, but then he'd read the book and realised this couldn't be the case.

Alarm bells instantly exploded. Months of living with Margaret's erratic behaviour meant Ray spent his life waiting for the worst to happen. A phone call later he'd established that Arabella hadn't taken Poppy as Eloise had planned. A second call and he discovered that the supply teacher had released Poppy to Margaret, unaware of the firm instructions to always question Margaret if she appeared at the gate and never to let the girls go with her.

Next, Ray rang Mark.

'Well, Mum's probably just taken Poppy for a cake and milkshake. She's munificent when it comes to sweet treats for the girls,' said Mark.

'Oh yes, probably, but even so.' Neither Ray nor Mark wanted to articulate any of the other possible scenarios but nor could they ignore them.

'How about you call some tea shops and I'll go and have a look around town,' offered Mark. He was already certain he wouldn't be able to stay at his desk.

Ray rang all the cafés and tea shops in Dartmouth, then joined Mark. Together they ran to the tennis courts to search there and the little park with the bandstand and then the library. There was no sign. Mark asked at the ferry crossing whether his mother and a child had crossed that evening, the pimply adolescent said not. They searched in the station, the castle and the museum. Dartmouth had never seemed so big. Time was ticking on. The shops and cafés began to close; as did their options of finding Margaret and Poppy somewhere safe and comfortable.

Mark began to feel ill with fear. This was it, this was the something dreadful that he'd been subconsciously waiting for, for all these months. Since the day Mark found Charlie all over Eloise in their kitchen and he'd stormed out – unreasonable and impetuous, not giving Eloise a chance to explain – he'd been waiting for a reprisal, a reckoning. Mark called Eloise but her phone was still switched off, as Ray had reported. Why the hell had she switched off her phone? That was unlike her. In the book she'd written that she was going to London. That she would be 'late'. What was she doing in London? She'd never mentioned she was going. She should be here. He needed her here.

At six o'clock he finally got through to Eloise.

'Where the fuck are you?' he barked down the phone.

'I'm – I'm . . .' Eloise was no doubt stunned; that was just not the sort of thing he said to her. 'I'm just getting into the car, actually. I'm on my way home. What's wrong?' she asked.

'Have you heard from Poppy or Mum?'

'No.' She sounded tiny. He knew she understood instantly. His panicked anger at her for not being available instantly dissolved into pity. She was four and a half hours away from where her world was being destroyed.

'You have to come straight away.' Without anger Mark was left with raw fear. 'They're missing.'

Lots of people helped with the search: the neighbours, Arabella's husband and Jackie's husband, Lydia, Graham and Hugh from Mark's office and others. Word spread around the village and people checked in their houses; over the past few months there had been more than one occasion when Margaret had turned up in someone else's bed or shed but this was unlikely if she was with Poppy because Poppy wouldn't let that happen.

They looked in the places they'd already searched, they combed every cobbled street and then groups set off to search in the woodlands. No one complained about the rain; no one wanted to mention it. So much had to be done on foot, as vast areas were not accessible by car; each footstep swallowed moments.

'Where can she be?' asked Ray for the hundredth time. He was ashen and desperate. Both men felt helpless as their gazes twisted and involuntarily turned towards the Dart. For the first time ever, Mark saw what Eloise had always seen: threat and danger, menace and potential peril. The Dart was enormous. And the sea, the sea beyond the Dart, it could hide monsters, shipwrecks and entire land masses. It went without saying that a frail old lady and a skinny little girl could be swallowed without trace.

'Where would she take Poppy?' Ray asked, letting his head drop into his hands.

Suddenly, it hit Mark. 'Our cove.'

'Where?'

'The cove we went to all the time when I was a kid. It's the best. She loved it there. I loved it there. I bet you that's where she's taken Poppy. Stay here, keep looking. Keep your phone on.'

Mark jumped into his car and set off. He drove at such a speed that the trees, hedges, lanes and walls tumbled by, blurring into one. Within minutes the outskirts of the town thinned out to bare grass fields; the fields had never looked so barren and bleak to him before. He couldn't reach the cove by car but drove as far as possible and then pulled to a violent halt, splattering mud as he skidded and swerved. He knew the track they used to take and he ran down it without a moment's hesitation. He was still wearing thin office brogues, as there hadn't been time to change; his feet slipped beneath him and he nearly fell over twice but he didn't care. He just longed to see them. He longed to spot their familiar shapes. It was nearly 9 p.m. No one had seen them for five and a half hours. He was beginning to truly fear he might never see them again. It was the worst thought in the world; a vile and abominable thought but also a vivid and real thought. The horrific idea pushed the blood around his body, his head. He'd never been so afraid in his life. He was sorry. Sorry for everything. This was his fault, all his fault. He deserved something like this to happen. He hadn't wanted her enough. He hadn't kept her close enough and now she was wandering around in the rain and cold with Poppy, his baby. In God only knew what state. He'd caused this.

And then he saw them. His mother was carrying something, staggering under the weight. The something was Poppy. He'd never forget it. His mother and child, broken, bloodied, blundering over the hill. Even in that instant Mark was grateful it was he who had found them, that Eloise had been saved from this sight. The horror would be tattooed on his mind for ever. But he had at least found them.

He ran, faster than he'd ever run in his life. Faster than when he was in the fathers' race on sports day because then his pride was at stake, now everything was.

When he reached them, Margaret let him take the weight of his little girl. She surrendered her charge to his superior strength and then she collapsed.

53

Margaret could feel pain in her back and chest, in her hand and bits of her body that she couldn't be bothered to summon the name for. Too much. Too much effort. She wanted to stay asleep but something else – something that was bigger than her – seemed to want to wake her up. The light. The noise, maybe. She could hear trolleys clattering. Was she in a station? Probably not, she wouldn't have fallen asleep in a station, would she? She could hear voices, people mumbling. There was a man's voice and she knew she knew it, just not right now, not just yet. As her eyes flickered she saw shapes that turned into people. They all looked very worried. Something terrible must have happened, Margaret wondered what.

'Nurse, nurse, she's coming round. Nurse.'

The man with the voice she almost recognised took her hand, which caused her to flinch. Her hand was tender because there was a tube coming out of it. The man apologised and laid his hand on her belly instead. He must know her quite well. A woman said, 'Mrs Hamilton, Mrs Hamilton, can you hear me?' Margaret nodded and decided she'd talk in a minute. Her throat felt like sandpaper, her lips were dry. 'You are in hospital, Mrs Hamilton, but there's nothing to worry about. Your family are all here. Your granddaughter is perfectly safe, Mrs Hamilton. You are a very brave woman.'

Margaret thought she might go back to sleep now for a little while because when she was sleeping she couldn't feel pain in her chest and back.

54

Having two people ill in hospital was a waking nightmare. Eloise and Mark found themselves constantly moving through the long, colourless corridors. They trailed from one bed to the next, swapping their vigil to watch over the generation that had gone before and the generation that should, by rights, follow. Poppy would follow. When Mark first laid eyes on Margaret and Poppy it had seemed as though his daughter was in the worse state of the two. What he'd assumed to be a lack of consciousness turned out to be a deep, exhausted sleep. She'd shut down and slept while her grandmother had staggered up the sandy bridle way. She'd nestled into the familiar warmth and trusted that it would all be OK, because Margaret had told her it would be. This was not Poppy's stop.

Still, Poppy had to stay in hospital because she had been concussed briefly; she'd also severely sprained her ankle, broken her right arm and fractured a rib. Not good. Not comfortable, but so much better than it could have been.

But Margaret? With Margaret it was harder to tell what the impact had been. No bones were broken, no serious cuts or bruises, but she seemed more dazed and confused than ever. They'd know more after they'd done some tests but it had been confirmed that she'd suffered mild hypothermia and it was clear that the trauma of the event would have consequences. She hadn't said a word since she'd come round.

Margaret's odd assortment of possessions had been found. No one understood why she'd had a bedside lamp with her, but the exact location of the accident was now known. The Hamiltons batted the details back and forth. They were scared and shocked, so they constantly rehashed the facts, in an effort to cope with and comprehend what had happened, what could have happened.

'If Poppy had rolled just two or three metres further she'd have been in the sea.' Mark couldn't bring himself to elaborate. Eloise shook her head; she didn't want to hear it, to think about it, to believe it. 'Mum took off her coat. She wrapped up Poppy and carried her over a mile. It's almost superhuman. How could she have done that?'

'She did it because of love, Mark. What isn't possible?'

'She made a sling. She bandaged her head.' He couldn't take it in.

'I know, hard to believe, when usually she can't make a cup of tea on her own.'

'Maybe she's been having us all on,' said Ray, trying to joke.

Eloise found it difficult to look at Ray, he'd shrunk. He wasn't the one who'd been out in the rain half the night but he seemed tinier since. For the first two days he'd stayed next to Margaret's bed and, although he'd asked after Poppy, he couldn't find the will to haul himself off the chair and go and visit her on the floor above.

'It's OK, no rush,' assured Eloise, understanding. 'But I think you'll like the kids' ward, you know, when you are ready. It's cheerful. They've tried in there. There're pictures of Disney characters painted on the wall. A nurse told me that one of the porters is very talented.'

Ray had nodded but hadn't taken his eyes off Margaret.

It wasn't until Poppy was discharged that Ray was finally persuaded to go home, to get a shower and have a nap in his own bed. They all wanted to stay round Margaret's bed 24/7, to coax her back to them, to help her find her voice again, but it was unreasonable. Arabella and Jackie and lots of the other school mums had been amazingly supportive; they'd filled the fridge and the freezer and taken the older two girls to and from school so that Mark and Eloise could stay at the hospital as much as possible, but now Poppy was home the Hamiltons needed to get back into some sort of normal routine.

No one knew when Margaret would be going home.

A week after the incident Ray finally admitted to enormous fatigue and said he might have to skip the evening visiting session. It was agreed that he should stay in with the girls and just Eloise and Mark would visit Margaret.

Margaret took food when it was fed to her, she could sit up, she even managed to walk to the bathroom with some help, but she still hadn't said a word; she was closed down. It was almost as if her Herculean effort to protect Poppy had sapped her. She was spent.

Tonight, when Eloise and Mark arrived at the ward, they found Margaret asleep. Neither would admit it but they both felt a tiny sense of relief. They'd been desperately hoping that she'd be sitting up, smiling, talking about what was on TV and what she'd just read but, failing that (and it was always failing that), then they both appreciated it when she slept. At least she was peaceful and whole when she was asleep; awake, she was a fraction of herself and it was hard to watch. Margaret didn't engage with what was going on around her in any way at the moment. She didn't seem to care what she watched on TV, if the radio was on or off, what she was fed, what newspapers, books and magazines were proffered. She didn't seem to recognise her family at all, any one of them, not even Ray or the children. For a few days she'd stared at them as though slightly perplexed by their presence and then she'd become resigned and didn't even bother to appear quizzical. She was simply indifferent. No one acknowledged this was the case. Every family member swallowed her impassive disregard, hoping that it would pass, that she'd come back to them.

'The ward's quiet tonight,' commented Mark. They'd thought about having her moved into a private room but then decided that having other occupants might provide a stimulus for her. There were five other beds in the ward and over the past few days generally three or four had been in use at any time. Tonight there was only one other patient; a woman in her late fifties, who was in the corner bed, diagonally opposite to Margaret's. Eloise knew that lady was in for a hysterectomy because they'd swapped a few words this morning and that was the sort of info people confided in Eloise after a few words. Tonight her daughter was visiting; they were talking in low murmurs and doing their best to give Mark and Eloise some privacy. They gave sympathetic glances which were a little more like winces. No doubt, the lady having the hysterectomy had found Margaret's presence disconcerting today. The staring and silence, the absence, could be disturbing. Eloise wished she had the energy to tell them how heroic her mother-in-law had been, how funny, caring, patient and skilled she used to be; she'd like to convince them that, *before*, they would've loved to have counted themselves in amongst her many acquaintances and friends. But, frankly, she didn't have the energy to convince strangers this was the case; it was all she could do to remind herself.

Eloise and Mark settled down in the bedside chairs. Fifteen minutes went by and neither of them could think of what to say beyond, 'She's got a bit more colour today, don't you think?'

'Yes. I think maybe she has.'

'Her charts say she's taken plenty of fluids.'

'Well, that's good, then.'

El wondered whether their time would be better used at home with the girls and Ray, rather than sitting by Margaret's bedside while she slept, but she found it impossible to make this suggestion. She sensed that Mark needed to be here. Close to his mum.

'Do you want a coffee?' asked Eloise.

'Not really.'

'No, nor me,' she admitted. Eloise was sick of trying to suck the warmth out of insipid, tasteless beverages. 'I blame myself, you know.' Eloise finally said what she'd been thinking for a week. 'I shouldn't have gone to London.'

The icy-blue fact had sat between them for days and Eloise knew she had to deal with it. The guilt and regret slit through her flesh like a knife every time she glimpsed Poppy hobbling on her crutch or struggling to cut up her food, every time she looked into Margaret's dead eyes and saw nothing. The pain wouldn't stop.

'This is *not* your fault,' Mark said firmly but kindly. 'You can't look after her every moment of the day. You were doing so much, probably too much, and you did try to set up alternative arrangements. Everyone blames themselves, El.' Eloise was grateful that Mark wasn't holding her responsible, but she didn't feel any better. He continued, 'The supply teacher blames herself for allowing Poppy to go with Margaret, but how could she have known any better? Arabella blames herself for taking Margaret's word that you were nearby. Ray blames himself for going fishing. But you called them all. You did everything you could.'

She hadn't called him. They both knew it.

'It wasn't enough, though, was it?'

'What is? Everyone blames themselves,' Mark repeated with a sigh. Eloise wondered what Mark blamed himself for but she didn't dare ask. They fell silent again. Eloise pulled the bed covers up over Margaret's shoulders. It was unnecessary; no doubt she was perfectly comfortable as she was, but Eloise couldn't fight the need to do something for her mother-in-law.

'Do you think she knows? At least, knew, I loved her?' Mark asked suddenly.

'Yes, Mark. Of course.' Eloise reached out and took his hand in hers. He clamped his other hand on top, grasping her as though she might slip away.

'Because, you know, I've been a total bastard since she told me about the adoption.' So that was what he blamed himself for, thought Eloise. 'I abandoned her. Left her. She never left me and I left her. This last year, I walked away from her.'

'Obviously you struggled with everything, but you didn't abandon her. You took her to lots of her hospital appointments. You did a whole load of the practical stuff.' Mark stared at his wife, wanting to be calmed and bolstered but doubting he could be. 'You invented that system to keep all the items she uses daily within easy reach and you cleared out the dangerous substances, the cleaning fluids and bleach and things. You checked that electrical wiring and appliances were safe throughout the house. You were very thoughtful and thorough.'

'Is that love?' Mark asked warily.

'*I* think it is, Mark. I *really* think it is,' said Eloise kindly.

'Will she?' Mark stared at his wife with an honest intensity that shocked her. He thought she had all the answers. He needed her to have at least some of them.

'Yes, no doubt.' Eloise paused. 'But that's not what's important. It hardly matters what I think or even what Margaret thought. *You*'re the one that knows for sure. Did you do it for love, Mark? Did it feel like love? If it did, you're OK, no matter what.'

The 'no matter what' in this case was the chance that Margaret might never again acknowledge anything he said. His opportunity to communicate with her, in the usual way, might have gone for ever. He was going to have to trust in himself. He was going to have to know he loved her and she loved him and the mistakes of this past year were not important in the grand scheme of their relationship.

'Would you know I loved you, if it was you lying there?' he asked abruptly.

'What?' Eloise couldn't understand why he'd veered off.

'I wish I could undo the last year, Eloise. I've made such terrible, terrible mistakes. My reaction was off-the-scale wrong.' Mark couldn't look at Eloise. He looked at their hands, still linked. He shook his head, drained. 'I'm so ashamed of myself. I got it so wrong. I didn't see how good everything was. I didn't trust in what I had.'

'Hey, shush now. This isn't helping.' Eloise pulled him into an enormous hug. He rested his head on her tiny shoulder.

'It was such a shock, you know. An enormous shock to find out that she didn't give birth to me.'

'I know.'

'Then the Charlie thing—' Mark broke off. 'I thought I was losing you too. It was the most appalling thing.'

Eloise rubbed his back. 'Hey, this is ancient history. Why go over it now?'

'I'm really so sorry, Eloise, because I let you down.'

'Well, you were a bit silent for a while and very focused on the search, but we're OK. We're through it,' she reassured him.

'I truly messed up. I was so lost and devastated that I wasn't theirs because I really, really wanted to be. You know? I want to be theirs. I want to be hers.'

'You are, Mark. She adored you. She's adored you all along.'

Mark uncurled from his wife and turned back to his mum. 'I wish I had more time. Time to tell her I love her. We're going to tell our girls every day. OK?'

'We do, actually,' Eloise pointed out.

'And we're going to make them tell us.'

'Make them?' Eloise smiled gently.

'Yes,' said Mark firmly, not seeing a flaw in his plan to hold them close.

'OK.'

'Eloise?'

'Yes?'

'I love you.'

'I know, and I love you too.' The words slipped out with easy familiarity. Eloise knew he loved her and she loved him. It was a given. A certainty.

'I am so sorry I messed up.'

'Yeah, you said.' Eloise wanted him to stop now. It was not a good idea to keep going over all this. She picked up the local newspaper and asked, 'Shall we have a go at the crossword?'

But instead of answering, Mark said, 'Eloise, are you having an affair?'

Her first reaction was to laugh, it was such a bizarre thing to ask, but then she caught sight of his face, dejected and serious. 'No. Why would you think that?' she replied, bewildered.

'Why were you in London?'

He'd never asked. Now he had, Eloise wondered what she should say. She decided not to lie but to offer no more than she needed to. She couldn't get into the whole Sara debacle now. 'I was seeing a friend who'd just had a baby. That's why the phone was off, because I was in a hospital and they make you turn them off.' Her voice fluttered.

Did he believe her? How could he think she was having an affair? Was it the stress? He wasn't thinking straight.

'I'd forgive you,' he said carefully.

'If I was having an affair?'

'Yes.'

'Well, thanks, I think.' Eloise hesitated. Was that the ultimate compliment or the ultimate insult? 'But I'm not having an affair.'

'Good. That's good,' he said simply, but he still didn't look very happy.

OCTOBER

55

It was wonderful to have Margaret home but Eloise was concerned that Margaret would no doubt have forgotten that Halloween was a custom passed down from heathen superstition, based on the idea that ghosts, witches and monsters were somehow funny, rather than sinister or scary. She might very well find a night of trick or treating an ordeal but the girls were bouncing with excitement over the treasures lying in store for them. Free sweets! So it was agreed that Mark would go out trick or treating with the girls and Ray and Eloise would stay with Margaret. One of them could answer the door and dole out mini Mars bars while the other could soothe Margaret and explain (no doubt several times) why there were so many people knocking.

Poppy made a virtue out of her bandaged arm and dressed as a mummy, Erin opted to dress as a little devil which meant red jeans and jumper and discreet horns and Emily wore orange and black tights (that she'd ripped) and a skimpy black dress (that Eloise was pretty sure she'd last seen in her own wardrobe about a decade ago). It was very short indeed; Emily's cloak only just fell below the hem, which caused Mark some distress.

'She's twelve, nearly thirteen,' laughed Eloise. 'Just be grateful it's you she wants to trick or treat with – next year it will no doubt be some pimply youth.' Mark looked aghast. 'That's a good look, you don't even need make-up to look horrified,' joked El. 'Now go and have fun.'

The girls posed as she took a few more snaps on her phone; each one edging the others out of view. Eloise left a box of sweets outside their own door. 'I hope they last and we don't get egged or flour thrown through the letter box,' she said as she set off for Margaret and Ray's and the others set off in the opposite direction.

'Love you,' Mark shouted.

'Love you back.'

She heard him prompt the kids and then with varying degrees of enthusiasm they shouted/mumbled, 'Love you, Mum.' Eloise smiled. It was all a bit gooey but she was glad Mark was keeping to his mantra.

As it happened, Ray, Margaret and Eloise had a lovely, peaceful evening rather than the fanatic one – up and down to the door – which El had anticipated. She assumed that most of the local kids had been told not to disturb Margaret (that, or Margaret genuinely terrified them in a way that plastic masks couldn't), because they only had four trick-or-treaters all evening. The three of them sat in front of the TV and gorged on the spare mini Mars bars. Eloise and Ray talked about holidays. Eloise and Mark both thought it might be a good idea for Ray to go on holiday at some point next year. Nothing too adventurous but maybe a long weekend's golf trip with his pals. The break would do him good as he was still bearing the brunt of most of Margaret's care. He was reluctant to relinquish his post, even for a few days, but he was sensible enough to know that he'd need a rest from his responsibilities at some point. Mark thought it might take several months to convince his dad to go, but El knew Ray's interest was piqued when he suggested nipping to the pub to chat to Bob and show him the brochures Mark had sourced.

'Mind you, Bob will have to get the nod from his Mrs, and I'm not sure how easy that will be.' Ray cast a glance at Margaret. Eloise knew he'd pay a king's ransom for her to be clear-sighted enough to ban him from a boys' weekend away.

'You go and have a pint,' Eloise encouraged. 'I don't think we're going to get any more trick-or-treaters and we're fine here, aren't we, Margaret?'

'Fine,' said Margaret.

Her speech was returning to her. A few words here and there. Nothing that suggested she was once witty and articulate, a lively chatterbox and a wise confidante, but enough to make sure that no one fed her soup when she wanted beans on toast, that no one took her to the bathroom when she just wanted to sit in the garden.

'Well, if you're sure.'

'Certain.'

Ray started to hunt around for his hat; it was a cold night. He and Eloise shared a smile when Margaret said, 'Table', which turned out to be accurate – his hat was on the kitchen table.

'Thanks, love,' he called as he pulled the door behind him.

'I thought Mark and the girls might have come by to show you their costumes,' Eloise mused to Margaret. 'Would you like to see them? I've photos.' Eloise put her hands gently on the sides of Margaret's face so that she could capture Margaret's full attention. 'The girls have dressed up for Halloween, would you like to see the photos?'

Margaret looked excited and Eloise briefly wondered whether Mark had been right after all. He'd wanted to take Margaret trick or treating. Maybe she would have enjoyed it. He wanted to take her everywhere with him nowadays, since the incident at the cove. He believed that Margaret must live life to the full and experience what she could, whereas Eloise was more careful, perhaps timid. The situation reminded Eloise of when the girls were babies. Mark would throw them high into the air and they'd squeal with delight but with every hurl Eloise's heart would skip a beat. She was always terrified that he'd drop them but he never did. He was the one who urged the girls to climb a little higher up the tree, while El nervously called, 'Be careful!' He encouraged them to go deeper, faster, higher, wilder. Eloise had always appreciated that the girls needed the balance; his encouragement, her caution. No doubt Margaret needed the same, it was just a matter of getting the balance right. However, El was delighted that Mark wanted to do so much with Margaret, that he was engaging with her, and all of them, so thoroughly once again.

It was only a matter of time before he'd be body popping at parties once more.

Eloise flicked through the photos on her iPhone. Margaret giggled appreciatively at the pics of her granddaughters pulling gruesome faces and silly poses to showcase their costumes. Whether or not she actually recognised Emily, Erin and Poppy was anyone's guess, but still it was fun. Eloise went into the kitchen to make them both a cup of tea; she was touched to see Ray had bought a box of Halloween cupcakes. Usually Margaret baked chocolate cakes in the shape of cats or witches' hats. Ray was doing his best to keep up traditions. Eloise was feeling a bit queasy after eating so much chocolate so didn't eat one, but she made a mental note to send the girls around to eat them tomorrow. They wouldn't need much persuading.

When Eloise took the tea tray back through to the sitting room, she found Margaret looking at the photos again. Margaret was concentrating on the snaps as though they were works of art, although they were the usual stuff: pictures of the girls beaming (or refusing to) at parks, near castles and at the beach.

'Oh, Mark. Lovely!' enthused Margaret suddenly. Eloise carefully lowered the tray on to the table and peeked over Margaret's shoulder. She was looking at the photo of baby Cooper. Eloise had forgotten she'd taken one.

'That's Cooper.'

'Coo-per?' Margaret looked perplexed.

'I know, strange name, huh? It's Sara and Charlie's baby.' Eloise felt slightly weird saying their names aloud. She hadn't thought of Sara since the day Cooper had been born. She'd set them adrift. She'd had more than enough to occupy herself with since.

'Not Charlie's baby,' said Margaret calmly and clearly. Eloise was shocked. It was odd that Margaret had stumbled on a truth through her confusion. 'Mark.'

Eloise felt the words in her gut before she could think about them in her head. 'You're getting it all muddled up, Margaret.'

'Mark,' Margaret insisted and then she dashed out of the room, leaving Eloise with the image of the baby on her phone. The baby with strong thighs and a mop of thick, black hair. Margaret returned within a few moments, and even before she looked up, Eloise knew what she'd fetched back.

Margaret handed El the baby photo of Mark, the one his birth mother had taken when he was a day old. Eloise held the two images side by side. Excepting that one was a slightly faded 1970s print and the other was a 5-megapixel digital image, they were identical.

Both babies were lying in exactly the same position. A fluke? Both babies were free of swaddling so that their body shapes were exposed. They both had big thighs, they looked strong and able. Their eyes were wide open and they were both staring at the photographer. Wrinkly and startled was universal. The same hair colour and hair line might be a coincidence, but the shape of the lips? Eloise stared at Cooper's lips and she knew they were lips she was familiar with. Lips she'd kissed a million times. They were her girls' lips. They were her husband's lips.

'Lovely baby,' said Margaret and she kissed the screen of the iPhone.

56

From: Sara Woddell [s.j.woddell72@kmail.com]
To: Eloise Hamilton
Date: 15 November
Subject: re: Cooper

Yes, Eloise, you are right. Mark is Cooper's father.

I can only imagine how you agonised over asking that question, hating having to put something so difficult into words. I'm quite surprised you ever had the courage; you've never been one for confrontation. I can only guess how many hours, days and weeks you must have agonised over Margaret's revelation. Dismissing it, believing it, rejecting it, being tortured by it. I suppose you were hoping I'd put your mind at rest by assuring you that the resemblance is passing, a coincidence. I considered doing so but I think part of me always wanted you to know.

You seemed angry in your email. Indignant. I think that's why I ultimately decided to tell you the truth. I can't bear it that you are so supercilious. So hypocritical, Eloise. After all, you accepted that Jeremy had fathered Cooper in a heartbeat. Jeremy has a wife and children too, but you didn't care about that, did you? Someone else's husband, someone else's problem. The irony is, it was *supposed* to be Jeremy. That's who I'd planned to conceive with but, on his way over to my place, Jeremy was called into his boss's office and Mark knocked on my door instead. Funny how things work out.

I don't think there's any risk in telling you the truth. You haven't got much room to manoeuvre, have you? I can't imagine that you are going to destroy your oh-so-perfect world. You'll have to find a way of dealing with the knowledge that your perfect husband is not so perfect after all. You'll have to do that for the sake of your girls. Learn to live with it.

Your girls were my everything until I had Cooper, now I understand what everything really means. However, because of the girls I've decided to tell you something that might help. It was only the once. It was that day he caught you kissing Charlie. By the way, it was Mark who told me all about that, not Charlie. He was devastated. So sure that you must be having an affair. It's funny that your actions sent him to me. He was very vulnerable, crazed with self-pity. I took advantage of him. And I don't regret it.

We all do what we have to do, don't we, in this imperfect world? I can't deny it, it has been rather fun being omnipresent, omnipotent. I've known all, controlled all. I knew about you and Charlie. I knew Mark would stop us meeting up after he'd been with me. And I knew you would not tell Mark that we *were* meeting up again, so wouldn't be able to tell him I was pregnant. I knew that when I introduced you to Cooper you were kissing your husband's son. I bet Mark still doesn't even know I've had a baby, does he, Eloise? You were all blind to it, weren't you? Too busy seeing everything from your own myopic point of view to see the entire picture.

Only Margaret, riddled with dementia, saw what was under your noses.

Don't be sad or angry, Eloise. Try and think about it calmly. You'd offered to be surrogate. What's the difference? Just a little donation. I will be a great mum. I *am* being a great mum. I want you to forgive him, and me and yourself – for not being perfect. This is what it is. Few people expect perfect or strive for perfect, the way you do.

Besides, what's your alternative? We've moved to Australia. We're on a visitors' visa at the moment but I don't plan on coming back to the UK. We can go anywhere in the world. And if we decide to stay in Australia you should know that Cooper is one of the most popular names here – I planned that – and we're in the process of changing our surnames. Even if you do tell Mark about Cooper, and you try to find us, be assured – you won't. All you'll be doing is condemning Mark to a lifetime of looking for another generation. I can't imagine you'll ever be that cruel. Leave it alone, Eloise. This isn't one you can fix.

I am closing this email account down. You will never hear from me again.

57

Eloise couldn't move. She sat for so long that the screen went black. She nudged her mouse and the words reappeared. She read them again. They were the same. They punched. The screen went black again. Nudge. The words reappeared, they wouldn't go away.

In fact, more words were crashing into Eloise's world. But not Sara's words. Sara had had too much say in her life so far, that was now blatantly clear. Eloise had always been plagued by an illogical guilt around Sara and that was why she'd indulged her time and time again. Eloise had it all when Sara had nothing. Now Sara had stolen from her. It was vile and cruel and desperate.

But Sara wasn't Eloise's problem.

Mark. Mark's words came to her. His apologies and explanations for this crime. Not for conceiving a baby that he was ignorant of, but for a drunken, self-pitying revenge fuck. He'd apologised to her so often over the last nine months, she could see that now.

He'd apologised with white roses, slow kisses, by cooking special meals when she was bored with her own convenience food, by being particularly attentive with the girls when she'd had an exhausting day with them or Margaret. He'd apologised in the hospital. 'I thought I was losing you too. It was the most appalling thing.' 'I'm really so sorry.' 'I let you down.' Eloise had thought he was talking about the stony silences and the manic search for his birth mother.

Now she understood. He had not dared confess. He had thought he might lose her. As well he might.

Eloise wanted to vomit with the shock. He'd put his dick inside another woman. It was such an ugly reduction but she couldn't see this any other way. He must have kissed Sara. She tried to comfort herself by thinking that there might not have been any kissing. Sara knew what she wanted and foreplay wouldn't have been a necessity but then Eloise couldn't imagine Mark getting down to it without at least a peck. She couldn't imagine it any which way. The pain was immense.

Her loving husband, the man she depended on, thought of as remarkable, passionate, responsible, incredible. The man who had always made her feel secure had betrayed her.

Once. He had betrayed her once. One mistake in sixteen years. Was that an acceptable level, a human frailty? Or was it the end?

Could she accept this? *Should* she accept this? And if so, should she stay silent about Cooper?

What was the right thing to do in amongst all this wrong?

58

Mark came in through the back door, bringing the chilly autumn evening with him. He was ruddy, glowing. Eloise noted there was something particularly animated about him this evening. She was sitting in the kitchen, like a statue, a parody of someone reading her email. Eloise stared at her husband across the screen.

'Where are the girls?' he asked, as he kissed her briefly on her cheek. His whiskers scratched a tad.

'Emily is at trampoline club, Erin is upstairs cleaning out her hamster's cage and Poppy is at your mum and dad's.' She couldn't believe she'd managed to get these words out of her mouth. Out of her head. *Hey, surprise, surprise, you're a daddy again* could have slipped out just as easily.

'Will Poppy be coming home for supper, or is she staying at theirs?'

'I think she's eating there.' She couldn't believe he looked the same. Sounded the same. This man who had fathered a baby elsewhere.

'So, just the four of us?'

'Yes.'

Mark glanced around the kitchen but didn't see any sign of supper being prepared. This didn't strike him as odd as Eloise often suggested they go out to eat on a Friday. It was a good way to kick off the weekend. He didn't mind either way, he'd never been sexist or felt entitled.

'Shall I put something on or do you fancy going to get fish and chips at Rockfish? We could pick Emily up on the way.' Mark glanced at the kitchen window. 'I'm going to have to have a look at that window frame,' he commented, poking the softened wood which the autumn rain had pounded and penetrated, exploiting the weakness. Mark then noticed that Eloise seemed strangely still and very pale. 'Hey, are you all right, love? Everything OK?' he asked, concerned.

'I was just reading my email. There was a surprise in my inbox.'

'Your bill from Boden?' he joked.

'A letter from Sara.'

'Sara?' Eloise wasn't sure if it was her imagination but she thought she saw him flinch, certainly he wasn't laughing any more. Mark walked to the kettle, picked it up and filled it. As he brushed past her she smelt the outside clinging on to his suit. He smelt fresh and strong. Wholesome. Was that fair? He paused, looked at his wife again and then considered. 'Would you like something stronger than tea?'

'Yes.'

He opened a bottle of full-bodied Bordeaux, poured healthy-sized glasses and handed one to Eloise. It was a garnet colour. Beautiful. She took a sip and found the courage.

'Sara had some news.'

'Oh yes.'

'They've moved to Australia.'

'Really?' Eloise wasn't imagining or mistaking his reaction now. She was certain that he looked relieved. He seemed to be focusing on a spot just above her head, anything to avoid meeting her eye. 'I hadn't expected to hear from her again,' he commented as he took a sip.

'No,' said Eloise. 'I don't imagine we will now. Her letter had an air of finality about it.'

Mark didn't ask for details. He had no interest in Sara. He wished she'd vanish. He wished he'd never met her. Eloise could see this and she wondered was it enough?

'As it happens, I have some news too,' said Mark. He plonked himself down in the chair next to Eloise's. 'I've had news from the adoption advisor.' He paused and took a deep breath. 'They've found my birth mother.'

Eloise gasped. They'd been anticipating this moment for a year now and yet she was still stunned. 'They have?'

'Yes.'

'Oh my God. So what now?'

Mark reached forward to take hold of Eloise's hand. She allowed him to because it felt natural; despite everything, they were joined in this moment. 'I know this is going to be hard to believe, after everything, but I'm not sure that there is a next. The truth is, I'm not certain I need or want another mother.'

'Because the one you've got is a handful?' asked Eloise, unable to hide her exasperation.

'I didn't mean that.'

She pulled her hand away. 'But you've been looking for a year. That's pretty much all you've been able to focus on.'

Mark was no fool and he could hear the criticism Eloise was lobbing at him. 'I know, I've got carried away with it and you've been really patient. Maybe I had to get this far to understand that what I've had all along is enough. Is wonderful, in fact. Or maybe things have just been different since Mum and Poppy went missing. Everything changed again, after that.' Eloise had to admit that since then Mark hadn't once mentioned searching for his birth mother. Mark shuffled closer to her; he draped his hand around the back of her chair, catching one of her curls between his thumb and forefinger. Shyly he said, 'This sounds so insane, but I sort of made a deal.'

'A deal?'

'With God or the fates. Whoever. It was probably superstitious nonsense but I bargained.'

'Go on.'

'If I was to only find one mother, I wanted it to be Margaret. I knew Mum would have Poppy. Despite everything, I knew she'd have kept her safe. I believed it because she's my mum. I haven't been in contact with the agencies since but because I'd previously registered, matters progressed at their own rate, without my input.'

'I see.'

'I miss Mum, you know. She's gone but she's here still, too. It's so bloody hard. But I don't want to replace her. She was amazing. Sort of still is. In here in my head, she's amazing. She's irreplaceable and it seemed like a betrayal to even try. She wanted me so much.'

'And that is enough, is it?'

Mark was surprised by Eloise's tone. He'd expected her to fling her arms around him and congratulate him for reaching this decision. Although she'd resisted ever saying as much, Eloise had somehow managed to give the impression that she'd always disagreed with his search.

'I think so.'

'And the fact that she wanted you so much justifies her silence, does it?'

Mark considered carefully. 'Yes. Truthfully, El, I think it does. I don't think anything has been made any better because she blurted out the fact I was adopted. It changed everything and nothing. Things were made harder and not necessarily better. The truth isn't always all.'

'That's an extremely unfashionable view,' muttered Eloise.

'Well, yes. Perhaps.'

Eloise was trying to take in everything he was saying. She was trying to use the information to decide what she ought to do next. 'So?'

'I'm OK. More than OK. I'm so fabulously lucky. I don't know how I could have forgotten it or taken it for granted. It's not just about my parents. El, I have so much. I have you and the girls and I'm so very lucky. I don't need anything more. Anyone more. I have everything I want and need right here. You don't swap a parent if they turn out to be a bit faulty.'

'No.' Or anyone else for that matter.

'I have the perfect family, Eloise. I think it's time I started focusing on it.'

For years theirs had been a wonderfully uncomplicated relationship.

There was no doubt, drama or palaver. They were meant to be and they'd both believed it from the start. Nothing but calm waters. In this past year they'd ridden storms, they'd been buffeted and battered. Did Eloise have any more in her? Could she wrap herself around the grenade, take the impact, protect her family?

Mark read her mind, or at least her face or eyes. 'I'm going to make it up to you, Eloise. I'm going to do everything in my power to get us back to where we should be.'

Mark stood up and put on the iPod. Heartfelt, melodic vocals drifted into their kitchen, oozed though their pots and pans, through their past and present.

'Are you dancing?' Mark stood in front of her, holding out his hand for her to take. He hadn't danced her around the kitchen for months; they hadn't had time to so much as think about such frivolities. His back was still broad and dependable; his shoulders were just as wide and willing to shore up Eloise.

Eloise looked at her husband and hit her biggest ever 'married moment'. She had a choice now. In one direction she could picture nothing but relentless grey. Today. Tomorrow. For ever. If she took the other route, there would be grey days and black days but many, many of her days would be glorious Technicolor.

'Are you asking?'

'I'm always asking.'

'Then I'm always dancing.' Eloise reached out and took hold of his hand, allowing him to sweep her around their kitchen, their home. Their life.

Thank you, Jonny Geller, who has been with me every step of the way. I'm so lucky to have benefitted from your perception, tenacity, support and friendship.

Thank you, again, to my fantastic editor Jane Morpeth and the entire team at Headline who all work so tirelessly and with such enthusiasm. You are a wonderful bunch of professionals; great fun and so full of determined intelligence. Thank you to the wonderful Jamie Hodder-Williams for inspirationally leading such a fine team.

Thank you to Emma Draude for gracefully telling the world when my books are out. Thank you to all at Curtis Brown for their industrious promotion of my work home and abroad.

Thank you to all my readers for giving me hours of your time; I hope I always make it worth your while. Thank you to my family and friends, my fellow authors, book sellers, book festival organisers, reviewers, magazine editors, TV producers and presenters, the Reading Agency and librarians who have so generously supported me in countless ways over the years. I wish I could name every one of you individually but it would run to pages. I think you know who you are.

Thank you, Jimmy and Conrad, because everything I do, I do for you.

ACKNOWLEDGEMENTS

I'd like to warmly acknowledge the generosity of a number of people who have supported charities which are close to my heart by bidding for the opportunity of giving a name to various characters in this novel.

Mark English, for his generous support of Alzheimer's Society, a membership organisation which works to improve the quality of life of people affected by dementia, as well as offering support to partners and families who cope with the demands of caring.
To learn more visit **www.alzheimers.org.uk**

Helen Ede, for her generous support of Zoë's Place Baby Hospice, a home from home for babies who have life-limiting or terminal illnesses.
To learn more visit **www.zoes-place.org.uk**

Alison Glover, for her generous support of Shooting Star CHASE, a children's hospice service, a charity caring for local families with a child or teenager with a life-limiting condition.
To learn more visit **www.shootingstarchase.org.uk**

Lydia Pluckrose, for her generous support of Relief for Japan, a project that disbursed funds to organisations providing relief and emergency services to victims of the devastating earthquake and tsunami.

The Leach Family: Andy, Angela, Arabella, Liberty and Hattie, for their generous support of Stepping Stones Down Syndrome Support Group, a group run by parents, for parents and carers of children with Down syndrome.

To learn more visit **www.steppingstonesds.co.uk**